The Flight of
Livi Starling

The *Livi Starling* series

The Flight of
Livi Starling

Karen Rosario Ingerslev

PURE&FIRE

The Flight of Livi Starling
First published in the UK by Pure & Fire in 2016
Pure & Fire, England
www.pureandfire.com

ISBN: 978-0-9934327-6-7
eBook ISBN: 978-0-9934327-7-4

'A large and mighty army comes, such as never was in ancient times nor ever will be in ages to come. Before them fire devours, behind them a flame blazes...'
— Joel 2:2-3

I will waste my life

When I get to Heaven, I will be in party mode for the rest of eternity. My short time on earth could be my only chance to change the world or impact a life or create anything of any significance. My name is Livi Starling and I'm sixteen years old.

Something happened this summer that changed my life forever. Contrary to the build up from our teachers, it wasn't getting my exam results (which were better than expected but not good enough for the photo of high achievers for the local newspaper). Nor was it Aunt Claudia's acquisition of a horse and my brief stint as a horse whisperer during our annual summer visit. No. As thrilling as those events were, they were nothing compared to a seemingly trivial encounter during a routine trip to the corner shop for milk.

I had paused to browse the chocolate bars when I overheard our elderly neighbour, Helen Tagda, announce to the shopkeeper, Raj, "My husband died last night."

As Raj turned red and offered his condolences, I dropped the chocolate bar I had been considering and looked up in shock. Mrs Tagda gave me a stiff smile. I forced a smile back and stepped aside as she shuffled out of the shop. Then I hurriedly grabbed a pint of milk, thrust some money at Raj and— without even waiting for my change— ran out of the shop after Mrs Tagda. Being rather old and frail, she hadn't got very far and I almost toppled into her as I sprinted round the corner. I steadied myself before tapping her on the shoulder.

"Excuse me."

Mrs Tagda turned and looked at me.

"I'm Livi. I live next door to you."

She kept staring which I took to mean that she either already knew or didn't really care.

"I heard you telling Raj that Mr Tagda died... I just wanted to say I'm sorry."

Mrs Tagda sucked in her cheeks and scratched her wrinkled neck. "Thank you."

"Are you alright?" I continued hesitantly.

She nodded but said nothing.

I eyed the packet of biscuits in her hand and imagined her eating them all alone. I wanted to say something else— something useful or meaningful. But nothing came to mind. I debated saying goodbye and walking off but, since we were both going the same way, the idea of suddenly striding off ahead of her seemed rather rude. In the end, I walked slowly beside her, alternating between noble pity for her loss and an uncomfortable social ineptness that almost made me regret stopping her in the first place.

We reached my house and I said, "Sorry," once again.

Mrs Tagda nodded.

"It was nice to walk with you," I added, turning to unlock my front door.

"You too."

I turned back to give her a quick smile.

Her next words caught me off guard. "I never told my husband that I loved him. What do you think of that?"

I blushed as I cleared my throat and grappled for a reply. "I'm sure he knew," I muttered finally.

"I hope so. We would have been married sixty six years this winter. Sixty six years..." I saw her blink rapidly as she composed herself and gave me a final smile. "Well, thank you, Livi. You take care."

"Thanks," I whispered. "You too."

I let myself into my house a little shakily and lingered in the hallway as I marvelled at Mrs Tagda's confession. Imagine being married for so many years and never hearing three little words, *'I love you...'*

My response jarred noisily in my head. *'He probably knew.'*

"How?" I wondered aloud. "How would he know without being told?"

My sister came out of the kitchen and jumped in surprise. "What are you doing just standing there?" she asked as she took the milk from me.

"Mr Tagda died."

"Oh?"

"Mrs Tagda never told him that she loved him."

Jill gave me a quizzical look. "How do you know?"

"She told me."

"Oh... I'm sure he knew."

"How?" I demanded. "How would he know without being told?"

Jill ignored me and pointed to the milk. "Was there any change?"

I took a deep breath and looked her in the eye. "I love you, Jill."

"I know." She chuckled. "I love you too."

I nodded and ran upstairs. When I reached my room, I picked up my phone and rang my best friend, Ruby Rico.

Within seconds, Ruby appeared at her window across the street dressed somewhat mysteriously in her father's brown dressing gown and a bicycle helmet. "Hey Livi!" she exclaimed as she answered her phone.

"Hey Ruby. Just letting you know that I love you."

She giggled. "Thanks. I love you too."

"Did you know Mr Tagda died?"

"Yeah. My mum made his wife a cake."

I bit my lip. Now Mrs Tagda had not only a packet of biscuits but a whole cake to eat by herself. "She never told him she loved him," I said.

Ruby cocked her head to one side. "Oh? That's sad." She paused before asking, "Do you think he knew?" Before I could reply, she continued more urgently, "Do you think he's in Heaven?"

I felt a pang of regret. What if Mr Tagda had never accepted Jesus and I'd known the truth all this time but never thought to knock next door to tell him? It was sad enough that he'd never heard his wife say that she loved him. But what if he'd lived his whole life never being told that God loved him even more? "I hope so," I whispered.

Ruby and I stayed silent on the line, staring at each other from our windows until Ruby said, "I'd better go. I promised Oscar I'd play space monkeys with him."

That explained the costume. I let out a splutter and said goodbye.

As I waved at Ruby and turned from my window, I debated calling my dad to tell him that I loved him. But in the end I decided against it. Partly because I wasn't completely sure if it was true, but mainly because I was afraid his wife, Erica, might answer. The last time I rang she mistook me for a cold caller, threatened me with a citizen's arrest, and slammed the phone down.

Instead, I lay on my bed and stared at the ceiling.

"I love you," I said aloud to Jesus. "I hope you know that."

I didn't hear a reply, at least not an audible one, but a quiet calm settled in my heart which I took to mean that he loved me too.

"Five more days," I continued, in case Jesus had forgotten. "So, if you want me to reconsider, then you'd better speak soon."

I was referring to the fact that in five days time Ruby and I would be enrolling at City Farm College, an agricultural centre on the outskirts of Leeds, to begin a course in Animal Behaviour and Care.[1]

If I'm honest, I only applied for the course because Ruby's doing it. I'd had half a mind to stay on in the sixth form at our high school alongside our close friend, Annie Button, who's retaking Maths, but the college course includes a week-long field trip to some mystery foreign destination so, having never been abroad before, that's what swung it for me.

My sister thought it was a peculiar course choice. "I understand why Ruby wants to do it," she said with a sniff when I announced my decision to apply. "She's obsessed with animals.[2] But when have *you* ever wanted to work with them?"

Aunt Claudia, on the other hand, was thrilled and offered me an unpaid apprenticeship with her sheep as soon as I graduated.

I had to break it to them that I have no intention whatsoever of working with animals. I simply wanted to choose a course that would allow for a little bit of entertainment before facing the arduous task of being a grown up.

"I'm not doing it for the qualifications," I told Jill. "I don't need any because hopefully Jesus will come back before I have to get a proper job."

My sister was so startled by my response that she dropped the mug in her hand and barely noticed when hot tea began to run across the carpet and under the TV. "Livi, don't say stupid things," she scolded.

---

[1] *'ABC'* for short.

[2] This isn't remotely true. Ruby's family simply own a dog, a rather scraggly one at that, and— having never had any fondness for animals— Jill seems to mistake Ruby's dutiful daily walk of Dennis for crazed obsession. In actual fact, Ruby only chose the course for the field trip too. She wants to be a missionary in Africa one day and thought spending some time overseas might prove useful.

"Well, he might," I said. When Jill didn't reply I continued, "Anyway, I'll probably be a writer. I don't need qualifications for that either."

But, far from praising my self assurance, Jill winced and said bitterly, "Don't waste your life, Livi. You only get one shot at it."

Since then, Jill had spent the summer bombarding me with magazine articles detailing the lives of various high-flying career women as she urged me to reconsider the direction of my life. I had initially responded to her efforts with polite smiling and the odd patronising nod. But, as more information came through about the animal course, I had been forced to rethink things. In particular, when I compared my reading list[3] with the business supplement from the Sunday paper, I couldn't ignore the nagging feeling that I might indeed be shrinking from my full potential. I found the double-page spread on *'Homes for the Aspiring Lawyer'* particularly enticing and I couldn't deny that the men and women featured in *'Britain's Brightest Bankers'* wore smiles that suggested their lives were better than mine. So I'd prayed diligently every day, allowing Jesus ample opportunity to give me a sign to aim higher.

But, following my encounter with Helen Tagda, as I lay on my bed counting the days down with Jesus, the idea of pursuing wealth or power or success suddenly seemed empty and futile. I didn't know what career Mr Tagda had once upon a time and I wasn't sure it mattered now. But, to never hear, *'I love you...'* To never have the opportunity to say it in return...

I sighed and turned to my bedside table where Jill's latest piece of scaremongering[4] sat neatly with my name on.

"I don't want to waste my life," I whispered to God as I absentmindedly scanned the article. "What am I meant to do with it?"

Quite unexpectedly, a line in the article leapt out and danced before my eyes. *'Put your whole heart into it and don't give up...'*

I bit my lip and read some more.

The writer of the article went into great detail about the necessity of devoting oneself fully to the fulfilment of one's goals. *'There is a single-mindedness that accompanies every true success story,'* they declared. *'Without such wholehearted devotion to the*

---

[3] Which included such titles as *'Inside a Rabbit'* and *'I'm a Dog. What are My Rights?'*

[4] A magazine article entitled *'Are You Wasting Your Life?'*

task at hand, one's full potential will always remain just out of reach.'

"I want to be a success story," I told God.

I expected him to say, *Then don't do the silly animal course.* But, instead, I felt him ask, *What is a success story?*

I turned back to the article for the answer but I felt God prompt even more strongly, *What is a success story, Livi?*

I put the article down and closed my eyes. "I don't know."

Nothing happened for a moment and then, in the silence that followed, three little words dropped into my heart: *I love you.*

I sat bolt upright and almost cried out in delight. *That's it!* I realised. *Jesus doesn't mind what course I do. What he wants is my heart!*

Glancing back at the article, the line jumped out at me once more. *'Put your whole heart into it and don't give up...'*

It dawned on me that the greatest tragedy in life wasn't never reaching your full potential; the greatest tragedy was pouring your whole heart into something that never even mattered in the first place.

I scrunched the article up and tossed it under my bed as I decided that I *would* waste my life after all. I would devote my heart to something, or rather *someone,* worth the cost. I would spend the rest of my life learning to love Jesus, the one who gave himself wholeheartedly for me. And it had to be my *whole* heart—the article was right about that. It couldn't be here and there, only on Sunday mornings, like a salad on the edge of my plate. If I was serious about being a success story then the task at hand demanded nothing less than all of me.

~ 2 ~

What if he doesn't?

"Did Jesus tell you what to do yet?" Ruby asked nervously.

I gave a triumphant nod. "He said I could do the animal course."

"Oh good! That means I can too!" She looked relieved.

"Yeah. It doesn't matter as long as we love him most," I added, reaching for a packet of multicoloured staples.

We were in town buying stationery for the new term. In keeping with the theme of our course, Ruby had chosen a pencil case in the shape of a furry goat. I had opted for a more sensible metal tin emblazoned with the slogan, *'I LOVES NOW!'* I hoped it would remind me to live each moment for Jesus.

She nodded. "Okay. Cool."

"So we've got to up our game," I continued as we made our way to the front of the shop.

"What do you mean?"

I shot her a quick smile as if to say, *'I'll tell you in a minute,'* as we joined the queue at the till.

The queue moved slowly and silently and Ruby kept throwing me anxious glances as she begged, "What is it, Livi? Tell me now."

"In a minute!" I forced a smile as if to pretend to nearby shoppers that we'd been discussing something ordinary like television shows rather than something strange like loving Jesus.

We paid for our things and hurried outside where I repeated, "We've got to up our game!"

"What do you mean?"

I grinned. "I've decided to live for Jesus."

Ruby looked at me in confusion. "I thought you did that three years ago?"

I shook my head. "I mean I want to give him *everything*. I know my faith has grown over the years but, to be honest, some days I barely think about Jesus at all. What if there's more than what we've known? If there is, I don't want to get to the end of my life having never tasted it."

"Okay..." Ruby still looked a little puzzled. Finally she muttered, "How are you going to do it?"

"Well..." I paused as I dug around in my bag and withdrew a scrap of paper I had been working on all morning. "I made a list."

Ruby took it from me and echoed, "A list?"

"Of things Jesus told his followers to do. I thought we could do them." I gave a proud beam.

Ruby raised her eyebrows as she read aloud,

"Five things Jesus told his disciples to do
1. Preach the gospel
2. Heal the sick
3. Cleanse the lepers
4. Cast out demons
5. Raise the dead."

She went a little pink.

I grinned. "So, where should we start?"

Ruby looked down at my list again and bit her lip.

"I don't know about preaching the gospel just yet," I confessed. "I'm not brave enough to stand on a bench and shout in the middle of the city centre."

Ruby looked at me in horror. "Me neither!"

"So we won't begin with that."

"Phew..."

"And I don't know how to go about finding lepers but, if the field trip for our course is in Africa, perhaps we'll meet some there..."

Ruby gulped.

"I wondered about raising Mr Tagda from the dead," I went on. "But I thought we should probably start small."

"Please start small!" Ruby squeaked.

"There are plenty of sick people about." I gave an awkward smile. "Shall we see if any of them want to be healed?"

She didn't say anything.

"See, there!" I nudged her. "There's a man with a walking stick!"

I was about to go running up to him when Ruby grabbed my arm and hissed, "Livi, what are you going to do?"

14

"I don't know... I suppose I'll just ask if I can pray for him." The look on her face instantly made me lose my nerve. "Or is that stupid?"

Ruby blushed. "I don't know. What if he doesn't get healed?"

"He has to. Why else would Jesus say to do it?"

Ruby went even redder. She seemed to be wrestling with something.

"What?" I demanded.

She squirmed. "Not everyone who gets prayed for gets healed."

I sighed. "I know. But Jesus said it... We should at least try."

"Maybe we should think about it first. Plan it properly, you know, and do it another day?"

I shook my head and tapped my new pencil tin. "Look!"

Ruby blinked. "You love snow?"

"No! I—" I re-read the message on the tin and frowned. "Oh."

Ruby shrugged and gave me my list back. "Did you have anything else to buy?" she asked gingerly as she pointed to my shopping.

I pursed my lips. "Can't we at least try this?" I begged. "It's what the Bible says." When Ruby didn't reply I continued, "I want more of God so I need to give him more of me. This is the best I can think of right now."

She chewed her thumb as she mulled it over. "Yeah, okay... Let's try..."

The man with the stick had gone by this point but it wasn't long before a lady walked past with both arms in a sling.

I nudged Ruby and whispered, "Her?"

She winced. "I'm scared..."

"Me too..." I watched in defeat as the lady wandered out of sight.

Moments later, a man walked past with a noticeable limp.

I poked Ruby. "Him?"

She shook her head.

I looked around. "That old woman with the lump on her face?"

Ruby's jaw dropped open. "No!"

We watched as the old woman walked right under our noses and into a nearby shop.

"That blind man with the guide dog?"

"No..."

"The guy with one arm?"

"*No!*"

I gave a heavy sigh. "Let's start with short term issues," I suggested. "People with broken arms and things like that. Then it won't be too bad if they don't get healed because they're likely to be better soon anyway so it's not like it's a life threatening illness like—"

Ruby dug me in the ribs as a lady went past pushing a very frail looking boy in a wheelchair.

My stomach churned as I whispered, "Yeah, like that."

Ruby nodded sombrely.

"There's a lady with a cast on her leg," I said, pointing to a woman hobbling on crutches a few yards away. "That's not too serious. Shall we try her?"

Ruby shook and muttered inaudibly.

"Come on," I insisted. "We have to start somewhere. She doesn't look too scary."

Ruby bit her knuckles.

"I'll do the talking," I promised. "You just come with me."

"Okay..." She looked about as frightened as if I had suggested apprehending an armed robber rather than approaching a timid-looking lady with crutches.

I gave a steely nod and trotted to catch up with the lady. Unsure of what to say once I got to her, I ended up walking alongside her for a while. Ruby dawdled several paces behind.

Eventually I squeaked, "Excuse me."

The lady turned. "Yes?"

I forced a smile. "I noticed you've got crutches and I wondered..." The words almost caught in my throat as I said hoarsely, *"CanIprayforyou?"*

The lady squinted in the sunlight. "What did you say?"

I bit my lip and whispered, "I asked... I mean, I was just wondering if..."

She waved a hand and shook her head. "You'll have to speak up. I'm a bit deaf." She indicated a hearing aid.

My stomach lurched. *Oh great.*

It took everything in me not to apologise and run away. I swallowed hard before trying again. "I saw your crutches," I yelled, pointing awkwardly. "And I... We..." I indicated Ruby who went bright red and ducked behind a nearby lamppost. "We wondered if we could pray for your leg... Or your ears." I finished with a stutter.

The lady looked a little taken aback and I braced myself for a scolding. To my relief she smiled and said, "That's very nice of you."

16

My heart beat double time. "Is that a yes?"

She laughed and said, "Thank you." Then she started to hobble away.

I felt myself blushing as I ran after her and said loudly, "I mean now? Can we pray now?"

She looked at me in surprise. "Oh! Okay."

I breathed a sigh and beckoned for Ruby to come and join me. Ruby shook her head and shimmied further out of sight.

"What do I need to do?" the lady asked.

I didn't know whether to confess that she was the first person I had ever done this with. I tried to sound confident as I said, "You don't need to do anything. Some people close their eyes but you don't have to. Is it okay if I put my hand on your cast?"

"Alright." The lady watched as I knelt down and put a tentative hand on her leg.

I had to put my other hand on the ground to keep myself from falling over. My heart was beating so loudly that I could barely hear myself think. Inwardly, I was praying frantically, *God I'm so scared... Please, please heal her. I have no idea what to do...* Outwardly, I cleared my throat and attempted a calm prayer, "Dear Jesus, please come and heal[5] this lady's leg... Amen." I stood up and gave a quick shrug.

The lady smiled. "Thank you."

I shrugged again. "It's alright."

She nodded and walked away.

"Have a nice day," I said awkwardly.

She turned back, cupping an ear. "Pardon?"

"Have a nice day!" I yelled, kicking myself for not being brave enough to pray for her ears too.

She grinned and walked on.

As I watched her hobbling down the high street, it occurred to me that I hadn't even thought to ask if she felt any better. Considering she was still using her crutches, I assumed not.

"Well done," Ruby whispered as she rejoined me.

I exhaled. Part of me was buzzing from the rush of actually daring to pray for a complete stranger in the middle of the street. But I couldn't help feeling disappointed that the lady hadn't thrown down her crutches with a jubilant cry. "Let's find someone else," I said before I could lose my nerve.

---

[5] I realised at this moment that I hadn't thought to ask the lady's name or even what was wrong with her.

Ruby turned pink. "Oh. Okay."

Another lady with crutches emerged from a nearby shop.

My stomach knotted. "Her?"

Ruby trembled as she muttered, "If you want."

I paused, checking for hearing aids, before darting over to the lady. In my haste, I tripped over one of her crutches and she tutted at me as I leapt to the side.

"Sorry," I said. "Er... Do you want, I mean, can I pray for you?"

"What?"

I gulped and repeated, "Can I pray for you?"

She gave a funny laugh before saying, "No," and hobbling off.

I returned to Ruby feeling rather crestfallen. "She said no."

Ruby gave me a little pat. "Well done anyway."

I looked around. "There's someone with a stick..." I pointed to an old man. "Shall we try him?"

"If you want..."

I nodded and stepped into the man's path. "Excuse me... I saw your walking stick and just wondered if I could pray for you?"

He raised an eyebrow.

"Because I follow Jesus," I added clumsily, digging my nails into the palms of my hands. "And he told his followers to heal people." Even as I said it, I wondered if I had got it all horribly wrong. After all, if Christians were really meant to be out healing people then why weren't more of us doing it?

The man smiled. "I need a hip replacement," he said. "I'm afraid it can't be healed without surgery."

"But Jesus can do anything," I insisted.

He chuckled. "You can try if you like."

"Yes please," I squeaked. "What's your name?"

"Mike."

I nodded and looked at the floor. I wasn't sure about touching him so I just waved a hand half-heartedly in the air as I mumbled, "God, I know you can heal Mike's hip. I ask that you would do it right now." I tentatively looked up. "Is it any better?"

Mike shifted his weight slightly and moved from side to side. "It could be a bit better," he said slowly.

"Really?" I gasped.

"It's hard to say... Like I said, it won't be fully better without surgery."

"But it feels better?"

He rocked from side to side again. "A bit... Who knows?"

I could hardly contain my excitement and just stared at him in wonder as a dopey grin landed on my face.

He chuckled again. "Well, thanks. Have a nice day."

"I will! You too."

As he hobbled off, I ran to Ruby and said, "He got a bit better!" She forced a smile and nodded.

We stared after Mike until he was almost out of sight. It didn't look like he was walking any straighter but, spurred on by this potential success and ignoring the nagging feeling that he had only said it to be polite, I took a deep breath and looked round to see who I could approach next.

Over the next hour I tried to offer healing to six more people but, unfortunately, Mike's slight improvement was as good as it got. Two people allowed me to pray but didn't report even the tiniest change, and the other four seemed rather affronted at my offer of prayer and walked off without even giving me a shot at it. I wasn't sure what bothered me most: praying and failing, or being regarded as a fool and not even getting the chance to pray in the first place. All the while, a war was raging inside me. *I don't want to do this... I do want to do this... I don't want to do this... I do want to do this...* If I hadn't just made a vow to waste my life for Jesus, I probably would've stopped right there. But, having been so determined to give God everything, I hated the idea of quitting so easily.

Ruby watched me from a distance, growing increasingly more fidgety as time went on.

As I was dismissed by a lady who snapped, "I don't do religion!" I headed back to Ruby and muttered, "Which is least offensive: *'I can heal you,'*? Or, *'Jesus wants to heal you,'*? Or just, *'Can I pray for you?'*?"

From the look on her face, they all sounded equally ridiculous.

I took a deep breath as another man with a walking stick crossed the road in front of us. As soon as he was within earshot, I called out, "I see you've got a stick!"

The man looked quite insulted. I had barely said, "Can I—" before he sniffed and strode off.

I turned uncomfortably back to Ruby.

She had gone rather pale and looked like she would soon need medical assistance herself. "Can we stop?" she pleaded. "I think you're upsetting people."

I sighed and followed her to a bench.

A lady sat nearby wearing a neck brace. I uttered a quiet prayer under my breath but nothing seemed to happen.

Ruby began rummaging around in her shopping, admiring her purchases as she pulled things out one by one.

My failed attempts went round and round my head as I watched the world rush past us. Suddenly it seemed that everywhere I looked there were people with crutches and sticks and wheelchairs. And those were just the ones with *visible* ailments. "So many people need healing," I said sadly.

Ruby blushed and put her shopping away.

We sat in silence, catching each other's eye whenever someone went past who looked particularly sick. *Was the power to heal them **really** sitting inside us?*

I wondered whether anybody had tried praying for my mum when she got ill. Had it been God's will for her to die at that time, in that way, on that day exactly, or had there been Christians around her with lifesaving power in their hands who just didn't know how to use it? I clenched my fists. *Could she have lived?*

"I don't get it," I said. "Jesus told his followers to heal people. So why didn't my prayers work?"

Ruby sucked in her cheeks. "Eddie and Summer talk about *living in the tension.*"

I looked at her in confusion. Our youth leaders were generally pretty wise. "What does that mean?"

Ruby shrugged. "I think it means God's Kingdom is here but not yet fully here. Sometimes people get healed and sometimes they don't. Like... We don't always know whether God wants to heal someone or not so we just have to pray and then accept it if they don't get better. I think that's what Summer said anyway."

I frowned. "You mean God might not want to heal everyone?"

She shrugged again. "I guess. We don't always know his will." She shifted awkwardly. "I don't really know. You should ask Summer sometime."

"Alright..." I gave Ruby a determined nod and dug into my bag.

She watched as I pulled my phone out and scrolled down to find Summer's number.

"Livi!" Summer answered after a few rings. "How are you?"

"Fine," I said. "I was just wondering about healing... How do we do it?"

Summer gave a bemused chuckle. "That's a big question."

Ruby nudged me and indicated herself.

I rolled my eyes. "Ruby says hi."

Summer laughed again. "Hi Ruby!"

"Summer says hi," I whispered quickly.

Ruby grinned and went to say something else.

"Anyway..." I gave Ruby a pointed look before turning back to my phone. "We tried praying for a few sick people in town—"

"Well done!" Summer sounded surprised. "That's very brave."

"I know. But it didn't work."

Summer sighed. "Healing is quite a complicated topic, Livi. All we can do is pray and trust the results to God."

"But he does *want* to heal everyone, doesn't he?"

There was a pause. "We don't always know what God wants to do."

I was aghast. "So he might *not* want to heal everyone?"

Summer sounded almost apologetic as she replied, "Like I said, it's not an easy topic."

My heart sunk. Why did Jesus tell his disciples to heal the sick if it wasn't God's will to do it all the time? How was I meant to know who God wanted to heal? What if I had just wasted a whole load of time pestering people who God wanted to keep sick?

Maybe I should leave healing for now...

I bit my fingernails as I pulled out my *Disciple To-Do List*. "What about demons?"

Summer gave a concerned hum. "It's probably best to leave that kind of thing to the ministry team."

I paused. "Can I join the team?"

Summer didn't reply for a moment. "We can talk about that at some point."

I felt crushed. Summer was meant to have all the answers. She always had done before. She'd been the standard by which I had measured my Christian life and she'd always been quick to spur me on, encouraging me that I was doing a good job and to keep going. Suddenly, it felt as though whole realms of the Kingdom were unattainable and unknowable. "Okay," I muttered. "Well, thanks..."

"Thanks for ringing, Livi."

I said goodbye and hung up. Then I turned to Ruby as yet another person hobbled past on crutches. "I don't get it," I moaned. "Why would Jesus tell us to heal people if he doesn't want to actually do it?"

Ruby shrugged and said nothing.

~ 3 ~

No going back

If I had been betting, I'd have reckoned it would have been Ruby and not me who would have fainted minutes into our first day at college.

According to our timetable, our first lesson was Small Animal Hygiene led by someone called Sharon Sheppard. After a frantic rush to register in the main hall (and almost accidentally joining the Horticulture course), we located our classroom where we were met by a lady of around Jill's age who had the appearance of a new age hippy.[6] By her desk sat a cage filled with squeaking guinea pigs.

I nudged Ruby and grinned. She gave a little grimace. Years ago, Ruby's cousin put a guinea pig in her Christmas stocking as a joke. Ruby was half asleep and, thinking it was a bobble hat, put it on her head. It almost clawed her ear off and, understandably, she has hated them ever since.

Rather than take a register, Sharon Sheppard introduced herself with the words, "I won't beat around the bush. If you can't stick a finger in a guinea pig's nose then you're not cut out for this course. Who wants to go first?"

Ruby gulped and gripped my arm.

I glanced around the room. None of the fifteen or so students in our class showed any signs of stepping up to the challenge so, keen to make a good first impression, I raised my hand.

Our teacher caught my eye, picked up one of the guinea pigs (a particularly hairy and fidgety one with red eyes and a menacing stare), and strode over.

I could feel Ruby shaking as Sharon nodded and held it towards me.

---

[6] She wore a long floaty skirt and the same crystal necklace as my new age stepmother.

I peered at the creature's scrunched up face and frowned. "Its nose is a bit small. Do you actually want me to stick my finger *inside—?*" However, before I could get all the words out, I caught a whiff of something foul protruding from the animal's nostrils and a wave of nausea rushed over me. The next thing I knew, I was staring up at our teacher from a splattered position on the floor. Ruby stood beside me, stroking the guinea pig which lay fast asleep in her arms.

Sharon squatted next to me, peering so closely that I could see the faintest specks of purple in her misty grey eyes. I kind of hoped she would help me up but she didn't. She just kept staring at me, leaning so close that I had no choice but to roll awkwardly into the centre of the room before scrambling to my feet. A few of my new classmates eyed me curiously as I blushed and made my way back to my desk.

"Are you quite finished?" asked Sharon.

"Yeah," I whispered.

"Good." She snatched the guinea pig off Ruby. "Would you like to try again?"

I gulped and debated telling her I had meant to join the Horticulture course. I half shook my head but she kept on staring at me so I sucked in my breath and delicately aimed a little poke up the creature's nose.

The guinea pig squeaked and went to bite me.

I quickly pulled away and Ruby almost fell off her chair as she eyed something green and slimy on the end of my finger. I grimaced and wiped it under the table.

Sharon gave a steely nod and marched back to her desk. "Now then..." She looked round the class. "You're all here because you desire a career in caring for animals..."

I caught Ruby's eye and we exchanged secret smirks. I wondered if it was too soon to ask where the field trip was going to be.

"Animals have certain differences from humans," Sharon continued. "What are they?"

A girl at the front raised her hand. "They can't speak English."

Sharon wrote it on the board. "What else?"

"They don't wear clothes," a boy called out.

I rolled my eyes as the rest of the class started shouting out suggestions.

After establishing that animals do not cook, iron, drive cars or write poetry, Sharon Sheppard handed out photocopies of diseased-looking guinea pigs and had us write down a list of all the ways their needs might differ from that of a human. Alongside this, she worked her way down the register, calling us to the front one by one to come and stick a finger up a guinea pig's nostril.

Unfortunately for Ruby, the guinea pig that she was assigned seemed to have more than its fair share of nasal excretion and Ruby wobbled back to her seat looking as green as the mess on her finger. I rubbed her back and tried to be sympathetic as she moaned that she wanted to throw up. But my attempt to assure her that our ordeal was over was interrupted by Sharon barking my name from the front.

"Livi Starling. Your turn."

I arose a little awkwardly and tried to excuse myself. "I, er... I did it earlier, remember?"

She gave a grim smile. "Are you or are you not serious about this course?"

I had no idea how to answer honestly to that so I gave a quick nod, shuffled over to her desk and poked the nearest guinea pig. Then I ran back to my seat, careful to avoid the small puddle of sick by Ruby's chair.

I had hoped the morning would get better but, after Small Animal Hygiene, we were baffled to discover we had a class called *'Ageing Dogs.'*

Our tutor was a hairy man who looked rather like an ageing dog himself. He introduced himself as *'Alf,'* which sounded like something a dog might say, before asking us to get into groups of four.

As the class broke into awkward muttering, I took a moment to assess our peers. On the whole, they were a rather bedraggled-looking lot with very little to attract anybody to them. Certainly, there was no *Kitty Warrington* type among them. I wasn't sure whether to feel pleased about this— perhaps I could rise to the role of most popular girl in college— or a little disturbed that we had chosen a course without the faintest whiff of *cool*.

Ruby and I were joined by a couple of girls and I smiled as they plonked their pencil cases down opposite ours.

"Hi," I said. "I'm Livi and this is Ruby."

Ruby joined me in offering the two girls a friendly wave.

"Hi Libby—"

"Livi," I corrected.

"Oh." The girls looked at me. One of them introduced herself as Maria. The other, Ellen, gave a shy smile and asked if we had any pets.

"She has a dog," I said, pointing to Ruby.

"Yeah, he's an *ageing* dog." Ruby giggled.

Neither of them laughed.

"Which high school did you go to?" asked Maria.

"Hare Valley," I replied, feeling an ache in my chest as I wondered what we were missing.

Maria turned to Ruby who nodded and said, "Same. How about you?"

"Copperfields."

We looked at Ellen.

"Roundwood."

We nodded politely. Since we knew nothing whatsoever about each others' schools, there wasn't much more to say about them.

I gave a little cough. "So... do you guys want, like, a career with animals and stuff?" I was unsure whether to accompany this question with a knowing smile that said, *'Yeah, yeah, we're here for the field trip too!'*

They both nodded.

My heart sunk. "Cool."

Alf got our attention and said we would be doing a bit of role playing. "If you will," he barked. "I'd like you to choose one person to be the dog."

I looked at my group. Ruby had gone bright red and Maria and Ellen were both staring at the floor.

After a very long silence, I volunteered.

Since I proceeded to spend most of the time on all fours, I'm not sure I learnt much in that lesson other than the fact that the Ageing Dogs classroom floor smells an awful lot like sprouts.

The day only got worse. After learning about parasites in Skin Anatomy, we were dismayed to discover that we had Sharon Sheppard again for Dissection. Studying our timetable, I couldn't help but feel disappointed. I'd had an illogical hope that Ms Sorenson, our favourite high school teacher, would be amongst our list of ABC tutors. She had left Hare Valley the previous year and, despite our careful stalking on the internet, Ruby and I had no idea where she was now. For a month leading up to the start of our course, I had entertained myself with wild daydreams of Ms Sorenson teaching us how to ride a horse.

We had barely sat down before Sharon went to fetch a tray of dead mice. By now, we were thoroughly convinced that Sharon was a witch. Besides her spooky attire, which was a dead giveaway, she also had scarlet hair and a cavernous black bag. She watched us with the sort of concentration of someone preparing to take over the world and, every so often, muttered something under her breath. She even had a huge book in her bag covered with cat stickers which we saw her sneak the odd peek at when she thought nobody was watching.

"I dare you to look," I whispered after betting Ruby five pounds that it was full of spells.

Ruby went red. "No way!" she spluttered. "I don't want to be turned into an animal, or whatever it is witches do!"

I rolled my eyes. "She can't do anything to us. We've got Jesus."

"Oh yeah... You're right. *She* should be scared of *us*."

"*Exactly!*"

So, for the rest of the lesson, we took every opportunity to drop little hints so that if Sharon *was* a witch she would know that we were Christians and that we weren't to be messed with. Ruby drew a big cross on her backpack and I scratched *'Jesus Rules!'* onto my new pencil tin. We loudly invited Maria and Ellen to come to church sometime.[7] Then, as soon as the lesson ended, we made a point of handing out Bible bookmarks to the rest of our baffled classmates.[8] Unfortunately, Sharon showed no sign of being intimidated and even brought a stuffed badger out of her cupboard which she held in the doorway as the class filed out.

Ruby went white at the sight of it and sprinted out of the room.

I tried to remain calm as I marched out, shooting Sharon a look which I hoped said, *'Your threats don't scare me, witch!'*

Sharon just patted the badger and gave a wicked smile.

We walked out of the college gates in utter despair.

"Do you think we've made a mistake?" Ruby moaned.

"No!" I insisted. "Trust me..." I ran a hand across my face and caught a whiff of guinea pig. I gulped before repeating, "Trust me... It will get better."

By the end of the week, however, I had to conclude that it hadn't

---

[7] They responded with unimpressed frowns and quickly looked away.
[8] I had recently acquired the bookmarks from a stash belonging to Ruby's mother as a small step in my efforts to start preaching the gospel.

got much better— unless you count checking a hedgehog for ticks and almost catching them ourselves.

We had Sharon the witch for at least two classes a day which meant being constantly on guard and remembering to whisper, *"Jesus is Lord,"* every time she spoke. The only thing that got us through was discussing possible locations for the mystery field trip. Ruby was holding out for Africa but I felt I'd be happy going anywhere with more sunshine than England.

As I poured over my Small Animal Hygiene homework that weekend, Jill watched me from the sofa and asked, "How was your first week?"

"It was great, thanks!"

She craned her neck to try to see the book I was reading.[9] "You're glad you chose the course?"

"Totally!" I forced an overexcited laugh. "Best course ever!"

She gave a quick smile. "Good. Whatever makes you happy."

I nodded and turned back to my book. There was a picture of a rotting tooth accompanied by the words, *'Does your hamster sneeze a lot? It could be tooth decay...'* I puffed out my cheeks and wondered whether it was too late to ask to go to the sixth form at my old school instead.

Right on cue, my phone started ringing with a call from Annie.

"Hey Annie," I cried, trying to sound cool. "How was your week?"

"It was awful!" she replied with a sob. "Fester gave us extra homework because apparently that's what happens in sixth form. And, now that we don't have to wear school uniform, every morning is a pain deciding what to wear. Kitty Warrington has just been elected Student Rep and Molly Masterson is the new Equalities Officer. Oh and Rupert Crisp says hello."

I hung up feeling worse than ever. Going back was not an option.

---

[9] *'Hamsters and their teeth.'*

~ 4 ~

How to fight a witch

After two weeks of pretending to want a career with animals, I wasn't sure I could take much more. My head was full of gruesome facts, my hands were covered in bites and stings, and my clothes were reeking of the smell of dead mouse. The sole perk of the course was the vast inspiration for animal noises from the various creatures on the farm[10] but, if I'm completely honest, after being exposed so regularly to whole rooms filled with shrieking guinea pigs I'd have been happy never to have heard another animal noise ever again.

As we endured another miserable Dissection class with Sharon the witch, I gave Ruby a solemn nod and said, "That's it."

"What's it?"

"I'm going to ask."

Ruby clamped a hand over my mouth. "Don't ask if she's a witch," she hissed. "She might put a curse on you!"

I shoved Ruby's hand away, retching and spluttering from the taste of dead mouse on her fingers. "I'm not going to ask *that!*" I snapped. "I'm going to ask where the field trip will be."

"Oh! Well, yeah... I kind of expected you to do that ages ago."

I rolled my eyes and glanced across at Sharon Sheppard. She was staring vacantly at the fish tank at the side of the room. I followed her gaze, half expecting the fish to pop out of the water one by one under her magical glare.

I raised a hand.

Sharon saw but said nothing.

---

[10] Already I had added *Indifferent Donkey* and *Embarrassed Dog* to my repertoire.

After a few minutes of waving my arm in the air, I took a deep breath and trotted over to her desk. "Excuse me..." I attempted a friendly smile. "Where's the field trip going to be?"

Sharon raised an eyebrow. "The field trip?"

"Yeah. We were just talking about it." I indicated Ruby who went bright red and put a hand over her face.

Sharon gave me a long look before saying, "Wait and see." Before I could beseech her further, she got up from her desk and walked away.

I sighed and returned to my seat, narrowing my eyes as Sharon the witch started prowling the classroom.

"How are you getting on?" she asked the group at a nearby table.

"Is this part of the mouse's liver?" asked a girl called Laura.[11]

"Mmm," Sharon replied. "Apparently it tastes of chicken. I'm not so sure."

I gulped and exchanged an uneasy glance with Ruby.

"What if the field trip's in Transylvania?" she whispered.

"Then we'll just have to quit the course."

"But what if that's what she *wants?* We can't let her win!"

My stomach churned. "You're right. Don't show her that you're frightened."

Ruby quivered as she attempted to exchange her grimace for a smile. "Is this better?"

I screwed up my nose. "You look like someone turned you to stone."

Right on cue, Sharon the witch looked over and grinned.

Summer was rather alarmed to hear that we were being taught by a witch.

---

[11] Of all the students on our course, Laura Ruffles is probably the one who is most cut out for a career with animals. Despite looking quite fragile— she has fluffy blonde hair, dimpled cheeks, a rather dainty frame and is only four feet tall— she is rather plucky and incredibly strong. Just last week, we saw her sprinting into the field to turn over an upside down sheep. We rather hoped she might like to be our friend but, when we asked if she wanted to hang out some time, she gave a noncommittal shrug and said, "I'll think about it."

"We think she's trying to scare us into leaving the course," Ruby told our youth group that evening.

"Today, she talked about eating mouse liver," I added.

Everyone recoiled and the younger members went white.

"That's so wrong," said Joey, shaking his head in disbelief.

"You've got to do something," Nicole warned.

We nodded and turned to Summer.

She looked rather concerned as she glanced at her husband and muttered, "What do you think, Eddie?"

Eddie chewed his lip and mulled it over. "What makes you think she's a witch?" he asked.

"She looks like one," Ruby retorted.

"She's always muttering spells under her breath and she has a stuffed badger," I added.

Eddie didn't look convinced. "I'm sure there's nothing to worry about. Anyway, you know Jesus is more powerful than anything, don't you?"

"We know," I said. "We've made it clear we're Christians. We made t-shirts and handed out Bible bookmarks."

Amanda Gipping, a newcomer to the group, put a hand to her mouth. "Don't draw attention to yourself!" she squealed. "She'll get you!"[12]

My stomach lurched but Eddie just said, "It's alright, Amanda. Nobody's going to get—"

"You have to fight her!" Bill piped up. "*She's* the one who should leave."

"Steal her spell book and burn it," suggested Kevin.

"We could do that," I said. "We know what it looks like and she's always leaving her bag unattended."

The group screeched in excitement.

"Don't look into her eyes!"

"Burn her shoes too!"

Joey and Mark were about to give us tips on starting a fire from scratch when Eddie interrupted loudly, "Guys! Calm down! Even if this lady *was* a witch, that's not how Christians fight!"

---

[12] At thirteen, Amanda is our youngest member. She joined after being invited by her next door neighbour, Kevin Moore, who got baptised at Kings Church just before the summer. Kevin's older sister, Grace, used to come to youth group and was probably on my list of *'Top Ten Favourite Christians'* but she left this year to go to university.

We fell silent and turned back to Eddie, feeling a little sheepish as he shook his head and repeated, "Calm down!"

After a moment's pause, Kevin put his hand up. "How do we fight then?"

Eddie gave a firm nod. "We pray."

"Let's pray now!" Kevin jumped up in earnest.

"We *have* to pray!" Amanda cried. "Can we?"

Eddie looked like he was about to refuse but, catching sight of our anxious faces, he said, "I suppose it can't hurt to pray. But don't get carried away."

"Hooray!"

Ruby and I joined the group in leaping to our feet and, within seconds, Eddie's discussion on *'Helping the needy'* was abandoned in favour of ardent petitions and exuberant chanting as we pleaded with God to come in power and *'defeat the witch.'*

"I wish Violet was here," Ruby whispered halfway through. "She'd have loved this."

I gave a withering smile. I had no doubt Violet the Zealot would have thrown herself headfirst into the commotion and taken no time in lecturing us on all the appropriate Bible verses to use as ammunition against Sharon Sheppard. As well-meaning as this would have been, the very presence of Ruby's sister at a time like this would have more than overshadowed the ordeal of having a witch for a teacher. I couldn't help feeling relieved that she was over a hundred miles away at Art College.

It didn't take long before our prayers ran out of steam and, one by one, we sat back against the sofas, grinning at one another as though we had just toppled a mighty foe.

"I wonder if she wears a black hat!" said Kevin.

"Maybe it won't fit now that we've prayed," Amanda suggested.

Ruby and I exchanged hopeful glances but Eddie interrupted with another rebuke. "Guys! Whether she's a witch or not, let's not forget that she's also a person! A person who God loves and wants to save."

We all fell silent once more.

I caught Ruby's eye and shrugged, trying not to giggle as she whispered, "We could sneak a Bible bookmark into her spell book."

Eddie checked his watch. "Right. We've still got a bit of time left. Let's look at the parable of the Good Samaritan..."

There was some noisy fidgeting as people reached for their Bibles and made themselves comfortable.

I found the story in my Bible and tried to concentrate as Eddie read from his but, pretty soon, his words became a blur as my mind drifted to thoughts of Sharon the witch. I wondered what she was doing right now. Perhaps eating a mouse or turning someone into a badger. I couldn't help but wonder if our prayers had actually *done* anything. Like with my futile attempts to heal the sick, I didn't want to throw up vain requests, never knowing whether God had heard me or whether I was doing things right.

I sighed and started to flick through my Bible where my eyes landed on the end of Mark's gospel. *'These signs will accompany those who believe: in my name they will drive out demons...'*

My *Disciple To-Do List* came to mind. *Drive out demons.* I was meant to be able to do that. If I wasn't sure how to defeat a witch, how could I ever face a demon? I didn't even know what one looked like. Were they tall? Did they wear clothes? A more terrifying thought struck me: *What if there are demons in Sharon's classroom?*

I turned back to my Bible, skimming the gospels for advice on the matter. Now that I was focusing on it, I could hardly believe how many references there were to Jesus casting out demons. It was everywhere. And his followers did it too. How could I have been a Christian for nearly three years and never heard a single preach on it? I looked up at Eddie in confusion.

He caught my eye and smiled. "What do you think, Livi?"

I blushed. "What?"

"Who is it?"

I bit my lip as I tried to guess from his facial expression what the right answer might be. I contemplated playing the odds and saying, *'Jesus,'* but, with thoughts of demons filling my mind, the answer could just as easily have been *'the devil.'* "I, er, I don't know."

Eddie gave me a concerned look. "Is everything alright, Livi?"

"Yeah! It's just a hard question."

He nodded slowly and turned to the rest of the group. "Anybody else?"

I felt my cheeks burning as Amanda answered what had obviously been a very simple question. "Your neighbour is anybody you meet."

Eddie thanked her and carried on with his talk.

I rubbed my forehead and turned back to my own Bible study. The more I read, the more confused I got. If there were that many demons around when Jesus was on the earth, then where were they all now?

Summer seemed to mistake my silent musings for fear of Sharon and came over as soon as the meeting ended. "Are you alright, Livi?" she asked.

"I was thinking about demons," I blurted out.

She looked at me in alarm. "Oh Livi... Don't worry about that."

"I'm not worried. I just want to know what they do."

Summer grimaced. "You shouldn't be thinking about things like *demons,*" she cautioned, saying the word *'demons'* really quietly, as though one might come if she spoke too loudly.

"But where are they?" I demanded. "And how do we drive them out?"

She shook her head and signalled for me to lower my voice. "It's a complicated topic. Leave it for now and we'll talk about it another time." She indicated Amanda and Kevin who were watching us wide-eyed, looking as though they were about to wet themselves.

I pursed my lips. "Okay. When?"

"Pardon?"

"When can we talk about it?"

Summer looked a little taken aback. She took me to one side and checked that nobody was listening before warning me, "I don't want you to get too curious about things that are unhelpful. Some people are convinced they see demons everywhere and they get themselves into all sorts of bother."

I opened my mouth and closed it again. I wanted to know who those people were. They sounded like people worth meeting.

When I didn't reply, Summer put a hand on my shoulder. "I understand your anxiety, Livi. It must be a bit startling having a witch for a teacher."

I shook my head. "It's not that startling," I said slowly. *Not as startling as learning my youth leader is more afraid than me.*

~ 5 ~

Dangerous circumstances

 W e decided it was best not to tell Ruby's parents about the witch issue. They were already a bit concerned about the course, having stumbled upon Ruby's drawing of the insides of a mouse,[13] and kept dropping heavy hints about a Bible school in Manchester that was accepting late applications.

Her father, Stanley, was continually slipping little notes into her lunchbox that read, *'I'm proud of you and I hope you're having fun but if you fancy learning some systematic theology then let me know!'*

And, in what I would consider a rather low shot, her mother, Belinda, even primed Ruby's six year old brother, Oscar, to declare loudly one dinner time, "Ruby, you need to wash your hands again. You smell like you've been handling dead chickens."

Unfortunately, it happened to be on an evening when Jill and I were round for dinner and, just as Ruby retorted, "I've not been anywhere near a chicken," Stanley asked my sister about her day at work.

"It was fine," Jill replied. "I visited the production house."

"What's the production house?" Belinda enquired meekly.

Jill forced a smile. "It's where the chickens are killed."

Oscar's jaw dropped open as he looked from Jill to Belinda. *"Mum!* It's not Ruby who smells. It's Auntie Jill!"

Belinda tittered as she said rapidly, "Nobody smells, my little pumpkin. Or, at least, nobody smells *bad."* She paused. "Jill, you smell lovely. What perfume are you wearing?"

"None."

---

[13] Splattered with real life blood and guts.

An awkward silence followed which Stanley attempted to fill with another chicken-related question. "Jill, am I right in thinking you're working for *Captain Barry's Chicken* now?"

Jill nodded.

"Well that's marvellous! Climbing the ranks, hey?"

Jill pursed her lips and said nothing. It was true that her new job with CBC was marginally better than her old one with CTC[14] but, having reached the peak of a career in local fast food PR, she was hardly '*climbing the ranks.*'

Stanley cleared his throat and continued, "And how's Andy?"

Before Jill could reply, Belinda corrected her husband, "You mean *Anthony*, dear."

"Andy is right," Jill said quickly. "We broke up."

Stanley gave an apologetic smile. "I'm sorry to hear that."

"It's fine," Jill insisted. "It was nothing serious. I'd almost forgotten about him actually!"[15]

After another painful silence, Belinda chuckled and said, "I don't know where I got '*Anthony*' from. I think I saw it written on the side of his motorbike."

Jill went pink.

"That *was* Anthony," I piped up. "Jill dated him last year. Then there was Jeremy. Or was it Grant—?" I caught sight of Jill's face and fell quiet. "Not that it matters."

"Of course not!" Belinda patted Jill on the shoulder. "You'll find somebody soon. Don't you worry."

Jill went even redder and stared at her food.

I looked across at Ruby and shrugged.

She gave a sympathetic smile. Then she poked her beef burger and announced to her parents, "We stretched out a cow's intestines the other day. I threw up."

Stanley raised an eyebrow and Belinda choked on a sprout.

Oscar squealed and yelled, "Cool!"

Jill, on the other hand, made no effort to hide her distaste. She gave Ruby a disgusted frown and pushed the rest of her burger into her napkin.

---

[14] *Colin's Tasty Chicken.*

[15] This was quite some artistic license. What she didn't add was that, prior to their very recent split, she had started stocking up on bridal magazines as she perfected her future signature as Mrs Andrew Banks. His reason for ending their three month relationship was that she was too clingy. She had responded by spending a whole week sobbing, *"We'd be so good together,"* into his answer phone.

I shot Ruby a pointed look and she grimaced. We had made an agreement not to mention anything about our course to any of our relatives— it was far too risky.

I tried to change the subject by congratulating Belinda on her homemade chips but, after receiving my compliment, she turned to Stanley and whispered, *"Darling!"*

Taking her hint, Stanley cleared his throat and said, "The two of you are learning lots on your course then?"

Ruby and I nodded.

"And you're enjoying it?"

I nodded extra hard, careful to shoot Jill a big beam. She looked like she still hadn't got over Ruby's intestine comment and just sniffed in return.

Stanley gave a soft smile. "Good."

Belinda didn't look convinced. "I don't like the idea of you being sick, my little carrot. Are you *sure* it's the right course?"

Ruby squirmed. "It's a great course! And I've only thrown up twice this week."

Belinda blinked at her before giving me a curious stare, as if trying to figure out whether I was the reason her little carrot was throwing her life away.

I shrugged and turned back to my food. I could hardly explain that we both hated the course and would have quit already if it wasn't for the mysterious field trip. With every passing day, our expectations had got grander and grander and, after handling a toxic-looking terrapin in that afternoon's Dangerous Circumstances class, we were convinced the trip would take us to the Congo.

I hoped the interrogation would end there but Belinda continued, "And what are your teachers like?"

I exchanged a glance with Ruby. That day, Sharon the witch had worn a floaty black dress and a scarf covered in what looked like embroidered beetles. While our classmates regarded the terrapin tank with terror, she muttered a swift spell under her breath and plunged her hand straight in.

"They're fine," I said.

"Completely normal," Ruby added. "Like normal people."

I coughed and had another go at changing the subject. "How's Violet?"

Belinda gave a worried sigh. "She has chicken pox."

At the mention of *'chicken,'* Oscar looked at Jill and tutted.

Jill stood up. "Well, this was lovely. Would you excuse us now? I have a headache."

"Oh, my poor dear!" Belinda jumped up to give Jill a hug. "You work so hard. Go and have an early night."

Jill forced a smile and grabbed her jacket.

The last thing we heard as we left the Ricos' house was Oscar warning Ruby, "That's where a career with animals leads: headaches and early nights."

"Have you actually got a headache?" I asked when we got home. "Or was it just an excuse to leave?"

Jill screwed up her nose. "I've actually got a headache."

I took a deep breath. "Can I try and heal it?"

"What?"

I smiled as if to say, *'Yeah, sure. I've always had this superpower, didn't you know?'* "Jesus told his followers to heal the sick," I explained. "So... If you like, I could pray for your head..." I held my breath. I knew I was venturing into dangerous territory. It wasn't often that I mentioned Jesus so candidly to her. We had an unspoken agreement that she wouldn't attack my beliefs as long as I kept as quiet about them as possible. This truce was relaxed around Christmas and Easter when Jill permitted me the odd comment about *'the true meaning'* of things without complaint. Although I prayed for her in secret and had a dim hope that *one day* she would seek Jesus for herself, I generally accepted that she was about as anti-God as anyone could be.

"Go on then," said Jill.

I blinked at her in surprise. "Really?"

"Well, yeah," she snapped. "My head hurts. If your God can sort it out then go for it."

I gulped, feeling my cheeks grow hot as I muttered a silent prayer. *Oh, Lord! You have to heal her! You just have to! Please show her you're real!* "Okay, er... I'll just put my hand on your head, if that's alright?"

Jill stared at me as I came towards her. I laid my hand on her temple.

"It's more *here*," she said, shifting my hand to one side.

"Okay." I tried to stay calm. *What if she doesn't get healed?* Jill closed her eyes as I started to pray. "Dear God, thank you that you love Jill. Jesus, you died for her and rose again—"

Jill opened her eyes. "I don't want a preach, Livi. Don't make my headache worse."

"Sorry," I said sheepishly. I cleared my throat and started again. "Jesus, please heal Jill's head. Please, please make it better. Amen." I took my hand away. "How is it?" I squeaked.

"About the same. Thanks anyway." She gave a quick smile and headed into the kitchen for some paracetamol.

I let out a frustrated sigh. *Well, that was pointless, wasn't it!*

When God didn't reply, I gave a growl and headed to my room. Once there, I pulled out my Small Animal Hygiene workbook and threw myself onto the bed. In my haste, I knocked my pencil tin onto the floor, sending pens flying everywhere. I gave a cry and bent down to pick them up. As I fumbled around under my bed, muttering and groaning and getting myself into a state, my hand brushed against a pile of scrunched up magazine articles. I pulled one out and unfolded it.

'Are You Wasting Your Life?'

My heart skipped a beat as I recalled my resolution to waste my life for Jesus. It had been several weeks and I wasn't sure I was living any differently. Abandoning my fallen pens, I rolled onto my back and lay on my rug, staring at the peeling paint on the ceiling.

"I want my life to count," I prayed. "But I don't know what to do. I'm trying to listen to you but I don't always hear you clearly. I'm trying to heal the sick, like you told the disciples to, but I can't do it right. Or maybe I'm just praying for the wrong people... But then I need you to tell me!" I squeezed my eyes shut. "What about Violet? Should I call her and offer to pray? Or is it your will for her to have chicken pox?"

I half reached for my phone then stopped and put my head in my hands. "I don't want to..." I moaned. "I'm bound to fail again. Oh God, I'm sorry for all the times I say I want to live for you but end up wimping out..."

I lay there for ages feeling like a hopeless case. All the while, my Small Animal Hygiene book sat waiting on my bed but I really couldn't care less about how to trim a hamster's toenails.

"There must be more than this," I muttered.

I was about to scramble off the floor and get ready for bed when a still small voice spoke into my heart. *I like you.*

I blinked, figuring I had just imagined it, but my heart pounded as it came again.

I like you. I don't just love you. I really like you.

A wave of relief washed over me as I closed my eyes and let this sink in. "I want my life to count," I repeated. "And I *am* trying..."

I expected God to reply, *Very trying,* as Jill often does. But, instead, I heard him whisper, *I know the plans I have for you. Plans to prosper you and not to harm you...*

It was the start of a popular Bible verse. I sat bolt upright and grabbed my Bible, eager to read the rest of it. "Where is it?" I threw the Bible open and started flicking through it. "Please God, help me find it..." I willed myself to stay calm as I turned to random pages.

It took me ages but, between kicking myself for not knowing the Scriptures better and texting Ruby to ask her to help me, I found it.

> *"I know the plans I have for you,' declares The Lord. 'Plans to prosper you and not to harm you, plans to give you hope and a future. Then you will call upon me and come and pray to me, and I will listen to you. You will seek me and find me when you seek me with all your heart."*[16]

The last line seemed to sparkle off the page. *'You will seek me and find me when you seek me with all your heart.'* My heart leapt as the words of the verse danced off the page and into the depths of my soul. A dangerous invitation confronted me: *Will you seek me with **all** of your heart?*

I paused and looked around, as if expecting Jesus himself to be watching from the doorway. "Help me. I want to but I don't know how."

The air felt thick with silence as I waited for God's reply.

"Help me," I repeated. "I want more of you. Do whatever it takes."

Had I known what would take place over the next few months, I might have thought long and hard before uttering such a dangerous prayer. But, as it was, nothing seemed to happen so I just picked myself up off the floor and went to bed.

I didn't know it then but sometimes God waits for permission before turning our lives upside down. I would soon learn that truly having faith in God would mean first fully losing faith in myself, and those four little words— *'Do whatever it takes'—* were to be the beginning of my great unravelling.

---

[16] Jeremiah 29:11-13.

~ 6 ~

Like salt and pepper

Ruby and I had hoped to make a few friends in time for our joint birthday party at the end of the month, but either none of our classmates liked us or else they were all genuinely busy, so we just ended up going to the park with Annie. We spent a few minutes spinning one another around on the swings before realising we were a little too old for the playground. In the end, we sat on a hill overlooking the city and picked at the grass.

"I feel so old!" I moaned, squashing a patch of dandelions with my fist.

"We *are* old," Ruby said. "We'll soon be adults!"

I screwed up my nose. There were so many things I wanted to achieve before then. I rooted around in my bag and pulled out my *Disciple To-Do List*. "I still haven't done any of these," I said glumly.

"There's a crowd down there if you fancy preaching." Ruby pointed to a group near the duck pond. "We'll watch from here."

"Nah," I muttered, throwing it back into my bag. Perhaps it was a silly list after all.

"Present time!" sang Annie, thrusting two poorly-wrapped identical packets in our direction.

I tore into mine with a grin and laughed as her gift rolled out. It was a salt shaker in the shape of a dolphin.

Ruby looked equally bemused. "Is it a pepper pot?" She gave hers a sniff and sneezed.

"Do you like them?" asked Annie. "They're friendship pots, you know? So, wherever you go, you'll know you're part of a set."

Ruby giggled as she clinked her pot with mine. "Cheers!"

I raised an eyebrow. "Thanks, Annie... But what about you?"

She beamed. "I kept the box."

Ruby gave her pot another sniff and almost choked. "Really... awesome... idea..." she gasped between sneezes.

I chuckled to myself, sprinkling some salt round my shoes before changing the subject. "How's sixth form?"

Annie frowned. "It's okay but everything's different without you two. Especially being on litter duty in the common room— it isn't the same now you're gone."

I giggled as I reminded her, "We never did litter duty."

Ruby grinned before asking, "How's The COOL Club?"

I shot her a quick look. The COOL[17] Club was the club Ruby and I had set up for Christians or people wanting to find out more. We had left Annie in charge of it but, considering we'd seen very little growth in the last two years, I had expected it to fold without us.

I was more than a little shocked when Annie said, "It's going great! Two new people joined last week!"

I stared at her. "Seriously?"

"Yeah. Georgina Harris and another girl."

"Georgina? But she never wanted to hear about Jesus!"

Annie shrugged. "She did after God healed her finger."

My heart stopped beating. "What?"

"She hurt it from using her calculator too much in Maths. I offered to pray for her and she let me. It got healed and she wanted to find out more."

My jaw almost hit the ground.

"The other girl came from Copperfields. Her name is—"

"You prayed for someone and they got healed?"

Annie grinned. "Yeah! Isn't it cool?"

"What did you pray?" I demanded. "Tell me word for word."

"I don't know. I just asked God to heal it."

"But how?" I insisted. "You have to tell me."

"I can't remember! It was so long ago."

"It was last week!"

"Yes, but I've said loads of things since then."

I growled. It wasn't fair that Annie had managed to pray an effective healing prayer without even knowing what she was doing. "I've got a guinea pig bite," I said, rolling up my sleeve. "Go on, heal it!"

Annie blinked at me.

Ruby raised an eyebrow.

---

[17] *Children Of Our Lord.*

I tried to calm down. "How many sick people have you prayed for?"

Annie shrugged. "I think that's the first one..."

"How come you can do it and I can't?" I blurted out.

She shrugged again. "I don't know. Jesus said to heal the sick, didn't he? So I just prayed."

I gaped at her. Ruby was looking a little bemused.

Annie gave an awkward smile. "I'm going to get a drink." She got up and headed for a nearby snacks hut.

I looked at Ruby. "I don't get it," I said.

Ruby grinned. "Why are you so upset about it?"

"Because it's not fair! I was a Christian before Annie. I should be able to heal people too!"

She giggled. "It's not a competition, Livi!"

I didn't want to say, *'Of course it is. I spent ages compiling my Disciple To-Do List and Annie doesn't even know what's on it!'* so I just sucked in my cheeks and looked away. "Did Annie get lucky?" I muttered. "Was she just in the right place at the right time? If I had prayed for Georgina would I have healed her too?"

"I don't know." Ruby twirled some hair round her finger. "Like Summer said; it's complicated. You just have to pray and trust the results to God."

"But surely we should be able to say, *'Hey God, do you want to heal this person?'* And he could say, *'Yes, go ahead,'* or, *'No, that's not my will. Don't even bother with that one.'*"

Ruby chewed her lip. "We live in a tension," she said unhelpfully. "Of God's Kingdom now but not yet. That's what Summer says anyway."

I wrinkled up my nose. I knew Summer was wise and had been a Christian far longer than me. She knew the Bible better and was married to a preacher. But she couldn't tell me anything about demons. I couldn't help but feel she had missed something with healing too. It just *couldn't* be the divine lottery she made it out to be. The thought occurred to me that maybe Annie was some kind of special Christian who had been granted this mysterious healing gift without even asking for it. I was about to complain to Ruby that it wasn't fair of God to pick Annie and not me but, before I could say anything, Annie came back with an armful of drinks.

"You probably won't like this," she said, "but the lady on the stall had a headache. I prayed for her and it got a bit better."

While Ruby leapt up in delight, I found myself seething. *Not fair, God! Totally not fair!*

42

My frustration lasted until my actual birthday the following Tuesday and I spent most of the morning's Dissection class scowling at the dead mouse in front of me. Sharon the witch was sitting at her desk reading sneakily from her book of spells.

I watched her for a moment before clearing my throat and declaring, "If I could have anything for my *birthday* today, I'd love *Jesus* to come for dinner." I said the words *'birthday'* and *'Jesus'* really loudly.[18]

Maria and Ellen looked a bit freaked out on the next table but Sharon Sheppard didn't bat an eyelid.

"I reckon she's scared on the inside," Ruby whispered as she prodded our mouse with some tweezers.

I gave a half-hearted grunt and picked at the mouse's tail.

Suddenly, Sharon got our attention with the words, "Class, I ought to inform you that our field trip is in three weeks' time."

I sat up in shock.

Ruby nudged me and grinned.

"You'll get a letter with more information shortly," Sharon continued. "But you might like to jot down the timings as we'll be travelling on a weekend and I'm afraid the dates are non-negotiable." She wrote some dates on the board before turning back to face us. "Any questions?"

I put my hand up. "Can you tell us where will it be yet?"

Sharon gave a wry smile. "Oh yes. It will be in Bryn Hapus."

I grabbed Ruby's arm. I had never heard of Bryn Hapus but it sounded mighty exotic. I could hardly contain my excitement as I imagined an early morning flight followed by many days trekking through the jungle in search of rare beasts.

"Anything else?" Sharon asked briskly.

My hand shot up again. "Will we need injections?"

She laughed. "No, Livi. You don't need injections to go to Wales."

My jaw fell open. *"Wales?"*

Ruby looked equally dismayed.

Sharon nodded. "South West Wales. There's a wonderful research centre specialising in sheep." She gave a grim smile.

---

[18] I figured that even if she *was* a witch, a little birthday greeting would have been nice.

"Anybody else?" When nobody responded she said, "Get on with your work then."

As the rest of our classmates broke into chatter, Ruby and I sat in stunned silence, neither of us daring to look at the other. I couldn't believe it. We had forfeited a place at sixth form for a field trip to *Wales*.

"What should we do?" Ruby whispered.

I shrugged helplessly. "Are they still accepting applications at that Bible school?"

"The deadline was yesterday."

My heart sunk.

"What should we do?" Ruby repeated.

I shook my head. "We either write this year off as a mistake... Or we get careers working with animals." I caught her eye and sighed.

She turned back to our dead mouse. "I guess I could be a vet," she said quietly. "Although *you*, Mr Mouse, are *way* beyond help."

I rolled my eyes and stared at the mouse. "If Jesus was here, could he bring it back to life?"

Ruby stuck out her bottom lip as she regarded the mouse entrails spread across our desk. "He *could...*"

I lay a finger on the mouse's chest and muttered, "Dear Jesus, please make the mouse come back to life."

Ruby gave me a baffled look before bursting into hysterics.

I ignored her and tried again. "Seriously, Jesus. Please make it live."

Ruby pounded the table so hard that our salt and pepper shakers rolled onto the floor[19] and the dead mouse nearly fell into my lap.

"Ruby!" I scolded.

She giggled as I chanted, "Come on Jesus! Raise it up! Raise it up!" I stared intently at the mouse but nothing happened.

"Maybe you should stop now," Ruby suggested.

"I don't understand!" I growled. "Jesus told his followers to *'preach the gospel, heal the sick, cleanse the lepers, cast out demons and raise the dead.'* Why can't I do it?"

At that moment, Sharon the witch appeared out of nowhere. "Is everything alright, girls?"

---

[19] We hadn't quite known what to do with Annie's bizarre gifts and had resorted to carrying them round college together, neither of us wanting to separate them.

44

I stopped my rant and prised my finger off the mouse's stone cold heart. "Yeah," I squeaked.

"What are you doing to the mouse?" She looked a little alarmed.

I was about to offer a more respectable explanation but, before I could come up with one, Ruby said feebly, "Livi wants to raise it from the dead."

I looked at her in horror before turning back to Sharon.

She had a rather funny look on her face. "Let's talk after class."

I started to shake as she walked away.

Ruby turned white as she muttered, "We're doomed."

Sharon waited until the rest of the class had left before coming over to our desk. We kept our heads low, determining not to look her in the eye.

After a short pause, she said, "I'm a Christian."

We were so stunned at her abrupt confession that we just gaped at her and said nothing.

Sharon pointed to Ruby's bag and our *'Jesus is gonna get ya!'* t-shirts. "I assume you are too?"

We nodded dumbly.

She looked at me. "I think it's great that you want to raise the dead, and by all means practise on my mice. But have you thought about starting small, with a headache perhaps?"

"I, er, yeah, I guess," I spluttered. I cleared my throat and tried to regain my composure. "I mean... You're a Christian? You're not..." I blushed.

She gave me a stern stare. "Not what?"

I shook my head and turned to Ruby who looked equally gobsmacked.

Sharon kept staring at us.

I pointed to our dead mouse and whispered, "You don't think it was silly?"

Sharon regarded the mouse. Half its organs were missing, its throat was ripped in two and it was covered in salt and pepper. "I suppose it's a little silly trying to resurrect *this* one," she said slowly. "But nothing's impossible with God."

My heart pounded. "So... do you believe in healing and stuff?"

Ruby looked rather wary as Sharon gave an ardent nod.

"And... can *any* Christian do it?" I continued. "Or is it just for... special ones?"

"It's for all Christians."

I breathed a sigh of relief. "How do..." The words caught in my throat as I asked in a whisper, "How do I do it?"

Sharon gave a thoughtful smile before replying, "For a start, you don't need to beg. Healing is God's idea. Just speak to the sickness and tell it what to do. If you're speaking in Jesus' name then you have the power to do all that God has promised."

I stared at the mouse. "So... I should say something like, 'Live in Jesus' name'?"

She pursed her lips. "Praying in Jesus' name means that you're praying in his authority. It's not a lucky charm that you wave about."

I blushed. "Okay then..." I took a moment to picture myself wrapped up in Jesus, my chest pounding as I tried again. "Live in the name of Jesus! Mouse, I command you in Jesus' name to get up!" I watched the mouse but nothing happened. I pouted. "It didn't work."

Sharon didn't look fazed. "Just keep practising."

I nodded and looked at Ruby.

She wore a somewhat sceptical expression. "Our youth leader says healing is a complicated topic..." she began a little pompously.

Sharon raised an eyebrow. "Well, I don't mean to show any disrespect to your youth leader but I would say they're wrong. Healing is a very *simple* topic."

My heart leapt. I was torn between a sense of loyalty towards Summer and a desperate desire to hear what Sharon had to say.

"But we don't always know who God wants to heal," Ruby insisted.

Sharon stared at her. "Don't we?"

Ruby frowned. "Obviously not because not everyone we pray for gets healed."

"Does everyone you pray for get *saved?*"

"No, but—"

"Yet it's God's will to save all?"

"Yes, but—"

"Should we change our theology when God's will is not done?"

Ruby sniffed. "God's will is always done, isn't it?"

Sharon kept staring at her. "Why would Jesus tell us to pray, '*Your will be done,*' if the Father's will was automatically done every time?" When Ruby didn't reply, Sharon continued, "We're in a battle to see God's will established. And the battle is not with God. He's made his will perfectly clear."

Ruby blinked at her. "Who does he want to heal then?"

46

"Everyone."

"But not everybody gets healed!" Ruby repeated.

She turned to me for help but I just shrugged. I liked what Sharon was saying and it made sense that God wouldn't actually *want* people to be ill. Yet I had to agree with Ruby that not everybody gets healed. That was plain to see. "I don't know," I muttered.

Ruby turned back to Sharon. "You honestly believe God wants to heal *everybody?*" she demanded.

Sharon nodded. "Yes, I do. I believe sickness is from the devil. I believe Jesus came to destroy every bit of the devil's work and gave his followers the authority to do the same. I believe that Jesus not only dealt with our sins on the cross but he bore our sicknesses and dealt with them too. After all, it was sin that brought sickness into the world in the first place so the provision for healing comes with forgiveness. They're inseparable." She gave a coy grin before adding, "Kind of like salt and pepper!"

I could hardly believe what I was hearing. Why had nobody told me this before?

Ruby frowned and tucked our salt and pepper shakers out of sight. "Do you have any books on the matter? I need to ask my mum."

Sharon gave a wry smile and rooted around in her bag. "Here," she said, handing us her book covered in cats.

We took it in alarm and threw it open. It was a Bible.

Ruby looked affronted. "The Bible doesn't say that God wants to heal *everyone,*" she snapped, slamming the Bible down.

"Are you sure?" Sharon challenged. "Or are you just going by your experience?" She picked up her Bible and thumbed through it. *"By his wounds we are healed... He forgives all your sins and heals all your diseases... I am willing."*

Ruby opened her mouth and closed it again. "But not everyone gets healed!" she exclaimed. By this point, she was bright red and closer to exploding than I had ever seen her. "We've tried it and it doesn't work!"

"That is true," I conceded. "We did try it."

Sharon pursed her lips. "How many people have you prayed for?"

"About five," Ruby retorted. "And none of them got healed."

"One man said he felt a bit better," I reminded her. "Remember Mike?"

Ruby screwed up her nose. "He was just saying it to be nice."

47

I scowled at her but, before I could respond, Sharon said, "Don't pray for five people and conclude it doesn't work. Pray for five *hundred* people and then come and tell me what you've learnt."

I let this sink in. "Five *hundred* people..?"

Ruby had stopped short but was still looking a little sceptical. "Does everyone *you* pray for get better?" she demanded.

"No," Sharon admitted. "But enough to convince me to keep going." She leant over to pick up the dead mouse and began to scoop it into a special box, turning her back on us as if to signify that the conversation was over.

Ruby and I took the hint and picked up our bags. My head was reeling as I walked to the door. I turned back to give Sharon one last look and caught her in the middle of trying to resurrect the mouse herself.

She grinned. "Well, we're all *practising* Christians, aren't we?"

I nodded in confusion and turned to go.

"Oh, and Livi?"

I turned back one last time. "Yeah?"

"Happy birthday!"

~ 7 ~

Will you be a trailblazer?

It took quite some effort to persuade Ruby to come out with me to try to heal people again. She was still convinced there was something dodgy about Sharon.

"If she's really not a witch then why does she dress like that? And why is she always so moody?"

"There's no time for questions," I said as I paced round her bedroom the following afternoon. "We've got five hundred people to pray for!"

Ruby screwed up her nose.

"Where would there be lots of sick people?" I continued, peering out of the window for inspiration.

"The hospital," she muttered.

I turned in surprise. "Do you want to pray for people in the hospital?"

"No way! I was just answering your question."

I sucked in my breath. "Where should we go then?"

She gave a careless cough and reached for her Small Animal Hygiene homework. "Don't know..."

"Come on, Ruby!" I begged, pulling her work out of her hands. "Don't you want to see people healed?"

She sighed and pulled herself off her bed. "Yeah... But I still don't know what I think about it."

"Me neither," I confessed. "But Sharon's right. We can't dismiss it till we've given it a proper go."

Ruby pouted and looked away. "I guess I just don't want to look stupid."

I bit my lip. I didn't want to look stupid either. But my fear of looking stupid was exceeded by an even greater fear— that of missing out on something incredible. "Imagine if God wants

49

everybody healed," I said. "Imagine if he's just waiting for people who dare to believe?"

Ruby shrugged. "I don't know. I asked my mum about it. She said healing is all very well but the most important thing is to make disciples."

I yanked my list out of my bag. "And what are disciples meant to do? *Preach the gospel, heal the sick, cleanse the—*"

"I know! I know!" She waved a hand. "It's just all so... complicated."

"But we've barely even tried! Don't you think if it's possible then it's worth trying? Imagine how amazing it would be if we could heal people! Nobody would need to..." A lump caught in my throat.

Ruby looked at me. "Nobody would need to what?"

"Nobody would need to die," I finished hoarsely.

She cocked her head to one side. "People would still die some time."

"But maybe not quite so soon." When Ruby kept staring I gulped before explaining, "If somebody had prayed for my mum she might not have died."

"Oh Livi..." Ruby looked uncomfortable.

"So, if it's possible to heal people, then I want to heal as many people as I can. Because I think it's probably too late to raise her from the dead..."

Ruby turned red.

"...But if I heal other people... then... it's the best I can do."

There was a long silence.

I swallowed hard.

Eventually Ruby whispered, "I don't know." She cleared her throat and reached into her bedside table.

"What's that?" I asked as she popped something into her mouth.

"Cough sweet."

"You've got a cough? Why didn't you say?" I went towards her with my hand outstretched. "Let me pray for you!"

Ruby blushed and shimmied away. "I already tried."

I stopped and stared at her.

"I prayed for myself last night. And my throat still hurts. So God obviously wants me to have a cough." She sounded a little bitter about it.

I raised an eyebrow. "Do you honestly think God wants you to have a cough?"

"Well he didn't heal it. So he must do."

I chewed the inside of my cheeks as I wondered what to say. "Why would he want you to have a cough?" I asked finally.

Ruby sat back down on her bed. "I don't know... To teach me something maybe."

"Okay... What have you learnt?"

She sniffed. "Nothing." She cleared her throat as she reached for another cough sweet. "These aren't helping at all," she moaned, turning to the back of the packet to check the ingredients.

I watched as she unwrapped a couple more. "If God wants you to have a cough then aren't you ignoring his will by trying to make yourself better?"

Ruby looked up from the packet and blinked at me. "What?"

I tried not to smirk as I repeated my question. "If it's God's will for people to be ill, then they're disobeying him every time they go to a doctor... Right?"

Her cheeks went pink as she gave a sharp intake of breath. "I hadn't thought of that..." She regarded the cough sweets in her hand and sighed as she put them down. "Okay, pray for me."

I grinned. "In the name of Jesus," I began, pointing to her throat. "I command this cough to leave right now!" I lowered my hand and shot Ruby a hopeful smile. "How does it feel?"

She cleared her throat and grimaced. "It still hurts."

I frowned before trying again. "Be healed in the name of Jesus!"

Ruby swallowed and cocked her head to one side. "I don't know. It's hard to tell."

I fought the temptation to give up there and then. "Well, shall we see if it gets better later?"

She looked relieved. "Yeah. It might just take time for the prayer to work."

"Yeah." I avoided her gaze.[20] "So... shall we go and pray for people?"

"Alright."

I pulled her off her bed with a grin. "Where would we find *loads and loads* of sick people?"

She gulped before suggesting, "The park?"

I giggled. "Sounds good to me."

---

[20] I didn't dare mention her cough again although, judging by the fact that her voice got croakier and croakier as the day went on, I would have to assume that she didn't get healed.

Ten minutes later, we walked through the great arches of Wormley park, shaking with fear and armed with Bibles. I kept my eyes peeled as I scoured the playing fields for wounded people. I couldn't see any.

"Nobody looks sick..." I said, torn between disappointment and relief.

Ruby looked back at the entrance to the park. "How about her?" She pointed to a lady who was smoking whilst perched on the stump of a tree. She wore a bright pink leather jacket, more bling than a Christmas tree and a big white cast round the bottom of one leg. She was the sort of person who, if it wasn't for the massive cast restricting her movement, I would generally avoid for fear of being beaten up.

I gulped. "Her?"

"Why not? Jesus loves everybody, doesn't he?"

I took a deep breath as I considered her words. "You're right. Jesus loves everybody and he wants to heal everybody. It's as simple as that."

Ruby nodded and shoved me forwards. "Go on then. I'll wait here."

"Ruby! You have to do this with me. We're a set! Like salt and pepper."

"Then you should have invited Annie," Ruby retorted. "She's the box, remember?"

I exhaled. I didn't want to confess that I had deliberately left Annie out of this. "She can come once I've cracked it," I muttered.

Ruby raised an eyebrow but, before she could say anything, I grabbed her arm and dragged her with me towards the lady on the tree stump. "Come on!"

The lady looked up as we got close and I felt myself blushing as I forced a smile. To my surprise, she smiled back.

I cleared my throat and curled my hands into balls as I said, "Hello... Sorry for bothering you. Er... How did you hurt your leg?"

She grinned and stuck her leg out. "Broke my ankle, didn't I? I was drunk and got my heels caught in a drain. I'm such an idiot!" She chortled and took a long drag on her cigarette.

I gulped as I wondered whether God wanted to heal even the stupidest of self-inflicted ailments. I took a deep breath before saying, "We're kind of praying for people today... Can we pray for your ankle?"

The lady gave me a curious look and I took a little step back, afraid that she might yell. "You're doing what?"

My cheeks burned as I tried to explain. "We're looking for people to heal..."

"Oh right? Like Brent Stubble?"[21]

"Er, no! We follow Jesus, so that means we can heal you."

The lady looked a bit confused. "You're gonna heal my ankle?"

"We can try," I squeaked.

Ruby was looking rather nauseous.

The lady sniffed before saying, "Yeah alright."

My heart beat heavily. "What's your name?"

"Well it's Tina really but my mates call me Apple Tart." She gave another grin.

I didn't want to ask how she'd got that nickname and just gave a quick smile in return. "Can I put my hand on your cast?"

She nodded. "Do you want me to put my cigarette out?"

"No, it's fine!" I insisted, forcing myself not to retch as smoke blew my way. I cleared my throat and started to pray. "I am speaking to Tina's ankle..."

Ruby, as red as her name, knelt down and closed her eyes as she pretended to pray with me.

My hand began to feel a bit warm as I continued, "Every bone be fixed in the name of Jesus..."

When we finished, we stood up and looked at Tina.

She wore a bemused expression. "I felt all this heat when you were doing that."

I nodded slowly. "Cool. How does it feel now?"

Tina stood up very carefully and put some weight on her foot. Her eyes widened as she exclaimed, "I can stand without it hurting!"

My jaw fell open as she danced from foot to foot, gaping at us in astonishment. "How did you do that?"

I almost said, *'I don't know!'* but composed myself in time to say, "Jesus did it. He healed you because he loves you!"

Ruby finally summoned up the courage to speak. "That's amazing..."

Tina shook her head in disbelief. "I can't believe it! So, you're... what? Like, just going round healing people?"

"Yeah, kind of!" I gave a coy shrug as Ruby nodded awkwardly.

---

[21] Brent Stubble is an illusionist who uses psychology, hypnosis and mind control to perform extraordinary feats. Some say he's a genius. Some say he's a conman. Others, like Violet, say he's got demonic powers.

"Wow!" Tina beamed before exclaiming, "Hey, you should go to the hospital! There are loads of sick people there!"

I shot Ruby a wry smile.

"I'm ripping this cast off when I get home," Tina continued. She held up a shopping bag. "Just bought a new pair of heels. I'll be hitting the town tonight!"

I giggled. "Well, it was nice to meet you... If you want to find out more about Jesus you could read the Bible or come to our church some time..." I wrote a few details about Kings Church on the back of one of Belinda's Bible bookmarks and handed it to Tina.

She took it with a smile. "Yeah, alright. I'll be telling my mates about this! Better than Brent Stubble, you are!"

My heart leapt. I imagined how impressed Summer and our youth group would be if Tina came to church with a hoard of friends that weekend. "Well, church starts at half ten on Sunday. So come along!"

"Alright," she repeated.

"Cool." I wasn't sure what else to say.

Ruby looked as dumbstruck as me. Our first healing! And it was so simple; we hadn't done anything special at all!

"Go on then!" said Tina, waving a hand. "You've got loads more people to heal."

Ruby and I nodded and said goodbye. Then we scampered into the park, salivating with excitement.

"She got healed! She actually got healed!"

"A proper healing as well, not just a headache or something little!"

Spurred on by this miracle breakthrough, we ran through the park, desperate for more people to heal. Almost immediately, we spotted a guy with a broken arm.

"Hi!" I sang. "Would you like us to heal you?"

The guy gave me a funny look and marched on.

I tried to stay cool as I glanced towards the skate park. "There's a boy over there with a cast on his wrist," I told Ruby.

She nodded and we ran over to the gang of moody-looking skaters lingering at the ramps. I couldn't wait to see their faces when we healed the boy's wrist. They turned to stare at us as we approached.

"Hello," I said, directing my attention to the injured boy. "We're healing people in the park today. Can we pray for your wrist?"

"What?"

"If we pray for your wrist, it'll get better."

The boy glanced at his friends and they all laughed. "Alright." He stuck his arm out, grinning as he did so.

Ruby had gone rather pale.

I took a deep breath, convinced that they were about to be utterly blown away. "In Jesus' name," I roared at his wrist, "be healed!" I nodded. "Give it a wave."

The boy gave me a funny look and shook his hand. I saw him wince as he said, "Ow."

My heart sunk as his friends nudged one another and burst out laughing.

"I can't believe you actually tried that, Gavin," one of them jeered.

"Let me pray again," I begged.

Gavin shook his head. "Nah, it's alright."

I blushed. "Sorry."

Ruby grabbed my arm and we trotted away as fast as we could, the taunts of the skaters echoing behind us.

"Don't worry," Ruby whispered. "Let's just try someone else."

I rubbed my head. Already the sense of victory was wearing off.

Over the next half hour, we summoned up the courage to stop three more people but, although they were friendly enough, none of them got healed. I couldn't understand it. Why did our prayers work for one person but not the rest?

"One healing is pretty good, isn't it?" Ruby said hopefully as we headed towards the playground.

I gave half a shrug as a dog ran towards us and began to sniff our feet.

"Cindy!" A man with a walking stick trotted over. "Leave them alone!"

"It's okay!" I told him. "We like dogs."

"I've got a dog," Ruby added.

He smiled. "She gets a bit overexcited. I can't get out as much as I used to."

I sucked in my cheeks and took a long time patting the dog as I considered what to say. Eventually, I said, "I see you're walking with a stick. We can heal you if you want."

The man looked me up and down and laughed. "Oh really?"

I tried to look confident as I said, "Yes."

"I've torn the tendons in my knee."

I had no idea what a tendon was but gave a nonchalant shrug. "That's no big deal. We just saw a broken ankle get healed."

"I also have diabetes and high blood pressure."

I felt my stomach churning as I insisted, "We can heal that too."

He laughed again. "Go on then! Give it your best shot!" He smirked, plonked himself onto a nearby bench, and stuck his leg in the air.

My heart pounded as I went towards him. I took a deep breath. "I command all pain in this leg to go in the name of Jesus—!"

I had barely said the word *'Jesus'* when the man sprang to his feet and pointed an angry finger at me. "No, no, no!" he roared. "That's not what you said! You reckoned *you* could heal me and suddenly you start talking about Jesus! I don't want that!"

I gaped at him. "I'm sorry. It's Jesus who heals. We just—"

"No!" The man shook his head, his face positively livid. "Jesus does not heal. Do *not* go around telling people that Jesus heals!"

Ruby had gone pink and looked close to tears. "We didn't mean to offend you..." she whispered.

He ignored her and continued his tirade. "Do *not* tell people that Jesus heals! You must not!"

I felt myself shaking as the man kept yelling at us to stop proclaiming Jesus as a healer. It seemed so bizarre; it was one thing that our mention of Jesus might offend him, but his insistence that we should stop praying for healing altogether was a little extreme. Unsure of what to do, I stared at him and tried to stand my ground.

He kept simmering and muttering until the colour in his face returned to normal and he said almost jovially, "My other leg hurts as well now! You made it worse!"

I gulped. "Sorry."

"Where's my dog? Oh, there she is. Come on, Cindy. Tea time!" He chuckled before hobbling off.

Ruby and I looked at one another.

"What was that all about?" she whispered.

I shook my head. "I have no idea."

"He was all friendly until you said *'Jesus.'*"

"Weird."

We walked on, feeling somewhat disorientated. Pretty soon, we passed a woman on crutches.

Ruby shot me a cautious glance. "What do you think?"

I gave a long sigh. The light was starting to fade. "I think I want to go home."

~*~

The next morning, I stormed into Sharon's classroom. "We prayed for six people yesterday," I told her hotly. "Seven if you count Ruby's throat—"

Ruby gave a little cough as if to prove that she still had it.

I frowned before continuing, "One girl was able to stand on her broken ankle but nobody else got healed and one man even shouted at us."

Sharon barely glanced up. "A girl's ankle got healed? Well, isn't that great?"

"But why didn't they *all* get healed?" I demanded. "Is it about how much faith I have? Because it's not fair if it is. I've got lots of faith."

Sharon gave a funny smile. "Why should everything be about *you?*"

I blushed. "Is it the people who are ill then? Should I make sure they believe before I pray?"

She shook her head. "Not necessarily."

"My mum says *partial* healings are quite common," Ruby piped up. "Maybe we should just look for small improvements?"

Sharon screwed up her nose. "I wouldn't settle for that. Jesus died fully didn't he? He didn't just partially die."

I chewed my thumb. "Perhaps people don't get healed because they've got to sort out their sin first?"

Sharon cocked her head to one side. "*Sometimes* a person might need to get right with God in a certain area of their life before healing will come, especially if there is a sin which brought the sickness on in the first place. If they are harbouring offence, for example, they may need to forgive. If they are stressed, they may need to change their thinking—"

"Lots of people are stressed!" I said in surprise.

"Yes. And lots of people are sick. Did you know there are many illnesses that are brought on by worry?"

"But we all worry sometimes," I insisted.

"It's not a sin," added Ruby.

"It is when the Bible tells us hundreds of times not to fear!" Sharon retorted. She sniffed before continuing, "*Sometimes* sin will hinder healing if left unchecked. But I wouldn't make it a rule. I wouldn't say that's the only reason for failure when we pray."

I was stumped. "What then?"

Sharon twirled a tuft of scarlet hair round her finger. "I can't pretend that I have all the answers, but I find it interesting that when Jesus walked the earth it was accepted that sickness came from the devil. Something has happened over the years to cause many Christians to now attribute sickness to God. I sometimes wonder if that shift in thinking has created a bit of a ceiling over the Church."

"A ceiling?"

She nodded. "We've accepted sickness as God's will. We believe we are powerless, and so we are."

I stuck my bottom lip out as I mulled this over. "So, healing will always be limited?"

"Not necessarily... There are many Christians around the world having tremendous breakthroughs in this area and throughout history there have always been trailblazers who dared to believe for more than the status quo. The question is: will you be a trailblazer?"

I nodded fiercely. "Yeah!"

"Really?" She raised an eyebrow. "It will be hard."

"I don't mind."

"You might have to step out when you don't want to."

"Alright."

"You might want to give up."

"I won't."

She gave a wry smile and looked away. Before she could busy herself with something else, I continued, "The man who shouted at us told us not to tell people that Jesus can heal."

"As soon as Livi said '*Jesus,*' he started going mental," said Ruby.

"It was like he was possessed," I added dramatically.

Sharon gave me a funny look. "Demon possession is quite rare," she replied. "It's more common to be under the *influence* of a demon. Sounds like something in him was riled by your witness. You should be encouraged; the enemy got frightened. Demons often manifest when threatened."

I looked at her in shock before quickly composing myself. "How do you drive out a demon?"

58

Ruby shot me a sharp look. I knew she thought I was wrong to be going against Summer's warning but I just had to hear what Sharon had to say.

Sharon didn't look fazed. "Perhaps we'll come to that later."

"Seriously?" I exclaimed. "Like, would you tell me where they are and what they look like?"

"I would tell you what you need to know," she snapped. "And trust you not to get carried away with needless extras."

I blushed. "That's what I meant."

Sharon gave a brisk nod as the rest of the class started to come in. "Maybe later," she repeated. "Sit down now."

"But when will—?"

She shook her head and pointed to my seat.

I felt a bit miffed as I headed to my desk.

Once the class had settled down, Sharon arose and started distributing dead mice. When she reached the table beside us, Laura gave a little moan and said, "Sharon, I've got a headache. Can I go and get a painkiller?"

Rather than answer her, Sharon glanced across at me and raised an eyebrow.

I gaped at her.

She kept staring at me as if to say, *'Well?'*

"Sharon?" Laura repeated. "My head really hurts." She followed Sharon's gaze and looked at me in confusion.

Afraid that if I stalled any longer more people would start to notice, I got to my feet and shuffled across to Laura. "Er, Laura... If you want, I could pray for your head to get better?"

She squinted at me.

"If you want," I repeated.

"Yeah, alright," she muttered, glancing at Sharon who just smiled serenely.

I took a deep breath, feeling extra nervous under Sharon's gaze, and took a moment to steady myself before whispering, "In Jesus' name, I command this headache to go right now." I exhaled quickly, hardly daring to look up.

"Hey, that's weird!" Laura exclaimed. "I kind of felt it leave."

Elation flooded through me as I gazed at her.

"Thanks, Livi," she added.

Maria and Ellen, who were beside her, gawped at me.

I tried to play it cool. "You're welcome..."

I stole a glance at Sharon, hoping for a little smile of approval, but she just nodded curtly and walked on.

~ 8 ~

The Great Leeds Skills Auction

"How many people have you healed this week?"

Annie looked up from a row of haphazardly folded shirts.[22]

I barely waited for a reply before adding, "I've healed two. One was a really tough-looking lady with a broken ankle."

"Wow!" Annie exclaimed. "That's cool."

Ruby gave a loud, *"Ahem!"*

"Oh yeah, Ruby was with me for the first one."

"I didn't mean that!" Ruby retorted. "I meant *Jesus* healed them, not you."

I pursed my lips. "Well, yeah, obviously. But *I* prayed." I pretended to admire a glossy shirt as Annie's manager went past before giving Annie a keen smile. "How about you?"

She kept grinning. "I had a good week. I passed my maths test on my second attempt."

I nodded, shamefully relieved that she had no healings to report. "Well done."

"Oh, and three more people joined The COOL Club!"

The glossy shirt slid out of my hands. *"Three?"*

She beamed. "Yeah."

I did the maths. "So there are six members now?"

Annie paused to count on her fingers. "Yeah, that's right... Well, seven if you count Miss Day. Turns out she's a Christian too! She asked if she can come occasionally."

I suppressed a frown. "How come so many people are joining? Have you done some kind of campaign?"

Annie giggled. "That's the weird thing. I haven't done anything at all. They just turned up and asked what we were doing."

---

[22] She has just started a Saturday job at Tizzi Berry where she spends most of her shifts chatting to me and Ruby under the guise of being our personal shopper.

I sucked in my cheeks as Ruby said, "That's cool."

"You mean, *'That's COOL Club!'*" Annie looked at us both and grinned.

I forced a laugh and was about to say something when Annie suddenly grabbed me and Ruby by the arms and yanked us through a clothes rail. I gave a yelp as we went crashing to the floor.

"What was that for?" Ruby cried as she scrambled to her feet.

"Hide!" Annie hissed, desperately pulling her down again. "Kitty Warrington just walked in."

I groaned and glanced at the shop entrance. I'm sure we would have gone unnoticed had Annie not caused such a commotion. Instead, I looked across to see Kitty staring straight at us. I got to my feet and forced a smile but she just turned her nose up and sneered.

"She tried to trip me up on the way to lunch yesterday," Annie whispered. "Luckily Mr Riley caught her." She shot Kitty a quick glance.

Kitty had wandered to the other end of the store where she draped a garish pink bag over her shoulder as though she were considering buying it.

"No way!" said Annie. "That bag costs over five hundred pounds."

Right on cue, Kitty looked over at us and smirked.

I rolled my eyes. High school politics suddenly seemed so petty. *Why had we ever cared?*

"Ignore her," I snapped. I cleared my throat. "So... What do you do at The COOL Club? Do you do Bible studies?"

"I don't know about *studies,* as such," Annie said. "We just read bits and then try to do what it says. Or we sing or pray or whatever feels right."

I nodded slowly. I wanted to quiz Annie on her capability of leading a growing group of new believers when she didn't know all that much herself. But I wasn't sure how to do this without sounding rude. "It's all going well then?"

Instead of answering, she screeched and yanked me and Ruby through the clothes rail again. Ruby gave a squeak as Annie's pile of freshly folded shirts landed on her head.

"Annie!" I exclaimed. "What is it now?"

"My mum!"

I rolled my eyes and looked towards the door.

Mrs Button had just wandered in, clad in a bright orange jumpsuit and oversized sunglasses. She caught sight of Annie and gave a cheery wave.

"She's seen me..." Annie groaned as her mother trotted over.

"Hello darling!" Mrs Button trilled. "Are you having a nice day at work?" She gave Annie a soppy kiss before turning to embrace me and Ruby. "Hello girls! Gosh, you both look so grown up. Livi, have you had a haircut?"

We said polite hellos and I flattened down my hair and said, "No... I just brushed it."

Annie's mother tipped her head back and laughed as though it was the funniest thing she had ever heard. Then she patted me on the arm and said loudly, "What a hoot!"

I felt myself blushing as nearby customers turned to stare. I hoped they wouldn't think she was *my* mother.

Kitty was at the till now. After trying out the expensive bag, some knee high boots and a couple of silk scarves, it seemed she had settled for a packet of Tizzi Berry scented tissues. She looked over in our direction and tutted as she waited to be served.

Clearly torn between serving Kitty and standing with her mother, Annie went a little pink as she scurried over to the till.

Ruby and I stayed where we were, shooting one another awkward glances as Mrs Button hunted around in her bag.

"Ah! Here they are," she said, pulling out a couple of shiny flyers. "Have you girls heard of The Great Leeds Skills Auction?"

I took the flyer with a smile. I recognised it as one Jill had brought home from work the week before. In order to raise money for local charities, a number of Leeds citizens were putting themselves up for auction, offering skills and services in return for the highest bids. They were mainly practical skills such as gardening and cleaning, but there were also a handful of creative offerings such as family portraits and piano lessons. In a desperate attempt to stop Jill crying about not having a date, I had promised to go with her. I had my eye on a lot that was mysteriously titled, *'Walk on water.'*

"I'm up for auction as a personal singer," Mrs Button told us gleefully.

I gave a quick nod. I knew better than to ask what a personal singer was. Knowing Mrs Button, she would quite likely give me a demonstration.

Annie got back from serving Kitty, looking a little beaten.[23] She brightened up when she saw the flyers in our hands. "Oh, are you going to that?" she asked hopefully. "The COOL Club are up for auction."

I blinked at her. "What for?"

She grinned. "We're going to pray for the winning bidder."

I screwed up my nose. "You shouldn't really make people pay for prayer."

She grinned even wider. "That's the best part! We're going to match whatever they pay so they can have their money back."

I looked at her in surprise.

Ruby gave an impressed nod. "That's a great idea, Annie!"

I forced a smile. "How are you going to afford that?"

Annie shrugged. "Don't know yet. But did you know Jesus can do *anything*, Livi?"

"Of course!" I felt rather peeved that she would think I'd need her to tell me.

"He can even walk on water!" she exclaimed.

My heart sunk. "That's the name of your lot, isn't it?"

She beamed. "Yeah! Cool isn't it?"

"Yeah... Cool."

~*~

The following Monday, we were meant to be analysing owl pellets to find out what some local barn owls had eaten. Besides the fact that Ruby kept throwing up, I was finding it hard to concentrate. I couldn't stop thinking about the sudden unprecedented growth of The COOL Club and the fact that it didn't feel fair that Ruby and I had ploughed so much into it yet hadn't been there to see it bear fruit. And it wasn't as though Annie really knew what she was doing; people just kept joining randomly.

"Shall we start up a Christian Union?" I blurted out.

"Ooh, yeah! The COOL Club College Years!" Ruby exclaimed.

I sucked in my cheeks. "'The COOL Club' sounds kind of, I don't know, *uncool* now, if you know what I mean?"

Ruby blinked at me.

---

[23] Apparently, Kitty had insisted on paying in pennies and had mocked Annie's maths ability when she took a while to count them.

"We should call it something a bit more sophisticated."

"Alright."

We stared at each other for a while until Ruby suggested, *"ABC for Jesus?"*

I screwed up my nose. "Sounds a bit basic."

Ruby shrugged and gave our tray of owl pellets a poke. "Well, what do you want to call it then?"

I took a deep breath. "I was thinking something like *'The Living Jewels.'* Or *'Livi-Ruby'* for short."

Ruby looked at me.

"Or *'Ruby-Livi,'* if you'd prefer," I said quickly.

Ruby kept staring at me.

"Because Ruby is a jewel and we're like... precious to God..."

"I get it... It just sounds a bit strange."

I sniffed. "What then?"

She shrugged again. "Do we have to have a name? Can't we just be a group of people who meet?"

"But then how will people know how to find us?"

"Maybe they'll just turn up. Like Annie said with The COOL Club."

I bit my lip. "I suppose..."

"The Early Church didn't have a name. They were just *'The Church.'*" Ruby paused. "Maybe we should just be *'The Club'?*"

I wrinkled up my nose. It sounded a little boring.

We sat silently for a while, taking turns with the owl pellets, until Ruby said, "It's a shame Tina didn't come to church."

"Hmmm," I muttered.

I had spent the first half of last week's youth group bragging about Tina's healing and the possibility that she might be coming to church that Sunday. Everyone seemed really pleased about it and I'd got to church extra early so I that could introduce her to everyone. But she didn't come. It had bugged me that she might have just taken the healing and not even bothered to thank Jesus for it.

"She must have forgotten," Ruby continued.

I shrugged. "Maybe she got drunk and broke her other ankle."

Suddenly, Sharon Sheppard gave a shrill cry behind me. "Livi Starling! Wash your mouth out!"

I looked up in horror, feeling my cheeks go crimson as a few of our classmates turned to stare. "What?"

Sharon shot me a stern look as she came up close and whispered, "How do you expect God to trust you with the power to raise the dead if you let that kind of talk come out of your mouth?"

I gaped at her. "All I said was—"

"Words are very important, Livi," she cut in. "The tongue has the power of life and death. Do you hear me?"

I nodded slowly.

I hoped she would stop speaking but she sat beside me as she went on, "With power comes responsibility. God needs to be able to trust you. Nobody in their right mind would give a sword to a baby. Are you a baby, Livi?" She ignored my wounded frown as she finished with, "God won't give you what he wants to give you if you're not ready to use it correctly."

I waited in case she was about to start speaking again.

She just stared at me.

"Okay," I said.

She stood up and smiled. "That can be your homework for today."

I raised an eyebrow. "Pardon?"

"Watch your words. And don't say anything that you wouldn't say to Jesus."

I forced a laugh but her smile turned serious. "I mean it, Livi. That's your homework." She paused before adding, "It starts now."

I gulped. "Alright..."

Sharon watched me for a bit longer.

As she sauntered off, Ruby whispered, "She's the weirdest teacher ever!"

I let out a long sigh and rubbed my head.

At youth group, Summer had asked how things were going with our 'witchy teacher.'

The others had perked up at her words and Kevin had rubbed his hands with glee.

I'd blushed as I'd confessed, "Actually she's not a witch."

"She's a Christian," said Ruby.

"Oh!" Summer had said in surprise.

Bill and Kevin looked disappointed.

Eddie had nodded, as if to say, 'There you go.'

"She's not an average Christian though," I'd insisted, keen to assure them we hadn't just been being stupid when we mistook her for a witch. "She's teaching us about healing and stuff."

At this, Summer had looked a little stunned, as though this was potentially worse.

Right now, I was tempted to agree. I watched Sharon out of the corner of my eye as I wondered whether the 'homework' she had set me was a serious assignment.

"Hey, it was weird when we saw Kitty, wasn't it?" Ruby piped up. "I can't believe she can afford to shop at Tizzi Berry."

I was about to retort that buying a packet of tissues hardly constituted shopping but the words caught in my throat. "I don't know. I guess she needed to blow her nose."

Ruby looked at me in confusion.

I shrugged. "I'm trying to watch my words."

She gave a bemused giggle and glanced at Sharon. "Do you think she'll ask you about it tomorrow?"

"I don't know. But, just in case, I'll make sure I don't say too much today."

"Are you and Jill still going to The Great Leeds Skills Auction tonight?"

My stomach sunk. "Oh yeah."

Ruby giggled again. "That will be fun."

The auction was held in the town hall, a large exquisite building filled with ornate paintings and high ceilings. Having never gone to any kind of auction before, let alone a skills auction, I hadn't been sure what to expect. I had dressed in a casual top and jeans and had slipped a rubber band round my wrist as a reminder to watch my words.[24] Jill, on the other hand, had gone all out and was wearing a black dress and little string of fake pearls. As we took seats towards the middle of the hall, my sister spotted a few of her work colleagues in the next row and exchanged friendly waves. I wondered if she had worn her nicest dress for their benefit.

Despite my misgivings about the popularity of the event, it turned out Jill was right to want to arrive early. It didn't take long before the whole hall was packed full. There were even people standing at the back. I gazed at the many eager faces and imagined

---

[24] Jill, ever the worrier, had insisted on leaving a whole hour to get to the town hall on time. I had started to mock her but as soon as I said, *"That's stupid!"* I remembered the homework Sharon had set me. As a punishment for speaking rashly, I had pulled the rubber band onto my wrist and given myself a big ping. I hoped the pain would remind me to be more careful.

how amazing it would be if the building was filled with people waiting to hear about Jesus. I stared at the stage, laden with purple cloths and pretty bunting, and imagined myself up there preaching.

After some health and safety notices and a brief welcome from the Lord Mayor, the auction got underway. It was being hosted by Mr Wong, a local councillor.

"It's great to have so many people here," Mr Wong said as he took to the stage. "Tonight is a wonderful opportunity for you, the people of Leeds, to raise money for local charities by bidding on things that you need..."

I gave a snort as I flicked through the evening's programme. I wasn't sure many of the items offered in the auction constituted things that I needed.

The first few lots were rather boring, with people offering their skills in DIY, computer maintenance and ironing. I stifled a yawn and entertained myself with seeing how high I could raise my hand without it being mistaken for a bid.[25] After that, I drifted into a daydream in which Mr Wong invited me up to tell the people of Leeds what they *really* needed.

'You need something you cannot pay for,' I would tell them boldly. *'Jesus already paid the highest price so you could have it for free...'*

My thoughts were interrupted by the sight of Annie and a handful of others making their way through the room.

Mr Wong was beckoning them up as he announced, "The next lot is called, *'Walk on water,'* and is offered by a group of students from Hare Valley High."

The audience applauded as Annie and The COOL Club joined Mr Wong on the stage.

Annie took the microphone. "Hello people of Leeds," she said shyly. "If you bid on us, you get the chance to have us pray for miracles to happen in your life."

Georgina Harris, who was beside her, looked into the audience. I frowned as she caught my eye and smiled. We hadn't been friends at school. I wasn't going to pretend now.

Mr Wong beamed. "Marvellous."

---

[25] I had to stop this after accidentally bidding fifty pounds for a fishing lesson. Fortunately, I was outbid rather quickly, but Jill's fierce rebuke forced me to sit on my hands for the rest of the night.

Annie started to hand him the microphone and then took it back again. "Oh, by the way," she added. "If you win, you actually get the prayer for free because we'll pay for it instead."

I rolled my eyes as a murmur of surprise erupted from the audience. I wondered how Annie could be so daft as to offer something for free.

"What was that?" Mr Wong asked. "You're going to pay the price?"

"Yes!" Annie grinned merrily. "Because Jesus said, *'Freely you have received, freely give.'* So you can always have him for free."

I felt my cheeks grow hot as I watched the audience consider her little preach.

"Well, there you have it!" Mr Wong exclaimed. "Your bid will be paid for by the lot themselves... Let's start the bidding at twenty pounds."

Hands went flying up all over the room and within seconds the bidding had reached over a hundred pounds.

On the stage, Annie and her friends were gripping one another in excitement as the bids went up and up. I watched in disbelief, wondering why they hadn't thought things through.

At one point, Jill nudged me and whispered, "Is that your friend, Annie, up there?"

I debated saying no, but realised this would be an improper use of my words. "Yeah," I muttered.

Jill stuck her lip out in disdain. "Is she rich or something?"

"Nope."

"Then what is she doing?" Jill looked at me as though somehow I needed to explain.

"How should I know?" I retorted, pinging the rubber band on my wrist. "It's nothing to do with me."

The bid reached five hundred pounds, the highest of the night. I felt a guilty kind of smugness as I wondered how on earth Annie was going to afford that.

Just as Mr Wong sang, *"Sold!"* the winning bidder stood up and made his way towards the stage.

The audience watched him, knowing this wasn't the proper protocol. Winners were supposed to wait until the end of the night to pay for their lots and exchange contact details with those whose skills they had bought.

Mr Wong squatted on the stage and leant over to hear what the man had to say. After a short conversation, Mr Wong stood up again and gave the audience a big smile. "Ladies and gentlemen," he said. "The winner of this item has just informed me that he is so impressed with the initiative and generosity of the Hare Valley students that he would not only like to pay for the bid himself, he would also like to double it."

My jaw dropped open. A cheer erupted from the audience.

Annie and her friends looked at one another and grinned. It was as though they had expected this divine provision all along.

"In all my years of The Great Leeds Skills Auction, I have never known a bid so high," exclaimed Mr Wong. "This is truly an exceptional night!"

The audience gave another cheer as Annie and The COOL Club left the stage.

I let out a long sigh as Jill gave me another nudge and whispered, "Well, I didn't expect that!"

I forced a smile. "Me neither."

I felt pretty miserable for the rest of the night. I know I should have been pleased for Annie but I couldn't help feeling mighty jealous. Not only had Annie managed to raise a thousand pounds for charity, but she had also fulfilled my daydream of proclaiming the name of Jesus to a room packed full of people.

As each new lot was announced, Jill uttered a sly comment beside me. "Looks like something Aunt Claudia would make!" she whispered as a photo was projected showing off one lady's knitting skills.

I tried to watch my words and responded to her remarks with the odd shrug or half-hearted smile but I couldn't help laughing when she suggested bidding on a lot entitled 'Doggy Hairdos' for Belinda.

"Yeah, Dennis is quite a scraggly dog," I said with a giggle.

"I meant for *Belinda.*"

I grinned and immediately felt guilty. "That's not very nice," I muttered, giving myself a sharp ping across the wrist.

Jill ignored me and continued to gossip about each item up for auction. She put in the odd low bid, as if to show her nearby colleagues that she was rich and charitable enough to do so, but pulled out well before any serious bidding could arise.

It felt as though the night would never end but, finally, the last lot was announced: Mrs Button's talent as a personal singer.[26]

---

[26] She demonstrated this 'skill' by warbling, *'Mr Wong, I will sing you a song. Your eyes are brown and your beard is long...'*

Within seconds, it had sold for fifteen pounds to Mr Button, the sole bidder.

A whoop erupted from the audience as Mr Wong announced, "Ladies and gentlemen, I am over the moon to inform you that this year's skills auction has raised over three thousand pounds for local charities!"

I pretended to look pleased as I joined in with the applause. Then I got to my feet, keen to leave before Annie could come over to talk to me. "Ready to go?" I asked Jill.

She nodded and picked up her bag. It seemed she was equally keen to avoid talking to her work colleagues, all of whom had won something in the auction.

We followed the crowd out of the hall, attempting to remain civilised whilst pushing our way to the exit. As we reached the main doorway, I was surprised to find myself shoulder to shoulder with Sharon Sheppard.

"How did you get on with your homework?" she asked.

I gulped and avoided her gaze. "I did okay..." I fiddled with the rubber band round my wrist. My skin was rather sore from the many times I had pinged it. I stole a glance at Jill but she was busy elbowing people on her way out of the hall.

Sharon nodded. "Hard, isn't it?"

I wasn't sure how to answer her so just gave a quick smile.

"Out of the overflow of the heart, the mouth speaks," Sharon continued cryptically. "Sometimes we don't know what's inside us until we're squeezed."

"I guess..."

"Did you bid on anything?"

I debated mentioning my fifty quid bid for a fishing lesson. Instead, I shook my head.

"Me neither." She grinned. "That group from Hare Valley did well, didn't they?"

My stomach lurched. *Why hadn't me and Ruby thought of doing something like that?* A million bitter vows went round my head and I hoped Sharon couldn't read my mind. In the end, I forced a smile and said, "They were cool."

~ 9 ~

Destiny Hill

It is clear that a class trip is not going to be very enjoyable when top of the list of things to bring are *'wellies'* and *'wet weather clothes.'* The first day of the much-awaited field trip had arrived and, as Ruby and I stood with the rest of our classmates, yawning in the fog at the crack of dawn, we found ourselves regretting once again our poor choice of course.

"Maybe it will be fun," said Ruby. "I've never been to Wales."

I gave her a withering look and reminded her that the letter had also warned, *'Bryn Hapus is a small rural town with little to offer in terms of entertainment. As such, it is not recommended that students bring excessive amounts of spending money.'*

"It won't be fun," I told her as a minibus pulled into the college car park. "We'll be working in the cold all week."

Right on cue, Sharon Sheppard got everybody's attention with a loud clap. "Is everybody here? Are you all ready for a week of hard labour?"

Ruby screwed up her face and lugged her bag onto her back. We pouted as we followed our classmates onto the minibus.

The drive to South West Wales took almost eight hours.[27] The minibus was so small that Ruby and I couldn't have a private conversation without fear of being overheard. On the bright side, this gave us a good chance to prove to some of the girls on our course that we were fun and friendly individuals. We had barely left Leeds before Ruby whipped out her box of *Travel Twister* and a bag of sour worms. We played the game for five hours straight and ate sweets until our gums were sore. By the end of the journey,

---

[27] It should have been six but we stopped a ridiculous number of times for Laura who got very badly travel sick. It made the journey something of an adventure to have her sat so near to us.

we were on reasonable terms with Maria, Ellen and Laura who sat with a bag on her head to stop herself throwing up.

We arrived at Bryn Hapus in the middle of the afternoon and drove straight to the research centre on the edge of the town. As expected, the whole place looked bleak and boring with nothing but hills for miles and enough sheep to feed Aunt Claudia for the rest of her life.

I exchanged a yawn with Ruby as we got off the minibus and lingered with our classmates outside a large grey building. It had started to drizzle.

"This is the Sheepsgate Centre," Sharon announced. "We'll be working here most days..." The rain got heavier as Sharon explained the week's itinerary which was jam-packed with sheep-related activities such as monitoring the dietary habits of lambs and improving the reproductive performance of ewes. Sharon finished with, "We're going to begin with a very important meeting tonight. Very, very important. We'll be setting out what's expected from you and projects will be allocated. I don't need to remind you that you'll be getting marked for every area of your involvement while on this trip."

I puffed out my cheeks at Ruby. She responded by wrinkling up her nose and pointing to a nearby pile of sheep poo.

After Sharon's introduction, a few people came out of the grey building and introduced themselves and their various roles at the research centre. One man assured us we were in for a treat that week as he gave an unnecessary lecture on methane emissions.

Sharon thanked him and ushered us back onto the minibus. We were going to be staying in pairs with host families around the town. I wasn't sure which I dreaded most: a week of sheep research or seven days of living with complete strangers.

The first few students were dropped off at homes very close to the research centre and Sharon warned them that they had no excuse not to arrive at the evening meeting on time. Next, we came to a large converted barn on the edge of a piece of farmland.

"Livi and Ruby," Sharon barked from the front. "This is where you're staying. Your hosts are Donny and Dana Roberts."

Ruby looked at me and grinned.

I gulped and followed her off the minibus, breathing a sigh of relief that at least the two of us hadn't been separated.

"Looks nice, doesn't it?" said Ruby.

I bit my lip as I regarded the sprawling barn with its rickety roof and tall imposing windows. A small dirt drive stood between us and our unknown hosts. *Were they friendly? Did they speak English? Were they being paid to have us?* I glanced back just in time to watch the minibus turn a corner.

The door of the house opened. "Ooh, I thought I heard a noise!" cried a middle-aged lady. She wore an apron and furry slippers and had chestnut brown hair flecked with grey. She was tall and a little plump. It made her welcome hug slightly overwhelming.

After telling us how happy she was to have us, Dana babbled on about the weather, the sheep and the fact that Donny had hoped to be there when we arrived but had been delayed by a meeting at some place called 'Destiny Hill.' Her Welsh accent was so thick that I struggled to keep up. I nodded and smiled, clinging onto my bag with one hand and Ruby with the other.

"Let me give you a tour," Dana continued, sweeping a cat out of her way as she beckoned us into her home. "Your room is down here. I hope you don't mind sharing..."

Ruby and I beamed at each other before following Dana down a narrow hallway.

"It's only small," Dana apologised. "I hope it will be alright." She pushed open a creaky wooden door to reveal a neat little guest room with twin beds, a rocking horse and a view of the field.

"It's nice," we replied.

After dumping our bags, we followed Dana through to the lounge where she told us to make ourselves at home. "Would you like a drink?" she asked as we shuffled to the sofa.

I looked at Ruby. "Are you having one?"

"Yes please," she said.

Dana smiled. "Tea? Coffee?"

"Tea, please."

"How about you, Livi?"

I blushed. "I'll have tea as well."

Dana nodded and popped into the kitchen.

I sighed and looked round the room. The ceiling was rather low with big wooden beams holding the house together. Family photos adorned the walls and I wondered if the two girls pictured were Donny and Dana's daughters. A wood burning stove sat in the corner and a nearby polish and duster suggested the house had recently been cleaned. The carpet was pristine white. I took my shoes off and looked up to see Ruby grinning at me.

"What?" I demanded.

"You don't like tea," she said with a giggle.

"Shh!" I muttered.

"Why did you say you wanted tea if you don't like tea?"

"Be quiet! She asked whether I wanted tea or coffee."

"You could have asked if she had juice or something."

I shook my head and hissed, *"Shh!"* again.

Ruby pointed to a little wooden cross on the wall. "Hey, do you reckon they're Christians?"

I shrugged, wishing she wouldn't talk so loudly.

Dana returned with a tray laden with mugs, a teapot and a plate of biscuits. "Do you take sugar?" she asked as she set it down.

I had no idea and watched to see what Ruby would do.

Ruby shook her head. "No thanks."

"Me neither," I said.

Dana poured the tea. She indicated a jug of milk and I had to watch Ruby again to make sure I put the right amount in.

"It's been rather busy round here," Dana said suddenly. "Excuse me not having done all the housework."

I took another look at the immaculate room.

"We're in the middle of an outpouring, see," Dana continued, giving us both a wide beam.

I glanced out of the window. Was that sheep-talk for something?

"Do you know what an outpouring is?" Dana asked as her cat leapt onto her lap.

I glanced at Ruby. She wore a curious smile. "Do you mean an outpouring of the Holy Spirit?" She shot me a grin as if to say, *'I told you they're Christians!'*

Dana nodded and stroked her cat. I couldn't help but think she looked like a jollier version of Aunt Claudia— with one cat and a family instead of a whole feline army. She turned to me and grinned.

I took an awkward sip of my tea. I still had no idea what *'outpouring'* meant.

Eventually, Dana explained, "Seven weeks ago, we were in the middle of our weekly prayer meeting when suddenly the presence of God came like nothing I've ever known. A lady got healed out of her wheelchair and started running round the room. We've had a meeting every night since! People are coming from all over the world to meet with God. Fancy that in little old Bryn Hapus!"

I let out a gasp. "Wow!"

Dana kept beaming. "You can come tonight if you'd like?"

Ruby's face fell. "We can't."

"We've got an important course meeting," I said.

As if on cue, the telephone rang.

Dana answered it before holding the phone out to me. "It's your teacher."

I exchanged a glance with Ruby as I took the phone. "Hello?"

"Livi, it's Sharon. Did Dana tell you about the outpouring?"

"Er, yeah."

"I think you should forget about tonight's meeting and go to church instead."

I gave a little splutter. "What?"

"Go to the outpouring. It will be good for you."

"But— What about—?" I opened and closed my mouth a few times. "What will we miss at the meeting?"

"Nothing." Sharon gave a wry chuckle. "You don't want a career with animals, do you?"

"Well, no," I said, shooting Ruby a quick glance.

Ruby raised an eyebrow as she mouthed, *"What's she saying?"*

I shook my head and turned back to the phone. "But aren't we getting marked on everything this week?" I asked Sharon.

"Yes."

"So you're just going to give us good marks anyway?"

I was about to give Ruby a big thumbs-up but Sharon retorted, "No."

"Oh." I glared at the phone. "You're suggesting we deliberately fail this module and go to church instead?"

Sharon hummed softly. "Why did you take this course?"

I bit my lip. "We kind of hoped the field trip would be somewhere exciting."

She laughed to herself. "Last year we went to Africa."

"Seriously?" I shot Ruby an incredulous stare.

"What?" Ruby hissed.

I batted her away again. "Why didn't you pick somewhere exciting *this* year?" I demanded into the phone.

This time, when Sharon replied, her tone was softer. "Livi, don't you get it?"

I stopped in confusion.

"You're more than welcome to join your classmates this evening. But you took the course for the field trip. Don't miss it."

A horde of questions filled my mind. Had Sharon guessed we'd only joined the course for the field trip? Had she known about the outpouring or somehow orchestrated it for our benefit? I cleared my throat. But, before I could ask anything, she hung up.

I gawped at the phone before handing it back to Dana.

"Everything alright?" she asked.

I nodded and turned to Ruby. "Sharon said we should go to the outpouring meeting."

Her eyes lit up. "Cool!" She paused before adding, "Hey, does that mean—"

"No. She's not going to pass us."

"Oh." Ruby gave a hum. "Fine then!"

I raised an eyebrow. "You wouldn't mind failing this module?"

She shook her head. "Would you?"

I stopped to think about it. "I guess not. It just feels weird to have a teacher actually encourage it."

Dana had been watching us this whole time. "So, would you like to come tonight?" she asked.

Ruby looked at me and grinned. "Absolutely!"

I was expecting a fancy church building, something to accommodate God's presence in an impressive way. So I was a little surprised when Dana drove us to a nearby warehouse and announced that we had arrived. There were no windows and the walls were a drab grey— as grey as the sheep research centre. Other than a sign bearing the words, 'Welcome to Destiny Hill,' there was nothing to suggest the building was even used for anything.

"This is it?" I asked, slipping out of the car and regarding the big concrete block in front of me.

"This is it!" Dana smiled. "Come in and meet Donny."

I sucked in my cheeks as Ruby and I followed her into the warehouse. I was waiting for something exciting to happen, like the appearance of an angel or some holy fire to fall from the sky. But there was nothing special about the surroundings and nothing peculiar happened to me when I walked through the door. The only thing that made this church different from any other was the fact that, even though we were half an hour early, swarms of people were already piling into the building looking as eager as anything. The front seats had already been taken and those entering sought to sit as close to the front as possible. It was a far cry from my experience of most Sunday mornings in which people were perhaps optimistic for what the meeting might hold but nowhere near as excited as this crowd. One thing was certain: nobody here had come out of routine or obligation. They all expected to meet with God. A sense of wonder hung in the air as people greeted one another and made new friends. From the sounds of it, some had travelled many miles to be there that evening. I even overheard one couple saying that they had come from Canada.

"Ah, there's my husband!" Dana led us to a gregarious-looking gentleman at the front of the church.

What Dana hadn't mentioned was that Donny was actually one of the pastors of Destiny Hill. In fact, he was due to speak that evening. After greeting Dana, he welcomed me and Ruby with a giant hug and said, "God bless you!"

We responded with shy smiles before shuffling away and squeezing into two empty seats at the side.

The meeting didn't have a clear beginning as the worship band had been playing since we arrived but, pretty soon, conversations ceased and loud singing took over. I knew the first few songs and sang along with great gusto, rather excited to be part of this 'outpouring' despite still not really knowing what it was all about.

The singing went on for ages. I didn't have the endurance to stand the whole time and ended up watching from my seat, marvelling at the passion of the people around me. Although there was the odd person who had sat down by now, most people seemed happy to carry on worshipping forever, lost in their own private praise to Jesus. I wished I had the persistence to sing so passionately for so long and wondered whether my lack of stamina meant I didn't love God enough yet.

The singing was still in full swing when Donny came up to the front and laid his Bible on a lectern. Unlike the preachers at King's Church who usually opened with a gentle welcome, Donny began his talk with a mighty roar. "Jesus! We love you!"

Several members of the congregation responded with similar shouts and spontaneous singing and it was a further five minutes before Donny could begin his preach.

I exchanged bemused smiles with Ruby as a man nearby started to shake.

When the noise died down, Donny gave another roar. "Let's keep things simple. We don't need new methods. We don't need fancy music or lighting or sound, as fun as those things are. We just need Jesus. And the world needs Jesus. Just Jesus. No hype, no hefty budget, no complicated outreach. Just the truth about our great big God— Jesus!"

I would usually find my mind wandering during church, no matter how inspired the teaching. But, this time, I couldn't take my eyes off Donny as every single word pierced like a sword.

"How big is your vision of Jesus? Is he big enough to live for? Is he big enough to *die* for?" Donny paused before adding, "Do you know, some people's God is so small, they only let him out occasionally. But we don't want a God as big as our brains, do we?"

I caught Ruby's eye and grinned. This guy was great!

"God is really, really big," Donny went on. "He's big enough to hold your atoms together. He's big enough to command the night sky. He's big enough to handle your problems. And, you know what? He's big enough to give you a starring role in an adventure made just for you... if you let him."

I sat up straight in my seat.

"If you want the fullness of a Kingdom life, then you cannot be best friends with God and best friends with the world. God can't do much through a lukewarm heart. You need to give him everything."

I nodded along as the people beside me chimed in with a loud, "Amen!"

I know this, God, I thought desperately. *I already want to give you everything.*

"If you completely devote yourself to God," Donny continued. "If you surrender everything to him... If you leave this world behind and follow Jesus, then there is no limit to the things God will do through you."

It was the clearest message I had ever heard: *Leave everything and follow Jesus. Simple as that.*

Just as I was debating whether I ought to quit my course, pack my bags and set off as a missionary, Donny added, "Of course, leaving everything is an attitude of the heart. It's about following Jesus wherever he wants you to be, even in the mundane and the ordinary."

I sighed. I wasn't sure whether I was relieved or disappointed to hear that Jesus might want me to remain exactly where I was.

Donny talked for a while longer before inviting anyone who didn't yet know Jesus to come to the front. "Jesus went to the cross for you. Will you stand up here for him?"

I watched as hordes of people rushed to the altar. I lost count pretty quickly. "Can you believe how many people are responding?" I whispered to Ruby.

She gave a wide-eyed nod. "It's amazing!"

Donny gave those who had come to the front a big beam before leading them in a prayer. When he'd finished, he told them, "Remember, it's not religion that saves. It's Jesus. Jesus, Jesus, Jesus! Keep it simple!" He invited members of the church to come and pray for the new converts before saying to the rest of the congregation, "We're going to keep worshipping. Feel free to stay as long as you want. If you want prayer for anything at all, then please come to the front."

The band started to play again and the congregation erupted in praise as all over the room people came forward for prayer.

I couldn't work out exactly what made this meeting an 'outpouring' rather than just a regular meeting, but I suspected it was something to do with the high number of salvations and the fact that all over the room there were people sobbing on their knees and many others rolling around with joy. I watched as a nearby lady sunk to the floor after prayer.

I nudged Ruby. "I don't get it. Why is God moving so strongly here and not in *our* church? I mean, nobody's doing anything special. They're ordinary people in an ordinary building."

Ruby shrugged. "I don't know. I guess they're just hungry."

"But *I'm* hungry!" I exclaimed. "I'm really, really hungry and I don't know how to—" The words caught in my throat and I burst into tears. After trying so hard for so long, this was something I could give my life to.

Ruby looked at me. "What's wrong?"

I rubbed my eyes. "I don't know," I blubbered. "I just want more. I want this. I want... I don't know." I paused before asking, "Ruby, do you ever feel like you're more of a theoretical Christian than a practical one?"

She raised an eyebrow. "What do you mean?"

I prodded my Bible. "Like... It all makes sense intellectually but not when you try to live it for real."

Ruby frowned. "Are you talking about healing? Because I knew that was going to lead to trouble."

"No! Well, yeah, a bit. But I mean *everything*. Trusting God day to day. Truly experiencing him. Like this..." I waved a hand.

Several people were sprawled out at the front of the altar and many others were dancing round the room.

"I want to feel God's joy like that," I whispered.

Ruby cocked her head to one side. "I guess this is something pretty special. Outpouring doesn't happen every day."

"Why not?" I demanded. "Shouldn't this be the norm? Shouldn't we be able to encounter God this deeply all the time?"

Ruby sat back in her chair. "Yeah, I suppose. But how?"

I let out a long sigh. "I don't know."

~ 10 ~

Have whatever you want

I awoke the next morning determined to put Donny's preach into practise.

Okay Jesus, here I am, I prayed as I sat up in my bed. *I'm leaving everything to follow you. Show me what that means today.* I listened but didn't hear anything. The sight of my course folder on the floor distracted me so I squeezed my eyes shut and tried again. *What should I do with my life today?*

My meditation was interrupted by Ruby who piped up from the next bed, "Hey, Livi, we should go to our lessons today."

I frowned at her. "I'm just praying."

"Oh." She grinned. "Sorry."

I closed my eyes again. *I'll do absolutely anything, Jesus. How should I follow you today?*

"We probably need to get up now otherwise we'll be late."

"Ruby!"

"I'm just saying." Ruby reached for her hairbrush and yawned. "We've got half an hour. And I'm not sure I can remember the way."

I growled and pulled my pillow over my face. *As I was saying, Jesus, what should I do today?*

This time, my thoughts were shattered by a knock on the bedroom door.

"Ruby? Livi? Would you like a lift to the research centre? I'll be driving past on my way to the shops?"

"Yes please, Dana!" Ruby called back. She poked me. "Looks like God has provided!"

I pummelled my fists into my ears as I tried to concentrate on hearing God's voice. *Come on, God. What should I do today? Tell me what to do?* The heavy ticking of the clock grew louder and louder as I waited in vain for God to speak.

I looked up to see Ruby staring at me. "Are you getting up or not?"

"Fine," I muttered. "Let's go to our stupid course."

She grinned and threw me my wash bag. "Hurry up then."

I scrambled out of bed and got ready as quickly as possible. Unfortunately, by the time I got out of the shower, Ruby had already had breakfast and was sitting in the lounge with Dana. I peeked into the kitchen before changing my mind and plodding into the lounge instead. I didn't want to keep Dana waiting.

"I'm ready," I said.

Dana smiled. "Did you sleep well?"

I nodded.

"And you found everything you needed? Did you have enough to eat?"

I forced another nod.

"Wonderful. Let's go."

I deliberately let Ruby have the passenger seat so that I wouldn't have to engage too much with Dana. There was nothing wrong with her. She was one of the friendliest people I had ever met. Donny was great too. When we'd got home the night before, he had made us hot chocolates and offered us brownies. If anything, they were just a little *too nice*. They were the sort of couple that exposed the lack of normality in my upbringing. Their kindness oozed from every nook and cranny of their house and I found it all very suffocating.

Our classmates eyed us suspiciously as we joined them for the morning's lesson. It was clear that we had missed the previous evening's meeting. For one thing, everybody else was wearing a bright blue bib emblazoned with the acronym 'SCRAT.'[28] For another, we had no idea where we were meant to go and arrived late after getting lost behind a herd of sheep.

"Where were you last night?" Maria whispered as we joined her, Ellen and Laura at a water trough in the far field. A man at the front was giving a dull talk about algae control.

I gave a coy smile as I told her, "We went to a different meeting."

"A different meeting?" She looked at us in surprise.

Ruby nodded. "At a place called Destiny Hill."

---

[28] Short for 'Sheepsgate Centre for Research and Training.'

"It was sort of a church meeting," I added, aware that Ellen and Laura were also listening now. Having taken so long to befriend the three of them, I was reluctant to say anything that would sully their opinion of us.

"Church?" Ellen repeated.

"It's alright," I said quickly. "Sharon said we could go."

The three of them stared at us.

"Seriously?" Laura piped up. "Sharon let you miss the meeting?"

"Yeah. She was totally fine with it."

All of a sudden, Sharon gave a loud shout from the water trough. "Livi Starling! Don't you think you ought to be listening to today's instructions, especially since you were absent from last night's meeting?"

I blushed before turning back to Maria, Ellen and Laura. They ignored my gaze as they gave each other little knowing looks.

The man shot me a frown before concluding his talk. "...to keep levels under control. So grab some equipment and that's what we'll do this morning."

Our class broke into chatter as they got to work. Since we'd missed the whole of the previous night and most of the man's instructions, Ruby and I had no idea what we were meant to be doing. It seemed everyone else had been split into groups and had already been briefed on how to use various utensils. We watched as Maria, Ellen and Laura distributed pieces of tubing amongst themselves and turned to some notes in a booklet that had clearly been handed out the night before.

I gave a small cough before asking, "Can we work with you?"

The three of them looked at us a little uneasily.

"We kind of got put into groups last night," Ellen explained.

"Oh, no worries!" I said, shuffling out of their way.

Ruby and I lingered for ages, shooting each other painful grimaces as we wondered what we ought to do.

I hoped Sharon might come over and give us some help, or at the very least ask us how the outpouring meeting had been. But it was ages before she gave us any attention. Even then, all she said was, "Livi, Ruby, do you know what you're doing?"

We shook our heads and looked at her blankly.

She pursed her lips. "Who do you want to work with?"

Ruby and I exchanged shrugs and glanced back at Maria and the others.

As if reading our minds, Sharon said, "Go and join them then."

"Okay," we squeaked, clutching hold of one another as we shuffled back to the girls.

The three of them looked up as we got close.

"Sharon said we could work with you," I said, knowing this sounded about as believable as saying Sharon had said we could miss the last night's meeting.

They stared at us.

"Alright," Laura said finally. "Here's a tube."

Ruby and I got through the day without having a clue what we were doing. After examining water samples in the morning, we moved on to cleaning water troughs in the afternoon. The sole perk of the day was Maria referring to us as her 'friends' to a member of the research centre over lunch.[29] We got back to Donny and Dana's extremely wet and worn out. I thanked Jesus that they weren't there to see us drip contaminated water through their house.

"Are you hungry?" Ruby yelled from the kitchen as I ripped off my wet clothes in the bathroom. "Do you want a snack?"

I pulled on some fresh clothes and padded down the hall. "A snack?"

Ruby grinned and opened the fridge. "Ooh, yoghurts!" I watched in horror as she pulled out a tray of posh-looking desserts. "Want one of these?"

"We can't eat their food!"

She looked at me. "Why not?"

"Because!" I spluttered. "It's not polite to creep into someone's fridge and eat their stuff."

"They told us to make ourselves at home."

"Well, yeah, that means making our beds and doing the washing up. It doesn't mean eating things without asking."

She shrugged. "They said if we get hungry we can help ourselves to whatever we want."

"But they might be saving that!" I pointed to the yoghurt in her hand. "Just have some bread."

Ruby blinked. "There are loads." She dug deeper into the fridge and pulled out a block of cheese. "Want some cheese?"

"Ruby!"

"What?"

---

[29] Her exact words were, "A couple of our friends need bibs because they bunked off during last night's meeting."

"Ask first!" I pulled out my phone and held it towards her. "Phone Dana and ask what we're allowed to eat."

Ruby took a long look at my phone. "Livi, what's wrong?"

"I don't know," I confessed. "I'm not used to staying with random strangers."

"But they're really nice! Dana said it was like having their daughters come to stay."

I sucked in my cheeks and looked away. Dana had made that remark on the way to the research centre and, although I knew it was stupid as she was probably just saying it to be polite, it had made me want to cry. "We're not their daughters," I muttered.

Ruby raised an eyebrow. "Do you want some juice?" She reached into the fridge once more.

"That hasn't been opened yet," I said quickly. "Just have water."

"But I don't want water. I want juice." Ruby pulled out a carton of orange juice and plonked it down on the work surface. Then, in her search for a glass, she stumbled upon a cupboard packed full of treats. "Ooh! Chocolates!" She held up a king-sized bar.

"You can't have that!" I lunged at her before she could get the wrapper off and was just about to wrestle her to the floor when Dana walked in.

"Hello girls!" she cooed.

I let go of Ruby in a panic and tried to divert all attention away from the stolen chocolate by asking, "Is it okay if we have a bit of bread?"

Dana chuckled. "Of course, my love. Have whatever you want. We have yoghurts in the fridge if you fancy one." She beamed and left the room.

I turned to see Ruby grinning at me, having already scoffed half the chocolate bar. "See?" she said. "Whatever we want."

I let out a grunt and went to get some bread.

~*~

I couldn't wait to get to Destiny Hill that evening. After Donny's preach the night before, I had great hopes that something amazing might happen.

84

As soon as we arrived, Dana dragged us over to meet a girl at the bookstall. "This is my niece, Rhiann. She got saved— when was it now?"

"Five weeks ago," said Rhiann.

"That's it! And she got baptised the week after."

"Cool," Ruby and I chimed in unison.

Rhiann grinned and asked whether we'd been to Wales before. We shook our heads.

"It's a lovely place," she said.

We nodded politely.

"It's dear to the Lord's heart, Wales is," Dana told us proudly. "Famous for its revivals."

My heart leapt as I informed them, "I'm a bit Welsh."[30]

"Ooh, are you, Livi?" Dana gave me a big squeeze. "Welcome home then!"

I gulped. "Thanks."

"Livi and Ruby are staying with us at the moment," Dana told Rhiann. "I'm their little Welsh mummy for the week!"

Something inside me ruptured at her words. I wanted to throw up.

"I told them this morning that it's like having my daughters come to stay," Dana added.

I bit my lip as she gave me another squeeze.

"They're a bit older than you," Dana continued to me and Ruby. "Liza's at university and Rosie's travelling."

"That's nice." I forced a smile before giving Ruby a little nudge. "I'll meet you in there. I need the toilet." I ran off and scurried through the building in search of the toilets. I didn't really need to go. I just felt uncomfortable with Dana hugging me every five minutes and was petrified that I might cry if she referred to herself as our mummy again.

When I entered the main hall five minutes later, worship was already underway so I took my place next to Ruby and closed my eyes to avoid further chit-chat with Dana or Rhiann.

The buzz in the room was just as palpable as the night before and it wasn't long before people were linking arms and dancing merrily. However, unlike the night before, this time I couldn't help but feel slightly on edge. I was afraid that Dana might suddenly try to link arms with me and I wasn't sure I would be able to cope with

---

[30] My mother's mother was Welsh. I never knew her, nor did I ever think I would one day be so proud of the fact.

the emotions that might surface if she did. In order to avoid this, I curled up on my chair and pretended to be lost in prayer.

As with the previous night, the singing went on for a long time, with large portions of spontaneous prayer and praise. Then there was a time of testimony in which hoards of people came to the front and shared stories of healing and provision that had taken place over the past week.

The first testimony was from a lady who had been healed of pneumonia— the very thing my mother died of.

I felt my stomach churning as everybody cheered.

Lord, why did you heal that woman but not my mum?

As soon as I started thinking about my mother, I couldn't stop. It wasn't long before I felt utterly miserable. What made it all the more uncomfortable was the fact that Dana was sitting beside me, shooting me a beam every few minutes and offering me tissues when my nose began to run. I found myself feeling smothered by the smell of her mysterious sweet perfume and the squishiness of her arm which bumped against me every time she moved, reminding me over and over that she, my *'little Welsh mummy,'* was alive while my real mother was not.

I blinked back the tears as more testimonies were shared and forced myself to ignore Dana's presence beside me.

A girl who looked about my age was in the middle of sharing a story in which she had prayed for several people at a party to be healed from various afflictions. "People kept lining up to be prayed for!" she exclaimed as the congregation applauded. "And they kept getting healed! It was crazy!"

I frowned. *Lord, why can't I do things like that?*

A wave of envy washed over me as the girl leapt off the stage. It had been a good two months since I had constructed my *Disciple To-Do List* and I was still so far from the superstar Christian life I'd envisioned— yet all of Wales seemed to have a story to tell. Even Annie was doing better than me and she wasn't even trying!

It's not fair! I told God bitterly as the long line of testimonies continued. *What about me? I want to see miracles too, you know!*

After a while, I started to feel a little nauseous. Part of me even wanted to get up and walk out of the room. I shook myself. *What's wrong with me? Why do I feel this way?* I was part of an outpouring. I was in the presence of God. I was supposed to be feeling happy.

As Ruby glanced at me and grinned, I shut my eyes and pretended to be praying.

I didn't know it but the discomfort I was feeling was all part of my great unravelling; part of God revealing things that needed to be purged from me. In that moment I was convinced he had thoroughly overlooked me. But later I would realise he'd had a reason and a plan for all that I was experiencing.

I jumped in surprise as a girl in the row in front suddenly burst into raucous laughter, rolling off her chair and loudly praising Jesus. She continued to squawk over the rest of the testimonies and didn't quieten down until about halfway through the preach. I was torn between disdain for her carelessness and jealousy for her freedom. I kept one eye on her and the other on the preacher.

She's still down there. What is she feeling? Is it God? Doesn't he mind that she's distracting everybody?

At one point Ruby nudged me and whispered, "She looks happy!"

I forced a smile and pretended to be engaged in the preach.

Tonight's preacher talked about Jesus being the only way to salvation. It was a good, solid preach, but nowhere near as gripping as Donny's had been the night before. Nevertheless, when he gave the altar call, many people rushed to respond.

I watched in awe as several people fell on their knees. How amazing it would be to see this in our church in Leeds! I went over the pastor's preach as I wondered how to replicate such results.

As with the night before, it was announced that anybody who wanted prayer could go forward as the worship went on. Figuring I wasn't experiencing God the way other people seemed to be, I got up and made my way to the front.

As I took my place at the altar, I warned God, *I don't particularly want to make any loud noises like that girl over there. And I don't want you to push me over either. But, other than that, I'd quite like something exciting to happen.*

A lady came over and asked if I was waiting for prayer.

"Yes please."

"What for?"

"Er... Just more of God," I said lamely.

"Beautiful. What's your name?"

"Livi."

She nodded and prayed for me,[31] giving me a serene smile as she held my hands in hers. Nothing spectacular happened but a sense of peace seemed to rest on my shoulders. When the lady

---

[31] Or rather, for *'Libby.'*

stepped away, I realised that my hands felt remarkably warm. I clenched my fists a few times as I asked God, *Is that you?* They seemed to grow hotter. I stared at them in wonder as I drifted back to my seat.

Ruby smiled as I sat down.

I put my hands on her cheeks. "Do my hands feel hot?"

She gave a careless shrug. "I don't know."

"They're burning! Can't you feel it?"

"I suppose..."

I sat back in my chair and pouted. Perhaps I was just imagining it. I let out a sigh and watched as the people around me continued in their passionate praise. My gaze fell on Rhiann who was swaying lightly with her eyes shut. A sudden picture popped into my mind of her in a sweet shop. Jars of every imaginable sweet filled the room and the owner beamed as he said to Rhiann, *'Have whatever you want.'*

In case I was just making it up, I tried to push the image from my mind. But, the more I ignored it, the more I felt as though God was waiting to give something special to Rhiann, if only I would dare to be his messenger.

"Are you alright, Livi?" Dana asked suddenly. "You're looking a bit thoughtful."

"Oh." I blushed. "I just thought I might have seen a picture for Rhiann."

"How lovely!" Dana trilled. "Well you ought to tell her."

"But I don't know if—" Before I could explain that I wasn't used to having pictures for people and couldn't be sure it was truly from God, Dana leant over and grabbed Rhiann's arm. "Rhiann, Livi's got a word for you."

Rhiann turned to me. "Oh?"

I gulped. "Well, I'm not sure really. I just had a little picture."

The two of them kept staring at me with beams on their faces.

I took a deep breath and shared what I'd seen.

To my amazement, Rhiann brought a hand up to her mouth and sobbed. "That's incredible," she blubbered. "I was just that second praying to God and I was asking him for the gift of tongues. And now you're telling me he wants to give me whatever I want! I can't believe it! Ooh, you have to pray for me, Livi!"

I was alarmed. I understood that tongues were a supernatural kind of prayer language and I'd frequently heard people speaking or singing in tongues at King's Church. I'd occasionally asked Ruby to do it just so I could hear what hers sounded like but I couldn't do it myself. I didn't even know if I wanted to. I'd certainly never prayed for anyone else to do it.

"I wasn't sure if it was really God," I confessed before Rhiann could get too excited.

"Well there you go," said Dana. "You're more powerful than you realise. God trusts you, see?"

I nodded blankly.

"Are you going to pray for Rhiann then?"

"Er..." I felt my cheeks grow hot. "I've never prayed for anyone to have tongues before."

"That's alright," Dana assured me. "Why don't we both pray?"

I gave a grateful nod. "Alright." At least then I wouldn't be fully responsible if nothing happened.

Rhiann stood in the middle as Dana and I prayed and invited the Holy Spirit to come and give her the gift of tongues.

After a while, Dana broke into tongues herself.

I squeezed my eyes shut, feeling like a fraud.

Rhiann started to mumble under her breath. "Ooh, it's happening," she told us. "It's like I can feel words trying to come out of my mouth."

"Keep going!" Dana exclaimed. "It will get easier." She gave us both little pats on the shoulder before wandering off to pray for more people.

I sighed and sat back down. I knew I ought to be over the moon after successfully praying for Rhiann to speak in tongues, but I just couldn't shake off the irritable sadness that had been bugging me all night.

Beside me, Rhiann went on and on until something resembling some kind of language started to flow from her mouth. She stopped and put a hand to her cheek. "Oh, this is amazing!" She gave me a massive grin. "Livi, isn't this amazing? Shall we pray in tongues together?"

I looked away as I confessed, "I can't speak in tongues."

I expected Rhiann to be confused or wonder why I had prayed for her to do something that I couldn't do myself, but she just took my hands and said, "Ooh, Livi! Let me pray for you!"

"But I don't know if..."

I was about to say that I didn't know whether or not God wanted to give me the gift of tongues, but Rhiann beamed and put her hand on my shoulder. She prayed for a while before whispering, "Give it a go!"

I opened my mouth to make a noise and the faintest, smallest, *could've-just-been-gibberish,* couple of syllables came out. I shrugged as if to say, *'Oh well.'*

Rhiann squealed and, before I could explain myself, leant over and tapped Ruby who was deep in prayer. "Livi just spoke in tongues!"

I blushed as Ruby looked up in excitement. "Really?"

"I don't know," I said. "Maybe."

"Cool." Ruby grinned. "We can pray together sometime."

"Alright," I mumbled, wishing the ground would swallow me up.

"Ooh!" Rhiann shrieked suddenly in my ear. "This is the song that was playing when I got saved!" She cocked her head towards the worship band before jumping into the aisle to join an emerging conga line.

All over the room, people were running to join in the dance, clutching hold of total strangers as if they were all one big happy family. My stomach churned as Dana trotted past and ruffled my hair.

"Livi, let's dance!" Without warning, Ruby grabbed me by the hands and pulled me off my chair.

I stumbled back and yanked my hands away. "No! I..." I didn't want to say that I wasn't in the mood or that I was an insecure dancer or, more to the point, that Ruby was an insecure dancer and ought to be shrinking back like she normally would. "I feel tired," I muttered instead.

Ruby giggled before skipping off and joining the conga line.

My chest ached as I sat back in my chair and watched her. I longed to feel whatever she seemed to be feeling. It wasn't that I couldn't feel *anything;* I was aware that the atmosphere was electric and that something powerful was happening all around me, but there was something about the intensity and the unity that I couldn't quite enter into.

I stayed stuck to my seat for the rest of the night, feeling a horrible combination of abandonment and anger. I knew there was more of God to be had; people all over the room were experiencing it. *Why couldn't I?*

I squeezed my eyes shut and prayed under my breath, "God, tell me what I need to do to have more of your love. I'll do anything... I'll tell everyone on the streets about you, I'll pray for five hundred people, I'll practise this tongues thing until I'm an expert. What are you waiting for? How can I prove that I'm serious? Just tell me what to do and I'll do it."

Suddenly, a gentle voice whispered to my heart, *Didn't we do this already?* It wasn't an angry reproach, nor was there even the hint of sarcasm. Just a simple, tender question. *Didn't we do this already?*

I bit my lip. "Do what?"

My love is priceless.

I paused and waited for God to continue.

You can't buy it.

"I know I can't *buy* it!" I snapped. "I'm not trying to *buy* it. It's just that I've come all this way for you and I don't seem to be getting anything..." Of course, I hadn't come *all this way* for God, but I hoped that he wouldn't notice in the heat of the moment. I grabbed a tissue from my bag and blew my nose before continuing bitterly, "You say you love me, but why can't I feel it like how Ruby feels it? Or like that girl who laughed all the way through the preach? Or Rhiann who only just got saved?" I squeezed my eyes shut and pulled my legs up onto my seat, alternating between shame and self-pity at my outburst.

I looked up to see Dana, on the other side of the room, staring in my direction. I held my breath, afraid that she had seen me crying and would soon be running down the aisle to give me a hug. I wrapped my arms around myself as I wondered what I should say. *'I've had a hard life and I feel so abandoned by God...'*

But then Dana turned and started talking to a lady at the side.

I sniffed, feeling both relieved and rejected at the same time. Perhaps she *had* seen me after all and had turned her back on me to make it clear that she wouldn't stand for any attention seeking.

I buried my head in my hands. *God, what's wrong with me?* "I shouldn't feel like this," I blubbered. "Something needs to change."

Yes.

I let out a long sigh. "What then?"

I waited for a while but God kept quiet. It was another five days before I would get his answer.

~ 11 ~

This is love

Our week in Bryn Hapus seemed to fly by, with every waking hour packed full of activity. Ruby and I joined in with sessions at the research centre during the day but always slipped off early so that we could go to the outpouring meetings in the evening. Our classmates seemed fairly settled on the idea that we were lazy rebels who were destined to fail the course.

Sharon did nothing to dissuade them from this view, giving us very little sympathy when we found ourselves struggling due to gaps in our learning. Only once did she actually ask us about the outpouring. And, even then, all she said was a brief, "Glad you came?" over lunch.

"It's amazing," Ruby exclaimed. "I've never felt God so strongly!"

At this, Sharon winked and walked off.

I'd wanted to run after her and explain that although I was pleased to be attending the meetings I wasn't experiencing the same level of joy as Ruby. But I was afraid Sharon might tell me off for wasting the liberties she had granted us so I sat still and said nothing.

I went to every outpouring meeting hopeful and expectant that maybe *this* time something wonderful would happen. At times I had glimpses, and several times my hands felt quite warm, but I still wasn't encountering God in any huge way. In fact, most nights I just felt sad for no good reason. Even so, something compelled me to keep going and I was hungrier than ever for more. I couldn't imagine going back to normal life, with regular church only once a week. At the same time, I was pretty sick of sheep. I was also struggling with not feeling at home at Donny and Dana's and was desperate to get back to Jill. She may not be as bubbly and warm as Dana but at least she was mine.

So it was with mixed feelings that I wandered round the research centre on our final morning. The day was cold and windy. I envied Ruby who had been given the job of feeding baby lambs with Maria and Ellen. I had hoped Sharon might let me join them but, instead, I had been paired with Laura and the two of us were tasked with collecting buckets of sheep poo from the field.[32]

Other than to bemoan how cold it was or how stinking our job was, neither of us talked for ages. Although Ruby and I had worked with Maria, Ellen and Laura all week, this was the first time I had hung out just with Laura. I saw her watching me rather carefully, as if expecting me not to pull my weight. I was determined to show her that I was not only a very hardworking individual but one who had found something far greater than ABC. I longed to tell her about Jesus or perhaps invite her to our last outpouring meeting, but I couldn't think how to begin. I prayed over and over, *What should I say, Lord? Help me start a conversation.*

The thought came to my mind, *Ask if she has any pets.*

I hesitated. I hated that it was exactly the kind of question someone from my course would ask. I shook my head and tried to think of something better but my mind remained blank so I took a deep breath and blurted out, "Have you got any pets?"

Laura grinned. "Yeah, I've got a rabbit."

"Cool. Er... What's its name?"

"Stampy."

I nodded politely. *Now what?*

There was brief silence before Laura asked, "How about you?"

"No, I don't have any." I forced a smile before bending down to shovel up a particularly big bit of poo.

"I know someone who had a snake," Laura said suddenly.

I looked at her. "Oh?"

"Yeah. I don't really like snakes."

"Me neither."

"Hey, didn't they used to have legs or something?"

"Legs?"

"Yeah, I think my grandma told me that. In the Garden of Eden the snake had legs but God took his legs away because it was naughty... Is that right?"

---

[32] As a 'treat' for working so hard, Sharon had invited a local artist to come in and show everyone how to recycle farmyard waste into homemade paper.

I couldn't believe it! The *'Have you got any pets?'* line had actually worked! My heart pounded as I said, "Yeah, sort of. The snake tempted Adam and Eve to sin against God."

Laura gave a satisfied smile. "I thought it was something like that."

I paused before asking, "Do you believe in God?"

"I don't know. Sometimes I do. That's selfish, isn't it?"

"What do you mean?"

"I mean... If he's real, I should probably pay him more attention."

I tried to choose my words carefully as I said, "Yeah, probably... Hey, can I tell you about Jesus?"

"Alright." Laura gave me a curious look and put her bucket of poo down.

I took a deep breath before launching into a hearty presentation of the gospel, combining all the best bits from the week of outpouring meetings as I drove the point home.

Laura stared at me the whole time. I couldn't read her expression. At one point, she reached into her pocket and I had the vain hope that she was hunting for a pen so that she could take notes. But she was just getting out her mittens.

I finished with something Donny had said the night before— "Life is shorter than you realise and some things are a matter of life and death,"— before asking, "So... do you want to accept Jesus?"

Laura puffed out her cheeks. "I don't know. I need to think about it."

My heart sunk. "Oh. Well... Ruby and I have a club if you want to join? It's for Christians and people who want to find out more."

"Yeah, maybe. What's it called?"

"Er... It's kind of called The Club." As Laura blinked at me, I kicked myself for not being more persistent with Ruby. "I mean, it doesn't have a proper name yet," I said hurriedly. "It will soon."

"Oh." Laura smiled. "That's nice. Thanks. I'll think about it."

I racked my brain for a way to persuade her further but nothing came and we spent the rest of the morning picking up poo in silence.

Later that afternoon,[33] Sharon announced that, contrary to the original itinerary, she had decided to give us all that evening off since it would be our last night.

---

[33] Incidentally, turning poo into paper proved to be far more exciting than it had sounded.

Immediately I tracked Laura down and invited her to the outpouring meeting, certain that she would meet Jesus if she came. To my great delight, she accepted my invitation and I sauntered out of the research centre brimming with joy.

Ruby almost fell over when I told her the news.

"And she might join our club," I added as we headed back to Donny and Dana's for dinner. "Although, we really should give it a proper name."

"Wow!" Ruby gasped. "How come she's suddenly interested?"

"Oh, I might've told her about Jesus earlier," I said casually.

I tried to look humble as Ruby gave an impressed nod.

Arriving early at Destiny Hill that evening, Ruby and I lingered eagerly by the door so that we could greet Laura. We had barely been there five minutes when I received a text saying that she was going to watch a film with Maria and Ellen instead.

I gave a cry of frustration as I held my phone up to Ruby. "Doesn't she realise this is a unique event? She can watch a film anytime!"

"Oh," said Ruby. "That's a shame."

I frowned. It was more than a shame. I had just been daydreaming about how great it would be to go home and brag to Annie that someone on our course had got saved.

Before I could grumble further, Dana popped up beside us. "Your last night!" she trilled. "I'm going to miss you!" I held my breath as she leant over and enveloped us both in a massive hug.

"Thanks for having us," I muttered, feeling a pang of guilt as I realised that, other than a card made from sheep poo, I hadn't bought them a thank you present.

"It's been so lovely having you to stay," Dana continued. "You have a home in Bryn Hapus any time. Just remember me as your little Welsh mummy!"

Ruby gave a gushing smile but I just swallowed hard and mumbled, "Thanks for having us," again.

As Dana held me at arm's length and beamed, I was certain she was secretly thinking that she would miss Ruby far more than me.

"I need the toilet," I said. "Save me a seat, Ruby."

When I wandered into the main hall several minutes later, the worship band was singing the same two lines over and over.

'More of you, less of me
Restore me to the person you always meant me to be...'

I found Ruby and squeezed in beside her, sitting down to listen to the song. The words wrapped themselves round my heart and I soon found myself singing along.

At the front of the altar, several people were kneeling, swaying or waiting to be prayed for. Apparently Donny had invited the congregation to come up for prayer at any point instead of waiting till the end. I spent a long time watching the people at the front, wondering whether I should go up and what I should ask for if I did. I had gone up for prayer every night since our second meeting but was yet to have anything impressive happen.

Ruby interrupted my thoughts with a poke. "Sharon's here!" She pointed to our teacher who stood with her arms raised several rows away.

I looked up and nodded. "Oh yeah." I pretended to be lost in worship in case Sharon were to look over and see me.

A few songs later, another of the pastors picked up the microphone and said, "I want to invite you up for prayer if you're a Christian, perhaps a new believer, who's not yet been filled with the Holy Spirit."

I sucked in my cheeks. I'd felt God's presence many times and Summer had assured me long ago that I'd been baptised in the Holy Spirit. But I wasn't sure I *truly* had him. After all, I wasn't living a life of miracles just yet. "I'm going up," I said.

Ruby looked at me in confusion. "You've already got the Holy Spirit, Livi."

"Have I?" I demanded.

"Yeah! Especially now that you can speak in tongues."

I pursed my lips. "I'm not sure I can quite call it that yet," I muttered. "Anyway, there's more. I just know it."

"Summer says—"

"I don't care what Summer says! There's more and I want it." I ignored Ruby's baffled frown and got up from my seat. I marched straight to the front and held my hands out.

Someone from the ministry team came over and prayed with me. Within seconds, I felt my hands grow a little warm. But, other than that, nothing happened. I gave a quick nod of thanks and went back to my seat, feeling rather disgruntled as I watched many others falling over at the front as they got prayed for.

The worship went on and, although I wasn't feeling anything in particular, I was sure my hands were getting warmer. I turned to ask Ruby to feel them but, before I could say anything, she giggled and slid to the floor as she fell under the weight of God's love. I stuck my lip out. People were laughing and weeping and rolling all around me. All I had was burning hands.

I stole a glance at Sharon. Even *she* was looking a whole lot jollier than I felt. My chest ached as my gaze fell on Dana. I was torn between wanting one last hug and yet feeling utterly unworthy to receive one. I found myself choking up as her words rang in my ears. *'Just remember me as your little Welsh mummy!'*

I covered my face with my hands. *Where are you God? Don't you love me anymore?*

Self-pity soon started pouring in. *It's because my mum died.* I thought bitterly. *That's why I'm such a mess.*

I rubbed my eyes and accepted that God had probably abandoned me. For some reason, he had no desire for me to know him as deeply as everybody else seemed to.

While Ruby continued to bask in God's presence from the floor, I sat cross-legged on my chair and waited for the preach to begin. I assumed it would be much the same as the rest of the week— a proclamation of the gospel, mainly for the benefit of those yet to receive Jesus. I figured I wouldn't need to concentrate too hard and could just practise speaking in tongues under my breath instead. Or maybe I ought to pray for Laura just so God would know I was serious about seeing her saved. But the moment Donny reached the stage I knew I needed to pay attention.

He began with a simple question: "Do you know God loves you?"

The congregation cheered and a few people said, "Amen," but his face remained quite serious.

"God really, *really* loves you," he went on. "Your parents had no choice about you. But God loved you and chose you and *imagined* you before the world began. He doesn't only love you when you behave. He loves you because he put his image and his glory inside of you. And he will never, ever, ever stop loving you. It's impossible. It's simply not in his character. One of the greatest tragedies of Christian life is so many people not living in the fullness of their adoption as God's child."

I felt sick as Donny continued, "I'm talking about an orphan spirit. If you're someone who's always trying to earn God's love then you'll know what I mean. Perhaps you compare yourself to other Christians and believe God must like them better. You try to get his attention but assume he's busy with all his other children. You don't feel part of the family. You don't realise the Father is pleased to give you his whole Kingdom. You eat scraps because you don't believe you're allowed to go into his fridge and help yourself to whatever you want."

I felt my stomach lurch. I knew God was speaking directly to me but what could I do about it? If I could change myself, I would have done so by now. Of course I *believed* that God loved me; I'd read plenty of Belinda's Bible bookmarks and I'd heard enough preaches. I knew he didn't have favourites and that I didn't need to work for his approval. But my inability to enter freely into his presence over the past week proved that, deep down, my heart still didn't have a full grasp of these truths.

"I was fine on the first day," I muttered to myself. "But then Dana got more and more *cuddly* and it messed me up..."

Tears pricked the backs of my eyes and I had to fight an overwhelming urge to get up and run away.

"If this is relevant to you," said Donny, "then Jesus wants to say right now: *'Do not exchange what I believe about you for a lie. Everything I have, I give to you.'* Do you realise that when Jesus was on the cross, he was thirsty for *you*? He is not just *the* Saviour; he is *your* Saviour. He is not just *the* Healer; he is *your* Healer. Even if you were the only one alive, Jesus would have come down and died, just for you. Even if you never noticed, it would have been worth it for him, for the chance that you might turn and choose him. That's how much he loves you. He's desperate for you to know his love. He desires intimacy more than you do! Do you know who you are? You are a precious child of the living God! You are worth every drop of Jesus' blood! You may dream of doing great exploits for God. But, I tell you now, you can't truly love others until you start to love yourself. And you can't love yourself until you know you're loved by God. No matter your gifts or your calling, if you don't *know* that God loves you— if you don't have his goodness as your firm foundation— then don't do a thing until you do."

I let out a long breath. Donny's words were nothing new. But there was something different this time. There was an urgency in my soul and a sickness in my bones. It was as though my heart had been sliced in two and laid out on the altar. I wanted to run and hide, yet I just knew I needed to respond.

Donny scanned the whole room before concluding his message. "If you know you need a deeper revelation of the Father's heart for you, then I want to invite you to come forward for prayer."

I swallowed hard and got to my feet. Ruby was still flat out on the floor and I carefully stepped over her as I made my way to the front. I was scared that I would stand out and look silly. But I didn't need to worry. All over the room, people were getting out of their seats and coming to the altar. It was one of the biggest responses all week.

The ministry team was rather stretched and it was several minutes before someone was free to come and pray with me. I waited with my eyes shut and my head down, feeling a little unsteady. By this point I had almost lost my nerve. *Was I just being daft, continually hoping for more of God? Perhaps I ought to be grateful for what I had?*

"Hello. Can I pray with you?"

I looked up to see a tall lady with bright blue eyes beaming down at me.

"Okay," I said quickly.

"I'm Evie. What's your name?"

"Livi," I mumbled.

"That's a lovely name."

I was certain she had misheard me so was rather surprised when she began to pray, "Father, I want to thank you for your precious princess, Livi..." Evie stopped and looked me in the eye. "Do you know you're his princess?"

I gave an awkward shrug. "I guess."

"I'm so happy I got to meet you tonight, Livi. You know why? Because I got to meet God's princess!"

She went on in this peculiar manner for quite some time and I tried to concentrate but found myself feeling more and more disorientated. The blueness of her eyes seemed to pierce my soul as she told me repeatedly that Jesus loved me. Eventually, I forced a smile and looked away.

"Hey, Livi. Will you look me in the eye?"

A rush of anger surged through me. "Why?"

"I think it's important."

I sighed irritably and looked back at her. Immediately, I felt a wave of nausea and almost lost my balance.

"Are you alright?"

"I feel sick."

Evie nodded. "Let it come out."

I wondered if she actually meant that I ought to throw up right there and then on the floor. "I need to sit down," I said weakly.

Evie led me to a chair and continued to pray as I put my head in my hands. I was beginning to feel tired.

What happened next was all a bit of a blur. I remember feeling a rising rage tinged with sorrow as Evie repeatedly told me that God loved me. At some point I heard her beckoning for someone else to come over. Then, as the two of them prayed, I was acutely aware of Evie saying, "Come out in the name of Jesus!"

She said this several times before I found myself retching and felt something like air rushing up through my body and out of my mouth.

"That's it!" I heard Evie say triumphantly. "It's out."

I sat back in the chair, feeling rather dazed. I felt about as weak as if I had been throwing up all evening, yet there was nothing physical to show for it.

Evie and her friend prayed for a while longer, asking the Holy Spirit to come and fill me up. As they prayed, a gentle peace seemed to seep through my veins. My whole body felt light and free, as though a massive weight had been taken out of me. I was too tired to think of anything other than, *This is love. Jesus loves me exactly as I am.* I curled up on the chair and closed my eyes as I bathed in this wonderful presence.

As some point, Evie and her friend must have slipped away and I looked up to see Sharon Sheppard sitting beside me. She gave me a big hug and asked if I was alright.

"Something came out when they prayed," I whispered.

She nodded.

"What was it?"

"A demon I expect."

I looked at her in shock. Fear and shame began to rise up inside me but Sharon said gently, "It's gone now. And it wasn't your fault. It's also very common." She pointed around the room to others receiving deliverance. Some of them were making much more of a scene than I had done.

I gulped and turned back to Sharon. "I didn't see anything."

"No, but you felt something go, didn't you?"

"Yeah."

"How do you feel now?"

"I feel great." I grinned. "Does that mean I've got the Holy Spirit now?"

Sharon gave me a curious smile. "I'm pretty sure you already had him, Livi."

"But I always feel like there's more."

She laughed. "Oh, there is. There's lots more."

My heart leapt. "So I'm right to want more?"

"You are."

"How do I—?"

"Let God lead you! He gave you that hunger and he will fill it. For now, just thank him for setting you free tonight."

"Okay..." I bit my thumb. "If it *was* a demon, why did I have it?"

"I would guess that it probably came in when you were quite young. Orphan spirits generally run very deep."

"Why did God let me have it for so long?

"That's not a helpful question. He's your Father; trust him to meet your needs in whatever way he pleases. He knows what's best. Do you truly know that he loves you?"

I let out a long breath. "Yes."

"Deep in your gut? Not just because you're feeling great right now."

"Yes, I know it." Peace flooded through me and a little tear of joy slid down my cheek. "I'm his child. He loves me as much as he possibly can."

"Could you go back to Donny and Dana's and eat anything in their fridge?"

I gave a slow nod as I wondered how she knew. "Yes. I think so."

Sharon smiled. "Good. Now you're ready to fly."

~ 12 ~

Jesus is the door

Μy whole life was changed by that one last evening in Wales. Something that had seemed so elusive and temporary was to be mine forever and ever: a final, certain assurance of God's love. No more striving for it. No more living as an orphan.

For the whole of the next week, I had a deep sense of my worth in God's sight. It was as though something broken inside me had been extracted and replaced with God's golden seal of approval. This didn't mean that I felt happy all the time or that I didn't sometimes find myself slipping into old habits of competing for God's affections.[34] But I quickly reminded myself that God loved me exactly as I was and on a fundamental heart level I knew this to be true. A new revelation of God as *my* Father (not just *the* Father) had suddenly clicked into place and, unlike occasions in the past, this time nothing could rob it. Not even Jill accusing me of being selfish when I accidentally ate the last chocolate bar.

I couldn't wait to tell everybody at youth group about the outpouring meetings. I was convinced they would all be as eager as I was to see the same thing in Leeds.

The moment Ruby and I got through Eddie and Summer's door the following Friday, I announced to those who had already arrived, "You'll never guess where we've been!"

Joey looked up from the tray of flapjacks at the side. "Ikea?"

I rolled my eyes. "Better than that."

He shrugged. "Where then?"

"We went to meetings for a whole week where hundreds of people came from all over the world to encounter God."

Amanda gawped at us from the sofa. "Really?"

---

[34] For example, when Annie rang to tell me that The COOL Club meetings had moved to a bigger classroom.

"Yeah." I grinned. "Wait till everyone arrives then we'll tell you all about it."

It turned out Eddie and Summer had heard about the Welsh outpouring through various church networks. They were thrilled to hear that Ruby and I had been there.

"Tell us about Bryn Hapus," Summer said once everyone had gathered. "What was it like?"

"It was amazing!" Ruby exclaimed before I could get a word in. "The church building was a massive grey warehouse, wasn't it, Livi?"

I nodded and opened my mouth to speak.

"God's peace was everywhere," Ruby went on. "And his love was so intense. Hundreds of people came and everyone was really excited to meet with God. Loads of people were getting saved. Oh, and Livi spoke in tongues!"

"Wonderful!" Summer looked at me. "Would you like to add anything, Livi?"

I sucked in my cheeks as I wondered how to follow Ruby's account. I figured it wouldn't go down too well if I announced I'd been delivered from a demon. I squirmed in my seat, feeling like I had some wonderful secret. I took a moment before saying, "Lots of people got healed from things."

The group exchanged excited murmurs.

"That's fantastic," said Eddie. "It's always amazing when God's presence comes powerfully."

Ruby nodded eagerly. "It was *really* powerful. I feel so refreshed."

The group listened wide-eyed as she recounted her experience of falling in the Spirit. I had to admit, she had been a lot bolder since our trip to Wales. I had never known her to hog the limelight so much.

"We need to have meetings like that in Leeds," I said when she finished.

Eddie chuckled. "That would be great, Livi. But we can't just manufacture it."

"Maybe if we press in for more..." I suggested. "The Bryn Hapus meetings started after a woman in a wheelchair got healed. We should pray for five hundred people and then maybe an outpouring would happen."

The group stared at me.

"We can be trailblazers!" I added.

Still nobody said anything.

"If it can happen there, then why not here?" I continued, longing for them to catch what I was feeling.

"I don't understand healing," Amanda piped up. "How do we know who God wants to heal?"

A surge of irritation went through me as Summer said, "That's a complicated topic."

"Oh." Amanda looked disappointed.

Summer was about to say something else when, quite without meaning to, I blurted out, "I believe God wants to heal everybody." My heart started to pound and I looked at Ruby for support but she just went pink and stared straight at Summer.

"I used to think that," Mark piped up. "But now I'm not sure."

"I know loads of people who haven't been healed," added Joey.

"Like my dad," said Nicole. "He never got healed. Lots of people prayed for him."

I tried to shoot Nicole a sympathetic glance as I muttered, "But if we press in for more..."

"We need to know God's will," said Bill.

By now, pretty much everyone except Kevin and Amanda had teamed up against me.[35] They watched the rest of us battle it out, both of them easily swayed as they nodded along with whoever was speaking.

Desperate to get through to *somebody,* I cleared my throat and declared, "Jesus said that anyone who believes in him would do greater works than him." I flicked through my Bible and then stopped, wishing I knew my way around it better. I nudged Ruby. "Where's the verse?"

She shrugged.

I turned to the group. "It does say it," I insisted.

"But there's no greater work than dying on the cross for the sins of the world, is there?" Joey retorted.

The others nodded in agreement. Kevin and Amanda looked across and grinned.

"Okay," I said. "So, if salvation is the greatest miracle, then why can't we do the lesser ones?" I paused before adding, "You know, like healing the sick and casting out demons."

I saw Summer give Eddie a quick glance.

Eddie nodded at her before asking me, "Livi, have you heard of the phrase, *'The Kingdom here but not yet'?"*

---

[35] Ruby was still staying quiet which irritated me.

"Yeah but I don't like it," I said. "I think it makes people settle for the *'not yet.'* How about *'The Kingdom here and coming even more'?*"

"Well, yes. That's another way of putting it. But, either way, there are some things that won't be completely restored until the fullness of Heaven."

"But if we press in for *more...*" My heart pounded as everybody stared at me. I couldn't understand why none of them shared my urgency.

Summer cleared her throat. "Shall we get on with tonight's meeting? We were thinking we'd look at what the Bible says about hospitality."

I stifled a sigh and pulled out my Bible. I had nothing against hospitality; it just sounded a little mundane following the week of explosive teaching in Wales.

"Do not forget to entertain strangers," Summer read from her Bible. *"For by so doing some people have entertained angels without knowing it."*

I blinked. *Well I wouldn't mind being more hospitable if it meant I might see an angel!*

I sat straighter, hoping Summer might shed some light on how to attract angels but, to my disappointment, she just said, "One way we can share God's love with others is by always being ready to serve..."

As Summer read another passage about the importance of generosity, I swallowed a yawn and began flicking through my Bible, pausing here and there to read various miraculous accounts: Jesus feeding the five thousand, Peter's shadow healing many who were sick, Paul's account of ascending to the third Heaven. How full of God's power would I need to be before I could do *those* kinds of things?

The study came to an end and Summer asked if anybody wanted prayer for anything.

Nobody spoke so I waited for a moment before taking a deep breath. "I want to be filled with the Holy Spirit."

Summer gave me a bemused smile. "You've already got the Holy Spirit, Livi."

I shook my head. "I mean *filled*. Like the people I saw in Wales. I need to be full of him. I'm still too full of myself." I thought about the orphan spirit and added quickly, "And maybe other things."

Summer looked a little taken aback. "We're all in the process of being sanctified. But you're definitely filled with the Spirit!"

I shook my head again. I wasn't taking no for an answer. I had glimpsed something at Destiny Hill and I wanted it— no longer because I felt I needed to earn it, but simply because a fire had been stoked within me and I wouldn't stop until I was consumed. It was true that God's love was more tangible and I was no longer in any doubt about his heart towards me, but I still wanted more. I knew my life didn't match up to that of the disciples in the Early Church.

"I don't have what they had when the fire fell at Pentecost," I said, flicking through my Bible in search of the account in Acts. "Oh, I don't know where it is," I muttered. "But I'm not changed like they were. You know, totally radical and stuff."

Summer gave me a somewhat patronising smile as she said, "We could all be more like that! But we need to let God be God."

"I'm not stopping God from being God," I retorted. "I just want more of him. What's wrong with that?"

I looked from Summer to Eddie to Ruby and the rest of our youth group. They were all staring at me as though I had gone mad. Perhaps I had turned into one of those extremists people sometimes joke about.

"There's nothing wrong with your passion," Summer insisted. "But you don't need to make things happen. God loves you exactly as you are."

"I know!" I exclaimed. "I don't have that problem anymore." I wondered whether this was the time to mention the demon but immediately thought better of it. I wasn't sure they would believe me. I felt a niggling annoyance that I'd been at this church for three years and nobody had spotted it. I could have had more of God sooner had they known what to do.

Summer leant over and put a hand on my arm. "Is everything okay, Livi? You sound like you're getting a bit worked up about things."

"I'm not!" I snapped. "I know I sound angry but that's because you're all staring at me. I'm just saying that things like outpouring don't have to be a one-off thing. We could have it every day if we wanted to."

Eddie took a deep breath. "What's happening in Wales is amazing," he said. "But God initiated it. We can't force his hand."

"Maybe not. But if we're hungry for him and empty of us then I reckon he'll come."

Eddie and Summer nodded but said nothing.

After a pause, Nicole piped up, "People have been waiting for revival for years. I remember my grandparents talking about it when I was little."

"It's like people keep saying Jesus is coming back soon," Joey said with a chuckle. "Like it's going to happen in our lifetime or something!"

I turned to Mark. "You believe that, don't you?"

"I guess..." he said. "But I've learnt God's idea of 'soon' isn't the same as mine."

"Like the way he sees blue might not be the same colour we see?" suggested Bill.

I frowned as the conversation switched to speculation about whether colours look the same to different people.

"I've had an idea," I began loudly.

Everyone stopped and looked at me.

I took a deep breath before announcing, "We should meet regularly to pray for revival."

"How regularly?" asked Joey. "Because I'm kind of busy with college."

"But aren't you hungry?" I implored him.

"A bit..." Joey grinned. "I could do with some chips."

I rolled my eyes as the others laughed.

"Well, anyway," I said irritably. "I'm going to start holding outpouring meetings at my house."

The group stared at me somewhat vacantly.

"Starting on Monday. You're all invited. We'll pray and sing and ask God to come."

"Thank you, Livi," said Summer. "That's a lovely idea."

I pursed my lips. It wasn't just a 'lovely idea.' Nobody ever changed the world with a 'lovely idea.'

I cornered Sharon on Monday morning. "You said there's more."

She looked at me. "Yes. I believe there is."

"My youth leaders don't seem to think so. When I talk about wanting more, they look at me as though I'm a crazy fanatic."

Sharon laughed. "What's wrong with that?"

"I'm not a crazy fanatic!"

"I know you're not. You're a normal Christian. But what if normal Christianity looks a little strange?"

I stopped as I thought about this. "My youth leaders are really strong in their faith," I said. "They know the Bible really well and they're usually quite wise..."

Sharon nodded.

I wrinkled up my nose. "But they don't seem to want more of God. They seem happy with the amount they've got."

Sharon shrugged. "There's grace for that."

"But *is* there more?"

"I believe so," she repeated. "I believe you can have as much of Jesus as you want. There are untold adventures in the Spirit yet to be discovered." Her eyes twinkled as she said this and I wondered what she knew.

"Like what?" I demanded.

"Oh, all sorts."

I frowned. "Tell me."

She chuckled. "God will show you. He wants to take you from glory to glory."

"Instead of comfort to comfort," I said wryly. "I don't want to settle for comfortable Christianity. But so many people do."

"That's because there's a price," said Sharon. "People may want the glory but they don't always want the homework. They don't want the sacrifices in the secret place— in the hidden things that nobody else sees."

"I do!" I exclaimed. "I'll do whatever it takes."

Her tone softened. "I know. I can tell you've had a lot of homework, Livi. God won't waste a single tear."

I gulped. I felt a lump in my throat and hurriedly changed the subject. "I can't wait to go to Heaven."

Sharon gave a curious smile.

"I can't wait to see Jesus face to face and be totally free and see everything how it should be. This world is so rubbish in comparison."

She kept staring at me.

"So I'm not scared of dying," I continued boldly. "Because then I get to go to Heaven."

I had hoped Sharon would be impressed by my valiant speech but she just pursed her lips and said, "Can't you have those things now?"

"Well, no... You don't go to Heaven until you die."

She gave me a long look. "But death is not the door. Jesus is."

"What?"

"Death was nailed to the cross. *Jesus* is your liberator into eternal life and eternal life starts now." I gawped at her as she went on, "When Jesus died, the veil was torn so that you could have access to the throne room *now*. Years of schooling have taught you that you're earthbound. But you're not part of this world anymore."

I stood in shock for a moment, afraid that I'd been taking lessons from a mad woman all this time. "Okay... So, how do I..?"

Sharon paused before saying cryptically, "I have come to learn that God is a little like a deer."

I blinked at her. "What?"

"If you want to know everything there is to know about deer, then you could go online and research them right now. But if you want to *experience* a deer, then you need to watch and be still." She grinned. "God wants to be sought and found. And you will find him if you seek him with all your heart."

"He told me that before," I said quietly.

"Good. He means it."

~ 13 ~

The Fire Brigade

As Ruby and I got the bus home from college, I sent several last minute reminders to our youth group about our first outpouring meeting that evening. In case I'd come across as a little intense on Friday, I added, *'Tonight we'll just be getting to know each other.'*

"Don't we already all know each other?" Ruby asked, giving me a bemused smile as she read my text.

"Well, Laura might come," I said. "She doesn't know everyone."

"Oh!" Ruby grinned. "Laura's coming?"

"She said she'd try."

Laura had actually said, *"I'll see if I'm free,"* in a way that had suggested she wouldn't be. But I was holding onto the vain hope that she would find herself compelled at the last minute to come.

"I suppose Annie doesn't know everyone," Ruby continued.

I resisted the temptation to wonder how many new converts Annie would announce that night. "Exactly." I coughed before saying tentatively, "Did you want to lead the meetings with me or should I do it by myself?"

"Oh!" Ruby looked at me in surprise. "I don't really mind."

"Well I'll lead it then and you can help."

"Alright."

I took a deep breath. "We should probably make sure we agree on some basics. For example, I believe God wants to heal *everybody.*"

"Yeah, I agree."

I pursed my lips. "Then why didn't you agree with me at youth group last week?"

She gave a quick shrug. "Because I know Summer doesn't believe that so I didn't want to be controversial."

"It's not being controversial! She's meant to be leading us. If she's got something wrong then we need to tell her."

"I don't know. I don't want to be disrespectful."

I gave a huffy sigh. "Fine. But when we meet at *my* house, I'm going to teach that God wants to heal everybody."

Ruby shrugged again. "Alright."

We got off the bus and turned the corner into our estate.

"Seven o' clock," I reminded Ruby as we reached our houses. "Don't be late."

She grinned. "I won't."

As it happened, Ruby wasn't late but everybody else was. As my clock struck half seven, my stomach sunk with the realisation that it was likely that nobody else was coming.

"Well…" I said glumly. "I guess nobody's very hungry."

Ruby was about to say something but was interrupted by a knock at the front door. I sprinted down the stairs and peered through the frosted window. It was Annie.

"You're late!" I said as I flung the door open.

"No I'm not." She checked her watch. "It's half seven."

"I said seven."

"You said half seven." Annie dug around in her bag and pulled out her phone. "See?" She showed me my text message.

"Oh!" My heart leapt as I realised nobody was late after all.

I ushered Annie up to my room where I exclaimed to Ruby, "People might still come! I said half seven in my text!"

Ruby paused the game that she'd begun on her phone. "Yeah, I know. I wondered why you wanted me half an hour early."

I threw myself onto my bed. "Phew! Just when I was thinking this was a silly idea."

Annie looked across and giggled. "It's a great idea, Livi!"

"Thanks."

"I've never been to an outpouring meeting before. I can't wait."

I gave her a quick smile. "Good."

Ruby looked up from her phone. "You could start outpouring meetings at The COOL Club," she suggested.

I forced another smile as Annie said, "Yeah!"

The three of us sat quietly on my bed as we waited for more people to come. I watched the clock on my wall, frowning as the minutes ticked by. By eight, we were still the only ones there.

"Are we going to start yet?" asked Annie.

I gave a disgruntled sigh. "I guess we should."

Suddenly, there was a little knock on the front door. I shrieked with joy and leapt off my bed, taking the stairs three at a time as I bounded to the door. I threw it open to find Amanda and Kevin shivering on the pavement.

"Hi," Amanda said nervously. "Sorry we're a bit late."

"My dad got lost finding your house," Kevin added.

"It's alright!" I assured them, just grateful they had come. "We haven't started yet."

Jill had come out of the kitchen to see who was at the door so I shot her a smile as I ushered Amanda and Kevin up the stairs. "Just having some friends round!"

Jill looked Amanda and Kevin up and down, clearly baffled as to why I was making friends with people so much younger than myself.

"It's a church thing," I said before she could ask.

Jill sniffed and went back into the kitchen.

"There aren't many of us tonight," I confessed as I led Kevin and Amanda up the stairs and into my bedroom. "I guess everybody else was busy or something."

They nodded and peered into my room.

I was about to introduce Annie but she beat me to it and leapt up with a cheery grin. "I'm Annie! Nice to meet you."

The two of them said their own names and lingered shyly in my doorway.

"Come in! Come in!" I exclaimed, clearing a couple of spaces on the floor. "Don't be nervous."

"Aw!" Annie gave the two of them little pats as they sat down beside her. "There's nothing to be scared of. We won't bite!"

Kevin turned pink. Amanda giggled and looked at me.

I cleared my throat. "Well, thank you all for coming," I said, shooting Ruby a sharp look to tell her to get off her phone.

She gave me a sheepish smile and put it away.

"So, the idea of us meeting is to show God that we're hungry for him," I explained.

The four of them nodded.

"Because that's all I saw that was different in Wales: people coming with hungry hearts and giving God the time to do stuff."

Kevin raised his hand. "Are we going to have a name?"

I looked at him. "Would you like a name?"

Ruby screwed up her nose as Kevin nodded keenly.

"Names are fun!" Amanda exclaimed.

"Everything should have a name!" Annie agreed.

I stared at Ruby. Eventually she shrugged and said, "If everyone else wants one."

The others grinned.

"Okay," I said. "What shall we call ourselves?"

The next few minutes were taken up with wild debate as various suggestions were put forward. They were as serious as *'The Revival Warriors'* and as daft as *'The Hungry Sheep'* but all of them were vetoed by one or more of the group. At one point, I heard Amanda suggest the name *'Livi's Army'* and I pretended not to hear, fixing a nonchalant expression on my face so that if it was put forward as a serious suggestion I could laugh and say, *'Sounds a bit daft but if you insist!'*

But she was quickly shouted down by Annie who said, "Oh, I know! We should call ourselves *'The Fire Brigade,'* except, instead of putting fires out, we'll pray until one comes!"

I gawped at her, surprised that she could propose such an intelligent suggestion. The rest of the group looked impressed.

"That sounds good," I said. "Is everyone agreed?"

They gave hearty nods and Amanda wrote it down in her diary.

"Cool. That's sorted. We're The Fire Brigade."

They all stared at me.

"What should we do now?" asked Kevin.

I sucked in my cheeks as I thought about it. "We could sing?"

"Yeah!" said Amanda. "God might like it if we sing."

"Feel free to start something..." I added, hoping someone else would take the lead.

They all nodded before looking away.

After an awkward pause, I cleared my throat and started to sing, *"Let your face shine on your children, we are waiting here for you..."*

The others joined me in a strained rendition of *'Waiting for You,'* one of the regular songs from the worship at King's Church. At one point, I put my arms in the air but felt embarrassed and promptly brought them back down. We got through the song without anybody making eye contact with anyone else. Kevin's voice broke here and there and we all sounded rather patchy in places when nobody could remember the words. Annie was hopelessly out of tune and I tried to set an example by singing sensibly.

Our singing trailed off after a while and Ruby whispered, "I'll bring my piccolo next time."

I gave a quick smile. "Does anybody play guitar?" I knew Annie couldn't but looked hopefully at Kevin and Amanda.

They shook their heads.

"It doesn't matter," I insisted, silently mourning Joey's absence. He would've been good at leading worship. I bit my lip and wondered what we ought to do next.

"The singing doesn't have to sound good," Annie piped up. "God looks at our hearts, right?"

Ruby broke into a grin. "Yeah!"

I breathed a sigh of relief. "Shall we sing it again?"

The others nodded and, after a slight pause, Annie and Ruby both started at the same time, beginning on two different notes. The rest of us stifled a giggle as we joined in. This time, we sang a little louder, humming joyfully over the bits we didn't know.

After we'd repeated the whole song, Annie took a deep breath and bellowed, *"Jesus is King of the jungle; the lion and the flea. Big and small, he made them all! Jesus is King of me. Oh oh oh!"*

The rest of us grinned and joined in. *"Jesus is King of the jungle..."*

"The horse and chimpanzee!" Amanda squealed.

"Big and small, he made them all! Jesus is King of me. Oh oh oh!"

Kevin got to his feet and clapped his hands together. "Skunk and killer bee!" he suggested.

We giggled and began again. *"Jesus is King of the jungle..."*

The others seemed perfectly happy to be squawking out of tune as they belted out the familiar children's song but, knowing my unbelieving sister was downstairs, I found myself growing anxious as the accompanying jungle noises got louder and louder.

After singing at least eleven impromptu verses of the song, I put a hand up and motioned for everyone to be quiet. "I think we should pray now," I said when everybody stopped to look at me.

They nodded and continued staring.

I took a deep breath. "Jesus, we're really hungry for you," I prayed. "Thank you for dying for us and giving us eternal life... which starts now." I thought about Sharon's claim that Heaven could be accessed this side of death. "Jesus, you're the door. Please... open yourself..."

Ruby joined in. "Yeah, Lord... We pray you would start a fire with us..."

The others murmured in agreement but nobody else prayed.

After a long silence, there was a knock downstairs.

"That will be my mum," Amanda said. She and Kevin got to their feet.

I stood up. "Well... Thanks for coming."

I was worried they would have found it all a bit awkward, so was rather surprised when Amanda asked, "When will we meet again?"

I exchanged a glance with Ruby. "What do you think?"

She cocked her head to one side. "I'm free tomorrow."

"Me too!" said Annie.

Amanda and Kevin both nodded.

My heart leapt. "Good. Same time tomorrow."

~*~

The five of us ended up meeting every evening that week from Monday to Thursday. To begin with, our meetings continued to feel a little dry or uncomfortable at times but we were committed to pressing in until God's fire fell and, by the end of the week, we had created a strong union. *'Jesus is King of the Jungle'* had become something of an anthem and we usually started our meetings with a few raucous renditions.

A slight complication emerged when it became apparent that Kevin was developing a bit of a crush on Annie. He went bright pink every time she looked at him and nodded along with even her most ridiculous of assertions.[36] He also started telling rather painful jokes, shooting Annie a quick glance each time to see whether she was laughing. Amanda, however, was clearly smitten with Kevin and tried to get his attention by laughing louder than Annie at all of his jokes. Knowing Annie, she was completely oblivious to the turmoil she was causing. This made for quite an intricate love triangle and I wondered whether I needed to lay down some rules but Ruby assured me it would all sort itself out if we pretended not to notice.

A couple of times in the week Jill had given me a curious glance over breakfast as she asked what we'd been up to the night before.

The first time I had replied that we were just meeting to pray together. The second time I was bolder and told her, "When we were in Wales, we went to this amazing church where hundreds of people have been encountering God every night for over seven

---

36 For example, on Wednesday, she mistakenly referred to Jesus as *'The Lion of Jonah'* and Kevin added a hasty, *"Amen,"* in agreement.

weeks. God's love has been falling powerfully and people have been healed and set free from all kinds of things. So we're starting our own thing in Leeds."

Jill just looked at me. "I'm not having you invite hundreds of people into our home."

I rolled my eyes. As if that was the one thing she had chosen to hear from my explanation. "There's just five of us for now," I assured her.

"Well as long as you keep the noise down when *'Gossip Town'* is on."

"Alright." I paused and wondered what to say next. Perhaps I could share a specific healing story from Wales or tell her about Ruby falling down in the Spirit. If it didn't freak her out it might just prompt her to want to find out more.

But, before I could think of anything, Jill changed the subject. She didn't ask about our meetings again after that.

A particularly noteworthy moment was Thursday night when Amanda asked how to speak in tongues. Neither she nor Kevin had ever done it before.

I discovered to my surprise that Annie had been doing it privately for the past year. I pushed the shock of this aside as I offered to pray for Amanda and Kevin to receive the gift. Within minutes, the two of them were muttering the beginnings of a new tongue and we spent the rest of the evening praying in tongues together.[37] A sense of God's peace was certainly evident after this which spurred us on to keep pressing in.

Nobody else from youth group joined us but I convinced myself that this didn't matter. Once the fire started falling, I was sure they would all come running. And, when they did, I would be the first one to say, *"I told you there was more!"*

_____

[37] By now, my own two little syllables had grown into a string of words as I continued to practise daily. At times I still feared that I was making it up but, the more I did it, the more I began to feel as though a deep part of me was truly communing with God. I had taken to practising every time I showered, although I had to be careful to keep my voice down after Jill started banging on the bathroom door fearing I was having a stroke.

The pride of Livi Starling

"Sharon... When are you going to teach us about demons?"

Sharon looked up abruptly and I blushed.

"I just wondered..." I mumbled. "Because I've felt really different since being set free in Wales so I think I'm ready to learn. Plus I'm kind of leading an outpouring meeting now so it would be good to be prepared, just in case."

Sharon stared at me for a long while and I was afraid she might tell me off for asking. But finally she said, "Soon."

I shuffled back to my desk and gave Ruby a nod. "She's going to teach us about demons soon."

Ruby looked a little wary. "Did you check with Summer?"

"Why?"

"Because she wasn't keen on you asking about demons before."

I waved a hand. "That's just because this stuff scares her. She won't mind me getting advice from an expert."

Ruby didn't look convinced. "If Summer doesn't want to talk about it then I would trust her."

I screwed up my nose. "Summer doesn't know everything."

Ruby sniffed and turned to that morning's assignment, a drab-looking worksheet on cat saliva.

"Anyway," I said. "Don't you want to learn about demons so that you can spot them and drive them out of people?"

She stuck her lip out. "Not particularly. I don't like thinking about that sort of thing."

"Whether you think about them or not they still exist," I retorted. "They won't leave you alone just because you ignore them. If anything, that would make you a prime target because you won't suspect them!"

Ruby shifted in her seat.

"*I* want to know *all* about them," I continued. "And then I'm going to make them pay for all the ways they've hurt people." I narrowed my eyes as I thought about the orphan spirit and wondered what other enemies might be lurking around. "Hey, do you think there are demons in this room?"

Ruby frowned. "I think we should be more interested in what God's doing than in what the enemy's doing."

"Yeah, obviously. It would just be good to have some understanding. We should be taught this stuff at church, don't you think?"

Ruby pointed to her worksheet. "I think we should get some work done."

"Okay…" I pursed my lips as I opened my pencil tin. I paused before adding, "I'm not a weirdo, you know."

Ruby forced a smile. "I know."

"I just want to be able to do the things Jesus talked about."

She nodded. "Hmmm."

"I want to see miracles."

"Yup…"

"And see God's power in action."

"Uh huh…"

"And Sharon seems to know more about this stuff than Summer."

Ruby glanced across the room at our teacher. "She's not as nice though," she said under her breath.

I followed her gaze.

Sharon looked rather hard-faced as she read from a devotional tucked into her Bible. Her lips were moving slowly and her brow was furrowed.

"She's just a deep person," I insisted.

When Ruby didn't reply, I went on, "We should write down everything she teaches us and make a book for other people to learn from. What do you think?"

Ruby screwed up her nose as she repeated, "I think we should get some work done."

I sighed and turned to my worksheet.

We had barely started when Sharon swooped over to our desk and took our worksheets away. "Forget this," she said in a whisper. "It's a load of nonsense. I've got a different exercise for you."

My heart leapt as she looked carefully to the side. I couldn't believe she was going to teach us about demons right in the middle of a Biology class!

118

Ruby looked stunned and shot me a worried glance.

"Here..." Quick as a flash, Sharon slid a couple of sheets of plain paper across the table.

I snatched mine up and turned it over. It was completely blank.

Ruby and I frowned at one another before turning to Sharon.

"Listen to God," she whispered. "And do what he says."

"But what about de—"

Sharon just pointed to our paper and sauntered off.

I nudged Ruby. "What's she doing?"

Ruby stared at her blank piece of paper. "No idea."

I puffed out my cheeks and wondered whether to ask for my worksheet back.

We spent some time trying to *'listen to God'* but didn't really hear anything. I had no idea whether Sharon was expecting an essay, or a picture, or a dramatic prophetic revelation, and was reluctant to make any careless marks on my sheet in case I messed it up and had to ask for another one.

By the end of the lesson, Ruby had folded her sheet into a paper bird and I had drawn a flower on mine. We waited for our classmates to leave before wandering over to Sharon's desk.

"Er, we did it," I said, holding up my pitiful drawing.

I expected her to quiz us on what we'd done and had already prepared a response,[38] but she just gave a serene smile and said, "Good."

I exchanged a baffled glance with Ruby before asking, "Do you want to keep them?"

"It's alright. Just keep practising."

"You want me to practise drawing flowers?"

"No. I want you to practise listening to God." She paused before adding, "It's essential in spiritual warfare. Otherwise you'll look for a method."

"You mean a method for casting out demons?" I asked tentatively.

She gave a brisk nod. "Or anything really. The Bible gives many examples and I could teach you a few principles, but anything you do must come out of relationship with the Father."

I looked at my flower. I wasn't sure I had heard God when I drew it. I was just trying to fill the paper. "I don't think I did this right," I admitted.

"That's alright. No child runs right away."

---

[38] *'God is like a flower because he's one with many parts...'*

I swallowed hard. "Give me some more paper. I'm sure I can do it properly if I try again."

Sharon laughed. "You're persistent."

I didn't know whether this was a compliment or an insult so I shrugged and insisted, "I'm a quick learner."

She didn't reply.

Ruby waved her paper bird in the air. "I'm not saying that I want to learn about demons or any of that stuff," she said, looking sideways at me. "But are you really telling us we should hear from God by making things out of paper instead of reading the Bible?"

"Of course not!" Sharon exclaimed. "Don't stop reading the Bible— it's God's word." She paused before peering at us. "You do know your Bible, don't you?"

I shot a glance at Ruby before muttering, "Yeah... Sort of."

To my surprise, Ruby confessed, "It's sometimes hard to get into."

Sharon didn't look fazed. "Ask the Father to give you a love for his word and it will begin to open up for you."

"Alright..."

"Just be aware that theology students don't always know God best. It's not *what* you know that counts; it's *who* you know. And how deeply. God hasn't stopped speaking and you need to learn how to keep in step with him moment by moment."

I nodded. "Like waiting for a deer?"

"Exactly."

I thought about it. "How can we be sure when God is really speaking to us? What if it's just our imaginations?"

Sharon seemed to smile to herself. "Sometimes it will be."

"But what if it's the devil?" Ruby piped up.

My stomach lurched. I hadn't even thought of that.

"Hmmm..." Sharon pursed her lips as she considered her reply. Eventually she said, "Many people stop listening to God for fear of being deceived. It rather elevates the devil's power in your life, don't you think?" Ruby went to reply but Sharon continued, "Jesus said that his sheep would know his voice, so trust him. The Early Church didn't always have access to the written word of God. They had to really listen to the living Word."

I gave a satisfied nod but Ruby didn't look so sure. "It's not always easy. What if we..." She gulped before whispering, "What if we fall into error?"

Sharon cocked her head to one side. "The greatest danger is not falling into error— although I pray that you won't. The greatest danger is falling out of love. Fix your eyes on Jesus and love him, love him, love him. If you give him everything, even if you get things wrong along the way, then I am sure you won't be found wanting when you stand before him."

Ruby let out a long breath. "Okay."

I bit my lip and flapped my drawing about. "How long do we have to practise for?"

Sharon chuckled. "How long do you *want* to practise for?"

I wrinkled up my nose. "I'm not very patient. I kind of want it all now."

She gave a wry smile. "I know."

"I just want God to use me," I insisted. "I want to do great things for him."

"Well that's quite simple. If you want to be used, then be usable. God uses the willing, not the smartest."

"I *am* willing!" I cried.

Sharon chuckled again. "I know."

I went to say something else but Sharon cut me off with a wave of her hand. "Class is over." She started busying herself in her cupboard.

Ruby and I waited for a moment before picking up our things.

As the two of us left the classroom, I muttered to Ruby, "Do you think we're getting marked on this?"

Ruby giggled and mouthed, *"She's so weird!"*

I smiled and glanced over my shoulder, watching as Sharon tied a knitted scarf around the neck of her stuffed badger.

There was no doubt about it. Sharon Sheppard was the weirdest teacher I'd ever had. But I had to admit I was starting to like her.

~*~

The Fire Brigade couldn't meet that evening since most of us had youth group at Eddie and Summer's. It had crossed my mind to suggest we skip youth group and continue with our own meeting instead but I knew this wouldn't be right. At any rate, I wanted to see how everyone would react to the news that Kevin and Amanda could now speak in tongues.

"Our first week of outpouring meetings went well," I announced when Summer asked if anybody had any news.

"Oh, fantastic!" She looked surprised, as though she hadn't actually expected the meetings to go ahead.

I poked Amanda. "Tell them what happened."

Amanda gave a shy smile before telling the group, "Me and Kevin spoke in tongues."

Kevin shrugged and added, "A little bit."

The group congratulated them and Summer said, "That's exciting!"

"Very exciting," Eddie agreed. He grinned at me. "It sounds like your meetings are a great success."

I gave a satisfied smile and leant against the sofa, figuring it wouldn't be long before I was able to set them straight on healing.

As the evening's Bible study got underway, I glanced across the circle and tried to catch Joey's eye. I hoped he felt bad for missing my meetings and shot him a big beam so that he'd know I hadn't been fazed by his absence.

He just blinked and looked away. To my surprise, he sat in silence for the entire evening. He didn't even laugh when Kevin accidentally called Summer 'Mum.' I kept throwing grins in his direction until eventually he buried his head in his Bible.

I couldn't help but feel a little smug. Perhaps he would come to our next meeting and beg for a second chance. But, when Summer ended the evening by asking if anybody wanted prayer for anything, Joey announced without even raising a hand, "My mum's got cancer. Please pray."

I stared at him in shock. Overwhelming guilt ripped through me as I realised how self-centred I had been to assume his silence revolved around *me*.

Eddie and Summer looked rather concerned.

"I'm so sorry, Joey," said Summer. "Of course we'll pray."

"What kind of cancer is it?" Nicole asked timidly. "Because my dad's was blood cancer."

Joey shook his head. His voice broke as he muttered, "Breast." Immediately his cheeks went red.

I sucked in my breath as I joined the rest of our group in huddling round Joey and praying for Janine, his mum.

"Dear God, please heal Joey's mum," Mark said sombrely.

"Your will be done," Bill added in a whisper.

I squeezed my eyes shut and tried to concentrate. From what Sharon had told me, there was a better way to pray than this. We needed to come against the disease with authority and power. I summoned up everything in me as I began loudly, "In the name of

Jesus..." I opened my eyes just in time to see a tear roll down Joey's cheek and quickly shut my eyes again.

God, please don't let Joey lose his mother. I instantly thought of *my* mother and wondered whether Joey and I would soon be forming a club of our own. *No, Lord!*

"In the name of Jesus..." I repeated. A lump formed in my throat and swallowed up every ounce of my bravado. "In the name of Jesus... Please heal Joey's mum."

"We're asking for a miracle, Lord," Summer prayed. "Come and make a way."

As Ruby echoed, "Yes, Lord. Please give us a miracle," I was reminded of my arrogant demand to God in Wales: *What about me? I want to see miracles too, you know!*

I stifled a sob as shame washed over me. How conceited to make it all a competition. *Of course everybody wants to see miracles. But nobody wants to **need** one.*

As the prayers continued, I got to my feet and went to the bathroom. Tears flowed like a fountain as I locked the door and leant against the bath. I couldn't pretend that I was selfless enough to be crying solely for Joey. Something had come unstuck within me and it felt like a little piece of my heart was once again grieving for my own loss.

I thought about mine and Ruby's recent attempts to heal the sick. *Perhaps that was our rehearsal,* I thought grimly, *to prepare us for healing Joey's mother.*

I imagined my own mum watching and cheering me on, urging me to do for Janine what nobody had done for her. *'You can do it, Livi!'* she would whisper. *'You can be a trailblazer!'*

I gulped. *If only I was ready.* I let out a long breath as the awareness of my frailty hit me. "I can't be a trailblazer," I said out loud. "I don't know how."

The tap dripped in the silence as I dragged a hand across my face and checked my reflection.

I was about to tuck my mother back into my heart and return to the others when an old saying of Belinda's danced into my mind: *'One bite at a time.'*

My heart caught in my throat.

It was Belinda's advice for tackling difficult tasks; simply do it bit by bit, one bite at a time.

I gave a steely nod as I considered that maybe I didn't need to devote myself to healing *loads* of people after all. Maybe if I could just heal Joey's mother it would somehow make everything alright.

~ 15 ~

The pure in heart will see God

The news about Joey's mother rather overshadowed my weekend. I spent most of Saturday rehearsing what I ought to say when I saw her at church on Sunday morning but, as it happened, none of Joey's family were there. Part of me felt relieved. Perhaps this would give me more time to practise praying for her before I offered to do it in person. Either way, I was determined to step everything up a gear.

"I want to heal Joey's mum," I announced when Ruby and I arrived at college on Monday morning. "We should pray for her regularly at our outpouring meetings."

Ruby nodded and turned a little pink.

"Oh, and by the way," I added. "We should have a club meeting soon."

"What club?"

"You know! Our college club. *The Club.* The one without a proper name."

"Oh." Ruby screwed up her nose. "Is there any point now that we're doing the outpouring meetings?"

"Of course. Annie's still doing The COOL Club."

"That's because she has lots of people in it," Ruby said carelessly. "If we start a college club, it will just be us."

"Laura might join."

Ruby didn't look convinced. "I don't know... Maybe you should find out how serious she is about it."

Right on cue, we entered the foyer and spotted Laura by the notice board.

Ruby nudged me. "There she is!"

I shot her an exasperated look as Laura turned and smiled.

"Oh, hi Laura," I said awkwardly. "I didn't see you there! How are you?"

"I'm fine. I was just thinking about signing up for the Rowing Club." She pointed to the notice board.

"Oh right!" I nodded. "Do you like rowing?"

"I don't know. I've never done it before but it sounds like fun. It would be something to do anyway!"

I took a deep breath. "Yeah... Clubs are fun. Oh, that reminds me, did you decide whether you wanted to join *our* club yet?" I pointed to Ruby who gave an embarrassed smile.

"I forgot about that!" Laura said gaily. "Remind me again what it's about?"

"Well, it's pretty chilled out... We generally chat about God and things like that. You know, exploring the meaning of life."

"When do you meet?"

I exchanged a glance with Ruby. "Er... We meet whenever really." I paused. "When are you free?"

Laura gave a little hum. "I'm not sure."

"Are you free today? This lunchtime. Or *now* even?"

"Hmmm..." Laura looked quite uncertain. "I'll have to let you know... I'll see you in Ageing Dogs." She shot us a quick smile before hurrying away.

I sighed and turned to Ruby. "She *will* come," I insisted.

Ruby rolled her eyes. "Well, when she does, I'll join."

I looked at her in horror. "Don't say you're leaving our club!"

"Yes, Livi. I'm leaving our club."

~*~

What made Ruby's resignation all the more cutting was the fact that, eleven hours later, Annie turned up on my doorstep with Georgina Harris.

"Hey Livi! Is it alright if Georgina comes to tonight's outpouring meeting?"

"Hi Livi," Georgina added as I stood gaping at the two of them.

"I told her that we're pressing in till the fire of God comes," Annie continued.

Georgina nodded. "It sounds really cool."

I took a deep breath before stepping aside to let them in. "Of course."

"Thanks." Georgina shot me an awkward smile containing a thousand unspoken words over our history of mutual ambivalence.

I gave an equally uncomfortable smile in return as I said, "Welcome to my house."

I bit my lip as Georgina followed me and Annie up the stairs.

"Don't mind the mess," I muttered, resisting the urge to feel self-conscious about the clutter on the landing and the peeling paint on the banister.

Ruby looked surprised as Georgina wandered into my bedroom behind me. "Hi Georgina!"

"Hi Ruby..." Georgina glanced round my room. I wished I'd had the foresight to hide my old teddy, Sausage-Legs, who was sprawled across the rug. Georgina almost sat on him as she asked, "So, what are you guys up to these days?"

"We go to City Farm College," Ruby replied.

"Oh!" Georgina raised her eyebrows. "Is that farming and stuff?"

"Animal Behaviour and Care," I said. "We learn about biology and veterinary care and animal sciences. It's quite varied actually."

She nodded. "Do you both want careers with animals then?"

"Er, not really," Ruby said sheepishly. "Actually we did it for the field trip."

Georgina looked confused as Ruby tried to explain about our trip to Wales. "You only took the course so that you could go to the outpouring?"

"No!" said Ruby. "We didn't know about the outpouring until we got there."

"So... You only took the course so that you could go to Wales?"

"It was more complicated than that," I said stiffly. I tried to think of a better way of explaining it but was saved by a knock at the front door. "That will be Kevin and Amanda," I said, leaping up from my bed.

"I'll get it!" Annie offered. "You guys have so much to catch up on."

"It's fine," I insisted, shoving past her and running down the stairs.

Being the impressionable youngsters that they were, Kevin and Amanda were thrilled to have a new addition to The Fire Brigade.

"Are you joining us from now on?" Kevin asked as they sat with Georgina on the floor.

I looked up for Georgina's response and was relieved to hear her say, "Just tonight, I think. I'll see."

"It's a fun group," said Amanda. "And Livi's really good at leading it."

A bubble of pride rippled through me as Georgina looked over and smiled.

"Well, we ought to start now," I said, clapping loudly to get everyone's attention. "I've got a good exercise for us tonight." I reached under my bed and pulled out a wad of plain paper. "Pass these round," I instructed Ruby.

She gave a bemused grin as she handed the paper out.

In the pause, Kevin shared one of his usual rubbish jokes.[39]

Not realising how much it would encourage him, Annie gave a big belly laugh and exclaimed, "Good one, Kevin! I love hedgehogs!"

This made Amanda roar extra loud, looking like a deranged hyena as she laughed until she cried.

"Right then!" I yelled, keen to avert any unnecessary distraction. "The idea with this is to listen to God and see what he says. Just draw or write down whatever comes to mind."

The group turned to their blank pieces of paper.

I held mine in one hand and grabbed a pen with the other. Then I closed my eyes and tried to focus on God. To begin with, I kept thinking about flowers but I figured that was probably because that's what I'd drawn in Sharon's class on Friday. Then I thought I saw a picture of a key but I wasn't sure whether that was just because I'd got my key stuck in the door that morning. I could hear the rustling of paper as some of the others started to write things down so, when nothing else came, I pursed my lips and began sketching a picture of a key.

Beside me, Amanda was giggling.

I looked over to see what was so funny but her paper was blank. "What's up?" I whispered.

"Nothing... I just couldn't stop thinking about hedgehogs."

"Well, if that's what you got... Put it down."

Amanda nodded and started to draw a hedgehog.

Beside her, Georgina had drawn a stick man walking a dog and, across the room, Kevin was still staring at a blank piece of paper. Ruby and Annie's papers both contained a line or two of writing.

I waited a little longer before asking, "How did it go?"

They replied with uncomfortable shrugs.

"Don't worry if you don't feel like it went well," I assured them, tucking my own doubtful attempt out of sight. "We just have to

---

[39] What do hedgehogs say when they kiss? Ouch.

keep practising." I leant over and pulled my *Disciple To-Do List* out from under a pile on my bedside table. "One day we'll be able to do all these things..." I cleared my throat and read aloud, *"Preach the gospel, heal the sick, cleanse the lepers, cast out demons, raise the dead."*

I looked up to see Amanda and Kevin looking stunned.

"Don't worry! We'll be able to do it all," I insisted. "We just have to put our minds to it."

Annie looked confused. After a slight pause, she piped up, "But aren't we meant to put our minds to loving God? How do we do both?"

"Oh yes!" Georgina nodded before quoting, *"Love the Lord your God with all your heart, with all your soul, with all your mind and with all your strength."* She grinned at me. "I learnt that at The COOL Club last week."

I felt a surge of irritation as the others beamed at her. "Yeah, obviously we need to love God," I muttered.

"So we don't need to put our minds to doing the things on that list," Annie said cheerfully. "We just need to put our minds to loving God. And he'll do the rest."

I exhaled as I realised she was right. "Yeah," I said quietly.

"It's like what Sharon said," Ruby spoke up as she poked me on the foot. "God uses the willing, not the smartest."

I nodded and pretended to examine my *Disciple To-Do List.*

Little did I know, God had a to-do list of his own and he was intent on ticking his tasks off as quickly as possible. Top of the list had been the orphan spirit. He was about to topple my pride.

"Oh, that reminds me," said Ruby. "I saw this amazing video the other day..." She reached into her bag and pulled out her phone. "See, look at this guy!" Ruby held the screen up so we could all see and pointed to a heavily tattooed man who was praying for a line of people.

"Who is he?" I asked, thinking that he looked like he ought to be in the circus, or a wrestling ring, or maybe even in jail.

"Leroy Pepper."

I shrugged at her. I was about to say that I'd never heard of him when some whooping erupted from within the video. My jaw fell open as a man in a wheelchair was helped to his feet. All around him, people were cheering and crying and praising the Lord. Some flashing text indicated that this man hadn't walked in twelve years.

"Wow!" said Annie.

"That's incredible," added Georgina.

Kevin and Amanda were wide-eyed.

I gaped at the screen as the man helped another lady out of a wheelchair. *Was this legitimate? Would God really use somebody like that?* "Is that God?" I asked aloud.

"Why not?" Annie responded.

"I don't know. He doesn't look very..." I was about to say *'normal.'* But then I realised I only define *'normal'* by what's normal to *me*.

The tattooed man started yelling at the crowd in a thick American drawl, "Jesus is here! Do you feel him?" I wrinkled up my nose as he bent down and pounded the floor, screaming, *"More Lord!"* in a rather undignified fashion. The crowd carried on whooping as he continued, "Salvation is found in no other name but Jesus Christ!"

"He's preaching the true gospel," said Ruby. "That's the test, isn't it?"

I opened my mouth and closed it again. It was true that I couldn't fault anything he was saying. It was just the way he was saying it. And the way he looked. "Yeah, I guess," I said. "I just wouldn't have thought God would use someone so..." I searched for the right word. "Unconventional."

Annie giggled. "God can use whoever he wants."

I forced a smile. "I know."

"God is too big to be contained in one expression," Ruby added. "That's what my mum says anyway."

By now, the tattooed preacher had turned his attention to the camera. Beads of sweat dripped down his face as he stared menacingly into the lens. "You want God to use you like this?" he exclaimed, pointing into the camera. "Well you gotta get your heart right with God. Sort out your character. God won't give you power if you can't handle it."

I pursed my lips. It sounded similar to Sharon's lecture about watching my words.

"Now character ain't what the world sees," the man went on. "Character ain't what you write on your resume. Oh no! Character is who you are when there's nobody around. It's who you are when you stub your toe or when someone winds you up. Yeah, that's the true measure of you. We gotta get rid of every vile thought in our hearts cos the Bible says that the pure in heart will see God. That's a promise! *The pure in heart will see God.* Purity, I tell you! That's the key!"

My stomach twisted. *I want to see God! Has this guy seen God? Is he really purer than me? Doesn't the Bible say something about tattoos?*

The video came to an end and Amanda turned to me. "That was amazing," she gasped. "Can we watch another one?"

"Yeah, why not," I muttered. It's not like I had any better ideas. My plan to discuss my *Disciple To-Do List* had flopped tremendously.

We continued watching videos for the rest of the meeting. Some of them got rather heavy on matters that Eddie and Summer would term 'side issues' and I found myself growing confused.

"Will there be a rapture?" Amanda asked after we listened to a short message on the end times.

"Er... I don't know," I admitted. "I tried reading Revelation but it's hard to understand. Maybe we should do a study on it sometime—"

"I've read bits of Revelation," Annie cut in. "It made sense to *me:* Jesus wins!" She grinned.

Kevin gave an enthusiastic nod and Amanda looked at Annie as though she was the cleverest person in the world.

I pursed my lips, fighting the compulsion to quickly assert myself. I managed to stay quiet but couldn't shake off the annoyance that I felt inside.

"We should probably be careful about what videos we watch," Ruby said. "We should ask Eddie and Summer which ones are alright."

"We don't need to ask them," I blurted out. "We can just ask the Holy Spirit. He'll tell us what to do."

As Ruby frowned and Amanda looked at me in surprise, I realised I had been a little abrupt. "I mean, obviously we can ask Eddie and Summer," I corrected myself. "But, also, if we practise listening to God then we'll be able to hear him for ourselves too."

Amanda gave a satisfied nod and Ruby smiled wryly before looking across at Annie. "Hey Annie, how's The COOL Club?"

I sucked in my cheeks as Ruby turned back to me and grinned. I would hate to be paranoid but I couldn't help feeling like she was deliberately winding me up.

"Yeah, it's going well!" Annie exclaimed.

Georgina nodded as she piped up, "We had a couple more people come today. They snuck into the sixth form common room just to ask if they could join our club!"

I swallowed hard. I wondered if it would be too harsh to remind her that it had been *my* club once upon a time.

"There are a few people who say they want to know Jesus but aren't quite ready yet," Annie added. "Maybe we can pray for them?"

The others launched into prayer, thanking God for growing The COOL Club and asking him to draw close to those who were coming. I wanted to be able to join in but my heart wasn't in it. The combination of Ruby quitting our college club, Georgina turning up and acting like long lost buddies, and Annie continuing to score fluke accomplishments infuriated me. It wasn't about trying to earn God's love. I knew that he loved me. I knew that I didn't *have* to lead a big club to make him happy. I just *wanted* to. And I knew for a fact that Annie hadn't asked for this.

After a while, I realised that everybody else had prayed. I didn't want them to wonder why I had stayed quiet so I said a brief prayer before looking pointedly at the clock. "Ooh, it's getting late."

The others got to their feet and started to gather up their belongings, chattering about how well our meetings were going.

"Wait!" cried Ruby. She looked at me. "We were going to pray for Joey's mum, weren't we?"

I gulped. I had been so consumed with myself that I'd completely forgotten about Janine. I nodded and shut my eyes as everybody else prayed. As much as I wanted to lead the prayers, I felt utterly incompetent. How could I heal Joey's mum? I couldn't even cure my own thoughts.

Ruby concluded the prayers with a hearty, "Amen!" and everyone got to their feet once more.

"Thanks for letting me come," Georgina said gingerly as she lingered in my doorway with Annie.

I tried to smile as I said, "Oh, you're welcome! It was so nice to catch up with you!"

"You too! Hopefully see you again some time."

"Hopefully!" I waited until she was down the stairs before letting my smile fall off.

When everybody had left I curled up on my bed, seething over Annie and Georgina and the undeserved explosion of The COOL Club.

"I want you to use me!" I told God. "What has Annie got that I haven't? I'm much more willing and I'm sure I'm hungrier than she is... It's not fair that her club keeps growing... I want it more!"

I ranted for a while longer before I heard God whisper, *Why do you want it?*

I was almost affronted by the question. "To bring you glory, of course!"

His quick response caught me off guard. *Do I need your help?*

"Well, no..." I tried another tactic. "I've proved that I can lead a group because the outpouring meetings are going really well. But there's only five of us and Annie's COOL Club keeps growing. What about *my* club?"

What about your club? There was a pause. Then God said, *I will build my Church.*

I opened my mouth and closed it again. I realised that however much I dressed it up, I couldn't fool God. I wanted a big club to make myself feel good and he knew it.

Suddenly it was very clear what Annie had that I didn't: *humility*. Annie never boasted about herself or tried to be sneaky or clever. She wore her heart on her sleeve and followed Jesus with a trusting childlike spirit. This meant that she was foolish enough to achieve great things for God and pure enough not to even notice when she did. I realised that if it was the other way round, and *my* club was growing faster than *hers*, she would have nothing but excitement for me. In fact, she probably didn't even consider The COOL Club her own. She was simply letting God take over.

I put my head in my hands as I realised how vain I was being. As if I had a right to be used more than Annie. And what exactly was I so desperate for anyway? Was it God himself, or simply displays of his power?

I'm sorry, Lord. I want to do amazing things so that I can brag about how great I am. But the truth is I'd be a mess without you...

I shuddered as I thought about how petty and obnoxious I had been ever since Annie first announced that The COOL Club was growing. "I should be pleased that it's going well," I muttered. "I don't want pride or envy in my heart."

The words of the tattooed preacher chimed in my ears. *'The pure in heart will see God! Purity, I tell you! That's the key!'*

A picture of Annie popped into my mind. She was singing wildly at the top of her lungs oblivious to how bad she sounded. I had always been embarrassed for her but I suddenly saw how much God loved it and how stupid I was for thinking that I could impress him with my sensible singing— as if he hadn't got a whole heavenly chorus at his disposal.

I want to be pure, God. I'm so sorry when I'm not. Please make me more like Annie.

As I sat repenting, my hands began to get quite hot. It caught me by surprise that God would be so gentle after I had been so proud for so long. But then I remembered the glorious truth: he had forgiven and forgotten all my mistakes. His love for me was endless.

I gave a long sigh and looked up at the ceiling. "Should I not bother with our college club then?" I asked aloud.

Instead of giving me a direct answer, I felt God ask, *Will you give me everything even if you never get any praise for yourself? Will you be unknown to the world but known deeply by me? Will you be dismissed by your peers but celebrated in Heaven? Will you give up every good idea you've ever had about how to bring me glory and let me glorify myself the way I choose?*

My heart almost slid into my stomach under the weight of this choice. After all my dreams of greatness, could I bear to remain invisible? Could I watch Annie's club grow bigger and bigger and maybe even take over the world while I watched empty handed from the sidelines? Would I lay down my own reputation and pick up whatever God gave me in exchange— however foolish, however undignified, however small?

I took a deep breath, tears trickling down my cheeks as I gave my answer. "Yes Lord, take everything. I'm sorry for trying to make it about me. Please make me pure in heart. I want to see you. More than power or miracles or clubs or any of those things, I just want *you.*" And once again I prayed that dangerous prayer... "Do whatever it takes."

My hands stayed rather warm while I prayed and I looked at them, wondering what it meant. Eventually, I rubbed my eyes and started to get ready for bed. On my way, I tripped on my drawing of the key. I stared at it for a moment before reaching for a pen. I added Annie to the picture, giving her a big smile and mighty fists that clenched the key with joy. Then I stopped and made a quick phone call.

"Hey Annie, it's me... I just wanted to let you know that I'm really pleased The COOL Club is growing... I'm sorry for not saying that until now. Also, I love you. I think you're great. And I want you to lead the Fire Brigade with me and Ruby... I need you to— you're the box."

~ 16 ~

Foolish things

That night, I dreamt I was a deer. I was galloping at high speed through a forest towards a bright white light. Suddenly, there were loads of other deer with me, running just as fast. I had the vague sense that the ones nearest me were Ruby and Annie and somewhere behind us were Kevin and Amanda, but there were also countless others, all moving as one. We reached the light and, immediately, a fire spread through the forest, consuming everything in sight. Although the deer were in the fire, we didn't get burnt. Instead, we ran even faster, almost as though we were a part of the fire itself and, as we did so, stars began to fall out of the sky. The dream got a little hazy but at one point there were loads of people running from the flames.

I sat bolt upright as I awoke with the urgent desire to keep running.

After coming to my senses, I yawned and rubbed my eyes, my heart dancing as I mulled the dream over. It had left me with a strong sense that something big was going to happen. Something far bigger than me or anything I had ever seen. Before, I had thought that if we did things right God would start a fire as our reward. The dream made me realise that the fire wasn't something we could control or contain. It was coming and *would* come in God's timing and, although we could position ourselves to be a part of it,[40] we could never legitimately claim that the idea had started with us. All we could do was stay hungry, grow in humility and seek God with all of our hearts.

However, the intensity of the dream also impressed upon me the need for *absolute purity*. The deer were spotless, selfless, totally unbounded. If I was serious about seeing a public revival,

---

[40] *Please God, let me be a part of it!*

then I needed to be just as committed to laying my heart open for a private one. And, as I had learnt the evening before, at times this wouldn't be easy.

I pulled myself out of bed, feeling as though I had just been dragged through a hedge, and looked out of my window. The stars seemed pretty fixed in the sky. Across the street, Ruby's curtains were tightly shut. This was no surprise since it was three in the morning.

I yawned and crawled back into bed. "I'm ready, Jesus," I whispered. "Ready for anything."

~*~

Over the next few weeks, I sought to take my hands off the reigns of The Fire Brigade as much as possible. The last thing I wanted was to squash whatever God might do by being self-seeking or controlling. Under Ruby and Annie's leading, we ended up doing some inventive things that I never would have thought of— such as spending a whole evening 'jumping for joy' round my room,[41] sharing a carton of juice and one of Annie's homemade cookies as communion, and praying for drooping plants as practise for raising the dead. We also spent whole evenings just listening to worship CDs as we basked in God's love.

On one of these evenings, we ended up giggling together as we received a shared revelation that Jesus is truly the happiest person on earth. He is not just serious all the time. He wants to have fun with us, like any good friend. There is always laughter in our Father's Kingdom.

As the five of us lay on my floor, giddy with joy, I heard the pounding of a television programme downstairs. From the familiar theme tune, it sounded as though my sister was watching 'Gossip Town,' recently hailed Britain's favourite show. It featured a dysfunctional cast of characters who were constantly at odds with one another as they sought successful careers in the media. Although it had its funny moments, the friendships were shallow, the successes were short-lived and every relationship turned sour. It was pretty devoid of any hope. It did have one token Christian

---

[41] This ended with Amanda falling off my bed.

character but this happened to be a lustful priest with a secret gambling addiction.

I was suddenly struck with a desire to take what we were experiencing out of my house and into the streets of Leeds. It was no longer about striving or trying to build a big club. I just knew that if the bleak morality of *'Gossip Town'* was the highlight of the average person's week, then our nation *seriously* needed Jesus.

"What would we do?" Amanda asked when I posed the suggestion to the others.

"We wouldn't do anything," I assured her. "We'd just watch and see what Jesus does!" If there was one thing I had learnt from practising Sharon's listening to God exercise it was that the key to *doing* was knowing how to be still. All we had to do was tell God that we were available and then listen out for what he might say.

Ruby cocked her head to one side. "So we'd just go to town and see what happens?"

I nodded. "Yup."

"But..." Kevin looked confused. "Nothing might happen."

"Or..." Annie leapt up with glee. *"Something* might happen!"

I ginned. "Exactly."

The five of us met the following weekend. The city centre was noisy and busy, packed full of restless shoppers gearing up for Christmas which was less than two months away. The *'Gossip Town'* Christmas movie was being advertised on the side of every bus and I sucked in my cheeks as I overheard a lady tell her friend, "I love that show! The characters are all so horrible."

"I made some Christmas cards," Annie announced once we had all arrived. She reached into her bag and pulled out a pile of haphazardly folded creations.

A sprinkling of glitter fell out as I took one from her and opened it. *'Dear stranger,'* it began. *'Have you heard the good news? It's a free present that lasts all year round...'* She had made quite a few spelling mistakes[42] but the gist of it was clear and her picture of baby Jesus riding on a reindeer was rather artistic.

"We don't have to do anything with them," she insisted as she passed them round. "But I just thought that, since there are lots of Christmas shoppers about, we might want something to give them."

---

[42] Such as asking the reader whether they would be going to *'Haven'* when they died.

I grinned. "They're great!"

"We could ask God who to give them to," Ruby suggested.

"Ooh, like a treasure hunt!" Amanda squealed. "Let's all ask God for a clue and we can see if they lead us to anyone." She smiled at me. "Then we're practising listening to the Spirit, aren't we?"

"Good idea, Amanda!"

We found an empty bench and sat quietly as we sought God for clues.

I closed my eyes and tried to clear my mind. I didn't see anything but the bottom of my back twinged a bit. I shifted uncomfortably and tried to concentrate. As the pain grew a little more intense, I found myself thinking, *That's weird. My back never hurts...* It struck me that perhaps this was what Summer called a *'word of knowledge'* or, in other words, God telling me something about somebody else. As I thought this, the pain seemed to recede. I waited a while longer but didn't get anything else. "Okay. What did everyone get?" I asked as I opened my eyes.

"I got the name *'Tom,'*" Kevin said proudly.

I pulled a pen and some paper out of my bag and gave an impressed nod as I wrote it down.

"I kind of saw an arcade," said Annie.

"I saw some big brown shoes," added Amanda.

"How big?" Ruby asked. "Like clown shoes?"

"Hmmm. No, just quite big."

I wrote down *'Arcade'* and *'Big brown shoes.'* "Anything else?"

"I saw different sports logos," Ruby said, chewing her bottom lip. "So, I don't know. Somebody sporty maybe." She looked at me. "What about you?"

"My back started hurting." I pointed to the base of my spine. "I don't know if it means anything but it's all I got." I wrote down *'Sports'* and *'Bad back'* and read the whole list aloud. "So this is what we're looking for. Where should we start?"

"Hmmm, we could just wander round and see if we spot anybody who fits the clues," Ruby suggested.

The rest of us nodded and got to our feet. We crossed the road and turned into the high street, eyes peeled like explorers in search of treasure.

"He's wearing brown shoes," Annie piped up, pointing to a man coming towards us.

Amanda shook her head. "Bigger than that."

"Ooh, him?" Ruby cried, pointing to a man on a bench.

"Yeah, maybe..."

I looked down my list. "Does he look sporty?" I asked uncertainly.

"Oh, he's got brown shoes too!" Annie pointed to a man at a bus stop. "And the man coming out of that shop!"

I exhaled slowly. When you start looking for them, big brown shoes are everywhere. So are sports logos. I found myself wishing God had been a little more specific.

"He's wearing brown shoes and they look *kind of* big." Kevin pointed to a man smoking in a doorway.

I had almost given up on the brown shoes clue and was about to suggest we focus on something else when Amanda shrieked, "Look!"

We turned to see what she was pointing at. An old rusted sign bearing the words *'The Arcade'* hung in the archway just left of the man's head.

"Arcade!" I exclaimed. "That was your clue, wasn't it, Annie?"

Annie nodded. "Let's go and talk to him!"

Before I could ask for more time to check the rest of our clues, the four of them bounded over. The man looked up in alarm as they came to a halt at his feet.

I followed at a trot, wincing as I heard Ruby tell the man, "We're a group of Christians on a bit of a treasure hunt..."

The man stared at her blankly.

"We think you might be our treasure!" added Annie.

He shook his head. "Sorry, I don't understand."

I held up our list. "We were praying earlier," I explained. "And we asked God for clues for who he wants us to bless today. We have *'Big brown shoes.'*" I pointed to his shoes, hoping the suggestion that he had big feet wouldn't offend him. "And *'Arcade,'* which you're standing under. Does anything else on here mean anything to you."

The man stuck out his bottom lip as he looked over our clues. "Not really."

"You don't know anyone called Tom?" asked Kevin.

"I used to work with a guy called Tom. Will that do?"

"Hmmm, maybe not," I said. I didn't want to clutch at straws. "Are you sporty? Or do you have a bad back?"

He shook his head.

I looked at the others and wondered what to do.

Finally, Annie piped up, "Well, can we give this to you anyway?" She rummaged in her bag. "And do you want prayer for anything?"

The man took the Christmas card with a bemused shrug.

Annie kept beaming. "Or we could just pray a general blessing over you?"

"Er... Yeah. If you want."

The five of us gathered round and prayed. I was aware of shoppers passing very near us and stared at the ground as I tried to stay focused.

When we'd finished, the man thanked us with a polite nod. We said goodbye and walked away, shooting one another little grins.

"I'm so happy we found my clue!" Amanda exclaimed, linking an arm in mine. She shot Kevin a huge grin but he didn't seem to notice.

As we wandered through the city centre, wondering where God wanted us to go next, we walked unwittingly into the path of a mobile phone salesman.

"Are you happy with your current tariff?" he asked with a cheeky smile. Before we could respond, he had whipped out a leaflet as he tried to convince us to change networks.

We listened as he told us about the various deals on offer. My fingers itched for the Christmas cards in my bag and I was certain that the others were thinking the same thing. The hope of sharing Jesus was the only thing that kept us from cutting him off.

The salesman came to the end of his spiel and grinned.

"None of us need a new phone," I said, looking round at the others who shook their heads. "But would you mind if we gave you something?"

He had barely responded when all five of us held out a card. "What are they?" he asked in surprise.

We giggled and put the rest away as he gingerly accepted Amanda's.

"It's a Christmas card," Ruby explained.

"Oh!" He opened it, jumping in fright as glitter covered his suit.

"Oops, sorry about that!" Annie tittered.

"If you died today, would you go to Haven?" He looked at us in confusion.

"Heaven," I corrected. *"If you died today, would you go to Heaven?"*

He swallowed hard as he looked at me. "Am I meant to answer that?"

"Er... If you want."

The salesman scratched his head. "I don't know really. I suppose I never think about it."

There was a pause and then Annie asked, "Are you thinking about it now?"

He laughed. "Yeah. I guess so." He glanced over his shoulder before adding, "Look I'm not meant to be talking to people unless it's about phones. I'll get into trouble with my boss."

"Oh, sorry!" We gave a step back.

"It's alright. Thanks for the card."

"Just think about it," said Ruby.

"I will. I will." He tucked the card into his jacket pocket as we started to walk away.

Kevin lingered a little uncertainly. He cleared his throat and asked, "Is your name Tom?"

The salesman slowly shook his head.

Kevin blushed. "Never mind."

"Don't worry," I said as Kevin joined us, looking deflated. I pulled our list of clues out of my pocket. "What do you reckon about *'Sports'?*" I asked the group. "There are lots of people in sporty clothes but it seems a bit daft to stop each one..."

"We could go to a sports shop?" suggested Annie.

No one had any smarter ideas so we turned the corner and headed for *Score Superstore,* the biggest sports shop in Leeds.

"Are we looking for somebody else with brown shoes or is that one finished?" Amanda asked as we entered the shop.

"I don't know," I confessed. I took a deep breath and looked around. The shop was huge and full of people. How on earth would we know who to talk to?

"No pressure," Ruby added, coming up beside me. "We don't have to do anything. We just watch and see what Jesus does."

"Oh yeah!" I sighed in relief, grateful for the reminder. I took a moment to commit it all to God. *I don't need to do anything. It's not about results.* As I opened my eyes, I found my attention drawn to a teenage boy who was sitting near a display of shoes. I scanned my list. There was nothing to suggest that he fit any of the other clues, yet I felt a little prompting to go over anyway.

"I know he's not on the list," I told the others. "But I feel like I should talk to him."

"Go for it!" said Annie.

"What should I say?"

"Ask if he's called Tom," said Kevin.

"Just say you felt God prompting you to talk to him," Ruby suggested. "Even if he's not on the list, God might still want to do something."

"So, I won't mention the list straight away?" I clarified.

"No, you should," Kevin insisted. "In case he's called Tom."

By now, we had lingered for some time and the boy was looking at me with a rather baffled expression on his face.

"I bet he thinks you fancy him!" Annie sang in my ear.

I batted her away and trotted over to the boy. "Hi," I said. "I know this will sound weird but I felt like I should come and talk to you."

The boy blushed.

"I don't mean—!" I spluttered. "It's not like I *want* to talk to you. I just felt God telling me to talk to you..."

He blinked at me.

I pulled out our list. "We're doing a treasure hunt," I said, feeling like a fool. "Does any of this mean anything to you?"

I handed him the list and he looked down it. "My back hurts," he said.

I stared at him. "Really?"

"Yeah." He pointed to his lower back. "Down here."

My jaw dropped open. "That's exactly where I felt it!" I exclaimed. "That means you're my treasure!"

He turned bright red. "What?"

"I mean God wants to heal you." I beckoned the others over. "He's the bad back clue!" I told them.

They exchanged astonished looks and came to join me.

"What's your name?" I asked the boy.

"Er... Sam." He looked startled to suddenly find himself surrounded by five grinning faces.

"Can we pray for you?"

He gave a slow nod. "If you want."

The five of us launched into a very short prayer, commanding his back to be better in the name of Jesus.

I bit my lip as we finished. "How is it?"

Sam turned in his seat. "Yeah, it's better."

"Seriously?" We gaped at him.

"Yeah, it's fine now." Sam shrugged.

He was being so blasé about it that I wondered if he was just pretending.

"Well, that's amazing!" I exclaimed. "Jesus healed your back."

He nodded.

Annie reached over and plonked a Christmas card on his lap. "Here you go!"

Sam watched as glitter ran down his trousers. "Thanks."

We didn't know what to say next so we just left Sam staring at Annie's card. His reaction had been so devoid of any emotion that I wasn't sure whether or not he was just having us on.

"That was cool!" Annie said as we left the shop and embraced the cold once more.

"He hardly reacted at all," Amanda remarked. "I'd be jumping up and down if I just got healed."

"Me too," I admitted. "I hope he was telling the truth."

Kevin looked uncertain.

"People are different," said Ruby. "Maybe he's just a serious person."

"I guess we have to believe something," Annie added. "We might as well believe he was telling the truth."

"Anyway," Ruby went on. "Why are *we* so surprised when people get healed? If we really believe in it then it should be the norm."

I nodded. "True..."

I was about to say something else when I happened to look up and spot Janine, Joey's mother, crossing the street in front of us. She wore a long dark coat and was heavily wrapped up in a fluffy hat and scarf. She looked so solemn that an awful part of me wanted to hide or pretend I hadn't seen her.

Before I could look away, Ruby called loudly, "Hey Janine!"

Janine stopped and turned. She broke into a smile. "Oh! Hello girls!" She sounded her usual jolly self. It was only a few extra bags under the eyes that gave away that anything might be wrong. After hugging me and Ruby, she gave Annie, Amanda and Kevin a cheery wave. I wondered if I ought to introduce her. *This is Joey's mother; the one we're praying for.*

I thought better of it and lingered uneasily as Janine reached for a tissue and blew her nose.

"How are you?" she asked.

I nodded as Ruby said, "We're fine thanks. How are you?"

I shot her a sideways glance. Surely it was a little absurd to ask a dying woman how she was.

Janine just smiled. "I'm doing alright. I have a bit more energy today so I'm making the most of it and getting my Christmas shopping done early!" She held up a bag and grinned.

I forced a smile in return. I wondered just how sick she was and whether she ever feared she wouldn't make it till Christmas. My own mother only lasted about three weeks when she got ill and she died just before Christmas. Apparently, she'd done a load of Christmas shopping and hidden it in the back of her wardrobe. Jill didn't find it for nearly two years. I wondered whether Janine had a plan in place in case her own gifts were hidden in vain, but of course I couldn't ask. I wanted to tell her we were praying for her every day at our meetings but it felt somehow wrong to draw attention to her sickness if she wasn't going to mention it herself.

Annie broke the silence by presenting Janine with a Christmas card. "Happy Christmas!"

I gulped as Janine opened it and read aloud, *"If you died today, would you go to Haven?"*

"Heaven," I corrected awkwardly.

She laughed. "Ah! Thank you." She put the Christmas card in her handbag and adjusted her shopping. "Well, I'd better carry on. It was lovely to see you."

"You too," I squeaked as Ruby gave her another tentative hug.

I watched as she walked away and wondered whether it would be the last time I ever saw her. I knew I was being a bit daft. I saw her most Sundays at church and, according to Joey, she was having some treatment which would last a month or so before more serious options were considered. Furthermore, if we continued to pray for her regularly, there was no reason why she shouldn't get miraculously healed. I'd been preparing for this with all the healing practice after all.

But still, what if she doesn't...

I shook this thought from my mind as I cleared my throat and turned back to the others. "Right then. Where were we?"

"Our treasure hunt," said Amanda.

I nodded and pulled our list out of my bag, humming to myself as I scanned the clues. "Well, we found everything... except for *'Tom.'*" I gave Kevin a sympathetic pat. "Should we ask God for new clues?"

"We could just hand cards out along the high street," Annie suggested. "We've got plenty."

"Is that keeping in step with the Spirit?" I asked. "We don't want to do anything in our own strength."

"We can stop if it feels wrong," Annie insisted. "But *any* of these people could be God's treasure!" She waved a hand at the bustling high street.

It was as good an idea as any. I looked round at the others who looked equally keen.

Kevin proposed we stand outside the pound shop because anybody shopping there was likely to need a bit of cheering up. So he, Amanda and Annie lingered in the pound shop doorway while Ruby and I waited outside a pub across the street.

"Merry Christmas!" we sang as we held the cards out to passersby.

A few people accepted our cards, some with quick smiles and others with vacant nods as though they were taking the cards by mistake. However, a great number of people ignored us, walking past our outstretched hands as though we weren't even there.

I feigned being cast aside as I said, "Don't they know who we are?"

I was only joking but Ruby replied, "Of course they don't. Most people don't even know who *they* are, let alone who anybody else is."

I grinned. "You're very wise, Miss Rico."

She grinned back and indicated the pile of Christmas cards in her hand. The top one featured baby Jesus tucked under a Christmas tree. "Or very foolish."

I laughed and offered a card to a couple coming out of the pub. They took it with a grunt and hurried off.

A chilly wind blew and I shivered and pulled my scarf tightly round my neck. Moments later, a serious-looking man in a long coat emerged from the pub.

I tried to catch his eye as I held a card out. "Merry Christmas!"

The man took the card without looking at me and carried on walking. Then he stopped and stared at it. "What's this?" he asked, turning back to the two of us.

"A Christmas card." I tried to smile, afraid that he might tell us off.

"Why?"

I felt myself blushing as I tried to explain that we were a group of Christians who wanted to bless people. As much as I believed it in theory, it sounded strange when I said it out loud.

I braced myself for a stern reproach but the man just replied quietly, "I feel like God's on my case."

I exchanged a glance with Ruby. "What do you mean?" we asked.

"I used to go to church," the man explained. "But I got put off by all the hypocrisy that I saw. I've been wondering recently whether I ought to go back."

Ruby and I stared at him.

"Well, maybe you should," I said.

He gave a little chuckle. "Yeah. Maybe."

We kept watching him, not wanting to do anything that would destroy the moment.

Eventually he shook his head and tucked the card into his pocket. "Thanks for that. You've made my day." He nodded and strode away.

I realised I'd been holding my breath. I let it out and whispered to Ruby, "I didn't expect that!"

"He looked quite scary when he came out of the pub," she agreed.

Rejection didn't matter so much after that. Just knowing one man had been touched by our efforts made it all worth it.

We had almost finished handing the cards out when Kevin came bounding over with a huge beam on his face. "I found Tom! I found Tom!"

Ruby and I exchanged grins as Kevin explained how he had asked every passing shopper what their name was and had finally come across one named Tom.

"We're going to do it, Livi!" Kevin continued. "We're going to start a revival!"

I smiled as Amanda and Annie crossed the street and joined us.

"Is anyone hungry?" asked Annie.

"Hungrier than I've ever been," I replied, giving Kevin a quick thumbs-up.

As I followed the others to the nearest chip shop, I looked down at the last card in my hand. Annie had drawn a reindeer with candles in its antlers. It made me smile as I remembered my recent dream. Although some might say that any hope of revival in our nation was a distant fantasy, I was convinced that one single hungry person fully yielded to God was enough to start one, and we had five of us which was more than plenty. As long as we fixed our eyes on Jesus and sought him with everything within us, then we were exactly the kind of foolish things God might change the world with.

~ 17 ~

The role of a princess

As Christmas drew closer, the five of us made it a habit to hand out Christmas cards at least once a fortnight. Still, we were careful not to make it a duty, choosing only to step out when we felt the Holy Spirit leading.

Annie's card designs got fancier and fancier and her most recent batch included statistics about loneliness cut up from her father's psychology journals. *'Do you have a deep arch inside?'* she had written clumsily. *'Let Jesus into your hearth.'*

Jill had bought herself a new scarf covered in little pink crowns which I borrowed from time to time to wear as a proud reminder that the five of us were secret royals bringing the Kingdom of our Father to earth. In God's Kingdom, there is no sadness or confusion or sickness, and our remit as heavenly children was to bring this reality to the world around us.

As we stepped out in faith, we continued to see the odd healing here and there, but nothing particularly spectacular happened until one unexpected Saturday at Tizzi Berry.

I was waiting with Ruby and Amanda by the Christmas display, smelling cinnamon scented candles and admiring the reindeer jumpsuits, while Annie finished her shift.[43] We had planned to find a quiet spot to pray together once Annie finished work so hadn't anticipated that God might have business to do in the store.

The shop was fairly full, mainly of *Kitty Warrington* types who brushed us out of the way as they stormed the aisles with attitude. We became aware of an elderly gentleman nearby who seemed completely out of place as he browsed the Christmas jumpers.

---

[43] Kevin was a little embarrassed about hanging around in a girls' clothing store and had opted for waiting outside. We saw him peering intermittently through the doorway as he tried to catch glimpses of Annie.

Amanda nudged Ruby and whispered, "Can we give him a card?"

Ruby nodded and rummaged around in her bag.

By this point, Annie only had a few minutes left of her shift. I watched enviously as her manager went over and handed her a small brown envelope. I wondered what Annie would buy with her wages and whether she could afford a Tizzi Berry jumpsuit. I considered asking whether there were any vacancies. Money had always been tight in our household and Jill had said she would cut my pocket money as soon as I finished college.

Before I could decide, Ruby pulled out a Christmas card. "Merry Christmas," she said as she thrust it at the old man.

He took it and said, "Oh! What's this?"

"It's a Christmas card," said Amanda. "Do you like Christmas?"

"Ah." He gave a soft smile. "Yes, very nice."

"What's your name?" Amanda continued.

I wondered if she was being a little too audacious but the old man kept smiling as he replied, "My name is Mr Clarence."

Amanda paused before asking, "Do you believe in God?"

Mr Clarence shook his head. "No, I don't..." He paused before adding, "I'd like there to be someone up there, you know. But I've never found proof that there is."

Amanda looked helplessly at me and Ruby.

I tried to come to her aid. "The Bible says that if you seek, you will find," I informed the old man.

"I've been seeking all my life," he said, turning to me. "I'm eighty four. And I've not found him yet."

I bit my lip. That was a very long time to seek. How could I tell him that he needed to try harder?

"Maybe you'll find him today," Amanda suggested. "Have you got any sicknesses we could pray for?"

He chortled. "I have plenty! I'm eighty four."

"Anything bothering you in particular?" Ruby pressed.

Mr Clarence gave us a thoughtful look. "Well, I'm having cataracts removed next Tuesday. I'm not looking forward to that."

"Could we pray for you?" I asked. "Perhaps God will heal you. Would that be a big enough sign?"

He laughed. "Oh, that would be quite a sign!"

I was about to pray and then reconsidered and nudged Amanda instead. "Do you want to do it?"

Amanda looked as though I had just suggested she grab a knife and operate on his cataracts herself. "Okay," she squeaked. She held both hands towards Mr Clarence's face as she whispered, "Cataracts, go away in Jesus' name."

Mr Clarence blinked at us.

"How is it?" I asked.

He shook his head and peered over his glasses. "Nothing's changed."

Amanda looked deflated.

"It's alright," I whispered. I turned to Mr Clarence. "Can we try again?"

He shrugged. "By all means!"

This time, the three of us prayed together.

As we finished, Annie joined us and added a hearty, "Amen!"

"No, nothing," said Mr Clarence, grinning as though we were all mad.

I let out a long breath. "We'll keep praying for you today," I promised. "I'm sorry it didn't happen."

"That's alright." He clearly hadn't expected anything. He gave a pleasant nod and made his way out of the shop. Kevin darted out of his way and joined the four of us as we exchanged disappointed glances.

"We have to keep believing," I told them.

Amanda gave a sad sigh and was about to say something when Mr Clarence burst back into the shop. "It's a miracle!" he exclaimed. "I don't know what you did but I can see!"

The five of us and half the shop stared at the old man as he came bouncing over. "I can see!" he yelled.

Amanda gripped my arm and squealed, "Wow, Livi!"

I composed myself enough to say, "That's amazing!"

"I just hope it lasts," Mr Clarence whispered as he pulled his glasses on and off.

"It will," said Amanda.

"Trust that God did it," Ruby added. "You asked for a sign and he's given you one."

Mr Clarence looked rather chuffed. "I can't believe it..." He pulled his glasses on and off once more before repeating, "I just hope it lasts."

I took a deep breath. "It's great that you can see," I said. "But the truth is that you're getting old..." The others shot me nervous glances as I told Mr Clarence, "Whether it lasts or not, you're probably going to die one day. The greater miracle is that Jesus died for all your sins."

Ruby gave me a quick jab and whispered, "Don't tell old people that they're going to die!"

But, far from scold me for my insensitivity, Mr Clarence chuckled and said, "Yes, you're right." He sighed. "You're right. Maybe I'll go to church this Christmas."

"While you're there, ask to meet Jesus," Annie counselled him. "Because just going to church isn't enough."

Mr Clarence nodded before thanking us all. He wandered out of the shop, stopping every few seconds to read signs on the walls as he marvelled at his new sight.

As the five of us jumped up and down, Annie's manager made her way over to us. "What was that all about?" she demanded.

"God healed his cataracts!" Annie said merrily. She paused before adding, "Do *you* need healing?"

Her manager looked a little taken aback. "Actually, my shoulder is a bit stiff," she admitted.

Annie beamed before pointing a finger at her manager's shoulder. "Shoulder, behave!"

I watched in astonishment as Annie's manager raised her arm and gasped. "Oh my goodness! The pain's gone."

Annie giggled and turned to the rest of us. Then, before any of us could say anything, she gave a loud whistle and yelled at the shoppers in the store, "Hey! Does anybody need healing? Come over here if you do!"

I felt myself blushing as people turned to stare. Some of them looked bemused. Others frowned as though Annie had just interrupted something important. I was torn between relief and regret as I scoured the shop and noted that there was nobody there that I knew.

There was a pause and then a young woman piped up nearby, "I've got asthma. Can you do anything about that?"

"Jesus can!" Annie sang. "Come here and we'll pray for you."

The young woman shuffled over and bent her head as we gathered round to pray.

If it wasn't for the fact that her shoulder had just been healed, I was fairly sure Annie's manager would have disapproved. But, as it was, she just gave us a quick smile and let us get on with it, presumably hoping that a few miracles might be good for business.

"I can't tell straight away," the young woman admitted when Annie asked whether she felt better. "But I'll know next time I play hockey."

Ruby handed her a Christmas card and said, "Either way, God loves you."

The young woman thanked us and turned to leave.

As a couple of other ladies came towards us, Kevin started to look uncomfortable. I wasn't sure whether this was because he was suddenly on show in a girls' clothing store or whether it was due to the fact that Amanda kept trying to get his attention by decorating herself with endless furry earmuffs. Either way, it wasn't long before he was waiting outside again.

It was another forty minutes before the rest of us left the shop. By this time, we were brimming with excitement and ready for a break. We had prayed for seven women between us and told a further six about the Kingdom of Heaven. They hadn't all been healed, or at least not right away, but they had all seemed touched by our prayers. We had also given away a number of Christmas cards and one lady was so impressed by them that she'd asked if she could buy a batch to hand out at her work.

Although it didn't seem to worry Ruby or the others, it bothered me that none of the ladies had asked us how they could get right with God. I wondered whether this was because we hadn't been definite enough about their need for salvation. I had found myself growing concerned as Annie eagerly told the women that they were all God's princesses. I felt she ought to focus on getting them to accept Jesus first. If they thought they were already princesses then they might not bother repenting. Surely, if we were going to properly represent the King, then the first thing people needed to know was that they were lost without him. I made a mental note to talk to her about it later.

"I'll get lunch," Annie said as we wandered into the nearest café.

I looked at her. "What do you mean?" I had just been adding up the change in my pocket and wondering whether I ought to skip lunch and have some toast when I got home.

Annie grinned. "I mean, I'll pay."

"For all of us?"

"Why not?" I watched in astonishment as she pulled out the brown envelope containing her wages and asked what we all wanted.

"Don't you want to keep that for yourself?" I spluttered. "It's *your* money."

"No it isn't. It's God's money. He gave it to me to share."

"But don't you want to save it?"

"What for? The world could end tomorrow!" Annie laughed before adding, "If I need more, God will give me more. I'm his princess."

I opened my mouth and then closed it again.

Ruby looked equally surprised.

"The early disciples shared everything, didn't they?" Annie went on. "It's not like I'm wasting it on a Tizzi Berry jumpsuit or something."

I blushed as she handed out menus.

Kevin and Amanda took theirs eagerly while Ruby and I remained cautious. I couldn't work out whether what Annie was doing was insanely generous or incredibly reckless. I watched Kevin and Amanda as they discussed which milkshake they wanted with their burgers. They seemed happy to let Annie pay for them without even questioning it. I rolled my eyes. Of course. They were younger. They hadn't yet learnt the value of money.

"Parents should take responsibility for their children, right?" Annie continued. "Well, God is my Father so I know he will look after me."

My heart thudded as I realised that maybe it was *me* who hadn't yet learnt the value of money. *'God is my Father so I know he will look after me.'* I hoped I would remember those words when I was old enough to feel as though everything depended on me.

"Wow," I said. "Thanks, Annie."

"It's okay," she replied cheerfully. "It's only a burger. You're worth more than hundreds of burgers."

My face grew hot.

"In fact..." Annie chewed the insides of her cheek. "You're worth more than all the money in the world."

My heart caught in my throat. I may have been delivered of the orphan mindset but in many ways I was still swimming in the shallow end of God's love. I realised I had a lot to learn about what it truly meant to be his child. I gave a quick sniff. I didn't want to start crying over a burger. "I'm not as carefree about money as you are," I admitted.

"That's probably because your sister is poor."

I blushed again. "Yeah..."

"So what do you want?" Annie continued, jabbing her finger at one of the specials. "How about the *Princess Burger Deluxe?*"

I sucked in my cheeks. "Alright. Thanks."

151

She grinned before declaring to the others, "Princess Burgers all round! Oh, not that I'm saying you're a princess, Kevin!"

Kevin gave an awkward squeal. "I don't mind being a princess if you are!"

Annie giggled and trotted over to the till. She returned a few minutes later with a tray laden with burgers, chips and various flavours of milkshake. I resisted the urge to add it all up and try to figure out how many hours of work it had cost her.

As I reached for the nearest burger, Annie grabbed my arm and said, "Hey wait!"

I looked up in alarm, afraid that she was expecting me to pay after all. "Oh, sorry..." I muttered.

She just blinked at me. "Can we do communion?"

I was taken aback. "Communion?"

"Yeah." She picked up a burger. "I got an extra burger specially."

I looked at the greasy bundle in her hands and gulped. Although we had occasionally used a cookie and some juice instead of bread and wine, I was afraid that substituting a chunk of processed meat for Jesus' body might constitute some form of heresy.

"Er, I don't know," I said. "What do you think, Ruby?"

She shrugged. "I suppose it's about our hearts, isn't it?"

"I guess..."

Annie grinned and held up a cup. "And I got some coffee for his blood!"

"Coffee?" Ruby and I looked at her in dismay.

"Nobody likes coffee!" Kevin protested.

"Exactly!" Annie kept grinning. "So it will be like wine; a sacrifice to drink it."

"Right..." I gave a splutter and watched as Annie divided the spare burger into five pieces.

I don't think she fully knew what she was doing or what communion was even all about but I nodded along as she handed me a piece of burger and said, "The body of Christ, broken for you."

I mumbled a quick, "Amen," before popping it into my mouth.

Ruby, Kevin and Amanda chewed their pieces with equal gravity, none of us quite knowing where to look.

When we'd finished, Annie raised the cup of coffee and said solemnly, "The blood of Christ, shed for you." She raised the cup to her lips, screwing up her nose as she took a loud slurp.

Then she handed it to me and I did the same before passing it on. One by one, the others took a little sip and winced.

Afterwards, there was a long pause before Annie clapped her hands together and said, "Right then! Let's eat!"

As Kevin and Amanda gave eager cheers and dove into the rest of the food, Ruby and I stopped and exchanged little glances. *Did we really just do that?*

"What would Sharon say?" I whispered as I reached for some chips.

"Sharon?" Ruby gave a bemused grin. "What would *Summer* say, more like!"

I let out a snort as I tucked into my food.

I had barely had two bites when Amanda gave me a tap on the arm and asked if we could talk privately for a moment. "I need to tell you a big secret," she whispered, giving me a serious stare.

I raised an eyebrow. "Alright."

We left the others eating their burgers and headed over to a couple of seats on the other side of the café where Amanda sat looking shifty as she summoned up the courage to speak. I tried not to look worried as I wondered what she was going to confess.

Eventually, she gave a small squeak. "Nobody knows this but..." She took a deep breath and looked away. "I kind of have feelings for Kevin."

I bit my lip and tried not to give anything away.

"I don't know what to do." She sniffed. "Should I tell him? Do you think he likes me?"

I glanced over her shoulder. Kevin was jabbering excitedly to Annie. It looked like he was in the middle of a joke.

I was about to reply that perhaps she ought to give up trying to impress Kevin and press in for more of God instead. I thought this would be rather sensible advice but, before I could get it out, God stopped me. If I told Amanda not to pursue Kevin, I was fairly sure she would try her best to take my advice. But then she might fail at it and end up feeling bad about herself. Far better than having all the right answers was the ability to lead her into the throne room so that she could hear from God herself.

"Have you prayed about it?" I asked.

"A bit. But I didn't get a clear answer."

I chewed my lip as I wondered what I ought to say next. "I don't know what to advise you about Kevin," I said finally. "But I do know that God loves you very much and cares about how you're feeling."

Amanda's eyes brightened. "That's good. I was worried that he might be angry with me for concentrating too much on Kevin and not enough on him."

I swallowed hard. "No, he's definitely not angry with you."

"Phew." Amanda beamed. "I'm glad I told you. I feel a lot better about it now." She looked across at the rest of our friends before adding, "Don't tell anyone."

I didn't want to break it to her that everybody except Kevin already knew. "Let's get back to the others," I said, offering her my hand as I stood up.

"Livi?" Amanda gave me an earnest stare. "Am I really a princess to God?"

I nodded. "Yes!"

"I know God loves me... but I hardly ever feel it," she confessed. "I always think I need to do things to please him. Do you ever feel like that?"

"I used to," I admitted. "But it's not true, I promise."

As Amanda scampered back to our table, I gave a sigh of relief and thanked God for not letting me go trundling in with words he hadn't told me to say. I realised Annie had probably been right not to get too heavy with the ladies at Tizzi Berry. My role as a princess was not to tell everybody how to please the King. Rather, it was to see the royal stamp within them and love them until they saw it for themselves. As Annie had just pointed out, one person was worth more than all the money in the world. Only when God's sons and daughters knew who they truly were would his Kingdom be established on earth as in Heaven.

Like Mr Clarence set free from his cataracts, I was finally beginning to see.

~ 18 ~

Pest control

Over the last few weeks, Ruby and I had made a special effort to work hard at college, hoping it would help improve our friendship with Maria, Ellen and Laura. The three of them had been rather reluctant to work with us after our perceived idleness on the field trip and it had taken them a long time to agree to team up with us for *'Clean and Comfortable Critters,'* our current Small Animal Hygiene module.

There were now less than two weeks left until the end of term and it seemed mine and Ruby's hard work had paid off. The five of us were happily washing a guinea pig at the sink, with me and Ruby doing more than our fair share of scrubbing, as we chatted and joked like old friends. Ellen was even talking about a Christmas sleepover as though we would be invited.

We were just about to wrap our guinea pig in a towel when Sharon stopped at our sink and asked if she could see me and Ruby at the end of class.

"What for?" I asked.

She gave me a firm look and swooped away.

Maria, Ellen and Laura eyed the two of us in suspicion.

"What did you do?" asked Maria.

"Nothing!" Ruby spluttered.

They shot one another quick smirks and avoided our gaze.

I looked over at Sharon and frowned. I hoped whatever she wanted would warrant us looking so stupid in front of our classmates.

The lesson came to an end and we tossed our guinea pig back into the cage with the rest of them and waited for everyone else to leave. Once the room was empty, Ruby and I exchanged anxious glances and went over to Sharon's desk.

"Grab a chair," she said.

We did as we were told, perching a little awkwardly as we waited to find out what she wanted.

She chuckled. "Don't look so serious! You're not in trouble."

I breathed a sigh. "Then what—"

"I just thought you might want me to answer your question."

We looked at one another blankly. As far as I could remember, we had struggled through washing our guinea pig without a single question.

"About demons," said Sharon. "And how to cast them out."

My jaw fell open and I gave Ruby a quick nudge. "Oh, yes please!" I exclaimed, hardly daring to believe that the day had finally come.

Sharon gave me a stern look. "First of all, you must not— and I mean *must not*— seek demons out. Only do what Jesus shows you and nothing else. Do you understand?"

I nodded.

"Don't give demons any unwarranted attention."

"No."

"I hope you haven't got curious about them and started looking for information from any source outside of the Bible?"

I shifted awkwardly.

She frowned. "Well?"

I blushed. "I kind of went online to see whether they wear clothes but—"

"Don't." Sharon pointed her finger at me and looked me in the eye. "You mustn't let curiosity lead you astray. There's so much rubbish out there. Do you understand?"

I felt my cheeks turn scarlet. "Okay. Sorry."

Ruby shot me an alarmed glance as Sharon continued frowning. I bit my lip and shrugged, suddenly afraid of what we were getting ourselves into.

After a long pause, Sharon composed herself and said, "When it comes to spiritual warfare, it's important that you stay in a place of rest. Don't try and do things in your own strength."

"We've been learning that when we go into town," I said, keen for Sharon to know how much we had all been practising.

She nodded. "Everything you do must flow out of your relationship with God. And it's about *his* glory, not yours."

"I've been learning that too," I insisted.

"Good. Now, too few Christians know how to deal with demonic attack and the Church is seriously suffering because of it..."

I glanced at Ruby. She looked like she was struggling with something.

Sharon gave her a gentle smile. "Ruby, I don't have to teach you about this if you don't want me to. It's extra curricular."

"I want to know..." Ruby said weakly. "I just wondered... Er..." She gave a small cough before blurting out, "Some people say that Christians can't have demons. Is that true?"

I frowned. After my experience in Wales, I had no doubt that they could. I turned to see how Sharon would respond. I hoped she wouldn't use me as an example.

Sharon pursed her lips and said nothing for a while. Eventually she muttered, "It would be very convenient if demons left at the moment a person became a believer, wouldn't it? Just as it would be very nice if all sicknesses left at that moment too, leaving the Christian exempt from the need for deliverance or healing for the rest of their lives." She cleared her throat before continuing, "Don't get me wrong; divine health and protection are available to us by the finished work of the cross. It's just rather plain to see that most of us are yet to experience that as a reality."

Ruby paused before clarifying, "So, Christians *can* have demons?"

I looked at her. "Who said they couldn't?"

"My mum."

I swallowed hard. It was one thing going against Summer's advice; were we going to disregard Belinda's opinion too?

Sharon looked a little uncomfortable. "You'll have to seek the Lord on it for yourself," she said. "But, as I understand it, Christians are not immune to sin or to the effects of sin so if a door is open then the enemy will seek to enter. Just like how Christians can still get sick. Did you know there are many sicknesses that are actually caused by demons?"

I exhaled. "Like what?"

She stopped and stroked her chin. "The way Jesus dealt with people suggests that anything outside of normal, reasonable functioning is an indicator of something that could need deliverance. You'll learn familiar signs: anything doctors can't diagnose, compulsive irrational behaviour, pain that comes and goes, many mental health issues..."

My stomach churned. "They're all caused by demons?"

Sharon shot me a quick glance. "Not always... Sometimes a person is just a person. And sometimes a person can be broken into pieces and need some help getting back together. But we're not dealing with that right now…" She looked away. "Don't make the mistake of thinking that every unreasonable person you meet needs to have a demon driven out of them. But don't be naïve either. Be aware of anything out of the ordinary and keep your spiritual senses open. Dealing with demons was a pretty regular occurrence for Jesus. There's no reason why it shouldn't be for you too. But, if you understand the truth about them, your dealings with them will bring neither fear nor unhealthy fascination. You'll treat them like the pests that they are." She paused. "Are you writing this down?"

I gulped and reached for a pen and some paper.

Sharon sucked in her breath and went on, "There are different degrees of influence that the enemy can have over someone. Sometimes, people are simply operating under a lie or trapped in a wrong pattern of thinking. These things are inherently demonic but, usually, just learning to stand on truth is enough to set that person free… Have you been getting into the word?"

We nodded. Over the last month or so, the two of us had been praying regularly that God would give us an increased love for the Bible. As a result, I was finding myself enjoying it more and more. I was even beginning to learn a few verses, although Ruby had taken to this far better than me and I still needed to ask her whenever I wanted to find anything.

"Good. Keep going. His word is a powerful weapon. For example, someone may have trouble believing that God cares about them. Often they will find freedom by learning a verse or two about God's faithfulness and meditating upon it until it becomes their reality. It's only when applying such truth isn't strong enough to bring about lasting change that one might need to look a little deeper."

I nodded and scribbled as fast as I could. Beside me, Ruby was biting her nails as she stared straight at our teacher.

"God can tell you if something demonic is happening and whether it's for *you* to deal with. Don't assume that you need to take action right away. It might not be the right time." Sharon gave me a sharp look. "Did you get that, Livi? Don't go wandering into a battle he hasn't prepared you for."

"I won't!" I squeaked.

"If there *is* a need to cast something out, then ask the Lord how to do it and follow his instructions completely." Sharon gave a broad smile. "There you go."

I dropped my pen. "Then what?"

"That's it. The rest is just listening to God. You've been practising that, haven't you?"

I gaped at her. "Yeah, but—! What do we do next? How do we drive them out?"

Sharon didn't reply.

I looked at Ruby. Her eyes were fixed on Sharon. I couldn't work out whether she was frightened, cynical, or just deep in thought. "Do demons talk?" she asked finally.

Sharon looked at her. "Sometimes."

I bit my lip. "Should we start by asking the demon questions? Like why it's there and what it looks like?"

"Absolutely not!" Sharon exclaimed. "Don't waste time conversing with demons. They may well lie. God can tell you anything you need to know."

I frowned. "Then... How do we drive them out?"

"The same way that you get rid of sickness. Command them to go in the name of Jesus." She paused. "And I mean standing in the *authority* of the name of Jesus. Not just using it as a lucky charm, remember?"

I nodded.

"Demons know they can't stand against the name of Jesus but they wait to see if you know it too." Sharon gave a disapproving sigh. "Unfortunately, many Christians don't."

I gulped. "But what if I tell a demon to go and it doesn't leave?"

"Easy! Ask God what to do next and do it. If he tells you to stop, then stop. There is always enough grace, time and revelation for anything God wants you to do."

My stomach tightened. "But what if we can't hear anything? What if it's all too confusing?"

Sharon gave a little hum. "Just praise Jesus until his peace comes. Don't focus on the enemy or get yourself whipped up." I was about to reply when she added, "I know it's serious stuff but there's no need to be frightened. The battle has already been won; Jesus finished it on the cross. Stand on that truth. Demons are more afraid of *Jesus in you* than you ever need to be of them."

I let out a long breath. Sharon made it sound so simple. I had been expecting some grand secret formula but it seemed that the key was simply listening to the Holy Spirit and doing whatever he said. I didn't know whether to be disappointed or relieved. I scanned my notes as I asked, "Do people need to be sitting down while I pray for them?"

I could tell from the look on Sharon's face that it was a daft question.

"Never mind," I muttered.

She smiled. "Whenever you can, try to empower people to be active in their own deliverance. For one thing, they'll know how to resist the enemy if it tries to come back. For another, they'll be able to set others free because they'll spot the same thing and be confident it's something they have victory over."

I thought about Amanda confessing that she wasn't always sure that God loved her. It sounded similar to how I had felt before. Perhaps this meant she had an orphan spirit too. "Our friend might have what I had—" I blurted out.

"Let God lead you," Sharon cautioned. "Whatever you do, don't start accusing people of having demons."

I blushed and shook my head.

"I know you keep saying that we need to let God lead us," Ruby spoke up. "But can you give us some practical examples?"

"Read the Bible. You'll find plenty." Sharon grinned. "Although, as you'll see, Jesus did things differently every time. That's why I tell you that the key is listening to the Father... Oh, and one last thing: always end by inviting the Holy Spirit to finish up." She gave a curt nod, as if she was giving advice on something as trivial as planting tomatoes.

I forced a smile and folded up my notes.

Ruby quivered as she voiced what I had been feeling: "I don't think I'm ready."

"If you're not ready then God won't ask you to do it." Sharon shrugged before adding, "Demons don't suddenly exist when you start learning about them. And opening your eyes to them doesn't give them more power. In fact, it's quite the opposite. It means you can deal with them if they come near you. You can also start to set others free."

I gave a slow nod as I realised she was right. If demons were indeed as real as they had been when Jesus walked the earth, then we probably encountered them all the time without even realising it. Surely knowing how to spot them could only be a good thing. I stopped to check, "Are you sure this stuff wasn't just for Bible times?"

"These *are* Bible times!" Sharon laughed before sauntering over to the fish tank at the side of the room. She gave us one last smile. "If you want to learn how to swim, you need to get wet." She started to hum as she reached for the tub of fish food on the windowsill.

Ruby grabbed hold of my arm. "What do you think?" she whispered.

I shot Sharon a quick side glance. "I guess we have to get wet."

Ruby puffed out her cheeks. "Sometimes I think she's crazy."

I stifled a giggle and put a finger to my lips as we arose and picked up our things.

"Thanks Sharon," we muttered, turning to leave.

As we reached the door, Sharon looked up with a twinkle in her eye. "Whatever you do, don't just listen to *me*. I could be crazy for all you know. Listen to God and do what he says."

Although I was far from being an expert, I couldn't wait to teach the rest of The Fire Brigade what Sharon had taught us. I'd been reviewing my notes all day, growing in confidence as I convinced myself that it would be easy once the five of us were stepping out together. I imagined us as a bit of a hit squad, marching in unity as we picked off demons one by one like the pesky pests that they were.

I meant to introduce the topic a little more sensitively but couldn't contain my excitement as I blurted out, "Ruby and I learnt about demons today!"

Annie's jaw dropped open and both Amanda and Kevin looked at me in horror.

I waved a hand. "Don't be scared. It's all really simple."

"So, demons are real?" Kevin bit his knuckles.

"Yes," I said. "But don't worry. The deliverance Jesus brings is real too."

Kevin gulped. "Oh."

Ruby dug in the ribs. "Don't frighten them," she whispered.

"I'm not frightened," Kevin insisted, shooting Annie a quick glance.

"Me neither," said Amanda, looking as though she had already wet herself.

"I guess if the Bible talks about them then we probably need to know about them," added Annie.

I looked at them. "Should we do it another time?"

"Tell us now," Annie pleaded. "Then, if we see one on our way home, we'll know what to do."

Amanda and Kevin gaped at her before turning back to me. "Tell us what to do!" they pleaded.

Ruby watched them thoughtfully before shrugging. "I guess if they want to know..."

"We'll learn about it together," I assured them. "God will help us..." I started to go through Sharon's notes, careful not to make it sound too scary or hard.

Despite my attempts to play it cool, Kevin gave a loud gulp every few seconds and Amanda chewed her finger until it looked quite pink.

"We just have to do what God tells us," I reiterated over and over.

The others hung on my every word as I flicked through my Bible and read aloud from different accounts of Jesus and his disciples dealing with demons. "With the authority Jesus gives us, we can fight anything." I lowered my voice before adding, "Demons tremble at the name of Jesus."

All of a sudden, something small and black sprinted across my room. I screamed and leapt to my feet. On either side of me, Ruby and Kevin started going hysterical and Annie shook as she shrieked, "Demon! Demon!"

The black thing darted like a shadow under my bed. Kevin took his shoes off and held them like clubs as he waited for the beast to resurface.

Only Amanda remained unmoved. "She's not a demon!" she yelled, giving the floor beneath her a little tap. "She's my rat."

I caught my breath as the black beast poked its head out from under my bed and scurried into Amanda's lap. Amanda scooped it up and gave it a kiss. "It's alright Polly, don't be frightened."

I clutched my chest, my heart pounding as I slid to the floor. Now that I had could see it clearly, the rat was as small and harmless as any of the creatures we had at college. More so, perhaps, since it was allowing Amanda to rub noses without making any attempt to bite her.

Ruby shuddered as she sat back down. "Oh, that scared me."

Kevin dropped his shoes and knelt down to peer at the rat. "That was hilarious."

Annie was still quivering in the corner. She covered her eyes as she cried, "Is it gone? Tell me when it's gone."

Amanda shot her a wounded look. "She's still here."

I shook my head in disbelief. "Why would you bring a rat to a prayer meeting?"

Amanda was wide-eyed. "Because you said we're to preach the gospel to every living creature!"

I laughed despite myself and exchanged a glance with Ruby.

Annie uncovered her eyes long enough to say, "I'm glad you know what you're doing, Livi. I thought we were doomed."

"She's not a demon!" Amanda cried.

Kevin sniggered. "I was about to bash it," he said. "At least it would have heard the gospel before it died."

After a quick glimpse at Amanda's horrified face, I put my notes away. "Well, that's enough for today. Any questions?"

I instantly regretted asking when Amanda gave a whimper and put her hand up. "Do pets go to Heaven?"

~ 19 ~

Fight or flight

Although I was excited that Sharon had finally told us about demons, I didn't expect to have to put things into practise quite so soon. The very next evening, Annie arrived with a rather thoughtful look on her face. She barely spoke and just picked at the paint on my wall as we waited for the others. I had never known her to be so quiet so I resisted the urge to ask her to stop and just watched with a grimace as flecks of lime green paint fell into my pile of dirty washing. By the time Ruby, Kevin and Amanda had arrived, Annie had scratched her way from my bed to the floor.

I frowned before asking, "Are you alright, Annie?"

She looked up and gave a pensive sigh. "You know demons?"

I nodded slowly. "Yeah..?"

"Well... Are there fear demons?"

The others looked a little startled.

"Fear demons?"

"Mmm." She sniffed. "You know, like demons that make everything scary."

I waited for her to elaborate but she fell silent and started picking my wall again.

Ruby leant over and put a hand on Annie's shoulder. "Are you talking about all your phobias?"

Annie gulped. "Yeah."

Kevin and Amanda watched open-mouthed as she listed things on her fingers.

"I get scared of the dark. I get scared of flashing lights. I get scared of bridges and worms and moustaches." She paused and looked at Amanda. "I get scared of rats..."

Amanda blushed and checked the zip on her bag.

I located my notes from Sharon's talk. *"Anything outside of normal, reasonable functioning..."* I read before giving Annie a

164

careful look. "It's not normal or reasonable to have so many phobias, is it?"

She gave a sad sigh and shook her head.

My heart started to pound. "This is so exciting! We have a real live demon to practise with!"

"But we don't know what to do," said Ruby.

"That doesn't matter. God does."

Annie gulped. "So it *is* a demon?"

"I don't know. But we should ask God and see what he says." I paused. "Do you want to?"

Everyone stared at Annie as she chewed her fingers. "What will happen?" she whispered.

"I don't know," I repeated. I turned to Ruby for support.

She sucked in her cheeks before grabbing my Bible off the floor. She flicked through at lightning speed before stopping somewhere in the Psalms. *"I will fear no evil,"* she read aloud. *"Because my God is with me."* She looked up at Annie. "Don't be scared."

"That's the problem!" Annie moaned. "I *am* scared!"

I leant over and grabbed her hand. "It's alright," I said. "You know God is good, don't you?"

She nodded.

"You're not scared of *him?*"

She shook her head.

"So how about we just pray and see what he says?"

"Okay..." Annie squeezed her eyes tightly shut.

I glanced round at the others. Kevin and Amanda were looking rather alarmed. "It's alright," I told them. "If God doesn't say anything then we won't do anything."

They gave quick smiles and closed their eyes.

I exchanged a glance with Ruby before starting to pray. "Dear God, thank you for being with us and for helping us in every situation. You've heard our conversation about Annie's fears. Do you want us to do anything?" I closed my eyes and opened my ears, desperate for God to speak.

Around the room, the others shifted as they waited for something to happen.

After a while, I let out a disappointed sigh. "I didn't get anything," I confessed.

"Me neither," said Ruby.

Kevin and Amanda shook their heads.

There was a pause and then Annie squeaked, "I saw a picture."

We looked at her.

"What was it?" Amanda whispered.

Annie took a deep breath. "I saw myself holding a big sack. It was full of all kinds of scary things like broccoli and garden gnomes... and rats." She quivered a little. "I saw myself tip everything out in front of Jesus and he took it all away."

Ruby grinned. "Then that's what you should do."

Annie looked at her. "How?"

"Just tell Jesus that you don't want to be scared of anything anymore and then tell him everything that comes to mind."

"Imagine Jesus taking each thing that you give him," I added.

"Okay..." Annie closed her eyes. "Hey Jesus," she mumbled. "I don't want to be scared anymore. I'm sorry for holding on to this stuff. I don't want to be scared of worms or moustaches or rats..." She began listing her fears one by one, growing more tearful as she went on. After a while, she paused and looked at the floor.

"Anything else?" I prompted.

Annie blushed. "I sometimes get scared of giant hares."

"Giant hairs?"

She nodded. "We were camping once and a giant hare pushed me over when I was peeing."

"Right..." I said. "Well, God can deal with that."

She nodded again and closed her eyes. "And giant hares, Jesus. I give you the giant hares..." She looked at me. "Now what?"

I closed my own eyes. "Now what, Lord?"

After a pause, I had a strong sense of God saying, *Now tell fear to go.*

I opened my eyes and blinked at everybody. "I think we just have to tell fear to go," I reported.

By now, Kevin and Amanda were looking more curious than frightened and Ruby was once again whizzing through the Bible as she hunted for a specific verse. "Here it is!" she cried. "I felt like I should pray this over you..." She shuffled over to Annie and put a hand on her shoulder. *"God did not give us a spirit of timidity, but a spirit of power, of love and of self-discipline."*

Annie gave a soft smile. "Amen."

I was about to command the demon of fear to leave when I remembered Sharon telling me that, wherever possible, we ought to let people be involved in their own deliverance. "Hey, Annie," I said. "I think *you* should tell fear to go."

She gulped before composing herself. "Alright." I was expecting her to mutter a nervous prayer so almost fell off the bed when she got to her feet and roared, "In the name of Jesus, fear leave me NOW! I DON'T WANT YOU!"

We watched in amazement as she bent over and started to cough. For a moment, she looked like she was struggling to breathe.

I got to my feet and beckoned the others to do the same. "Come out in the name of Jesus!" I commanded.

Kevin and Amanda joined me in rebuking the evil spirit while Ruby read the same Bible verse over and over.

Annie exhaled sharply and then dropped to her knees as though in a bit of a daze. She looked up with a grin. "I think it's gone."

We continued to pray for her, laying hands on her shoulders as we asked the Holy Spirit to come and fill the spaces where fear had been. Her whole body began to relax as God gently ministered to her.[44]

"How do you feel?" I asked.

"I feel good. It's like a weight has gone."

"Ooh let's test it!" Amanda cried, whipping her rat out of her bag.

While the rest of us screamed, Annie looked over and giggled.

I gawped at her. "Annie, this is incredible!"

"I know!" she yelled. "I feel like I can do *anything.*"

I was almost giddy with excitement. I looked round at everybody else and wondered what we should do next. My gaze fell on Amanda who looked crushed as Kevin told Annie how brave she had been. I was about to ask if she knew God loved her yet and whether she wanted us to pray for her but fortunately I stopped to ask God first.

Not today.

I closed my mouth and sat back down. I didn't want to fall out of step with whatever Jesus was doing.

"Our first deliverance down!" Ruby exclaimed, giving me a nudge.

I grinned. Learning to swim was easy when you simply let God carry you. "We didn't even get too wet," I agreed.

---

[44] She told me later that Jesus had taken her through various memories of occasions in which the door of fear had been opened. As each door was closed, Jesus gave her a little gemstone of love in exchange.

~*~

It hadn't occurred to me when we were praying for Annie that I might have to answer to Eddie and Summer for going against their warning. It wasn't until Ruby and I were on our way to youth group on Friday night that I realised they might want to know we'd been learning about demons.

"Should we tell Eddie and Summer about what happened to Annie?"

Ruby's eyes widened. It seemed she hadn't thought about it either. "We have to tell them," she said. "They're our youth leaders."

I sighed. "How should we tell them?"

"At the end. Wait till everybody's gone and explain it really carefully."

I nodded and began to script a conversation in my head. I decided I would begin by explaining what had happened to me in Wales and then go on to talk about how God had been teaching us how to listen to him. It would flow quite naturally that some of listening to God might involve spiritual warfare. I hoped that once Eddie and Summer heard how easy and successful our first deliverance had been their fears would be relieved and they would give us their approval to continue.

Most people were there when we arrived. Summer greeted us at the door and took our coats from us.

As we followed her into the lounge, I tried to prepare the ground for what I'd be sharing later. "We've been practising listening to God more this week."

Summer looked pleased. "Fantastic!"

I beamed. Perhaps it wouldn't be a problem after all.

Just as I was about to explain that we were learning how to pray more effectively, Amanda danced into the room and exclaimed, "Has Livi told you yet? We got a demon out of our friend!"

The whole room fell silent and everybody turned to look at me.

Eddie and Summer looked at one another in horror as Amanda continued, "Livi taught us how to do it." She pointed at me, as though I needed further attention.

I cleared my throat and tried to think sharp. "We just did what Jesus told us to do!"

"How do you know it was a demon?" asked Mark.

"What did it look like?" piped up Bill.

Before I could reply, Eddie coughed and said loudly, "Guys, I don't think this is a conversation we should be having." He gave me a pointed look, as though I had started it.

I shrugged and kept my head down as I wandered over to the plate of cookies at the side.

"A few more minutes," Eddie went on. "Then we'll start."

Everyone glanced at me before continuing their previous conversations.

Ruby joined me at the cookies. "Well, that didn't quite go to plan," she whispered.

I rolled my eyes and turned slightly. A few yards away, I could see Summer talking to Amanda. She was looking very serious. I tried to crane my ears to listen but couldn't hear anything. Then Summer exchanged a quick word with Eddie before looking up and catching my eye. I felt myself blushing and pretended I hadn't been staring. It made no difference as Summer made her way over to me anyway.

I tried to make it look as though I was chatting with Ruby. "Have you done your Dangerous Circumstances homework yet?"

"Er... Did we have any homework for that?"

"Yeah, you know..."

I fought to stay cool as Summer came and stood beside me. "Livi, could I have a word with you please?"

I gulped and forced a smile. "Sure. What's up?"

She cocked her head towards the kitchen. "Can we speak privately?"

I exchanged an anxious glance with Ruby as I followed Summer into the kitchen, my face burning with the shame of being watched by everybody.

She closed the door behind us and turned to me with a worried look on her face. "Eddie and I have been talking," she said. "We're concerned about what you're teaching people in your little meetings."

I didn't like her use of the word 'little' but tried to sound mature as I replied, "May I ask what exactly has concerned you?"

"All the..." Summer lowered her voice. "All the interest in the demonic. It's really not healthy."

"We've not focussed on it much," I insisted. "We only just started learning about it. And then my friend had a demon of fear so we set her free from it." When Summer didn't reply, I added irritably, "Was I meant to leave her with it?"

169

Summer bit her lip. "We're worried that you're getting carried away."

"I'm not!" I tried to stay calm, knowing that if I had a meltdown I would be displaying exactly the kind of unreasonable behaviour she was concerned about.

"Amanda said you told her that her pet rat was a demon."

"I never said that!"

She carried on as though I hadn't spoken. "She and Kevin are very impressionable. They haven't been Christians for long."

"But that's good," I blurted out without thinking. "It means they can learn how to be proper followers of Jesus before they pick up too many churchy restrictions."

Summer looked a little affronted. "What do you mean?"

I blushed. "I didn't mean... I just think sometimes Christians are scared of this stuff because nobody ever talks about it." I paused. "The Bible says we're to heal the sick and cast out demons. But, until recently, I didn't realise I was actually meant to do it." Summer didn't say anything so I went on, "I just want to do what the Bible says. If people have demons in them then we should set them free!" I wanted to add that I was sure there was something afflicting Amanda but I knew that wouldn't go down well.

Summer kept staring at me.

I wished I was better at explaining myself. I was starting to feel like an idiot. "We've got this teacher at school," I said. "She's been teaching us about listening to the Holy Spirit. She told us a bit about spiritual warfare so we're trying to put it into practise."

"This is the lady you thought was a witch," Summer reminded me.

I grimaced. "Well, we were wrong about that." I felt my chest tighten as I muttered, "We just want more of God."

Summer exhaled. "Perhaps we should talk to your teacher."

I was very happy with the idea of Sharon setting Summer and Eddie straight and went to find her early on Monday morning to see what had happened.

I was more than a little horrified when Sharon told me, "They would like it if you would stop teaching about spiritual warfare. And stop praying for people to be delivered from demons."

"What!" I cried. "I don't have to stop, do I?"

Sharon screwed up her face. "If God tells you to do something then he's your highest authority. But he's also put leaders above us and we should honour them. They're your youth leaders, Livi. You need to listen to them."

"But they're wrong!" I had to bite my thumb to keep myself from yelling.

Sharon sighed. "I probably shouldn't have taught you about demons without checking they were alright with it. That was my fault."

"Don't be silly!" I exclaimed. "We need to be taught about this stuff! I've got the same Holy Spirit in me as the disciples, haven't I? I don't just have a junior version."

The sides of her lips curled slightly but she didn't say anything.

"What should I do?" I continued. "Should I make a petition and get people in my church to sign it? Or should I find all the Bible verses about demons and post them on Summer's FriendWeb page?"

Sharon gave me a stern look. "That's not how Christians fight."

"What then?"

"Pray."

I bit my lip. I was aware of the painful irony that that was exactly how Eddie had suggested Ruby and I combat Sharon when we'd thought she was a witch.

"But they're wrong," I repeated.

"Try to walk in love."

"But I'm right!"

"That's when love is especially needed."

I opened my mouth and closed it again. My mind was racing. "What church do you go to?"

Sharon gave a quick laugh. "I could tell you. But I don't want you to come."

I stared at her. "What? You can't stop me from going to church. They're public places."

"I'm not going to stop you. It's your choice. But I would advise you to keep going to your own church."

"But my church is rubbish! I feel like a bird in a cage. I need to be where I can fly." I knew I was being dramatic but I tried to look serious as I gave Sharon a beseeching stare.

"You need to be where God puts you," she said. "And I believe, right now, he wants you where you are."

"But how can I go to a church if I don't agree with absolutely everything the leaders say?" I was aghast.

She shrugged. "Do you agree with absolutely everything *you* say?"

I looked at her in confusion. "What?"

"Never make a mistake? Never reassess your ideas about something? Never learn anything new?"

I thought back to our communion with the coffee and Princess Burger. Did I agree with that? I still had no idea. I opened and closed my mouth a few times before changing the subject. "I would have been set free from that orphan demon years ago if they'd known what to do."

"Hmmm."

"Just like so many people wouldn't have to be sick if enough Christians bothered to fight for healing."

Sharon gave me a thoughtful look. "God has you in that church for a reason."

I frowned.

"And you're to love and honour them because we're all in the same family. We have the same Daddy and the same big brother and the world is watching to see if we'll all get along."

I snorted. "If God cared enough about his family, he'd pick better leaders."

"Don't give the enemy a foothold, Livi," Sharon warned. "You can be honest with God about how you're feeling. But don't speak lies against his character."

I blushed. *Sorry, God.*

Sharon pulled some work out of her desk. Just when I thought our conversation was over, she muttered, "What if you're wrong anyway?"

"What?"

"What if you're wrong about demons?"

My mouth fell open. "But you said—"

"What if I'm wrong?"

I stared at her in disbelief. "Well... *Are* you wrong?"

"Of course I'm not wrong!" she said indignantly. "But I *could* be."

My head spun as I took this in. "I'm not wrong," I said. "I know what I've experienced..."

She nodded. "Even so... Let love be stronger than the issues that threaten to divide."

I frowned. "But this is *important*."

Sharon looked at me. "God gives you tests that you can pass. He wants to see if he can trust you enough to take you to the next level and the way you choose to deal with offence will determine that."

I breathed sharply and tapped my fingers against her desk.

"There's a difference between those who fight and those who are really ready to fly," Sharon continued. "What will you choose? Fighting talk or taking flight?"

"That's an anagram," I muttered.

"Pardon?"

"'Fighting talk' is an anagram of 'Taking flight.'"

Sharon stopped to mull it over before chuckling. "God must have had fun when he made you."

I blushed. "What?"

She kept laughing. "Choose wisely, Livi. The whole of Heaven is watching you."

~ 20 ~

Keeping the peace

'*If I have a faith that can move mountains, but have not love, I am nothing...*'[45] I read the same verse over and over, desperately trying to forgive Eddie and Summer.

I knew that Sharon was talking sense and I really wanted to walk in love but it was just so difficult! I couldn't believe they had the audacity to ask me to stop making progress with spiritual warfare. I had many an argument in my head as I went over the previous Friday and rehearsed what I should have said instead.

'*Why don't you pray and ask Jesus for yourself whether I should be learning this stuff.*'

'*Oh, good idea, Livi. We didn't think of that.*'

'*See, I'm more mature than you realise...*'

The painful thing was that up until a few months ago I'd had a great relationship with them, especially Summer. I hated feeling like it had all been ruined. But I just didn't know what to do to make it right. They were wrong and I knew they were.

I tried getting Ruby's support but she grew uncomfortable whenever I mentioned it.

"Can you believe how awful they're being?" I exclaimed during Ageing Dogs.

She shrugged and said, "Hmmm."

"They want people to stay trapped with demons!"

"No they don't. They just don't think *we* should be dealing with it."

"Well they're not exactly doing anything about it themselves, are they?"

"Maybe God hasn't told them to."

"Jesus tells them to!" I retorted. "In the Bible!"

---

45 1 Corinthians 13:2.

Ruby puffed out her cheeks. "I don't know..." She went pink as she added, "I asked my mum about it."

My stomach lurched. "What did she say?"

"She got a bit scared."

"Oh Ruby!" I scolded. "Why did you have to ask her?"

She shot me an affronted frown. "Because I ask my mum about everything."

I rolled my eyes and looked out of the window.

"Anyway, she said to be careful."

I gave a sniff. *Why does everybody want to control us?* "I wish I knew which church Sharon goes to," I muttered.

Laura looked up from the next table. "Does Sharon go to church?"

"Yeah," I said flippantly, too irritated to even bother trying to evangelise her.

"Oh, right." Laura nodded and got on with her work.

Ruby cleared her throat. "What are you going to tell the others?"

I sucked in my cheeks. I had begun many a daydream about that too.

'I've got some bad news. Summer and Eddie are banning us from praying for people to be set free from demons.'

'Oh no!'

'That's right, Kevin. They think you and Amanda are too impressionable. As if you can't hear from Jesus without them.'

'That's not very nice.'

'I know, Amanda. I guess they just don't trust you.'

'Who are Summer and Eddie?'

'Well, Annie, I'll tell you who they're not. They're not people you should go to if that fear demon tries to bother you again!'

Ruby poked me with the bone of a dog. "Livi? What are you going to tell the others?"

I exhaled. "I don't know."

In the end, I thought it was best not to say anything. I wasn't sure I would be able to explain myself without resorting to bitterness so I stayed quiet and let Ruby do the talking.

"Eddie and Summer are a bit worried," she said once everyone had arrived. "They don't want us to get carried away. It's probably best if we wait before doing any more spiritual warfare."

I breathed heavily out of my nose as the others nodded.

"We don't want to upset your youth leaders," said Annie.

I pursed my lips and looked away.

Amanda turned to me. "Well, what should we do today?"

I shrugged. "You decide," I mumbled to Ruby.

"Let's put some worship music on," she suggested. "And just soak in God's love." She pulled her phone out of her bag and located her music. "I'll put it on shuffle so we get a good selection." She grinned and set it down in the middle of my room.

"God can be the DJ!" Kevin agreed.

Amanda gave an overenthusiastic giggle as she stretched out next to Ruby's phone. I shuddered as her rat, Polly, poked its nose out of her pocket and scurried onto her tummy.[46]

The rest of us made ourselves comfortable as the first song began. *'Let your face shine on your children, we are waiting here for you...'*

I pretended to be lost in worship as I curled up on my floor hugging Sausage-Legs. I tried to clear my mind and listen to the songs but I couldn't stop thinking about Eddie and Summer. We had one more youth meeting before Christmas. I decided that I might not go.

Several songs later, Kevin was snoring lightly in the corner, Amanda was sucking her thumb and gazing at my ceiling, Ruby and Annie wore dreamy expressions as they hummed along to each tune and I was still simmering with anger.

Suddenly, a noise like a foghorn erupted from Ruby's phone following by a lively harmonica solo.

Kevin awoke with a jolt and spluttered, "What's happening?"

The rest of us sat up as a chorus of chipmunks began to squeak.

'A world full of love is a world full of songs
For love is stronger than the greatest of wrongs...'

"Oh sorry!" Ruby exclaimed as the others burst out laughing. "That one's in there for Oscar..." She giggled and reached for her phone. "I'll skip to the next one."

"Who was the band?" Amanda asked.

"Bible and Squeak."

---

[46] I had attempted to ban Amanda from bringing her rat to our meetings but she had almost burst into tears as she exclaimed, "But God loves Polly! And she's really clever. You just need to get to know her." I still struggled to understand why God would make something as creepy as a rat but promised to *'try to see God in her'* as long as Amanda didn't let her come too near me.

I forced a smile as the others roared with laughter.

Ruby skipped to a more contemplative song but it was too late. The words had already etched themselves on my heart. *'Love is stronger than the greatest of wrongs...'*

How could I justify being so angry with Eddie and Summer? At worst, they were acting out of fear. At best, they were concerned for us. It was hardly the greatest of wrongs. I squeezed my eyes shut and lay back down. I knew I had to keep going to youth group.

~*~

Attending youth group that Friday proved to be a greater ordeal than I had expected due to the fact that Ruby was away at a welcome home meal for her sister, Violet.

When she had announced it, I'd breathed a sigh of relief as I concluded this meant I didn't have to go to youth group either. I pretended to be super-excited about Violet's meal in the hopes that Ruby might invite me along.

"She says she's got loads of artwork to show us," Ruby said with a grimace.

"Sounds nice!"

"I don't know... Apparently this term she was experimenting with painting with her nose."

I gulped and tried to look excited.

"I wish I could go to youth group with you instead."

"I don't mind keeping you company at the meal, if you want?"

"No way! I'd never ask you to miss youth group!"

I paused. The subtle tactics weren't working. I needed to be more blatant. "Ruby, please can I come to dinner with you? I don't want to go to youth group."

She stared at me. "Oh... This is about Eddie and Summer, isn't it?"

I rolled my eyes. "Obviously."

"I think you need to go, Livi."

"But—"

"I'll ask Violet to show you her artwork another time."

I opened my mouth and closed it again. "Great."

So it was with a heavy heart and a very fake smile that I arrived at youth group, all by myself, half an hour late after accidentally-on-purpose missing the bus.

I lingered for a moment on Eddie and Summer's front step, listening to the sound of laughter coming from inside. Then I rang the bell and reapplied my smile.

Summer answered the door a few moments later. "Livi!" She gave me an awkward hug as I came through the door.

"Hello." I pulled my shoes off and hung up my coat, aware of her staring at me the whole time.

"Have you had a nice week?"

I gave a nod. "Yup." I paused before adding, "Have you?"

"I have, thank you." She started telling me about something funny that had happened with her boys. It was a rather longwinded tale but I tried to be polite as I nodded along.

"Good," I said when she finished.

"We weren't sure if you were coming," Summer continued as she followed me into the living room. "We've just started."

"Oh?" I feigned surprise. I didn't want to add that I had deliberately come late so that I could avoid this awkward chat.

Everybody else was sitting in a circle. Amanda caught my eye and waved. I sat down beside her.

Eddie shot me a smile before explaining, "We were just talking about what the Bible means when it says we are *'seated with Christ in heavenly places.'*"

"Okay."

"Do you have any thoughts on it?"

"Nope."

Eddie looked round the room. "Anybody else?"

"It doesn't feel like we're actually sat with Jesus in Heaven," said Nicole. "It feels like he's up there and we're walking around down here."

The others agreed.

"What can we do to help ourselves be more aware of who we are in Christ?" Summer asked the group.

I shrugged as she caught my eye.

"You have to say *'in Jesus' name'* at the end of your prayers," suggested Bill.

While Nicole nodded, Joey and Mark didn't look convinced.

"Just saying it isn't enough," Kevin retorted.

"It's not a lucky charm," Amanda added. "Is it, Livi?"

I shook my head and looked away.

"That's right, Amanda!" Eddie grinned. "Jesus' name is not a lucky charm."

178

"Because the name *'Jesus'* is different in different languages anyway," said Joey.

"Yeshua!" exclaimed Mark. "That's in Hebrew."

"What will we call him in Heaven?" asked Nicole.

I stared at the floor as the conversation drifted to the fact that God could speak every language and speculation over which one was his favourite.

"Let's get back on track," said Eddie. "Is everyone clear on what it means to be seated with Christ?" The others nodded as he explained, "Being seated with Christ means that everything that belongs to Jesus now belongs to us as well."

"Our prayers should be from the viewpoint of Heaven as we seek to see God's will established on the earth," added Summer.

I frowned. If that much was clear to them, then how could *'everything that belongs to Jesus'* not also include healing and deliverance and the authority to set people free? How would non-Christians ever know that we were so powerful in Christ if our lives looked just like theirs? It couldn't all just be *talk;* there had to be *action* too.

As Summer asked if anybody wanted prayer for anything, I excused myself and went to the toilet. I spent as long as I dared in the bathroom, pacing up and down as I willed myself to forgive them. "They're saying all the right things," I muttered. "Why aren't they letting us actually *do* it?"

I went back downstairs, keeping my steps light so as not to interrupt the faint murmuring of prayer coming from the lounge. They were praying for Joey's mum. From the sounds of it, the cancer treatment wasn't working.

My stomach churned as I heard grim-sounding words such as *'radioresistant'* and *'chemotherapy.'*

Oh Lord, I begged. *Why aren't my prayers good enough?*

Mark concluded with a loud, "Amen!" and patted Joey's arm.

Joey sniffed and said, "Thanks everyone."

I rejoined the circle in time to see Amanda put her hand up.

Summer looked over at her and smiled. "Amanda?"

"Sometimes I don't feel like God loves me..." Amanda admitted. She went to say something else and then stopped.

Summer nodded. "Let's pray for you."

One by one, the others gathered round and asked God to help Amanda feel his love more.

"Thank you, Lord, for loving Amanda," Nicole began.

"Thank you for filling her with your Holy Spirit," said Mark. "Please draw closer to her."

"In Jesus' name," added Bill.

Their words were all noble enough but they seemed to be lacking any real power.

I tried to join in with a silent prayer but felt a little sick. I glanced at Amanda. She looked like she was trying not to cry.

When everybody had finished praying Summer asked Amanda how she was feeling now.

Amanda shrugged. "I don't know."

"Well, don't beat yourself up about it," said Summer. "God really loves you. He's doing a great work in your life."

Amanda sighed as Summer leant over and gave her a squeeze.

I frowned. Was that it? Wasn't she going to pray and ask Jesus if there was anything lurking deeper?

The meeting came to an end and I went straight to fetch my coat, keen to leave as quickly as possible. Unfortunately, one of my shoes had fallen out of sight behind the shoe rack and, in the time it took for me to find it, everyone else had already left.

Summer came and stood by the stairs, watching as I hurriedly tied my laces. "It was nice to see you, Livi."

I forced a smile. "You too."

"Do you have anything planned for Christmas?"

I got to my feet. "Just seeing my aunt. Well, thanks for having me." I turned to go.

"Livi?"

I turned back.

"I know there was a bit of... confusion last week. Eddie and I were just a bit concerned about what this teacher of yours had been telling you." She paused. "I hope we're alright?"

"Yeah, we're fine. Don't worry about it."

She looked a little hurt. "How are you getting home? Do you want a lift?"

"No, no. I don't mind getting the bus."

"Okay... See you soon, Livi."

"Yup." I didn't even glance at her as I pulled the door shut behind me.

I immediately regretted not accepting a lift home when I reached the bus stop and saw that there wasn't a bus for ages. I debated going back to their house and asking if the offer was still there but pride kept me rooted to the spot. Instead, I rehearsed my right to remain angry as I shivered in the cold.

The bus finally came and I spent the whole journey begging God to teach me how to love more. It seems that the homework God sends is sometimes quite unexpected. I had been hoping he would give me strategy on how to love Eddie and Summer better. Instead, I felt him say, *Send Erica some flowers.*

"Erica?" I said aloud. "You want me to send my stepmother flowers?"

Yes. Big ones.

I screwed up my nose. *But flowers are really expensive. I don't even know if Erica likes them.*

She's worth more than all the money in the world.

I tried to reason with God. *She doesn't believe in you. She goes to psychic fairs and she's into crystal healing and other weird new age things that you surely don't approve of.*

She has no peace.

I stopped in surprise. I hadn't expected God to say that. I had always thought that Erica was a dreadful sinner, embracing all manner of darkness as she courted the enemy. She had even admitted once that she believed she had enough inner power not to need Jesus *'or any other deity.'* I was struck by the sudden realisation that, despite where it had led her, Erica was seeking something that would fill a deep void. The supernatural lifestyle she was living was probably very real, but it would also be twisted and limited and would come at a price because she was entering by the wrong door. The only true door to peace is Jesus.

I got off the bus and wandered into my estate, marvelling at the extravagance of God's love; that he would interrupt my turmoil about Eddie and Summer to involve me in his pursuit of somebody else. Somebody so hardened and lost and deliberately living in direct opposition to all that Jesus died for. I realised it must truly pain God to know that one of his precious children was ensnared by so much darkness.

"But still..." I said. "Remind me to pray for Erica later or something. This is about me loving Eddie and Summer."

I let myself into my house and went to kick my shoes off. In my haste to leave youth group, I had tied a knot in one of my laces. I spent the next ten minutes groaning as I tried to unpick it. Finally it came loose and I tossed my shoes into the corner. Then, hoping God would have forgotten about Erica, I turned to go up the stairs.

Remember the flowers.

With another groan, I went into the living room and switched the computer on. I found an online flower delivery service and asked God which ones he wanted. I hovered the mouse above the cheapest bunch but God pressed upon me to get the next size up.

"Fine," I whispered. "Whatever you say." I clicked on the link and filled in Erica's details.

I wasn't sure what to write for my 'personal greeting' and spent ages running things over in my mind. In the end, I wrote, *'Dear Erica. Peace is not a concept. It's a person. Hoping you encounter the love of Jesus this Christmas. Love from Livi.'*

I wanted to go for the cheapest delivery option but followed God's prompting to choose the mightily extortionate *'next day express'* instead.

"Lord, I hope you help me pay for this," I muttered as I calculated how much it would all cost.

I've already paid for everything, I felt him reply.

The next day, I got a phone call from my dad.

"Erica says thanks for the flowers," he said when I answered.

"Tell her she's welcome," I replied, wondering why she couldn't thank me herself.

"She wants to know how you're getting on at college."

"Er, yeah, fine."

"Was it Chemistry you're studying?"

"No... Animals."

"Ah, yes."

I took a deep breath. "So... How are you?"

"I'm fine, thanks. I was over in Leeds last weekend for a football match. I thought about you."

"Oh." I wasn't sure whether to feel flattered or hurt. He had thought about me but clearly not enough to see whether I was available to meet up. "Was it a good match?"

"Nah. We lost. Flipping clowns."

I forced a laugh. "How's Erica?"

"She's fine too. She's at a chuckling weekend. Apparently it's like a laughing workshop but not as intense."

"Right..."

"They learn how to chuckle for three days straight. It's meant to relieve tension." Dad gave a heavy sigh. "She gets back tomorrow night... She wants us to take up Couples Chanting."

"What's that?"

"I don't know. Something to do with channelling energy between two people."

"Oh."

He sounded tired. "I'll find out more when she gets back."

I was about to give an absent grunt when I suddenly realised that if Erica had been away all weekend then she wouldn't have seen my flowers yet. For some reason, Dad was using the excuse to call me.

"Sounds a bit daft to me but it keeps the peace," Dad continued.

I thought about the message on my flowers. "Peace isn't a concept..." I began.

"Oh yeah. I read that on your note. Very clever."

I took a deep breath. I was used to conversations with my dad being rather uncomfortable but something was different this time. He sounded quite lost. "Peace is Jesus," I said, in case he hadn't understood.

He gave a distracted hum before asking, "So... What's the weather like where you are?"

I pursed my lips. "It's cold... Probably the same as for you in Hull." I paused. I was about to ask my dad what he thought about Jesus but what came out was, "Dad, do you ever pray?"

"I don't believe in God."

I took a deep breath. "What's he like?"

"Who?"

"The God you don't believe in."

I heard the confusion in his voice as he replied, "I don't know. Angry, I suppose."

"I don't believe in that God either," I whispered.

After an awkward silence, Dad said, "Well, I'd better let you go. I expect you're too busy to talk to me!"

I let out my breath. "I don't mind... Dad?"

"Yeah?"

"Why did you ring?"

When he finally replied, his voice sounded rather hoarse. "I just saw the flowers and missed you. I feel like I hardly know you..." He coughed. "I guess that's my fault really."

I didn't say anything.

"Well, anyway, have a nice Christmas."

"Thanks... Oh, Dad?"

"Yeah?"

"I love you." I hung up, feeling the weight of his chains. It's so much harder to hate people when the demons that ensnare them get worse and worse at hiding.

~ 21 ~

Jill's regrets

The Christmas holidays were due to begin with a festive party featuring Ruby's extended family. It had been in the diary since July as Belinda had been disappointed to be told by Jill, "I'm afraid all our weekends are booked up this Christmas," for the last two years.

"I'm letting you know with lots of warning," Belinda had told us this time. "You can't possibly be booked up yet!"

Jill had grimaced as she confessed, "No, I didn't think I'd need to be..."

I had anticipated this wouldn't be the most enjoyable of occasions, not least because Belinda had already posted a couple of scripts through our door for the *'Rico-Starling Nativity'* in which Jill had been cast as Mary.[47]

However, unknown to us, one ingredient was needed in order to make a party round the Ricos' a complete nightmare: Aunt Claudia.

We weren't meant to be seeing our aunt until the following day when we planned to drive down to her battered old farmhouse in Suffolk. So the last thing I expected to find when the doorbell rang at seven in the morning was Aunt Claudia waiting on the doorstep with a box of lamb, a bag of Christmas pudding and a trailer of cats.

"What are you doing here?" I blurted out before composing myself and giving her a quick hug. "I mean, what a nice surprise!"

"Hurry up, Livi," Aunt Claudia retorted. "I need to put this in the fridge." She thrust the box of lamb at me and started to yank her trailer of cats up the step and into the house.

---

[47] I was a sheep.

Jill came down the stairs looking like she'd just awoken from a bad dream. "Aunt Claudia!" she spluttered. "What are you—? I mean, what a nice surprise!"

"I took the overnight bus," our aunt replied gruffly. "I can't tell you how awful the man beside me smelt."

Despite stating that she couldn't tell us, she did an awfully good job at trying. Twenty minutes later she was still going into great detail about her fellow passenger's oral hygiene. "I've never seen such yellow teeth—"

Jill cut her off to ask if she wanted a cup of tea.

"Get me two. I need it after the journey I've just had."

I stood with Jill in the hallway as she rang Belinda to explain that we couldn't come to their party after all as we'd had a last minute visit from our aunt.

I heard Belinda squawking on the other end of the line.

"Are you sure?" said Jill, shoving one of Aunt Claudia's cats off her face. "We don't want to cause you any trouble... Well, thanks then, if you're sure it's alright." She put the phone down and grimaced. "She's invited Aunt Claudia."

Aunt Claudia perked up at the mention of her name. "What's this?" she called from the living room.

"A party," Jill said through gritted teeth. "At our neighbours' house tonight."

"Very well." Aunt Claudia sniffed. "I could do with some cheering up."

Oscar was the first to greet us when we arrived. He answered the door wearing nothing but a pair of white pants.

"I'm Jesus," he announced.

"Lovely," said Jill as Aunt Claudia looked him up and down and frowned.

He pointed a podgy finger. "Who's that?"

"This is our aunt," I told him. "She's staying with us at the moment."

"Oh." Oscar grinned and ushered us into the living room where a handful of Rico relations had already gathered, including Violet who wore garish earrings in the shape of bulbous mince pies. I guessed they were homemade but didn't want to draw attention to them by asking.

"Livi! Jill!" she exclaimed as we came in. "It's so nice to see you."

"You too," I muttered as she almost suffocated me with her embrace.

"Have you met our cousin, Henry?" Violet indicated a tall red-haired guy in his early twenties.

"Er, I don't think so." I exchanged a polite nod with Henry and shook his hand.

"And that's Uncle Nigel and Auntie Fiona."

The couple on the sofa stood up and said hello.

I glanced over at Aunt Claudia and wondered whether to introduce her. I thought better of it when I caught sight of her sneering at the Ricos' family tree tapestry on the wall.

"Which one are you then?" she asked Violet.

Violet located herself on the tapestry.

"Violet Iris Rico," Aunt Claudia read aloud. "I had a cat called Violet. She lost a leg."

Violet looked like she didn't know whether this was a compliment or an insult and just nodded before shuffling away.

Then Ruby appeared with an old couple who she introduced as 'Nooni and Pops.'

I gave an awkward smile and wondered whether we were expected to call them that too.

"You must be Livi!" said Nooni. "We've heard so much about you."

"Thanks..." I paused and realised I knew nothing whatsoever about *them*. Perhaps Ruby had told me and I had never listened.

"*Nooni?*" Aunt Claudia piped up. "Is that French?"

Ruby's grandmother was about to reply when Dennis the dog ran in and knocked Aunt Claudia to the floor. My aunt screamed as Dennis lapped at her face. Ruby's relatives quickly ran to her aid, laughing as they apologised for Dennis being '*a little jumpy.*'

"Jumpy my foot!" Aunt Claudia shouted as she finally broke free. "It ought to be shot."

The room fell silent as she stood fuming.

Jill shot Ruby's aunt and uncle a polite smile before asking, "Do you have any pets?"

"We have a dog too," Fiona admitted, blushing as Aunt Claudia snorted.

Before the small talk could get too painful, Belinda entered, dressed in a sparkly Christmas gown. "Dinner's ready!" she trilled. "Oh, Jill, you look lovely. Have you done something new to your eyebrows?"

My sister raised a self-conscious hand. "No. I don't think so." She paused before adding, "This is our Aunt Claudia."

Aunt Claudia barely cracked a smile as Belinda came over and cooed. "Hello Claudia! It's wonderful to have you with us. Please make yourself at home."

Aunt Claudia took this invitation far too liberally and broke wind as we followed Belinda into the dining room.

I noted rather ominously that the table was set for thirteen and took a seat as far away as possible from the sprouts. Stanley looked up from opening a bottle of wine and gave me a friendly smile. He wore a luminous orange jumper bearing a giant fluffy reindeer with a flashing red nose.

"Nice jumper," I said.

He winked. "Belinda's choice."

Ruby had already informed me that the Christmas meal would be a lentil pie due to her grandmother being a vegetarian. Unfortunately, I hadn't thought to warn Aunt Claudia. She swept into the dining room and gave a great sniff. "Where's the turkey?"

Belinda tittered. "My mother doesn't eat meat."

She pointed to Nooni who gave Aunt Claudia a timid wave.

Aunt Claudia looked as though she had just been introduced to an alien. "Not even at Christmas?" she asked in disbelief.

Nooni shook her head. "I'm against any form of cruelty to animals."

"It's not cruel to eat meat!" Aunt Claudia retorted. She pointed to the lentil pie. "It's cruel not to."

"Why don't you come and sit over here," Stanley said quickly, patting a seat on the other side of the room.

Aunt Claudia frowned and shuffled towards him.

The rest of us took our seats and gave Belinda encouraging noises as she dished out the lentil pie.

My aunt screwed her nose up as her portion was passed to her and took it without a word of thanks. She kept shifting in her seat, bashing elbows with Stanley and Jill who were either side of her. "It's a bit of a squeeze, isn't it?" she whispered loudly to my sister.

"They didn't know you were coming," Jill hissed back.

"Let's say grace!" announced Pops.

"Oh goodness me!" Aunt Claudia exclaimed as everybody held hands.

"Aunt Claudia, be quiet!" Jill snapped. "Just hold my hand."

I exchanged an awkward glance with Ruby as I held hands with her and Violet.

"For what we are about to receive," Ruby's grandfather continued. "May the Lord make us truly thankful!"

"And may he keep us from spitting it out," my aunt muttered as she hacked at her pie.

"Wait!" Oscar shrieked. "We have to pull our Christmas crackers! Nobody eat until we've done the crackers!"

Aunt Claudia dropped her cutlery onto her plate as the rest of us picked up our crackers. After a few moments of jostling around, the crackers were pulled apart. A little green whistle fell out of mine, along with a yellow hat and a rubbish joke which I saved for Kevin.

"What on earth is this?" Aunt Claudia demanded, holding up a shiny plastic coil.

"It's a paper clip," said my sister.

Aunt Claudia pursed her lips and mumbled something under her breath.

"You have to wear your hats all day," Oscar commanded everyone as his own oversized hat slipped down his neck.

While everybody else entered into the spirit and put their hats on, Aunt Claudia left hers in a folded heap by her plate.

I pulled my own hat on and turned to Violet, keen to do anything to drown out the sound of my miserable aunt. "How's college going?" I asked.

"It's amazing!" she replied. "I feel like God must have felt when he created the universe."

"Oh?" I took a bite of lentil pie and almost spat it back out.

"Yeah." She gave a dreamy sigh. "I painted a whole series of landscapes using just my nose."

"Ruby said something about that... Sounds interesting."

"Thanks. I'll give you a presentation after dinner."

Ruby nudged me and grinned. "I told her you wanted to see them."

I forced a smile. "Thanks."

"In fact," said Violet, "we ought to use them as backdrops for the nativity." She paused before adding, "Did everybody learn their lines?"

I nodded. "Baa."

Violet looked across at my sister. "I hear you've got one of the starring roles."

Jill blushed. "I wasn't sure if I wanted to do that actually."

Oscar gave a shrill cry. "We always do the nativity!" he yelled. "I got dressed as Jesus specially." He poked his pants.

"You can do it," Jill retorted. "But I think I'd just like to watch."

"Oh Jill!" Belinda snivelled. "I think you'd be smashing as Mary."

At this, my aunt gave a loud guffaw. "Jill's the Virgin Mary?" she roared. "And I'm blooming Santa Claus."

Jill went bright pink as the whole table fell silent.

"Who's the lucky man who gets to play Joseph?" Aunt Claudia continued.

After a brief pause, Ruby's cousin Henry put his hand up. He turned crimson as Aunt Claudia nudged Jill and said, "Ha!"

Jill got up and stormed out of the room, muttering something about needing the toilet.

I exchanged a grimace with Ruby and tried to change the subject. "Does anybody want my whistle?"

Ruby's relatives looked up and smiled but nobody took me up on my offer.

Stanley turned to Ruby's aunt and uncle. "How's Hector getting on in China?"

Nigel and Fiona beamed as they started to talk about their eldest son who was halfway through an expedition in Asia.

Aunt Claudia kept her nose out of this conversation and I breathed a sigh of relief, hoping she had finally gained some self-awareness. However, it transpired she was simply waiting for my sister to come back in. "Are you dating anybody?" she asked, the moment Jill sat back down.

Jill took a deep breath. "No. Violet, can you pass the potatoes, please?"

"Simple carbohydrates," my aunt said with a tut. "Deadly killers."

I shot her an angry scowl before blowing on my whistle. "Let's take a few moments to remember the true meaning of Christmas," I said loudly. "For God so loved the world that he came into our mess to give us the gift of life."

"Jesus is better than Santa Claus," Oscar added, giving my aunt a pointed look.

Within seconds, almost everyone was talking about the wonders of God's grace and the beauty of his plan to come as a helpless baby. The conversation achieved my main aim which was to shut Aunt Claudia up. Unfortunately, it also irritated Jill in the process. I saw her looking uncomfortable as Ruby's grandfather asked whether she attended church.

"No I don't," she replied stiffly. She cocked her head at me. "My sister does. You can talk to her about it."

Pops nodded and turned back to his food.

I forced down a few more mouthfuls of lentil pie before spreading the rest round my plate and covering it with my napkin.

Across the table, I saw Belinda looking upset as Aunt Claudia said to Jill, "This dish makes me miss the pies your mother used to make."

"My mother never cooked," Jill muttered.

"Exactly. Now, where's that wretched dog? She can eat my lentils."

"HE not she!" Oscar yelled. "How would you like it if I said you were a man?"

Aunt Claudia looked across at him and frowned.

Before she could say anything, I shouted out, "If Jill doesn't want to be Mary, I'll do it!"

Jill shot me a grateful smile. "Yeah, you do it, Livi."

"Ooh! That means you have to kiss Henry!" Oscar squealed.

I looked at Ruby's cousin in horror. He was as red as his hair.

"You don't have to kiss anybody," Stanley assured me.

"Unless you want to," Violet added.

"I don't want to!" I spluttered.

"Pass Livi a script," Belinda said to her husband. "She can learn her lines while she eats."

I felt myself blushing as a script was passed round the table. I hoped Jill appreciated I was only doing this to spare her. After tucking the script under my plate, I turned casually to Violet. "By the way, did Ruby tell you about our meetings?"

I'd expected Violet to approve of our pursuit of God but she just gave me a long look before asking, "Do you do Bible studies?"

Her question had the ring of someone who was trying to catch me out. I knew because it hadn't been long since I had asked Annie the same thing.

I shrugged. "Why?"

Violet's reply was rather more blunt than mine would have been. "So you don't fall into sin."

"What?" I stared at her. "We're just trying to love God more!"

"Ruby's been a lot more jolly recently."

"And that's a bad thing?"

"Being frivolous is a sin. It's one step away from irreverence."

"Excuse me?"

"The Bible warns us to be sober-minded."

"But not *miserable,"* I retorted. "God isn't miserable!"

"You need to be balanced." Violet sniffed. "And the only way to stay balanced is to stick to what the Bible says."

"We *are* sticking to what the Bible says. We're living by the Spirit. As it says in Galatians, *'Since we live by the Spirit, let us keep in step with the Spirit.'"* I grinned. I had read that verse that very morning and felt mighty proud of myself for remembering it.

"Just don't get carried away," Violet warned.

"I thought you'd be pleased," I muttered.

As Violet gave a disapproving shrug and turned back to her food, I started to feel unsettled. What if God wasn't so impressed with our pursuit of him after all? What if we had fallen off the teeny tiny tightrope of 'perfect balance' and somehow slid into error? Sharon had said that falling into error was not as dangerous as falling out of love, but what if she was wrong? What if that was precisely the sort of misguided statement someone would make if they were already too far gone? Was God rolling his eyes at our hopes for revival? Did he groan every time we mistook a random thought for a sign from Heaven? Did he think we were spending too much time together? Had he grown bored of our company by now?

I frowned. *Is the danger of being a little frivolous really so bad?* "God loves us," I said. "And he's not afraid of us getting it wrong. If we're being too *'frivolous'* then I'm sure he'll help us."

Violet barely looked up. "It's still a sin."

"It's not that bad," I snapped. "It's not like murder."

"Sin is sin," she sang.

I rolled my eyes and resolved not to speak to her for the rest of the meal.

We had made it to dessert when Aunt Claudia announced, "I'm going to have my teeth done. I want a whole new set of dentures."

Nobody said anything.

"Well, why not?" she demanded, although no one had challenged her. "I've got enough money for it and you can't take it with you."

Ruby's relatives nodded politely and Stanley said, "That's true."

"You can't take your teeth either," I said under my breath.

Aunt Claudia turned and guffawed. "Good one, Livi!"

I shrugged and poked my apple crumble. "Well, you can't. People ought to think about these things. Life goes really fast and then—" I blew my whistle. "Game over!"

Jill glared at me. "Put that whistle down, Livi!"

I frowned. Once again, I had intended to silence Aunt Claudia but had ended up annoying Jill instead.

My aunt kept watching me. "Have you got a job lined up yet for when you finish your course?"

I shook my head.

"The invitation is still there if you want to come and work on my farm."

"I'll bear that in mind."

"Well, be quick about it," she retorted. "I won't wait forever." She turned her attention to Ruby. "That goes for you too, Ruby. I have a whole field of sheep that won't shear themselves."

Ruby went pink. "Thanks."

"And, of course, I take them to be slaughtered." Aunt Claudia shot Ruby's grandmother a snide glance. "I have a box across the street if anybody wants any."

I cleared my throat. "Actually, I can tell you now that I won't want to work on your farm. I'm going to live for Jesus."

I braced for her reply but she just carried on as though I hadn't spoken. "People underestimate the importance of good quality meat."

"It looks like everyone's finished eating," Stanley said loudly, rising from his seat. "Shall we go through to the living room?"

"It's time for the nativity!" Oscar screeched. He whipped an old blue shawl off the sideboard. "Wrap me up in this, Nooni!"

Ruby's grandmother dressed Oscar in the shawl as the rest of the family shuffled through to the lounge.

Belinda took on the role of director, telling the performers where to stand as she ushered everyone else onto the sofa. "Livi and Henry, you need to start from the hallway riding on the donkey." She handed us a purple hobby horse. "Stanley, come and be the shepherd. You need a tea towel for your head..."

As Henry and I made our way to the hallway, Violet came running in with a pile of paintings. "Don't start yet!" she yelled as she began pinning them to the wall.

I tried to hide my confusion as I gazed at the one nearest me. It looked like she had fallen asleep in a bucket of paint and rolled across the page.

"Ready!" Violet exclaimed. She pinned up the last of her paintings before plonking a lampshade on her head and taking her position as the *'Narrating bright star.'* Then she cleared her throat and addressed the audience, *"In a tiny little town in the middle of the earth, the Saviour of the world was about to be birthed."*

I peered round the door to see what was happening.

"Not yet, Livi!" Violet scolded.

I blushed and ducked back out of the way.

"Mary and Joseph arrived on a donkey; soon Mary began to feel a little wonky." Violet paused before yelling, "Now, Livi!"

Henry and I waddled into the room, the hobby horse held uncomfortably between us.

I hadn't managed to learn my lines over dinner and turned to the script in my hand. *"My darling Joe,"* I read. *"You ought to know... I'm in quite a bit of pain. I'm not being funny but the baby is coming. And I don't want to give birth in a drain..."*

Ruby arose to play her piccolo as Henry led me round the room asking various family members if they had somewhere we could stay. While the rest of the audience responded with playful shakes of the head, Aunt Claudia noisily unwrapped a toffee.

Henry led me back to the middle of the room where Violet announced, *"And so baby Jesus was born in a stable; to a poor peasant girl and a lad who made tables..."*

Oscar ran through my legs and splattered onto the floor, writhing around in Belinda's blue shawl. I was so startled that I fell over and Henry had to catch me. I expect it would have been a rather tender moment had Aunt Claudia not given a loud belch on the front row.

The drama concluded with Stanley the shepherd arriving with Ruby who wore a white swimming cap covered in cotton wool as his sheep. *"The angel was right; the Saviour is here! Oh happy night! This calls for a beer!"*

"Baa," said Ruby. She paused before adding another one for the line that should have been mine. *"Baa."*

"Fantastic!" Belinda arose and gave us a standing ovation.

"Wait!" Violet darted across the room and plonked a Christmas cracker hat on Dennis' head. "Don't forget the wise man."

Dennis, who had been fast asleep, awoke with a jolt and started barking.

Aunt Claudia frowned and gave him a kick as he darted past her.

The rest of the family applauded, giving Oscar an extra clap as he pulled off his shawl and bowed many times in his underwear.

"Well, that was marvellous," Nooni said, rising to her feet.

"Who wants a hot drink?" asked Stanley.

"Not yet!" Violet exclaimed, before anybody could go too far. "It's time for my presentation." She grinned at me. "Livi asked for it specially."

I blushed and avoided Jill's incredulous stare.

The Rico family sat back down and gazed at Violet.

"The theme of these landscapes is *'My Travels through Life,'*" Violet explained as she pulled her biggest painting off the wall. "This one's all about my birth and my earliest memories." She swept a hand across the painting. "This line might look like blood but it's meant to be red flowers from the field outside my primary school."

I screwed up my nose as Violet pulled several more pictures off the wall, each with convoluted titles depicting her schooldays, her childhood memories and the significant moments of her life to date. I turned to see what Jill made of it but she was hardly paying attention and just sat picking her fingernails.

"This one is called *'My Wedding will be Pretty,'*" Violet continued, holding up a painting of what looked like a polar bear walking down a yellow path towards a gorilla in a top hat.

"You did this all with your nose?" Pops asked carefully.

"Well, I smudged that bit with my chin because I slipped." She pointed to the polar bear's extra leg.

Her relatives made encouraging noises.

"Very clever, darling!" Belinda cooed.

Violet nodded smugly and held up another one. "This is *'I Want at Least Three Children.'*"

I tipped my head to one side. Her future children seemed mightily deformed, almost like crabs walking on hind legs.

Oscar took it from her and turned it upside down. He grinned at the rest of us before asking, "Auntie Jill, how many children will *you* have when you grow up?"

Jill looked up in alarm but said nothing.

Violet glared at her brother for interrupting her presentation and drew our attention to a painting smeared with giant blue painted tears. "I called this one *'Violet's Valley of Regrets.'* Not that I really have any regrets... Other than never learning piano. But maybe when I'm *your* age." Although she was indicating the older generation, she seemed to look straight at Jill when she said this.

My sister frowned and looked away.

Violet was midway through an explanation of a painting entitled *'When I'm Old and Grey in the Wilderness of Weeping'* when Aunt Claudia gave a loud groan. "Jill, we need to go home."

Jill shot her a sharp look. "What?"

"My stomach is killing me. It's that wretched lentil pie. It won't leave me alone."

I saw Belinda exchange a glance with Stanley. "Would you like a herbal tea?" she whispered.

"No," Aunt Claudia retorted. "I'm going to need something stronger than that." She got up and marched out of the room. A few seconds later, she called from the hallway, "Come on Jill! Livi! I've got fireworks inside me."

Jill went red as she shot the guests an awkward smile and quickly left the room.

I said goodbye to Ruby and turned to thank her parents.

"Thanks for coming, Livi," Belinda said as she came over to hug me. "It was lovely to meet your aunt." Her voice shook slightly as she said this.

I gave her a sympathetic smile. "Thanks for having us. Ignore my aunt— the lentil pie was really nice."

"Oh, thank you!" Belinda took my hand in hers. "I'll make it for you and Jill again some time."

I gulped. "Okay." I gave the rest of the guests a wave before hurrying out of the house and across the street.

Aunt Claudia had already thrown up on our doormat.

"Not to worry," said my sister. "The rain will wash it away."

Our aunt grunted. "It's at times like this that I wish you weren't single. A man would mop that up no problem."

Jill pursed her lips and pushed open the front door.

"Well, I think I need an early night," Aunt Claudia said as she flung her coat into my arms.

After a pause, Jill said, "Go on then."

Aunt Claudia wrinkled up her nose and headed for the stairs. On her way, I handed her one of Annie's homemade Christmas cards and told her I hoped she would feel better in the morning. She sucked in her teeth and told Jill not to wake her until after six.

"I'll probably let you sleep in," my sister replied.

Aunt Claudia nodded and stomped away.

I looked at my sister and smirked. She rolled her eyes.

I was about to go up to my room and read when Jill asked if I wanted some Christmas pudding. I almost said no, preferring to eat a cake made of my own hair than try Aunt Claudia's Christmas pudding. But something about the look in Jill's eyes made me want to stay with her a little longer.

"Er... I'll have a tiny bit," I said, following her into the kitchen.

Jill nodded absently and hauled the pudding out of its bag.

I cringed as she filled up a whole bowl. "Thanks..."

Jill scooped herself a portion and pulled out a chair. We ate in silence for several minutes. The whole house was still apart from the ticking of the clock and the distant sound of Aunt Claudia snoring in the spare room.

I tried to think of a light-hearted conversation starter. "If you could be any animal for a whole day, what would you be?"

Jill raised her eyebrows. "I don't know. Probably a dog."

I laughed in surprise. "A dog? What for?"

She shrugged. "They get to sit around on the sofa all day."

"You can do that now!" I exclaimed. "I was thinking of something exciting like a bird or a koala bear." Still, it was better than Annie's answer. She'd said she would want to be a 'mince.'[48]

"Oh!" Jill chuckled before falling silent. "I don't know... Maybe one of Aunt Claudia's cats." She sneered as a couple of them padded into the kitchen. "Then I could pee in her shoes."

We exchanged a grin as Aunt Claudia's snoring grew louder.

Halfway through her Christmas pudding, Jill picked a magazine up from the work surface and flicked through it.

I tried to think of another question before she started reading. "If you could do anything with your life and you knew you wouldn't fail, what would you do?"

Jill frowned and put the magazine down. "I don't know. I think it's a bit late for that."

"What do you mean?"

"I've already failed."

I stared at her. "No you haven't!"

Jill reached for a piece of kitchen paper and blew her nose. "Course I have."

"You've got your whole life ahead of you!" I exclaimed. "You're only..." I quickly did the maths. "Thirty three?"

"Thirty four."

"Exactly! It's never too late to make something of your life."

Her voice wobbled as she said, "I can't change the past."

"Well, forget about the past. You live in the present."

"No I don't." She reached for more kitchen paper. "The past is my present every single day."

I frowned. "Are you alright?"

---

[48] "Because I've eaten them loads of times but I've never seen one in the wild."

She forced a smile and looked away. "You've got to follow your heart, Livi. I know I don't understand why you wanted to do that animal course but I really admire you going after your dreams."

I wondered if she had drunk too much wine at the Ricos'. "Thanks," I said.

"Follow your heart," she repeated. "There are lots of things I'd have done differently and it's too late for me now."

I leant closer to her. "Like what?"

She shook her head. "I'd have made better choices when I was your age, for a start. I wouldn't have... You know..."

"Wouldn't have what?"

She rubbed a hand across her head. "I always think about it at Christmas."

"Think about what?"

"What I did." Tears rolled down her cheeks as she grabbed several more reams of kitchen paper. "It was around this time of year."

"When Mum died?" I clarified.

She shook her head again. "I can't believe Oscar asked about children..."

I was about to ask what on earth she was talking about when it hit me. She was alluding to the fact that she'd had an abortion when she was a teenager. She had told me in not altogether pleasant circumstances a few years ago and neither of us had dared to mention it since. I bit my lip, not wanting to do or say anything that might upset her further.

She stared straight ahead for ages. Eventually she muttered, "People say it's alright but I don't know. I've never been able to forgive myself. A life's a life, isn't it?"

I went to say something but thought better of it.

Jill turned and rolled her eyes. "You're going to tell me murder is the worst sin, aren't you?"

I blushed. What was I meant to say to that? I was reminded of my conversation with Violet over dinner. She had made me feel like I was treading a dangerous line in my pursuit for more of God. I had retorted that it wasn't as bad as murder. Was there anything that was even worse? My mind raced for an answer. I didn't want to validate Jill's belief that God could never accept her. Yet I wasn't sure I could get away with a lengthy gospel presentation.

"King David was a murderer," I stammered. "And Moses and Paul..."

I stopped as Jill frowned. Comparing her with biblical heroes didn't appear to be helping.

I bit my lip as Violet's words rang in my ears. *'You need to be balanced.'* How could I give Jill a *balanced* view?

I was about to reply that *'all sin is sin,'* when it struck me that God had done greater things through wild men like David and Moses and Paul than he had through multitudes of reasonable, balanced men. It wasn't their ability to live a balanced life which caused God to use them. It was their faith and hunger for him. In fact, very few heroes of the Bible could accurately be labelled *'balanced.'* To be perfectly balanced, after all, means walking in a straight line and never going anywhere new. Most churches are full of balanced people and perhaps that is the problem. Balanced people don't usually believe in the impossible. For example, Joey and the others scorned the idea of revival because they didn't believe it could happen in our lifetime; Eddie and Summer didn't teach us about demons because they didn't believe we could face them; and Violet didn't press in for more of God because she didn't believe there was enough grace for her to get it wrong. If being *'balanced'* meant being scared to take God at his word, then I wasn't sure it was all that holy after all.

I took a deep breath and stared hard at my sister. Jill had done many wrong things in her life, and this one act in particular haunted her, but none of it was enough to stop her from entering into God's Kingdom. Nor did it disqualify her from being someone who God could use as mightily as King David. The only thing that kept her from knowing Christ's saving love was a heart that refused to believe. "I don't think murder is the worst sin," I told her. "I think it's unbelief."

Jill's eyes flickered slightly. Then she turned back to her magazine. "Oh."

~ 22 ~

For such a time as this

Jill's depressing confession haunted me for the rest of the Christmas holidays. I knew I had no idea how she felt and no right to advise her as though I did but I desperately wanted to tell her that there was enough forgiveness and love in Jesus to cover every mistake. As much as I prayed, there never seemed to be an appropriate opportunity to raise the issue again. At any rate, I feared my words would be too simple and too shallow to truly reach her. I longed to talk to Ruby about it so that I could have some advice on what to do but I had to keep quiet. I could hardly ask Jill, *'Can I tell Ruby your secret?'*

The holidays felt even drearier due to Aunt Claudia's extended stay and I avoided her as much as possible by pretending to do homework at Ruby's. Of course, this then meant dealing with Violet and her hideous artwork.

"Would you like me to paint you?" Violet asked one evening.

"Sure," I replied, thinking it would be rather fascinating to have a portrait of myself done by somebody's nose.

Without warning, Violet came towards me and slapped a handful of red paint on my face. "It's my new project," she said when I screamed. *"Life Painting."*

After checking that Aunt Claudia would be gone in time, Belinda issued me and Jill with an invitation to spend New Year's Eve at theirs. Jill replied that she wanted a quiet night in so I went alone and spent most of the evening playing cards with Ruby and dodging Violet who was wandering round with a tin of paint.

As the end of the night approached, Ruby and I snuck up to her room to hang out. Annie, Kevin and Amanda had all gone away for Christmas so we had suspended our outpouring meetings until the start of the new term. I had missed them during those cold dark evenings although, given Aunt Claudia's tendency to waltz into rooms uninvited,[49] it had probably been for the best.

"Have you made any New Year's resolutions?" Ruby asked as she leant against her bed.

"I've been thinking about it," I said.[50] "But I haven't come up with anything... except for healing Janine."

Ruby inhaled sharply. She went to say something and then thought better of it.

"I can't understand why she isn't healed yet," I continued glumly.

Ruby sighed. "I don't know. I guess it's all a bit comp—"

"Don't!" I cried. "Don't say it."

She looked a little taken aback. "Don't say what?"

"Don't say 'complicated.'" I felt myself getting choked up as I shook my head. "Let's just pray for her— one last time before the New Year."

Ruby nodded and closed her eyes. "Dear God, you are good. Please help us to pray..."

I bit my lip before muttering, "In the name of Jesus, I command all cancer to leave Janine..." I wanted to say more. I wanted to launch into a passionate outpouring of faith-filled proclamations as I petitioned for full and immediate healing but we'd been praying for so many days that it seemed there were no words left. I swallowed hard before turning to Ruby. "What about you?"

"What about me?"

"Have you made any New Year's resolutions?"

"Oh. Not really. Except for getting closer to God."

"That's good."

She smiled. "Yeah."

"How do we do it?"

"I don't know! I suppose we just keep pressing in, like in our meetings."

"I guess that's all we can do."

We talked about it for a while longer before playing a few more rounds of cards. Then suddenly it was midnight so we ran downstairs to sing in the New Year with the rest of the Rico family.

---

[49] At one point, she had trundled into my bedroom in the middle of the night in search of a working light bulb.

[50] It had been on my mind ever since I saw Aunt Claudia's suggestions for Jill stuck to the fridge: '1. Get boyfriend. 2. Keep boyfriend. 3. Learn to cook.'

I squeezed my eyes shut as I locked arms with Ruby and Belinda and, instead of singing, I prayed my first prayer of the year. *Lord, whatever happens with Janine or anybody else, help me get closer to you this year.*

It didn't occur to me that anything might happen any time soon. That very night, however, God met me unexpectedly as I lay wide awake in my bed. The hours were ticking by and morning was dawning but my mind was racing as I went over all the homework that lay incomplete on my floor.

All of a sudden, I saw what appeared to be fireworks falling across a night sky. Far above, was a castle hidden in the clouds. I saw the scene in my head, the same way I usually received pictures from God, but this time it was far more vivid. As the fireworks fell, it was as though my vision was growing sharper and sharper and I felt as though I was being plunged deep into a very real landscape. Before I could decide whether it meant anything, a great presence fell upon me and I realised I couldn't move. I tried to turn my head or even wiggle a finger but my whole body was locked into position, as though pinned to the bed. Then I noticed I couldn't open my eyes either, nor could I speak. Far from being alarmed, the presence that surrounded me was so peaceful that I simply lay there in wonder. As the fireworks continued falling, I felt myself being yanked into the night sky, almost as though someone had reached down and pulled me out of my bed. My whole body felt as though it was whooshing up through the sky and a holy fear overwhelmed me as I thought, *I'm going to Heaven!* Fear was replaced by ecstasy and I tried to call out but I still couldn't move and my mouth wouldn't open. Instead, I cried with my spirit, *Jesus! Jesus! Jesus!* I was certain I would see him face to face at any moment.

Then, as quickly as it had begun, it ended. I opened my eyes and sat up, wriggling my fingers and gawping into the darkness. "What was that about?"

I received no reply and just sunk back against my pillows, breathing heavily. Sharon was right. There was more; so much more. I still had no idea what any of it was but I was certain I had just glimpsed it.

I awoke the next morning hungrier than ever for the presence of God. Since visiting Wales, I had done my best to let God out of the box that I'd kept him in. But it seemed he was bigger still. The more I sought to know him, the more I discovered there was to find.

I lay in bed and looked round my room, blinking at my Western walls with its twenty first century décor, British books and contemporary clothing. I realised, for perhaps the first time, that *God is not an English gentleman.*

"You're bigger than me," I whispered as I pummelled my fists into my duvet. "Open my eyes. Help me to see..."

What struck me more than anything was that I hadn't asked for this sudden encounter. Of course, I had been begging and pleading for more of God for months. But, on that particular night, Ruby and I hadn't prayed for very long or done anything holy. In fact, I had spent quite some time being rude about Aunt Claudia who had finally left that afternoon.

I jumped out of bed and started to pace my room. "More, God... More of you..." I remembered one of the songs we had sung in Wales and recited it under my breath, *"More of you, less of me. Restore me to the person you always meant me to be."*

I stopped for a moment as I thought about this. I wondered whether God had some divine blueprint of how he'd intended my life to pan out and who I could be if I gave him full access. Then, as I heard my sister bustling about downstairs, another thought occurred to me: *Who was Jill meant to be?* I realised that I had probably never known the real Jill. For as long as I had been alive, my sister had lived under the shadow of her past. Whoever she had been before that point, and whoever she could have been now, was buried deep in a sea of regret.

I left my room and padded down the stairs, entering the kitchen with a leap as I sang, "Happy New Year!"

Jill shot me half a glance and muttered, "You too."

I paused and wondered whether to tell her about my encounter. "I had an amazing experience last night..." I began.

Jill just grunted. "I dreamt I was being eaten by a shark." She turned her back on me and started hunting in the cupboard for teabags.

~*~

Ruby and I arrived at college the next day with very little enthusiasm for the new term. A new lesson called *'Hooves and*

Hair' had been added to our timetable bringing several more dreary books to our reading list.

We tried to look interested as Maria, Ellen and Laura raved about a recent television programme about being kind to insects but I think they realised we weren't being genuine after Ruby absentmindedly squashed an earwig.

"Did you have a nice Christmas?" I asked during the silence that followed.

They nodded but didn't say anything.

I forced a smile and wondered whether to ask why the Christmas sleepover Ellen had promised had never materialised. I thought better of it after I peeked on FriendWeb on Ruby's phone and realised from Ellen's profile picture that the three of them had done it without us.

I was pretty resigned to the fact that none of them wanted to be our friends so was rather surprised when Laura came to find us at break. "I think I might join your club," she said.

"What club?"

"You said you had a club where you talk about the meaning of life?"

"Oh! That!"

She blinked at me. "Well, can I?"

I exchanged a quick glance with Ruby. "That club never took off," I admitted. "But we have another club, if you're interested?"

"What's that one about?"

I stopped and wondered how to best sum up The Fire Brigade. "It's for people who are hungry for God... And we..." I looked at Ruby for help.

"We love God and we love each other," she filled in.

I gave an impressed nod. "Ooh, that should be our motto!"

Ruby grinned. "I hoped you'd say that."

I glanced back at Laura. She was looking curious.

"Sounds interesting," she said. "Although I don't really know much about God."

I thought back to my experience on New Year's morning. "Me neither," I confessed. When both Laura and Ruby looked at me in surprise, I added, "I mean I know *some* stuff about God. But he's massive. We can always discover more."

"Oh right!" Laura smiled. "When do you meet?"

"Pretty much every night."

"Every night?"

"But you can come as much or as little as you want."

"Oh."

I wrote down my address and gave it to her. "Half seven tonight. We'll probably pray and maybe sing some songs. You can just watch if you don't feel ready to join in."

"And feel free to ask if you have any questions," Ruby added.

Laura sucked her thumb. "Thanks. I'll think about it."

I assumed that, like before, when Laura said she would *'think about it'* she would end up finding an excuse not to come. This time, however, it didn't bother me. I knew it wasn't about numbers or building a huge club. The five of us were having an amazing time pressing in together and if God wanted to add to us then he could do it without our help. I'd been so sure that Laura wouldn't come that I forgot we had even invited her. The five of us were in the middle of praying through the Lord's Prayer when there was a knock on the front door.

The others stopped praying and looked at me.

"Must be someone for Jill," I said, waving at them to carry on.

Ruby peered out of my window. "It's Laura!"

I jumped up in shock. "Laura?"

Annie, Amanda and Kevin looked at one another. "Laura?"

"She's a friend from college," I explained as I sprinted out of my room.

Jill had beat me to the door. I heard her asking Laura what she wanted.

"It's alright!" I said as I galloped down the stairs. "She's my friend. Hi Laura!"

Laura gave a shy smile as Jill stepped back and let her enter. "Hi Livi."

"Come on up! We've just started."

Jill frowned as Laura began to follow me up the stairs. *"Shoes!"* she mouthed behind Laura's back.

"Oh, Laura, can you take your shoes off please?" I said.

Laura blushed and kicked off her boots.

My sister gave a terse smile and wandered into the living room. A few seconds later, I heard her switch the television on.

I grinned at Laura and led the way up the stairs. "It's great that you've come!" I said.

"I just want to watch," she whispered. "Until I know what I think."

"Of course! No problem."

It seemed Ruby had filled Annie, Kevin and Amanda in on who Laura was. The three of them gawped at her as she came into my room.

"Do you believe in God?" Amanda blurted out, before Laura even had a chance to sit down.

"Er... I don't know. A bit." Laura looked petrified.

"That's Amanda," I told her. "And that's Kevin and Annie. Everyone, this is Laura. She's just going to watch tonight and see what she thinks about it so nobody ask her any difficult questions."

Laura shot me a thankful smile and sat down on my bed. The others kept grinning at her.

"Pretend Laura isn't here," I told them.

"Well, not completely," Ruby piped up. "Don't ignore her."

"No," I said. "But don't put her on the spot either."

"People are allowed to say hello and things like that."

"Obviously! I just meant don't draw too much attention to her."

Laura looked uncomfortable as the two of us went backwards and forwards.

"Anyway," I said, giving a quick cough. "Where were we?"

"Give us today our daily bread," said Kevin.

"Oh yeah..."

The five of us did our best not to be put off by Laura's presence as we carried on with our prayer.

"Lord, feed us with food from earth and food from Heaven," Annie cried.

"We need fresh bread..." continued Ruby.

"Not yesterday's crumbs," I added.

Recently, we had started to build up our stamina by praying as much as we could and then a bit more. The aim was to pray through to the end of the Lord's Prayer and then keep going. However, it wasn't long before I heard the *'Gossip Town'* theme tune ringing out from downstairs. I stopped praying and sunk to the floor. I couldn't concentrate on enjoying God when I knew Jill was downstairs feeling so sad.

After a moment, Ruby sat down beside me. "You look worried," she whispered. "What's wrong?"

I turned to face her. "My sister." I sighed.

Ruby raised her eyebrows. "What about her?"

The others stopped praying to listen.

I shifted as they stared at me. "She just really needs God. She's depressed because of..." I paused. "Because of something that happened years ago."

"What was it?" Amanda was wide-eyed.

I felt myself blushing as I wondered what to say.

"You don't need to tell us," said Ruby. "God knows."

I nodded. "Thanks."

Ruby took my hand and closed her eyes. A tear trickled down my cheek as she started to pray. "Dear Lord, we love Jill so much but not as much as you do. Only you can fill her deepest needs and heal the pain in her heart. Please help her..."

It was such a beautiful prayer that I immediately felt hope awaken inside me.

"Yeah, Jesus!" Annie exclaimed. "Save Jill! Save Jill!"

As the others picked up her chant, a holy boldness overtook me and I got to my feet. Years ago, I'd had high hopes that Jill would be radically saved. But, as time had gone by, her walls had seemed ever impenetrable as my efforts were greeted with contempt. It had become the norm to play down what God had done in my life or to add an apologetic smile onto the end of my stories so as not to offend. I entertained the hope that she would be saved *'one day in the distant future'* but I'd stopped believing that it might happen any time soon.

But why not now? Why not suddenly? Why not today?

"Lord, come and reveal yourself to Jill!" I begged.

Laura wore a bemused expression as the rest of us marched round my room, petitioning God for breakthrough.

"What is the key to Jill's heart?" I prayed. "Show us what to do. I hate seeing her so sad... I know you do too..."

I found myself growing angry as I realised this wasn't a battle against Jill. It was a battle against the liar, the thief, the murderer, the enemy who had bound her up for so many years and convinced her that she was unworthy of God's love. I was suddenly aware of the authority I had as her sister to break those chains and usher the Kingdom of God into our household.

After a while, I felt God whisper, *Silence depression.*

I paused. Would that count as spiritual warfare? I was about to ask Ruby but then I reconsidered. Jill was my sister. I was going to fight for her and I didn't care what Eddie and Summer would think. Besides, Sharon had said God was my highest authority. If he was telling me to fight then I had every right to do it. I took a deep breath before announcing, "God says we need to silence depression."

Annie, Amanda and Kevin nodded.

Ruby looked a little stunned. She seemed to be weighing things up in her head. "Okay... Let's do what God says."

I took a deep breath before muttering, "Depression, I silence you in the name of Jesus." I had no idea if this was what God meant. I looked at the others. "Should we tell depression to *leave*, not just be silent?"

"We should do exactly what God says," Ruby said before anybody else could answer. "Maybe Jill isn't ready for it to leave completely yet... Or maybe she needs Jesus first so that it won't come back."

"Are you saying depression is a demon?" Annie piped up.

Kevin and Amanda suddenly cottoned on to the fact that we were partaking in spiritual warfare and looked at me in alarm.

"I don't know what Eddie and Summer are so worried about," I said. "If God tells us to do something then surely we can do it."

"But that's why we must *only* do what God says," Ruby insisted. "And not add to his words."

I nodded. "Well, I felt God tell me to silence depression. So that's what I'm going to do." I cleared my throat and started again. "Depression, I silence you in the name of Jesus. I command you to be quiet and not speak to my sister..."

After a pause, the others joined in.

"Depression be silenced!"

"Depression be still!"

"Save Jill! Save Jill!"

I grew in confidence as we marched round the room praying at the tops of our voices. At one point, it felt as though our prayers were cutting through the atmosphere like lasers and I could hardly contain the feeling of expectation that wrapped itself round my heart. Laura continued watching us from my bed but I forced myself not to wonder what she was thinking.

When we ran out of words, we picked up Annie's chant, "Save Jill! Save Jill! Save Jill!"

Our prayers reached quite a crescendo and it struck me that I could no longer hear the television. I signalled for everyone to be quiet. I was afraid that Jill had heard us chanting her name and would come up to ask what we were playing at.

Everyone stopped and looked at me.

After a pause, I heard the sound of a news report downstairs and breathed a sigh of relief.

"It's fine," I whispered. "She's just watching the news."

The others grinned and carried on praying.

Before I joined them, I stopped to wonder what the headlines might be that evening. I don't mean the headlines Jill was listening to— I was pretty sure *they* would be all about wars and rumours of wars and money and politics and sport with a sprinkling of celebrity gossip. No, I wanted to know what headlines were making the news in Heaven.

The world doesn't know it yet... An army is rising... For such a time as this.

~ 23 ~

The King's Arms

Laura had left our meeting a little abruptly so Ruby and I didn't have the chance to ask her what she'd made of it. I was concerned that she may have found our warfare for Jill disturbing and wondered whether I needed to prepare a defence in case she started spreading rumours. But it turned out she had loved every minute of it. She ran over to me and Ruby the moment we got off the bus.

"Last night was amazing!" she exclaimed. "I was so excited that I couldn't sleep."

I exchanged an astonished glance with Ruby.

Laura kept grinning. "You seemed to really know God. I'd love to have faith like that."

I was about to scrape my jaw off the ground when Maria and Ellen came trotting over. "Can we join your club?" they sang.

I gripped Ruby's arm. "What?"

"Laura told us about it," Maria said, giving us perhaps her first ever genuine smile.

"It sounds fun," Ellen added.

They kept staring at us.

"Please let them join," said Laura.

"Of course you can join!" I said in disbelief. "If you're sure you want to..." As they continued to stare, I felt I needed to clarify. "We're Christians. We follow Jesus... We pray and sing and try to heal the sick and sometimes cast out demons..."

They nodded in excitement.

Before I could say anything else, Ruby pinched me on the arm.

"Ow!" I looked at her.

"Just checking we weren't dreaming," she whispered.

I rolled my eyes before turning back to the others. "We didn't think you were interested in Christianity."

"We didn't think you liked us," added Ruby.

"That's because we never knew being a Christian could be fun," Laura explained.

"We thought you were just weird," said Maria.

"And boring," said Ellen.

"And lazy," said all three.

"So... You don't think we're weird or boring?" I asked.

"Or lazy?" mumbled Ruby.

They shook their heads.

"Well, good... Welcome to our club."

I exchanged another baffled glance with Ruby as the three of them beamed and led the way to our first lesson.

"What if they change their minds when they come and realise we *are* weird and boring after all?" I whispered.

Ruby shrugged. "I guess we wouldn't have lost anything."

I laughed. "At least they no longer think we're lazy."

We wandered into the Biology lab where Sharon Sheppard was lining up pig parts on her table. I wanted to run up to her and tell her what had happened but, instead, I followed Maria, Ellen and Laura to their desk.

"Sit here, Livi!" Laura whispered, patting the seat beside her. "I've got loads of questions to ask you."

I nodded dumbly and sat down.

Opposite us, Ruby looked rather chuffed as Maria and Ellen pulled her into a seat between them.

The lesson got underway but Laura, Maria and Ellen made no effort to do any work. The three of them bombarded me and Ruby with question after question about religion and the universe and whether church was boring. Sharon came by at one point, looking as though she was about to scold us for not doing any work. But, just as she reached our table, Ellen asked, "Does everybody go to Heaven?" so Sharon gave me a quick wink and kept walking.

Ruby and I did our best to answer their questions, presenting the gospel in the clearest way we knew: "God loves us and created us to know him. We've all messed up and broken our relationship with him. Jesus came to restore all things by taking the punishment for our sins. If we turn back to him, we can have eternal life, beginning now, and find out who we were truly meant to be."

They nodded along and Laura even asked, "So what do we need to do?"

"You just tell God that you want him," I said. "And that you're sorry for the things you've done wrong."

"And accept Jesus into your heart," added Ruby.

Laura took a deep breath. "Oh. I'll have to think about that."

I resisted the urge to implore her to think about it quickly. I realised God wanted a heart response, not one manipulated by me pressuring her. He knew what was going on inside her and could lead her in his own timing.

"Tell us about demons," Maria said suddenly. She wore a slight grin.

I blushed and looked up.

Sharon was staring straight at me.

"I can't tell you just yet," I replied. "They're not a game. You'd need to learn how to listen to God first. Plus, you can only defeat them if you've got Jesus inside you." I checked to see whether this was the right answer but Sharon had gone back to pretending not to listen.

"Oh." Maria looked disappointed.

My heart sunk as she and Ellen turned to their work. Perhaps they hadn't been interested in Jesus after all.

"There are cooler things than demons though," Ruby piped up.

Maria looked at her. "Like what?"

"Like angels, for a start."

Ellen's eyes widened. "Have you ever seen one?"

The three of them gawped at Ruby as she said, "I think I heard some singing once."

Ellen turned to me. "How about you?"

I shook my head. I'd recently spent twenty minutes talking to a random man on the bus after mistaking him for an angel. I'd realised my error after he offered me a cigarette.

"But, even cooler than angels," Ruby went on, "is knowing the Creator of the universe."

Maria looked uncertain. "I knew some Christians at high school who were really judgemental. They always made me feel like God was angry with everyone."

I took a deep breath. "Well, on behalf of those Christians, we're sorry."

Ruby nodded. "Yeah, we're sorry."

Maria laughed. "It's not *your* fault!"

"But I've done it too," I confessed. "I don't always represent God well. That's why you need to discover him for yourself."

She still didn't look convinced. "I'm a spiritual person," she explained. "I sometimes sense stuff about, if you know what I mean?" She paused. "I don't know about *God* or *Jesus* but I think there are friendly spirits around." She nudged Ellen. "Like the one that sometimes knocks on my wall."

Ellen giggled. "Oh yeah!"

I took a deep breath. "There are only two teams: God's team or the devil's team. Anything spiritual that doesn't come from God isn't good."

Maria bit her lip. "How do you know?"

"The Bible says so."

Ruby spouted a verse she had learnt recently: *"Every spirit that does not acknowledge Jesus is not from God."*

"So you should be careful," I warned.

Maria exchanged an uncomfortable glance with Ellen.

"Isn't the Bible really complicated though?" Laura piped up.

"Some bits," I admitted. "But some bits are really easy. Like the stories about Jesus. If you want an easy place to start, just read about *him.*"

Laura nodded. "Okay. I'll think about it."

I grinned. "Take as long as you need."

Jill beat me to the door again that evening. I heard the surprise in her voice as she asked Maria, Ellen and Laura whether I was expecting them.

"Yes, yes, yes!" I exclaimed as I bounded down the stairs. "Come in everyone!"

Jill looked at me in alarm as the three of them traipsed into the hallway.

"Take your shoes off," I told them.

They did so and followed me up the stairs.

I looked back to give Jill a smile. I saw her counting the pairs of shoes in the hallway but she didn't say anything.

"Just having our usual meeting!" I said cheerily.

Jill frowned and marched back into the living room.

Ruby, Annie, Amanda and Kevin looked like they were trying not to burst as the four of us came into my room. They shuffled onto the floor so that our guests could sit on the bed.

Maria and Ellen perched awkwardly as I introduced them to the others. "And you know Laura," I added, shooting Laura a smile.

"Welcome back, Laura!" Annie cried as Amanda and Kevin nodded.

Laura gave a shy grin and squeezed in beside Maria and Ellen.

"Do you have any questions before we start?" I asked them. "Or would you rather just watch?"

While both Maria and Laura said they would like to watch, Ellen bit her lip and put her hand up.

I turned to her. "Yes?"

"Can you pray?"

"What do you mean?"

She blushed. "I've never heard anyone say a prayer before."

"Oh! Do you want to hear one?"

She nodded.

I looked at Ruby. "What should we pray?"

Ruby smiled at Ellen. "Do you want us to pray for *you?*"

Ellen turned pink. "Oh, not for *me*. I wouldn't know what to do."

"You don't have to do anything!" I said.

"You just sit there, like this." Annie demonstrated sitting still.

Ellen stared at her.

"So, do you want one?" Amanda asked.

"Hmmm... Maybe later."

We ended up talking about prayer for most of the night. Ellen couldn't get her head round the idea that God was able to watch over and listen to every single person all at the same time and kept asking for examples of times we'd prayed and received an answer. She finally agreed to have one of us pray for her so Ruby put her hand on her shoulder as she prayed a short blessing.

"Lord, please show Ellen your love and fill her with peace..."

When Ruby had finished, Ellen looked round at us and grinned. "Wow. My first prayer."

Next, she wanted to hear us sing so we sang a few awkward verses just for her benefit.

Maria and Laura watched in silence and I couldn't quite read their expressions. I was aware the meeting hadn't been as exciting as the one Laura had been to the night before and I felt rather self-conscious as I called the evening to an end.

"Well, I hope you had fun," I mumbled as the eight of us went down the stairs together.

Laura nodded and gave me a quick smile.

"Can I see if my sister wants to come next time?" Maria asked as she located her trainers.[51]

---

[51] Jill had moved everybody's shoes into a heap in the corner.

I looked at her in surprise. "Of course! Bring anyone you want."

Annie squealed. "Really? Because loads of people from The COOL Club want to come but I wasn't sure if they were allowed."

"Of course they're allowed!" I said. "Why wouldn't they be?"

She shrugged. "When Georgina came, she said she got the feeling you didn't really want her here."

I felt a pang of guilt. "That was wrong," I said. "Tell her she can come. Everyone can come."

I hadn't noticed my sister lingering in the living room doorway. She gave a cough as the others chatted. "Livi, can I have a word?"

I followed her into the living room. "What?"

"You're going to have to stop your little meetings."

I felt a surge of anger at her words. I wondered if she'd been talking to Summer. "They're not *little*," I snapped.

Jill rolled her eyes. "You can't have them anymore."

"But we're not casting out demons!" I exclaimed. "We're just doing whatever God says."

"You're not *what?*"

I blushed as I realised she hadn't been talking to Summer after all. "Nothing... Why do we have to stop?"

"I can't stand having so many people in the house."

"We're in my room! It's not like anybody's in your way!"

"The shoes get in my way," she said shortly. I opened my mouth to protest but she put her hand up. "Either you tell them or I will."

I gave a growl. "That's not fair."

My sister sniffed and looked away.

I felt frustration rising inside me. Depression or no depression, I couldn't believe how unreasonable she was being. After giving a loud sigh, I went out to break the bad news to the others.

To my surprise, they all wore big grins.

"My parents own a pub," Ellen said proudly.

"So?" I wondered whether she was suggesting we abandon our meetings and take up drinking instead.

"They have a function room that's empty most week nights. I'm sure they'd let us use it."

I gaped at her. "Really?"

"Yup."

I turned back to my sister who was looking rather uncomfortable in the doorway. "We don't need to meet here anymore," I told her. "We're upgrading."

~*~

Ellen's parents' pub was a battered old building in a rundown area of the city. The moment Ruby and I stepped off the bus, I felt uneasy.

"Where are we?" I muttered as I eyed a smashed up car nearby.

Instead of replying, Ruby nudged me and grinned.

"What?"

She pointed to the sign on the pub. 'The King's Arms.'

I let out a long breath. "Right."

Ellen met us at the door and, after introducing us to her parents, led us down a skinny hallway to the pub's function room.

"Isn't it amazing!" she exclaimed.

I felt my stomach sink as I looked round the room. It was cold and dreary, with dusty grey curtains, patchy orange carpet and the aroma of spilt beer. How on earth could we expect God to meet us here? I was about to suggest to Ruby that we cancel the meeting but then I remembered the warehouse in Wales. If God could turn up there, he could turn up anywhere.

We were just setting up[52] when Annie arrived with half a dozen members of The COOL Club. I recognised a few of them who had been in the years below us at Hare Valley. They chatted eagerly, trotting into the room as though they couldn't believe they were in a pub on a school night. A few seconds later, Georgina Harris arrived looking rather wary.

I took a deep breath and strode over to her. "Hi Georgina."

"Hi Livi."

I blushed and looked at the floor. "I just want to say that I'm sorry for not making you feel welcome when you came to my house. I just..." I was about to excuse myself by reminding her of occasions in high school when she'd made me feel like she didn't like me. Instead, I gritted my teeth and said, "You can come whenever you want."

I looked up to see Georgina smiling. "Thanks."

I nodded and turned to go.

"Oh, and Livi..."

"Yeah?"

---

[52] By stacking all the chairs and tables at the side to create a big empty space in the middle of the room.

"I'm sorry for the times I wasn't very nice to you in high school. Like when I told Miss Day that it was you who broke the oven."

I bit my lip. I hadn't even known she'd done that. "It's fine," I muttered.

I gave her a quick hug before wandering back to Ruby. Several more members of The COOL Club were starting to arrive along with Maria and her sister and, as the room filled up, I found myself growing nervous.

"This feels like an official meeting," I whispered to Ruby. "What are we going to do?"

She thought for a moment before giving me a big smile. "We're not going to do anything, remember? We're going to see what Jesus does."

I grinned. "That's cool."

She giggled. "That's COOL Club!"

I thought for a moment. "Are we still The Fire Brigade? Or is this The COOL Club now?" I indicated the swarm around Annie.

Ruby shrugged. "Do we need a name?"

I gave her a playful nudge. "Fine... We're just whatever we are."

Laura arrived next, followed by Kevin, Amanda and an anxious-looking lady in a suit.

Amanda came running over, her cheeks bright pink as she asked, "Is it okay if my mum watches?" She pointed to the anxious lady. "She didn't want me to come to a pub by myself."

"I suppose so..." I gulped, suddenly afraid again.

I waited till quarter to eight before summoning up the courage to get the meeting started. Then I stood at the front of the room, clapping my hands several times before I got anybody's attention. I felt a little sick as everybody stopped and looked at me.

"Welcome to The King's Arms..." I began. "I hope you all experience being in the King's arms tonight!"

I thought that was rather witty but most people seemed to miss the pun and just stared at me blankly.

I coughed. "Anyway... We're going to start by thanking God for being with us and asking him what he wants to do tonight." I squeezed my eyes shut and started to pray. Outwardly, I declared, "Jesus, we want to meet with you tonight. We give you this whole evening to do whatever you want..." Inwardly, I begged God desperately, *Lord, I am totally out of my depth. If you don't do something, I'm going to look so stupid.*

It crossed my mind that God's silence might be exactly the kind of thing I needed to keep me humble but, fortunately, Annie put her hand up and said, "I think we should sing *'Waiting for You.'*"

I shot her a thankful smile. "Alright…"

Annie began to sing, *"Let your face shine on your children, we are waiting here for you…"*

I shuffled back to my place and sang along. It seemed it had been a regular song at The COOL Club too as Georgina and the others quickly joined in.

When we reached the end, I glanced at Ruby to see if she had any idea what we ought to do next. She just shrugged.

To my surprise, Kevin came forward and started reading from John's gospel. *"Whoever comes to me I will never drive away."* He caught my eye and blushed. "I felt like God was telling me to read that out."

"That's great!" I encouraged him. I ran to the front and looked round the room before declaring, "That's a promise for everyone. Whether you're already a Christian or whether you're coming to him for the first time, Jesus won't drive you away."

I caught Laura's eye and smiled.

She smiled back and whispered something to Ellen.

"Can we sing *'Jesus is King of the Jungle'?*" yelled Amanda.

I paused, wondering whether that song would be too daft for our first big meeting. But, before I could reply, half of The COOL Club let out a cheer and launched straight in. *Oh, whatever, God,* I conceded. *I give you full control.* I wandered back to my place where I determined to stay for the rest of the night.

As we bellowed *'Jesus is King of the Jungle'* at the tops of our lungs, several of the pub regulars popped their heads in to see what all the noise was about. Many of them looked round in confusion and quickly walked back out but quite a few stood at the back for a moment with curious expressions on their faces.

One lady in particular stayed for a very long time and I saw Annie go over to talk to her. I wondered whether I ought to check that everything was alright but, moments later, my jaw dropped open as the lady put her hands out and nodded along to Annie's prayer. Annie then moved on to Amanda's mum who looked a little taken aback but closed her eyes as Annie put a hand on her head.

At one point Ellen's dad came in with a mandolin and started strumming along as we sang. I had no idea whether he believed what he was singing but he joined in with a cheery smile and roared like a lion during the chorus.

We were singing the song for the umpteenth time when I felt a sudden presence come into the room and rush past me. I opened my eyes and looked round to see who it was. Nobody was there. Even so, I could feel the weight of glory in the air as I stared at the empty space in front of me.

Nearby, a few members of The COOL Club fell about laughing.

Georgina came up beside me, her eyes wide with shock. "Can you see that, Livi?" She pointed in front of me.

"See what?" I whispered.

"A massive angel!" If it wasn't for the fact that her eyes were glowing, I might have thought she was having me on.

I glanced back but still couldn't see anything. "I can't see it," I confessed.

She kept staring. "He's massive and he's smiling and his wings almost touch the ceiling."

I resisted the urge to feel jealous and just glanced back in awe. "Er... If there's an angel there," I whispered. "Then I welcome you to our meeting."

Although I didn't see or hear anything in response, the presence grew thicker still and I felt a bubble of delight erupt within me.

Ruby came bounding over. "I felt God say he's releasing joy," she gasped.

I turned to say something but started laughing instead.

Ruby and Georgina began to giggle and pretty soon they couldn't stop. The laughter was contagious and it wasn't long before most of the room had caught it.

The rest of the evening flew by. Spontaneous songs erupted here and there, interspersed with prayer and the odd moment of silence. Not everybody joined in; Maria and her sister spent a lot of time just chatting at the side. But they seemed cheerful enough so I left them to it.

According to Ellen's parents, our meeting had brightened up the night for many of the punters in the pub. Even those who hadn't made it as far as the function room seemed happier simply as a result of being in the same building. Ellen's father put this down to the theory that singing releases happy hormones and brings about a sense of unity. Whilst this might have played a role, I was fairly certain it was something to do with the overflow of God's love and the whooping great angel of joy he had sent.

~ 24 ~

The real world

The following week, we met at The King's Arms on Monday, Wednesday and Thursday. We couldn't go on Tuesday as that was the pub's poker night and, of course, most of the original Fire Brigade still had our own youth group on Friday. It pained me to have to keep going to youth group when God appeared to be doing far more exciting things outside it. Although I was doing my best to forgive Eddie and Summer, I still didn't much like being around them. Everything in me wanted to brag about our week of meetings at the pub but I held my tongue and let Ruby, Amanda and Kevin do the sharing instead.

"We must have had about... twenty people there last night?" Ruby looked at me.

"Twenty two," I said. I had counted.

"Wow," Nicole gasped.

"Sounds good," said Mark.

"What do you do?" asked Bill.

Kevin replied, "We mainly sing."

Eddie gave an encouraging nod before looking at Summer. "We'll have to come one night."

I frowned. I didn't want them interfering.

"Do you need a guitarist?" Joey piped up.

"Er..." Ruby nudged me. "Do we?"

I looked at Joey. "You can come and play it if you want," I said. "But we don't have a worship band. Everybody leads it together."

Joey raised his eyebrows. "How does that work?"

"It just does." I stared at my lap, desperate to know what Summer was thinking. "Someone starts singing and we all join in. It means nobody's on stage except Jesus."

"You should all come," said Amanda. "It's really fun."

I shot Summer a quick glance. She was smiling at Amanda. I resisted the urge to feel bitter as she said, "Well done you guys. It sounds great."

Three days later, Joey, Mark and Nicole turned up at The King's Arms to check things out. Joey gave a cheery wave as he pointed to his guitar. I nodded and told him he could play it whenever he wanted as long as he didn't stand at the front like a performer. He gave a serious nod and shuffled over to the back of the room. Mark went and stood with him, muttering something about bringing his bass, and Nicole headed over to sit with Amanda and Kevin. It crossed my mind that all we needed next was Bill and our Friday youth group could be officially cancelled.

As the meeting got underway, I had to admit that Joey's guitar was a nice addition as it helped keep the singing in tune. But by no means was it an essential ingredient. I decided it was rather fortunate that Joey hadn't joined The Fire Brigade from the outset. I was sure we'd all have relied on him to lead the worship if he had. As it was, the five of us had learnt how to worship spontaneously without needing it to sound perfect. To his credit, Joey didn't play too loudly and kept glancing over at me to check whether to continue.

Over the next few nights, quite a few people started coming with musical instruments and they played them from wherever they were stood round the room. It was chaotic to say the least but everyone was free to worship as they desired.

We began each evening with the same prayer: *"Jesus, what do you want to do tonight?"* and did our best to follow whatever the Holy Spirit said.

Some nights were more exciting than others. At one meeting, for example, at least four people reported minor healings such as the relief of toothache or muscle pain. A few of the pub regulars also joined us that night after remarking that some of us seemed drunker than them.

Other nights were a lot less dramatic. We didn't always hear God clearly and sometimes ended up with lots of people standing around talking as a few of us attempted to pray. Occasionally, I would feel a bit of pressure as I feared the day would come when everyone would get bored and decide they weren't getting anything out of it anymore. But then I'd catch sight of Ruby, Annie, Amanda and Kevin and realise that, even if everybody else left, the five of us could just carry on as before. I knew God would rather have a handful of sold-out believers than hundreds of names on a list. Our mission was first and foremost to keep loving God. Whether anybody else came or not was not to be our concern.

~*~

Within a couple of weeks, both Maria and Ellen made tentative confessions of faith.[53] Laura said she still needed more time to think about it and came into college every day with a list of questions for me and Ruby to answer. One question in particular stumped us both— it was the same question that Amanda had got stuck on— and we stopped to asked Sharon's advice at lunchtime.

"Do pets go to Heaven?"

Sharon chuckled and reached for her Bible. She opened it to the book of Proverbs and read aloud, *"It is the glory of God to conceal a matter; to search out a matter is the glory of kings."*

I frowned and glanced at Ruby who asked, "What does that mean?"

"It means there are many mysteries in this universe and God loves it when you seek his ways. But he is also within his rights to keep things hidden." Sharon smiled before continuing, "I believe you're having quite an effect on some of your classmates."

I tried to be humble as I said, "It's all God."

"Of course, their grades are suffering slightly." She held up a recent essay written by Ellen. It was less than half a page long.

"It's because we're having meetings nearly every night," I explained. "There's no time for homework." A sudden idea struck me. "You should come and be our guest speaker!"

Sharon gave a little laugh.

"Seriously!" I insisted. "You have loads to teach us."

She pursed her lips as she considered it. "I'll do it—"

"Yes!" I grinned at Ruby.

"If you can give me your word that your youth leaders are happy for me to do so."

I stared at her. "But it's nothing to do with them! It's our own thing."

"Who's in charge?"

"Me!"

She kept staring.

"I mean God."

---

[53] During which they both repented from an unhealthy interest in the wrong kind of spiritual life. Maria was thrilled to discover that with the Holy Spirit inside her she could finally command whatever was knocking on her bedroom wall to stop.

She nodded. "And God loves honour. I know I upset your leaders in the past by undermining their teachings. I'm not going to do it again."

"But you don't need their permission to go to a pub," I retorted. "You can just say you popped in for a pint. Not that they'll ever know."

I turned to Ruby for support but she just went pink.

Sharon gave me a pointed look. "How are you getting on with your test?"

I looked at the mock biology test she had set for that night's homework.

"Not that one. Your real test: how you deal with offence."

I sighed. "Fine," I muttered. "We'll ask Summer."

Ruby and I left Sharon's classroom and found a quiet place to talk things through. We came to the agreement that Summer was likely to ask Ruby less questions than me since it was me she held responsible for causing problems before. So I sat praying while Ruby made the phone call nearby. I could see her shaking her head as she answered Summer's questions. I had half a mind to snatch the phone from her and see what Summer was saying.

Just as I was about to conclude that Summer was going to be unreasonable, Ruby hung up and gave me a thumbs-up. "Sharon can come and talk as long as she doesn't get into anything too heavy."

I grinned and sprinted back to Sharon's classroom.

Sharon looked up from marking some papers.

"Our youth leader says you can speak."

"As long as it's not too heavy," Ruby added as she followed me into the classroom.

I rolled my eyes and turned back to Sharon. "Will you do it?"

I whooped with joy as she gave a quick nod.

"When?" I pushed. "Tonight?"

She looked down and carried on marking. "Give me the address."

When Ruby and I arrived at The King's Arms that evening, we were shocked to discover several of our college mates waiting for us at the bar. It turned out that news had spread pretty quickly and a FriendWeb event had even been created advertising the fact that Sharon Sheppard was going to be talking about Jesus in a pub.

"Is Sharon here yet?" asked a guy from the Horticulture course.

"Er... I don't know," I muttered. "Have you seen her?"

"Is she for real?" another guy piped up. "Like, is she really into God and all that?"

"Yeah she's... for real." I gave him an awkward smile and glanced round the room.

I counted thirteen people at the bar and a further five scattered round the pool table. Several others were clustered round Laura who, judging by the proud look on her face, was the one who had advertised the event.

I clutched Ruby's arm, unsure whether to be excited or worried at how many people had turned up. From the look on her face, she was just as torn as me.

Behind the bar, Ellen's parents were looking a little peeved as many of our classmates attempted to order alcohol.

"Right!" yelled Ellen's mother. "You can't all hang around like this. Who's in charge?"

Every eye turned to me.

"God's in charge," I squeaked.

"If you're here for your little meeting then can you please go through to the function room?" Ellen's dad pointed towards the corridor.

I gave a quick nod, wishing for the first time that it really was only a *'little'* meeting. "Follow me!" I yelped as I led the way down the hallway.

Fifteen minutes later, Sharon still hadn't arrived. Those who had come from City Farm more than outnumbered the members of The Fire Brigade and The COOL Club and my stomach churned as I overheard people muttering impatiently and asking one another what was meant to be happening. Another ten minutes passed and I was about to apologise and tell everybody from college to go home when Sharon swooped into the room, holding her Bible in one hand and a pint of lemonade in the other.

I breathed a huge sigh of relief and ran over to her. "I thought you weren't coming!"

She gave a wry smile. "And then what would you have done?"

I blushed. "Shall I introduce you? Then you can just take over."

Sharon pursed her lips, oblivious to the stares she was getting. "How do you usually start your meetings?"

"We ask Jesus what to do and we do it."

"Well, don't do things differently just because I'm here. He might not want me to speak."

"Oh!" I was rather alarmed at the idea of Sharon not speaking. What would everyone from college think? I shuffled to the front of the room and took a deep breath as everybody turned to stare at me. "Hello everyone..."

A few of the newcomers sniggered when I explained we would be starting with a prayer and maybe a song or two. Fortunately, Ruby and Annie and the others backed me up and joined me in welcoming the Holy Spirit and asking the Father what we should do.

After we had sung a couple of short songs, I shuffled over to Sharon and said, "I feel like you should speak now."

"Very well." Sharon took her time setting her coat and bag down and making her way to the front. Then she stood for ages without doing anything.

I exchanged a baffled glance with Ruby.

Some of our college mates giggled in the corner.

Finally, Sharon flicked though her Bible and read, "*So we fix our eyes not on what is seen, but on what is unseen, since what is seen is temporary, but what is unseen is eternal.*" She looked up and smiled. "Human beings can be very short-sighted, can't we?" She paused before adding, "I was engaged once. His name was Ollie. He had a great job and he was very handsome."

A few people chuckled, hardly daring to believe we were hearing such private information from a teacher.

"We took a long time to get engaged because we wanted everything to be perfect. We wanted a fancy wedding but, before that, we wanted a nice house. We worked extra hours to build our deposit quickly and eventually put in an offer for a lovely little house in Hebden Bridge." She paused and took a sip of her drink. "When our dream home was ready, Ollie finally proposed although we never got round to setting a date for our wedding. We wanted more money. I wanted an expensive dress..."

Laughter melted into awe as Sharon's story turned serious. "We kept putting it off because, well, you would wouldn't you?" Sharon stared hard at the floor as she gathered her thoughts. "I didn't believe in God at that point. I just believed in myself and I thought that was enough. I thought I had all the time in the world. One day, I got a call from Ollie's mother." Sharon swallowed. "He had been in a car accident."

There was a gasp as Sharon said quietly, "He didn't survive."

I hardly dared to blink. I was afraid tears would come rolling out if I did.

"Everything we were living for— all our plans, our promises, all that toil— over just like that." Sharon stopped and blew her nose. "Life is so fleeting... And then reality hits."

Our classmates hung on her every word and I rather hoped she would do an altar call. I expected it would be quite spectacular if she did.

Instead she finished with, "Did you know, some scientists reckon that we only see about four percent of the universe? The rest is unseen... It's not enough to believe only in yourself. It's not enough to be so short-sighted." She looked at me. "I hope that wasn't too heavy."

I felt my cheeks burn as I shook my head.

Sharon nodded before stepping away from the front. "I'm done." She went to collect her things.

I gaped at Ruby who looked as stunned as me.

After a hushed pause, Joey began to strum softly on the guitar. Those who knew it joined in as he sang 'Amazing Grace.'

I turned to talk to Sharon but she had already gone.

"Wow," Ruby whispered. Her eyes had gone all puffy. "Poor Sharon."

I bit my lip. "What do we do now?"

Most of our classmates had left as soon as Sharon finished but many others had stayed behind and were talking quietly or watching as pockets of people prayed around the room.

Before Ruby could reply, Laura came up beside us, tears streaming down her cheeks. "I'm ready," she whispered.

My heart leapt as I joined her and Ruby in kneeling down on the patchy floor.

Laura had just finished praying her first ever prayer to Jesus when something happened that blew the hinges of my box wide open: both she and Annie discovered what looked like flecks of gold on the tips of their fingers.

Annie spotted it first and started shrieking as she ran over and waved her hands under my nose.

I was so confused that I just stared at her.

Ruby leant over and exclaimed, "Gold dust!"

I was about to ask Annie what she had been touching when Laura looked down and whispered, "I've got it too!"

As the news spread, everyone in the room crowded round to inspect their hands with some jumping in excitement when they saw it and others concluding that there must have been glitter on the carpet. Those from college who had stayed to the end immediately demanded to know more about Jesus and it was Laura who stepped up to tell them.

Ruby and I couldn't stop grinning all the way home.

"Call your sister!" I said, as soon as we got on the bus.

Ruby giggled and reached for her phone.

Violet had shown no enthusiasm when we'd rung previously to tell her about the angel of joy. "I hope you didn't talk to it," she had warned. "It's a sin to worship angels."

"Saying 'hello' hardly constitutes worship," Ruby had retorted.

Violet had hummed down the line before giving us some very solemn advice: "Just don't get carried away."

As naughty as it was, I couldn't wait to tell her about the gold dust.

After going into detail about Sharon's sad story and Laura's conversion, Ruby took a deep breath and said, "Oh, and a couple of people got gold dust on their hands!"

"What's the point of that?" Violet snapped.

"Because it's fun!" I pressed my cheek against Ruby's as I yelled into the phone, "God loves having fun."

Violet grunted. "God isn't a fairy godmother."

"No, he's not," Ruby told her sister. "He's much, much better than that!"

"But what use does it have in the real world?"

Ruby shrugged and handed me the phone. I was about to tell Violet that I wasn't completely sure. But then I remembered the verse that Sharon had shared that evening. '...*What is seen is temporary, but what is unseen is eternal...*' Suddenly everything clicked. The world we see is not the real world. The real, true, eternal world is the one God sees. And his world is much wilder than ours.

"Well?" Violet demanded down the phone. "What have angel sightings and gold dust got to do with the real world?"

"I don't know," I said. "I guess we'll find out when we get there."

~ 25 ~

I know best

Our numbers seemed to double after the gold dust incident as several people brought their curious friends along. Those who wanted a quick sign were miffed when they didn't get one and a few people stormed out after claiming we were weird. But those who were genuinely hungry for God had many questions about how to get to know him better. Ruby led a couple of sessions on the basics of the Christian faith and, to our delight, a handful of people responded.

As the nights went on, our numbers grew. I could hardly believe it when I looked round the room one evening and counted more than forty people. As exciting as this was, our sudden growth brought more challenges than I would have expected. Our original format of listening to the Holy Spirit grew harder and harder to implement as more and more people came. Many who had never been to any kind of church meeting before found it hard to stay quiet and came with genuine but disruptive questions which they blurted out as soon as they arrived. I found myself struggling as people grilled me on all manner of issues ranging from suffering to sexuality to predestination.

To add to this was the slight problem of discerning between the things of God and the things of the flesh. One evening, for example, a whole line of people fell over while singing. Whilst some seemed to have truly encountered the power of God, I suspected that most of them were simply hyping themselves up— especially the ones who were looking round to see who was watching them fall.

Unfortunately, we also attracted those who enjoyed the excuse to hang out in a pub. There were several clusters of people who used our meetings as a social club, chatting and making snide comments while the rest of us tried to sing or pray. I didn't want to turn people away if there was any chance they might hear about

Jesus but, at the same time, things were getting a little out of hand. I even spotted a couple of guys making inappropriate advances on some of the girls under the guise of offering prayer. I was at a loss at what to do. After working so hard to create an atmosphere of freedom with the original Fire Brigade, was I now supposed to start laying down rules?

"I think we need to talk to Eddie and Summer," Ruby said when I asked for her advice.

I bit my lip, desperate to solve things without their involvement. "Let's give it a bit longer."

As it happened, that very Sunday something happened which took the decision right out of my hands.

Ruby and I arrived at church with quite a trail of people behind us including Annie, Georgina, Laura and a few of the new converts. I headed straight for the front of the room and reserved the entire front row. In the past, the youth had taken to sitting at the back. I think this was something Joey and Mark initiated a couple of years ago as it meant we could chat through worship without anybody noticing. Today, however, the two of them came and joined us at the front.

Joey gave me a little poke. "Hey Livi."

"Hey Joey. How are you?"

"I'm fine thanks..." He paused. "The last couple of weeks have been cool."

"The pub meetings?"

"Yeah. Are we meeting again tomorrow?"

"Of course."

Joey was about to say something else when Kevin popped up beside us. "What do you call a fly without wings?"

I raised an eyebrow. "I don't know."

"A walk."

Joey and I groaned. "Good one, Kevin."

He grinned as he craned to catch Annie's attention.

Then Amanda came running over and plonked her stuff down as close as possible to Kevin's coat.

I saw Summer looking bemused as she glanced at our long line from the other side of the room. I hoped she would wonder who all the new people were. Perhaps she would even feel jealous that their youth group had been swallowed up by ours. Even as I thought this, I felt a pang of shame. It bothered me that something seemed to happen inside me whenever Summer and Eddie were near. I'd find myself wanting vindication for them closing down our progress with spiritual warfare. I wanted to prove I was more capable than they realised. Or I would devise arguments in my head to defend our meetings. Of course, they were arguments that I always won.

I forced myself to ignore them as the worship band stepped onto the stage to begin the meeting. The first song happened to be *'Waiting for You,'* and smugness rose inside me as I wondered what Summer and Eddie would think when they saw that the group we had brought already knew it.

As I looked up and down our row, I spotted Amanda looking a little teary as she perched on a seat at the end of the line. I assumed this was because she hadn't managed to sit as near to Kevin as she would have liked so I shot her a kind smile before closing my eyes and attempting to sing. Suddenly, a picture popped into my mind of Amanda with a huge metallic spider clinging to her shoulder. I frowned and glanced back at Amanda. There was nothing to suggest that my picture meant anything so I shook my head and closed my eyes again.

I had just got back into the singing when I felt a tap on my arm. I opened my eyes to see Kevin white with fright.

"What's wrong?" I asked.

He pointed to Amanda who was quaking on the floor nearby. "Something's wrong with Amanda."

A wave of sickness washed over me as I watched Amanda shaking and crying as though under the grip of an invisible force. I didn't have time to process anything but somehow I just *knew* it was the spidery creature I had seen.

I knelt beside her, my heart pounding as her sobs grew louder. I could sense the spider tormenting her as she rolled about on the floor.

"Amanda?" I said. "Can you hear me?"

Amanda moaned even louder. As I looked into her face and wondered how long she had been afflicted by this thing, I was really, really glad that Hell existed and that one day God would deal with evil once and for all.

Since we were on the floor, we were obscured from most of the church but the worship band had full view of Amanda and I saw the drummer waving as he tried to get someone's attention. I glanced up and saw Eddie on the other side of the room looking over in confusion.

"Lord, help," I muttered. I held Amanda's hand as I prayed. I wished I knew the Bible as well as Ruby. I recited a couple of verses as they came to mind. *"Who the Son sets free is free indeed... In all things, we are more than conquerors through him who has loved us..."*

Amanda continued to writhe and moan and, in my mind's eye, I could see the spidery creature wreaking havoc inside her. Eddie and Summer were walking over. I knew I didn't have long.

I took a deep breath before saying fiercely, "Whatever is afflicting Amanda, I command you right now to come out in the name of Jesus!"

Immediately, Amanda's body jerked and twisted before she fell still. After a moment, she sat up in a daze. Eddie and Summer reached us just in time to hear her say, "Something crawled out of me."

I avoided looking at Eddie and Summer as I whispered, "Something spidery?"

"Yeah."

"Is everything okay?" Eddie knelt down beside us.

I nodded before continuing to Amanda, "Can I pray for the Holy Spirit to come and fill the space where that thing was?"

She gave a breathy sigh. "Please."

Before Eddie or Summer could say anything, I put my hand on her shoulder and started to pray.

Within seconds, Amanda had a great grin on her face. "I can feel God's love, like really *feel* it. I know I'm his princess!"

I smiled and left her to enjoy God's presence before turning to face Eddie and Summer. I couldn't work out their expressions. "I didn't mean to do warfare," I tried to explain. "God showed me a picture and then I saw it in front of me... It just happened."

"It's alright," Summer said quietly. She went to say something else but the worship came to an end at that moment and everyone fell silent as Jim arose to preach.

Out of the corner of my eye, I saw Eddie exchange a quick word with Summer. He went to take their children off to the Kids' Club while Summer remained next to me.

It was perhaps the most uncomfortable half hour of my life. I didn't concentrate on a single word Jim said. All my energy was going into not looking at Summer as I went over what had just happened with Amanda. A part of me marvelled at how dramatic the deliverance had been and the calm authority that God had given me in the moment. Months ago, I would never have dared to believe that I could handle such a situation. However, I was rather miffed that it had happened right in the middle of church instead of during our pub meetings out of Eddie and Summer's sight. I wondered why God hadn't thought about that.

As soon as the preach came to an end, I got to my feet, determined to leave before Summer spoke to me.

"Livi, wait!"

I turned and forced a smile. "Yes?"

"Have you got a minute? We need to talk."

Frustration exploded inside me. After I had just set Amanda free, I was about to be told off! "I'm really busy right now," I said, indicating Laura who had come over with a notepad full of questions.

Summer pursed her lips. "Are you free this afternoon?"

I shook my head. "I've got loads of homework."[54]

"When are you free? How about tomorrow night?" She pulled her diary out of her bag.

"I'm leading an outpouring meeting at the pub."

She sighed. "Well, perhaps Eddie and I will come. It will be good to see what you're up to."

My heart sunk as she asked for the address.

I had prayed that Eddie and Summer would be unable to find a babysitter or perhaps have a last minute minor emergency like the bath overflowing— anything that would delay their visit to The King's Arms. I was mightily disappointed when they arrived on time and full of energy. Amanda was ecstatic to see them and ran straight over, blissfully unaware that they were there to inspect us. It transpired that someone from college had been exaggerating about the miracles we had seen and it didn't go down too well when the first thing Summer and Eddie heard was someone asking how much it cost for a pot of gold dust and an angel feather.

"We've got lots of non-Christians here," I tried to explain as I hurried over. "Sometimes people ask strange questions."

---

[54] This was true in the sense that I *always* have loads of homework. I didn't actually end up doing any of it.

Eddie stroked his chin. "We'll have to sort out how to disciple them."

I frowned. I hadn't asked for their input. "We should start our meeting now," I said loudly to Ruby.

She nodded so I grabbed her hand and led the way through the crowd. We had a pretty good turnout and I found myself wondering how I could twist God's arm to induce a spectacular healing or a horde of conversions.

I cleared my throat as we reached the front. As usual, most people fell silent and looked at us while those who were using us as a social club carried on talking.

"Good evening everyone," I said over the chatter. "Thank you for coming. It's a wonderful pleasure to welcome you all to The King's Arms to meet with God tonight..."

The formal nature of my address was for Eddie and Summer's benefit. They lingered at the back like dark shadows, scrutinising our every move and ready to pounce if we did something wrong. I longed for everybody to sing loudly and pray fervently so they could see how great it all was.

Despite my high hopes, the meeting was pretty tedious. We sang a number of songs and spent some time praying in small groups. Ruby gave a short talk about God's love and several of our college mates heckled all the way through. There was no gold dust, no angel sightings, no healings, and I didn't feel remotely peaceful.

As people started to leave, Eddie and Summer cornered me at the side.

I took a deep breath and turned to face them. "So, that's what we're doing," I said with a shrug.

Eddie gave an encouraging smile. "We think it's wonderful," he began, much to my surprise. "We're just a bit concerned..."

My heart sunk.

"There doesn't seem to be much order." He pointed to a group of college students who were dancing wildly nearby.

"God's in charge," I muttered.

Summer put a hand on my shoulder. "We want to help you."

I almost scoffed in her face. "It's alright," I said. "We know what we're doing."

At this, Eddie turned a little serious. "It's dangerous to disconnect from the body," he warned.

"The body?"

"The body of Christ. The Church."

"I haven't disconnected from the Church!" I retorted. "You're welcome to come as long as..." I stopped short of saying, 'As long as you let me lead it.'

As if reading my mind, Eddie said, "If you want to be a leader, Livi, then you need to learn how to be led."

I gave a petulant shrug. "Who says I want to be a leader?"

"You're a great leader, Livi," Summer said, shooting her husband a quick glance. "We're just concerned that this is all taking off without any real covering."

I blinked at them. "Covering?" I figured this was church-speak for something.

"Protection," Eddie added. "And accountability."

I frowned. "It's not an official church meeting. We don't need 'covering' or any of those things. We're taking God out of the religious box."

While Eddie looked affronted by my words, I could see that Summer was feeling uncomfortable.

"We're not trying to control you," she insisted. "But we're your leaders and we take our responsibility seriously. We'll have to answer to God for how we've looked after you."

"For how safe you kept us?" I demanded. "Or for how far we flew?"

Eddie exhaled sharply. "Are you meeting again tomorrow?"

"It's poker night."

They looked at me in alarm.

"I don't mean us!" I spluttered. "The pub has a poker night. We have a night off."

Eddie breathed a sigh as Summer asked, "Then would you like to come for dinner?"

I pursed my lips, noting the concern in Summer's eyes and the frustration in Eddie's. "I'll think about it."

The moment Ruby and I boarded our bus, I sent Summer a text stating that I couldn't come for dinner as I had so much homework to do. As I waited for her reply, I found myself growing more and more annoyed as I tormented myself over what they might say. Would they tell me to close down the meetings? Did they have a right to make me do that? Does honouring your leaders mean doing everything they ask, even when it sucks?

"They're probably a bit scared," Ruby suggested when I offloaded on her. "They're not used to this sort of thing. They're used to the youth just... being youth." She shrugged. "When people

233

have been in church for a long time they get kind of fixed on how to do things."

"Then they need to deal with their religious baggage!" I said hotly.

Ruby raised her eyebrows. "What if they had said the same about you and your... *emotional* baggage?"

Her words struck me like a slap in the face. I shot her a wounded look before turning away. "I'm right though," I muttered.

As Ruby shrugged, I heard God whisper, *Your attitude isn't.*

I was stunned. *But I forgave them, didn't I? And I only did what you told me to do.*

When God stayed silent, I thought back to how abrupt and defensive I had been with Eddie and Summer that evening. I certainly hadn't shown them the honour and love that Sharon had told me to walk in.

Eddie's words rang in my ears. *'It's dangerous to disconnect from the body.'*

My stomach churned as I realised that, even if they had all the good advice in the world, I still wouldn't want their help. I liked doing things my way. I liked not needing them. I liked not having *'covering.'* I had disconnected without even realising.

I fought to defend my actions. *They're too scared of getting it wrong. They don't encourage us to fly. They think we can't handle spiritual matters.*

But God interrupted with the words, *I don't like independence.*

I gulped. What did he mean by that?

My phone beeped with Summer's reply and I quickly pulled it out of my pocket. *'Livi, please consider coming for a bit. We'd really like to talk to you. Summer.'*

My thumb hovered over my phone. Everything in me wanted to reject her but a little voice told me not to be so hasty. That night hadn't been as good as previous meetings. Would God withdraw his hand completely if I refused Eddie and Summer's counsel?

I shoved my phone back into my pocket and sighed. I would deal with it later.

"Everything okay?" asked Ruby.

I nodded and forced a smile. "I think Joey had a new guitar strap," I said, clutching at the first thing I could think of.

Ruby giggled and recounted a joke Mark had told her.

I did my best to pretend to be interested but my heart was heavy with the conviction of God's words. *I don't like independence.* By the time we got off the bus, I felt as though I was going to throw up.

We reached our houses and I said a hasty goodbye, desperate to go to sleep and ignore it all. I couldn't stand the idea that God didn't approve one hundred percent of everything I had done.

Unfortunately, God followed me all the way up to my bed and I tossed and turned for ages, unable to quieten my soul.

"I'm not being independent," I told him. "I just don't like being told what to do."

That's independent.

"But Eddie and Summer are wrong! I know best."

I felt like God was almost laughing as he retorted, *I know best.*

"No you don't!" I blurted out. "If you knew best, you'd have told Eddie and Summer not to interfere. You'd have done an amazing miracle so they'd know that you're happy with our meetings... You'd have let me see the angel of joy instead of only showing it to Georgina... You'd have healed Janine instead of putting her through such a horrible disease... You'd have saved Jill by now... You'd have let my mother live..." I sobbed as grudges I didn't even realise I was holding came gushing out. God seemed to sit back and watch as I ranted and raved at him. Pretty soon, I forgot what I was even arguing about. God had pulled all the right strings to expose the raging rebellion deep in my heart. I ran out of words and lay panting as tears streamed down my cheeks.

I know best, said God. *I love you and you need to trust me.*

I rolled around and moaned, unravelled and broken. "I'm sorry," I blubbered. "I don't know what came over me." I sat bolt upright as I wondered, *Is independence a demon?*

God didn't reply so I prayed a hasty prayer and commanded it out just in case.

I let out a sigh of relief and lay back down, hoping it had been dealt with. But, as my clock ticked past midnight, I realised I needed to take some responsibility for my actions. I couldn't just blame the enemy.

I grabbed my phone and sent Summer a text. *'Can I still come for dinner tomorrow?'*

The Church in Leeds

"I am sorry. I was wrong."

It had taken me a whole day to get to the point where I could actually say those words out loud. To begin with, even the idea of saying it had been enough to induce a near fit of rage.

In our household, *'Sorry'* was not a commonly used word. Arguments were generally brushed aside with neither me nor my sister accepting responsibility although I was usually left with the feeling that Jill had the upper hand since she was in charge. Everything wrong in me wanted to run away from my conflict with Eddie and Summer. But everything right in me knew that I had to face them.

It was hard enough summoning up the courage to tell them that I was sorry. But, even worse was the idea of saying those three little words: *'I was wrong.'* Every time I thought about it, I could think of a million reasons why I wasn't wrong or, at the very least, why I was only wrong because of my upbringing and should therefore be exempt from any blame. Finally I could just about say it without excusing myself or demanding an equal apology in return.

I had one last practise as I stood outside Eddie and Summer's front door. *"I am sorry. I was wrong... I am sorry. I was wrong..."* Then I took a deep breath and rang the doorbell.

I could hear Summer singing to herself as she came down the stairs and resisted the urge to run away.

She opened the door with a cheery smile. "Hi Livi!"

I fixed a serious expression on my face and stepped into their house. "Good evening."

Summer cleared some toys off the doormat and I nodded as she excused the mess. "The twins decided to send their toys skydiving before bed..."

I meant to save my noble apology for a quiet moment after dinner but, out of nowhere, I burst into tears.

"Oh Livi!" Summer threw the toys down and enveloped me in a hug.

"I'm sorry!" I sobbed. "I was wrong!" Remorse, sorrow, frustration and confusion all came pouring out and Summer just held me for ages, stroking my hair and rocking me slightly as I wept on her shoulder.

When I had cried about as many tears as Yorkshire's annual rainfall, I stepped back and gave a little whimper. I felt like I had been tipped upside down and given a good clean.

Summer handed me a tissue. "Are you alright?"

I looked at my feet.

"Let's go and have some food." She took my hand and led me through to the kitchen where Eddie was retrieving something from the oven.

"Summer, I took the potatoes out because I thought I heard the oven beeping but then I put them back in because—" Eddie took one look at me and stopped. "Is everything alright?"

I gave sniff and nodded.

Summer put her hand on my shoulder. She seemed to be mouthing something to her husband but, by this point, I didn't really care. I felt worn out from crying but, strangely, I also felt light and free. I had psyched myself up with carefully scripted conversations and strategic devices for keeping my heart guarded but, even though it had involved losing every ounce of my dignity, somehow it felt a whole lot better this way.

"Have a seat, Livi." Summer led me to the kitchen table before asking what I wanted to drink.

"I don't mind," I whispered.

"Orange juice?"

I nodded.

She passed me a glass and sat beside me. I stared at my lap as Eddie dished out our food and came to join us.

"Let's say grace," he said. I was scared he might ask me to do it but, to my relief, he did it himself. "Heavenly Father, we thank you for the pleasure of having Livi here with us tonight and we ask that you would bless our time together..."

I sniffed and almost burst into tears again.

When Eddie finished, I picked up my cutlery and slowly started to eat. Summer and Eddie attempted to fill the silence by talking between themselves about their kids and their garden and their work.

Eventually Eddie turned to me. "How was college today, Livi?"

"It was fine," I mumbled.

He nodded and glanced at Summer.

Before I could lose my nerve, I looked at Eddie and said, "I'm sorry..." I gulped. "I was wrong. I don't know it all."

Eddie seemed rather taken aback. "Thank you." He gave me a warm smile before turning serious. "About what happened to Amanda on Sunday..."

I braced.

"We think you handled the situation really well."

I blinked at him. "Thanks..."

Summer leant over and put a hand on my arm. "I know you found it hard when we asked you stay away from learning about demons," she said. "It was never our intention to crush you. We just wanted to keep you safe. We still do."

I nodded. "I know."

Summer glanced at Eddie before continuing, "But we've been talking about things and we have to confess that we don't know it all either. We do our best but we don't know everything."

"That's why we all need each other," Eddie added. "We're a family. We learn together."

"We love you, Livi," Summer finished.

A tear ran down my cheek. I quickly wiped it away and said, "Thanks."

Summer got up to clear our plates and Eddie asked if I wanted ice cream with my dessert. I nodded and fiddled with the tablecloth as I wondered whether the conversation was over. Should I mention the pub meetings?

When they came back to the table, Eddie said, "We want to support you in stepping out in the things you've been pursuing. We just want you to be careful and walk under appropriate covering..." He caught sight of my confused expression and turned to Summer for help.

She nodded and looked at me. "I guess what we're saying is... You have our blessing to step out when God is leading you. But don't go wandering into things by yourself. Keep us in the loop."

I almost fell off my chair in amazement. "Thanks. I will."

"Just don't overdo it," Eddie cautioned. "An understanding of spiritual warfare is all very well but make sure you focus on Jesus more than you focus on the enemy."

I nodded. "Okay."

"And, Livi..." Summer wore a worried expression. "We've heard you talking a lot about healing and how you think God should heal every time."

"Not *'should,'*" I corrected. *"Wants to."*

She blinked at me. "Yes... Well... We just worry sometimes that you'll find yourself growing disheartened if things don't work out the way you think they ought to."

"Do you remember Harry Turner?" Eddie asked suddenly.

I stopped to think. "The guy who died last year?"

Eddie nodded. "I can't remember the name of his condition but he was suffering for many years and his last three months were a nightmare. We prayed for him as a church. People even fasted for him regularly. For a while, we all thought God was going to bring about a miracle. But Harry died."

I swallowed hard and dug my nails into my hands.

"The point is that we press in for these things but if we don't see a healing we just have to accept that God is bigger than us and his ways are higher than ours. There's a right time for us all to die. For Harry, it was last year. And, if you think about it, he's now fully healed and restored and in a whole new body. Death has given him the fullest healing possible!"

I bit my lip. "But death is not the door... Jesus is."

They looked at me.

"I really, really believe it's God's will to heal everyone," I said.

"We all have to die at some point," Eddie insisted.

"But it doesn't have to hurt, does it? And it doesn't have to happen early." I gulped before blurting out, "It's not God's will for Joey's mum to die! I pray for her every day."

Summer looked at me in concern. "It seems to be having a big impact on you."

"Yeah..." I took a deep breath. "It's just... I often wonder whether anybody ever told my mum about Jesus, or whether anybody tried to pray for her when she got ill, and I..." I swallowed hard. "I thought that if I could heal Joey's mum then it would somehow make it better." I wiped my eyes and looked away.

"Oh Livi!" Summer came round the table and put an arm around me. "I don't know what will happen with Janine but the responsibility doesn't rest on you to heal her."

"But you have to believe!" I exclaimed. "You have to believe God wants her well!"

Sorrow filled Summer's eyes as she insisted, "We do, Livi, and believe me we're all praying as hard as we can. It's just…"

"Complicated," I whispered. "I know."

She squeezed my hand.

Eddie rubbed his chin. "You're right to persevere for healing, Livi," he said. "I'd even go so far as to say you're right to expect it. But God is sovereign and it doesn't always happen. There's a tension that we don't understand."

I frowned. How could they hold to both opinions; that God wanted everyone well and yet sometimes desired to take them early. It didn't make sense to me.

"We might have to agree to disagree," Eddie finished with a smile.

I paused. Could I accept that compromise? I wondered whether I needed to be more persistent.

"We could be wrong," Summer added. "But we agree about the main things, don't we? We all want to love Jesus and know him better. We can disagree on side issues… like whether pets go to Heaven, for example."

I blinked at her. *"Do* they?"

She laughed. "I have no idea!"

Eddie cleared his throat before changing the subject. "Livi, do you know Adrian Cooke? He's the vicar at St John's."

I looked at him blankly.

"The old Anglican church on Brunswick Street. You must know it? It's near the city centre."

"Never heard of it." I didn't add that I didn't even know what *'Anglican'* meant.

"Well, anyway, we mentioned what God was doing at The Kings Arms and he said we could have full use of their church building every night of the week if we wanted."

I raised an eyebrow. I wasn't sure I understood what he was proposing.

"I've told him we'd love that," Eddie continued. "Although, perhaps we'll begin with the same three days you've been doing at the pub. We can always add more later if it feels right to do so." He grinned. "Isn't that wonderful?"

I gulped. I wanted to ask who would lead it and how exactly it would work. "Sounds interesting… But what's wrong with the pub?"

Eddie screwed up his nose. "It's a little out of the way," he said. "And it's not the nicest location for you all to be hanging out in so late at night. I've already had a couple of phone calls from Amanda's mother about the things she sees when she comes to pick her daughter up. Plus, St John's is much bigger and is well suited for large gatherings."

I paused.

Independence lingered at the door, screaming out for recognition for what I had started. *'Listen to them talking as though they had approved all along!'* it seemed to whisper. *'Don't let them come and mess things up!'*

I resisted the temptation to be stubborn. Our meetings had already become too big for me to handle. I could do with their help, especially with all the unexpected problems like people pretending to fall in the Spirit and guys putting their hands on girls under the guise of praying.

"Okay..." I said. "Sounds good."

Eddie pulled some paper off the work surface and started to jot things down. "Now then... What will we need? I assume they already have sound equipment in place. If not, I'll have to ask Jim..."

I bit my lip. "Do we need all of that? Can't we just keep it simple? The early disciples didn't have complicated sound systems and they coped fine."

Eddie and Summer looked at one another and burst out laughing.

"I've been saying that for years!" Summer exclaimed.

"So, you're suggesting an acoustic worship band?" asked Eddie.

I shrugged. "I don't know. We don't even have a band. People just play or sing from all over the room." I took a deep breath. "We can have a band if you want. It doesn't really matter. The main thing is everybody loving God and loving each other."

Eddie grinned. "Good motto."

I smiled. "It was Ruby's."

Eddie scribbled down a few more notes before saying, "Great. Well I'll give Adrian a ring and let you know when we can start meeting there." He glanced at his watch. "We should take you home soon. I expect you've got lots of homework to do?"

"Yeah," I said. "But it doesn't matter. Sharon doesn't mind if we do it or not. She knows following God is more important."

I had hoped this would go some way to restoring their image of Sharon. Unfortunately, they both looked a little worried.

"We wouldn't agree with your teacher not pushing you to work hard," Eddie said. "Whatever you do, you ought to do it as though doing it for the Lord. He doesn't want you to be lazy."

I paused. I could see their point. "I guess nobody knows it all?" I suggested.

Fortunately they smiled. "There's grace for each one of us," they agreed.

Before going to bed that evening, I picked up my *Disciple To-Do List* and read it through several times.

'Preach the gospel, heal the sick, cleanse the lepers, cast out demons, raise the dead...'

My pursuit of those things had definitely intensified my Christian walk. But, at the same time, it had also caused a lot of unnecessary friction. I'd had to battle pride and frustration when I compared my progress with others and I hadn't realised that different Christians believed different things about healing and deliverance until I started trying to put them into practice. How could I know for sure which opinions were right? And how could I keep myself from getting carried away?

What if I've got it wrong? Should I just leave it all for now?

I bit my thumb as I mulled it over. Eddie and Summer's theology on healing was certainly safer than Sharon's. Following their view, if healing doesn't manifest then we can simply resign ourselves to sickness or even death being God's perfect will for that person. In Sharon's view, we don't have that option. Every failed healing leads to the painful question of why our prayer did not work. But just because a certain theology makes you feel better, it doesn't mean it is true. I couldn't choose Eddie and Summer's belief just because it was *safe*.

I thought back to Sharon's counsel that I ought to pray for as many as five hundred people before I drew any serious conclusions about healing. I was still a long way off from that and my experience with the rest of the list was even smaller. It was too soon to call it a day. Plus, I simply *couldn't* give up hope that Janine might still be healed. And, if she wasn't, then it would surely be better to face God with my disappointment than to live with unbelief.

"Don't quit!" I told myself. "Have faith and keep practising."

Even so... *I could have a faith that can move mountains but faith alone won't heal the world...* If I'd learnt anything over the last few months it was that the pursuit of great exploits does not necessarily guarantee a life that pleases the Lord.

I read through my list one last time before folding it up and tucking it into my starling box. Then I grabbed some fresh paper and made a new list.

The greatest thing Jesus told his disciples to do
1. LOVE

~*~

Six days later, thirty three people met at St John's Church for the first outpouring meeting in Leeds. Along with many of our regulars, we were also joined by several people from King's Church, Adrian Cooke and a handful of his congregation, an older couple who happened to be walking past when we were setting up and Sharon Sheppard who came towards Summer with a hand outstretched and said, "You must be Summer. I'm Sharon."

Without a pause, Summer gave Sharon a hug and said, "I'm so pleased we could finally meet in person!"

Sharon looked relieved as she welcomed Summer's embrace and I exchanged a thankful glance with Ruby as the two of them found a seat together.

The church was big and airy, with traditional pews and beautiful stained glass windows. I realised I had passed it many times on my way into Leeds but had never thought to go inside. It had simply been some random church, not one I'd ever dreamt we would one day be partnering with.

I glanced round before the meeting began and realised we had lost quite a few people in the move. But these were mainly college mates who had been coming as an excuse to hang out in a pub. Those who had remained were serious about encountering Jesus.

Eddie was at the front, shuffling some notes about on the lectern. I understood from Summer that he was intending to include a short talk if the Holy Spirit allowed. He had come over to me earlier, looking a little awkward as he suggested he lead the meeting. "I hope that's alright," he'd said. "We just thought it would be good to have a bit of order to things."

I had shrugged and replied, "Whatever you think is best."

The fear had crossed my mind that bringing 'order' would stifle the freedom that God might want to release. But I chose to lay that fear down and trust God to continue what he had started. In a strange way, I was rather glad for the pressure to be taken off me and breathed a sigh as I kicked off my shoes and waited for the meeting to start. I sat with Ruby on the front row, giggling as we overheard Belinda complimenting Sharon on her hair in the pew behind us.

"It's so red. Can I touch it?"

Fortunately for Sharon, Eddie cleared his throat at that moment and announced that we were about to begin. "Hello everybody and welcome to St John's!" He laughed before adding, "Or should I say, 'King's Church at St John's'?" He paused. "We'll have to think of a name later."

I exchanged a quick smile with Ruby. "Do we have to have a name?" I called out. When Eddie raised his eyebrows, I continued, "Can't we just be 'The Church in Leeds'?"

A few people stared at me in bemusement.

I took a deep breath as I went on, "There's only one Church, isn't there? We have the same Daddy and the same big brother and the world is watching to see if we'll all get along."

I turned to catch Sharon's eye and she grinned.

Eddie chuckled. "Very true," he said. "Right then. Welcome to The Church in Leeds!"

The congregation gave a little cheer.

As Eddie confessed that he wasn't quite sure what to expect that evening, Ruby and I nudged one another in excitement. "Let's see what Jesus does!"

~ 27 ~

Priceless

Our first night at St John's was a roaring success. Of course, this is only if success is deemed a room full of people growing in intimacy with Jesus and seeking after the Father's heart. If success means an impressive career, a gorgeous face and the promise of wealth then it was just a bunch of people singing and praying together.

Within a few days, our numbers had tripled as several churches from across the city heard about what we were doing and asked if they could join us. Eddie shared the role of leading with a number of pastors from the other churches but the basic premise was the same: a time of prayer followed by singing, more prayer and a short talk. In the end, they had opted for a small worship band in the corner although anyone who wanted to was free to play their instruments around the room. Songs still began spontaneously and so did prolonged periods of silence and anyone who heard a word from God was allowed to bring it, although we were generally encouraged to run it by the leader first instead of just blurting it out. It was rather more formal than I would have liked it but I prayed that God wouldn't hold it against them. At any rate, on the odd occasion, God would disrupt the evening and one or more of these elements would be abandoned as the Holy Spirit had his way. For example, during a meeting on the second week, we were halfway through a song when what sounded like a mighty wind rushed through the building.

I turned to see who had opened the door but it was tightly closed. A sense of majesty hung in the air and, around the room, several people started to sob. Several others began to laugh with joy. The weight of God's presence forced me to my knees and I spent most of the night facedown on the floor.

Seven people were saved that night and at least five more were healed, including a lady whose deaf ears popped open without anyone laying a hand on her.

Eddie and Summer came up to me at the end and confessed they were giving the whole healing thing more thought.

"We think you might be onto something," admitted Summer.

"And we need a bit of your spark," added Eddie.

I listened in surprise as they told me that God had insisted they take their hands off the reigns that evening.

"I was about to preach," Eddie confessed. "But God pushed me to the floor and told me to keep quiet. Moments later, that lady was healed." I giggled as he went on, "We'll try to keep it simple from now on."

After that, it wasn't long before we were meeting every night.

The Church in Leeds had been running for three weeks and Ruby and I were in town handing out paper flowers for Valentine's Day.

The flowers served two purposes. Firstly, it gave us a chance to tell the women of Leeds that God loved them and wanted to romance them. Secondly, we were able to invite anyone who might be interested in coming to the outpouring meetings.

As with the Christmas cards, there were quite a lot of people who dismissed our gesture. However, we also had a number of sincere conversations with many women, young and old, who were touched by our words. As we summoned up the courage to stop each woman who passed us, we could never tell which ones might be the treasure ready to hear God's good news for them. Appearances can be deceptive and sometimes it was the hardest faces who revealed the softest hearts.

One lady had her face set in a scowl but started crying when Ruby offered her a flower. "For me?" she asked, wide-eyed. "I've not been given flowers in years."

As she stopped to sniff it, I confessed, "It's only paper."

"I know!" She laughed. "It's just habit, isn't it? What are you giving them out for?"

She listened as Ruby and I told her that Jesus loved her and found her beautiful.

"Oh, that's lovely," she said when we finished. Then, as though she needed to explain herself, she added, "I've always believed in God, you know. I'm just a bit naughty and don't go to church."

"Because it's boring?" I ventured.

"Well, yes!"

"Would you come if you knew you could experience God instead of just experiencing religion?"

She thought about it. "I'd love to experience God."

Ruby grinned and invited her to The Church in Leeds.

"The Church in Leeds?" the lady echoed. "I like that. Because it gets so confusing with there being hundreds of different churches, if you know what I mean?"

I shared a smile with Ruby as I explained, "We're keeping things simple. Loving God and loving each other."

The lady looked like she was considering it. We gave her a couple more flowers and left her reading a Bible bookmark.

As we went on our way, we were halted by a tramp in a nearby doorway. "Can you spare 37p, girls?"

I was about to shake my head and keep walking. The tramp was a familiar sight whenever we were in town and I was pretty sure he was wasting any money he got given. But, as my shadow drifted over him, I suddenly remembered Annie's generosity with the Princess Burgers and realised Jesus would never turn down an opportunity to love. To me, this man had always been *The tramp who asks for 37p.'* But God didn't see him like that. God knew his name and his deepest heart's desires. God knew his past and the heartbreaking story of how one of his precious children had ended up begging on the streets. He knew the plans he had for this guy, plans to prosper him and not to harm him...

I nudged Ruby. "Can we stop?"

She looked at me in surprise. "Yeah. Sure."

I took a deep breath before turning to the tramp. "Hi, er... What's your name?"

He looked up and squinted. "Alan Rose."

"Hi Alan." I took another tentative step towards him. "I'm Livi and this is Ruby." I held out my hand.

Ruby blushed and gave a little wave.

Alan shook my hand. "Nice to meet you."

I pointed to the cup of copper coins at his feet. "What do you need?"

"I'm saving up for some shoes."

"Oh!" I glanced at Ruby before feeling for my purse. I bit my lip as I said, "I'll buy you some shoes if you like?"

Alan looked at me in alarm. "Don't be daft."

"I'd like to," I insisted, crouching down beside him as I grew in confidence.

"What? Are you rich or something?"

"No. But my Daddy is."

"Oh yeah?" Alan sneered. "What is he then? A businessman?"

"Better than that. He created the universe."

Alan looked at me as though I was mad. "What's she on?" he asked Ruby.

"He's *your* Daddy too," Ruby told him. "And he loves you very much."

"God," I clarified when Alan screwed up his nose. "God loves you. You're his child."

Alan turned away. "Nah. God don't love me. It was God who ruined my life."

"No it wasn't," I said. "It was the devil. And also... possibly you." I coughed before adding, "But God still loves you."

Alan frowned. Now that I was so close, I could smell the alcohol on his breath and I tried not retch as he gave a long sigh.

"Well, let's go and get some shoes," I continued. "What sort would you like?"

Alan winced before admitting, "I don't want shoes. I just want the money." He ran a grubby hand across his face.

I pulled out my purse. "Okay," I said quietly, handing him a five pound note.

He took it with a gulp. "Thanks."

"Do you want one of these?" Ruby held out a flower.

He paused. "Go on then." He put it in his cup. "Looks good there, don't it?" He peered at it before asking, "Is it a rose?"

We nodded.

"Like my name."

Ruby giggled before saying seriously, "God will never give up on you, Alan Rose."

"You'll find him," I added. "If you seek him with all of your heart."

Alan nodded. "Thanks."

I got to my feet. "It was nice to meet you, Alan."

"You too... Livi."

I gasped. "You got my name right!"

"You told me it."

"I know!" I blushed. "It's just people often think I've said 'Libby.'"

"Oh." He grinned and patted his head. "Not just a pretty face, hey?" He nodded at Ruby. "Nice to meet you too, Ruby."

We smiled at him and started to walk away.

"See you again some time!" Alan called after us.

I turned to wave, taking one last glance at the man named Alan Rose, a man worth far more than 37p.

"Well," I said, once we were out of earshot. "Do you think that counts as cleansing a leper?"

Ruby gave a splutter. "Maybe..."

"It's a start at least."

As we turned a corner, Ruby gave a sudden squeal and gripped my arm. "Look!" She pointed to a nearby food stand. "It's Ms Sorenson!"

My heart skipped a beat as I spotted our former Personal and Social Development teacher paying for a hotdog. We shrieked at one another before running over like giddy schoolgirls.

Ms Sorenson had paused to add ketchup to her food and didn't notice as we lingered behind her. I was about to tap her on the shoulder and ask if she remembered us when she looked up and exclaimed, "Livi! Ruby! How are you?"

"We're fine," we said shyly. "How are you?"

She waved her hotdog at us and grinned. "A lot happier now I've got some lunch. What are you girls up to?"

I wondered whether she meant *today* or just in life generally. "We're free right now," I said, in case she wanted to hang out.

Ms Sorenson smiled before turning to ask the man on the stall if he had any mustard. "It's usually on the counter," she told him.

I bit my nails as the hotdog man laughed like old friends with Ms Sorenson. "Here you go, Audrey." He handed her a bottle.

I wondered if she was a regular. For a moment, I debated whether to ask if there were any jobs going.

Ms Sorenson squeezed a line of mustard onto her hotdog before turning back to me and Ruby. I gulped as I noticed she was wearing a tiny cross round her neck. *What did the cross mean? Was it a statement of faith? A symbol of hope? Or a simple fashion accessory? And would it be extremely weird if I asked?*

"I hope you're still writing, Livi?" She looked at me.

I nodded.

"Great. I'll be buying your bestsellers one day." My heart leapt as she winked. "And you're still collecting banana stickers, Ruby?"

Ruby giggled. "Yeah. I've also got quite a lot of limited edition egg boxes."

Ms Sorenson chuckled. "That's brilliant."

I took a deep breath before handing her one of our flowers. "Ruby made these."

"Oh, that's very creative." She turned it over in her hands before attempting to give it back to me.

"You can keep it," I insisted. "We're handing them out as Valentine's roses to let people know how valuable they are to God and also to invite them to get to know him better..."

She nodded as I explained about the meetings at St John's.

"You should come," I finished awkwardly. "We meet every night."

She smiled.

"And um... Jesus loves you," I added.

She chuckled again. "Thank you." She raised her hotdog before saying, "Well, I'd better find a safe place to eat this before I spill sauce down myself! It was lovely to see you both."

"You too," we squeaked.

"Take care of yourselves."

"You too..."

My stomach churned as we watched her walk away. My favourite high school memory would always be Ms Sorenson telling me she was proud of me. It pained me not to know whether she was saved yet, whether she ever would be, and whether I would see her again.

As Ruby and I linked arms and went to hand out some more flowers, the ache was soothed slightly as I felt God whisper deep inside, *I'm so proud of you, Livi.*

I had great hopes that Ms Sorenson would come to the outpouring meeting that evening and packed my bag with a couple of my recent short stories just in case. The very thought of her coming and getting saved filled me with shivers. *Please Lord, it would be priceless!* I was halfway out the door when Jill stopped me to ask where I was going.

"Do you know St John's?"

She shook her head.

"The old Anglican church on Brunswick Street."

"What's 'Anglican'?"

I blushed. "I don't know. It's just a big church."

"Oh. What are you doing there?"

"We meet to sing and pray and stuff." I felt embarrassed and resisted the urge to play it down.

"Every night?" She looked confused.

"Yeah..."

"Why do they make you go every night?"

"Nobody *makes* us. We want to. It's really cool." I paused. "It's not just for Christians. It's for anyone who wants to encounter God... You're welcome to come if you ever want to."

She shook her head. "'*Gossip Town*' is about to start."

My heart sunk but I tried to smile. "Well, have fun."

"Thanks. You too." Jill wandered into the living room.

I had closed the front door behind me when I felt God whisper, *Tell her that her baby is in Heaven.*

I stopped in shock. *Seriously? Is that really you, God?* I waited for a moment but didn't hear anything. I frowned. *If that's you, tell me again later.*

I was about to keep walking when I felt a deep sense of urgency rise within me. *Tell her that her baby is in Heaven.*

I swallowed hard and turned back to my house. I unlocked the front door before walking slowly into the living room.

My sister looked up. "Are you alright?"

"Yeah," I whispered. "I just... This might sound weird but..." I took a deep breath. "I believe that God wants you to know that your baby is in Heaven."

Jill's eyes filled with tears as she stared at me.

Immediately I feared that it wasn't true and that I had just given her some huge deluded lie to try and make her feel better. I sucked in my cheeks. *Oh, Lord, why did I say that?*

Tell her that the blood of Jesus is stronger than anything.

I opened my mouth and closed it again.

The blood of Jesus is stronger than anything.

"The blood of Jesus is stronger than anything," I repeated like a puppet.

And you were worth every drop.

I gulped. "And you were worth every drop."

Jill blinked and shook her head, looking confused.

I exhaled and pulled the last paper flower out of my bag. It was a little battered so I smoothed it out before laying it down on the sofa. "Here... See you later."

~ 28 ~

The great shipwreck

As people arrived for that evening's meeting, I overheard Adrian Cooke telling Eddie that in all his years as vicar of St John's the building had never been as full as it was now. I turned round in my seat, trying to count as people came in, and kept my eyes peeled for Ms Sorenson. The pews filled up pretty quickly and quite a lot of people were looking around, as though they had never been in a church building before. Several of our college mates had come back and, this time, it wasn't just to socialise. They sat with Maria, Ellen and Laura in one of the middle pews. I smiled as Sharon went to greet them.

Ruby and I were on the front row with Annie, Amanda and Kevin. As I glanced at the four of them, I could hardly believe that what had begun so haphazardly in my bedroom was now a citywide event hosting over a hundred people.

Amanda sat stroking her rat. "Isn't this amazing, Livi?"

I nodded and peered at Polly. "Is she purring?"

"She's praising God. I told you she was clever. You just need to give her a chance."

"Hmmm."

"I hope pets do go to Heaven," Amanda continued. "God loves her more than *we* do, doesn't he?"

I chuckled. "Much more than *I* do, definitely!"

She frowned. "Don't you think she's cute?"

"Maybe..." As I leant closer, Polly sneezed. I screamed and jumped sideways onto Ruby's lap.

She cried, "Ow!" and shuffled across to the next seat.

Amanda giggled. "Don't be scared. That means she loves you."

"There's no fear in love!" sang Annie. "That's what the Bible says."

Joey came wandering over, swinging his guitar. He paused in front of me, an anxious expression etched across his face.

I patted the seat between me and Amanda, grateful to have some distance from her rat. "Hey Joey."

"Hey." He sat down and gave me a serious stare.

"What?" I spluttered.

He blushed. "I just wanted to say that your hunger for God is so inspiring. It kind of makes me want to dream bigger."

I felt my insides squirming. "Thanks Joey."

"How did you do it?" He gestured to the packed room.

I thought back over the last few months. I certainly hadn't earned it by my good behaviour. Nor had I figured out what to do through years of intellectual study. "We didn't really," I confessed. "We were just hungry... For more than chips."

Joey blushed again. "Me too," he muttered. "I mean... I am now. I think you've done great." As he sat beaming at me, I felt the temptation to feel proud or puff myself up.

I quickly shook my head as I begged God, *Let the greatest thing I ever do be to love you with all my heart.*

Joey was still staring at me so I asked carefully, "How's your mum?"

He forced a smile. "She's tired. She had more chemo today."

I gulped and nodded. I wondered whether I ought to ask for more information but I wasn't sure I could stomach it.

Joey gave it to me anyway. "Her hair has all fallen out now. She looks like a shiny version of my granddad and she's still got another four months of it..." He paused before adding, "Unless she gets healed."

"I'm still praying."

"Thanks."

In the corner of the room, the worship band had started making music. I gave Joey a tentative pat on the arm before getting to my feet and joining in with the first song.

'Let your face shine on your children, we are waiting here for you
Fill our hearts with expectation for what's holy, good and true
For you're the one who made me, you gave your all to save me
I'll believe, I will believe
If you say you love me, if you say I'm lovely
Then I'll believe, I will believe
Help me to believe...'

Joey stood and strummed his guitar.

On the other side of me, Ruby gave me a sudden nudge and cocked her head sideways.

I turned to see what she was pointing at and gasped: Amanda and Kevin were holding hands.

We shared a giggle before throwing ourselves back into the worship.

We were halfway through the second song when a picture formed in my mind. I saw many people on boards and rafts and bits of wood being washed along a wave on the ocean. The people were of all different ages and from different backgrounds but they had one thing in common: they would have drowned had they not clung to the wood that now carried them. Along the water's edge, I was waiting with many others to help the people come to shore. As the picture zoomed out, I saw that the many pieces of wood had all originated from one big cross. I had the impression that the people coming on the ocean were part of a great wave of salvations that God was about to pour out across the country. Although I wondered whether I was making too much of it, I felt a little prompting to share it so, after a pause, I shuffled over to Eddie who was leading the meeting.

He smiled as I leant over and whispered my picture in his ear. "That's brilliant, Livi. You need to share that."

I nodded and waited for him to tell me when.

A short while later, the song came to an end and Eddie got everyone's attention before another one could begin. "Keep pressing in," he said. "I just feel Livi has something that God wants us all to receive." He handed me the microphone.

I blushed as I turned to face the congregation. I had a quick glance across the rows but couldn't see Ms Sorenson.

"I saw a picture," I began. I took a deep breath before sharing what I had seen. I was about to explain what I felt it meant when I glanced up and saw something that almost made me fall over.

Jill was sitting on the back row.

She had a whole pew to herself and looked anxious and unsure of herself as she watched me.

I was so stunned that I forgot what I was going to say and opened and closed my mouth several times as I summoned up the courage to keep speaking. "Er, anyway, it will be like a great shipwreck," I squeaked, avoiding Jill's gaze. "And people will come to church buildings like these." I waved a hand around. "Because that's where they'll hope to find God. We need to be ready."

I handed Eddie the microphone and started to go back to my seat. Then I reconsidered and walked up the aisle towards Jill.

She shot me a small smile as I slotted in beside her.

"Hi," I whispered.

"Hi."

I wanted to ask her what she was doing there but fought to play it cool as I stood for the next song. I closed my eyes and tried to concentrate on Jesus.

At one point, a few people started to laugh with joy and I glanced at Jill, afraid that she would be put off. She looked rather uncomfortable. I was about to lean over and explain that the people were just enjoying God's presence when a lady in the row in front of us began praying loudly in tongues.

I bit my lip and hoped Jill would just assume she was foreign.

Moments later, Stanley Rico arose and gave the interpretation for the lady's tongue. *"More, Lord, more. You are worth more than a million stars, a million dreams, a million men. I can't please two lovers, Lord. So I'll choose you— my husband, my King, my one true lover. No man will ever be enough. Let me have you..."*

At this, many more people were gripped with holy laughter and spontaneous praise erupted round the room.

Jill had gone white. My palms grew sweaty as I realised how bizarre it must have sounded to hear Stanley Rico call God his *'husband'* and *'one true lover.'* No wonder the world thinks Christians are mad.

After a few more songs and a lot of raucous prayer, Eddie took his place at the front. He looked like he was still thinking about what to preach on and paused for a long while before looking up. Finally he said, "Thank you for the tongue that was brought earlier." He waved at the lady in front of us before indicating Stanley. "I feel we ought to spend some time meditating on the interpretation."

My stomach churned. *Do we have to?*

"No man or woman will ever be enough," said Eddie. "Only Jesus can satisfy. Only Jesus is worth it. He is the perfect lover, the perfect brother, the perfect friend. He will never let you down." He paused and looked around. "You might have heard this many times before. But maybe it has never yet sunk in that it's for *you.*"

I watched Jill out of the corner of my eye as Eddie shared the gospel. She looked bored.

"You don't have to be clever or rich or popular or of a certain age to enter the Kingdom of Heaven," Eddie continued. "You don't have to have your act together or be like anybody else..." The congregation laughed as he added, "Of course, you don't have to be stupid or poor or unpopular either! This message is for you, whoever you are. Maybe you're waiting for the perfect moment or perhaps you're scared because you don't know what following Jesus will entail. But I want to ask you: Will you trust God for today? Just today? Right now, have you heard enough to say, *'Yes, God. I need you, I want you. Come to me today.'?*"

I nibbled my fingers as I prayed desperately that Eddie's message would somehow reach a deep part of Jill. I found myself overanalysing his every word as I wondered whether he was being too loud, too forceful or not forceful enough. I tried to surrender it all to the Lord. *God... You saved me. Surely you can save Jill.*

Eddie reached the end of his short talk and finished with an altar call. I watched as several people got out of their rows and made their way to the front. This had to be the biggest response we had seen in our meetings so far. I counted at least fifteen people.

I peeked at Jill out of the corner of my eye but she didn't join them. I closed my eyes and pretended to be deep in prayer, hoping that she would get up if she didn't feel like I was staring. I visualised her getting up from her seat and walking down the aisle but, when I looked up several minutes later, she still hadn't moved.

I rubbed my eyes. *Lord, I really thought she might.*

The number at the front had grown to twenty and people continued to come in ones and twos as Eddie led them all in a short prayer.

I mumbled along on autopilot, feeling deeply aggrieved that Jill wasn't down at the front. *"Dear Jesus, I believe you died for me and rose again. I'm sorry for all the things I've done wrong. Come and be Lord of my life..."*

The congregation cheered as the new converts finished praying with Eddie and the worship band started to play a song.

"The meeting is officially over but please stay as long as you want," Eddie called over the noise. "If you want prayer for anything then come to the front..."

A flood of people rushed to the altar and Summer and a few others leapt into action as they organised prayer teams. Around the room, most people stood to worship for a bit longer and many others prayed or talked quietly in small groups.

Not far from us, a few people began singing spontaneously, *"Jesus says he loves me, Jesus says I'm lovely, so I'll believe... I will believe..."*

I expected Jill to gather up her things and leave before anybody could come over to talk to her but she just sat quietly in her seat. She still looked bored so I resisted the urge to ask if she wanted prayer for anything. I didn't want to irritate her.

I could see Ruby and the others dancing together at the front and felt a pang of joy mixed with sorrow. I was torn between a desire to join them and a sense of pity for Jill.

Ruby turned as though looking for something. I saw the shock in her eyes as she caught sight of my sister. *"Jill's here!"* she mouthed, as if I hadn't seen her.

I shot her a look, as if to say, '*Don't freak her out.*'

Ruby left the others and made her way up the aisle towards us. "Hi Jill," she said.

Jill smiled. "Hi Ruby."

"It's nice to see you."

"Thanks. You too."

"Are you keeping well?"

"Very well, thanks. And you?"

I bit my lip and tried to smile, hardly daring to breathe as Ruby engaged in cautious chit-chat with my sister.

It was all very casual until Annie came running over. "JILL!" she shrieked. "What are *you* doing here?"

I tried to catch her eye but Jill just gave another smile as she said, "Hi Annie. How are you?"

Annie didn't reply and kept staring at Jill until I nudged her in the ribs. *"Annie!"*

Annie blushed. "I mean... It's really nice to see you and not at all strange."

Jill nodded and picked up her bag. "Do you want a lift home?" she asked me. "Or are you coming back with Ruby?"

"I'll come with you," I said. "I'll just get my coat."

"Alright."

I was about to run and fetch my things when Summer popped up beside us. "Livi, are you free to come and pray for people?" She indicated a line at the altar. "We could do with some help."

"Er..." I shot Jill a wary glance.

She shrugged. "Go ahead. I'll wait here."

"Okay." I gave Ruby and Annie quick looks, warning them to play it cool, before following Summer down the aisle.

On our way, we passed Sharon Sheppard.

"I've not done my Hooves and Hair essay," I told her. "I hope that's okay."

"You'd better do it," Sharon retorted, sharing a smile with Summer. "Otherwise I'll give you a detention."

"We don't have detentions in college!" I laughed.

"We didn't have miracles either," she said, pointing to a row of my classmates who were waiting for prayer at the front. "Until you came."

I laughed again. "Thanks for everything, Sharon. I wanted more of God and you were part of the answer to my prayers."

She grinned. "And you were part of the answer to mine."

I looked at her in surprise. "What do you mean?"

She blushed. "I hadn't spoken about Ollie before. That evening at the pub brought up a lot of emotion for me... I needed to do some business with God that I'd been avoiding for many years." She smiled softly. "We all have our tests, don't we?"

"We're all practising Christians," I agreed.

Sharon winked as I followed Summer to the altar. A girl called Sophie was waiting for prayer for an upcoming medical appointment.

"Just pray they find out what's wrong with me," she begged.

"Can we also pray that God heals whatever it is?" I asked, more to Summer than to Sophie.

Summer nodded as Sophie said, "Yes please."

The three of us held hands and prayed. I followed Summer's lead, marvelling at the compassion that flowed from her lips. In previous months, I had been so angry with her that I had forgotten how wise and insightful her prayers could be.

"Thank you Lord for your precious child, Sophie. You know every hair on her head and every thought in her heart. Come with your presence to bring perfect peace..."

I nodded along before commanding full healing.

Sophie gave us thankful smiles as we finished. Her affliction wasn't something that could be tested right away so we had no way of knowing whether or not she'd been healed. But Summer didn't focus on the sickness. She just kept telling Sophie how much Jesus loved her and she took a long time making sure that Sophie felt alright before moving on to the next person. She didn't seem fazed by the large crowd waiting to be prayed for. I was overcome by a new depth of respect as I watched Summer giving all her time and attention to loving the one person in front of her. I made a vow, there and then, to never cut myself off from the body again. I needed Summer. I needed Eddie. They needed me.

We prayed for a few more people before Summer looked round and said, "You can go now, Livi. There aren't many people left."

I'd have gladly stayed all night had it not been for the fact that Jill was waiting for me. "Alright," I said. "Let me know if you need me to pray another time."

"I certainly will."

"Does this mean I'm on the ministry team?" I grinned.

Summer laughed. "I suppose it does. I'll see you tomorrow."

I gave her a hug before making my way back to Jill.

Ruby and Annie were still beside her, looking about as awkward as when I'd left them.

Jill and I made it all the way home without either of us mentioning the church meeting. We talked about the weather and college and *Captain Barry's Chicken*. We talked about Aunt Claudia's latest parcel of lamb and how it had leaked all over the doorstep. We talked about Helen Tagda who had recently acquired a dog. We talked about cinema releases and speculated over which films would be worth watching. Then Jill asked my opinion on a new haircut she was considering and I nodded politely and told her it would suit her. We pulled into our street having covered more topics than the two of us would usually get through in a month.

"Quarter to eleven," Jill remarked as the car came to a stop.

"That's right."

"I must remember to put a load of washing on."

"Yup."

"I'll do a white load so if you've got anything to add you'll need to bring it down."

"I will..."

I fixed a carefree smile on my face as I followed Jill into the house. Everything within me was screaming to know what she had thought of the evening but I was desperate not to be the one to raise it. One false move and I could put her off God for life. I kicked my shoes off and lingered by the stairs as Jill checked the answer phone for messages.

"Livi? Don't forget your whites."

"Oh yeah..." I sped up to my room, grabbed a heap of dirty clothes off the floor, and sprinted back down.

Jill was in the kitchen loading up the washing machine.

I shoved my clothes in and watched as she located the softener.

"Do you want a cup of tea?" I asked.

She smiled. "I'd love a cup of tea. Thanks."

I switched the kettle on, humming to myself as I grabbed the teabags. "Any particular mug?"

My sister shook her head and sat at the table. "Any is fine." She pulled a magazine off the work surface.

I pursed my lips and grabbed the two nearest mugs.

"Are you having one?" Jill looked up as I handed her a mug and poured another for me. "I didn't think you liked tea."

"I just fancied it for a change." I didn't want to admit that I was only having it so that I could stall my bedtime a little longer.

"Oh, alright." Jill turned back to her magazine. "Apparently there's going to be a musical episode of 'Gossip Town.'" Any hopes that Jill might engage in a conversation about church evaporated as she held the article up and grinned.

I gave a murmur and pretended to be interested. Then I sat for ages waiting for my drink to cool down while Jill flicked through her magazine. It looked as though my window of opportunity was over so I had a couple of sips of tea before giving up and pouring the rest down the sink. "Goodnight then," I said quietly.

As I left, Jill called after me, "Oh, by the way, I said that prayer."

I turned so fast that I almost smacked my head on the doorframe. "What?"

"You know... What that man prayed at the end."

"You... You prayed it?"

"Yeah. I just knew I needed to. Everything he was saying made sense." She frowned. "Well, not all of it. I didn't understand why Stanley Rico was referring to God as his lover..."

"Don't worry about that," I said quickly.

She shook her head. "I'm not. And I'm not saying... I don't know..." Her voice cracked. "It's not that I know what I believe or even if... I don't know..." She stopped and wiped her eyes. "There just has to be more than this and... if there is, then I need it. Do you know what I mean?"

I wanted to grab her with both hands and shriek with joy. Instead, I whispered, "Yeah, I know what you mean."

She gave a funny smile and turned back to her magazine. "Anyway, I just thought you'd like to know."

~ 29 ~

Through the veil

It's been several months and our evening meetings are still going strong. People have come from all over the country to catch a glimpse of what God's doing in Leeds and many have gone on to start similar fires in their own hometowns. According to Eddie, over a thousand people have come to know Jesus in our meetings during the last four months. We're catching up with Bryn Hapus— they've baptised more than fifteen hundred new converts and, as far as I know, they're still meeting daily. We regularly see bigger crowds than what the town hall held for The Great Leeds Skills Auction and it's even been reported on in the news. Very few people know how it started and nobody's mentioned me. They just say that it must have begun with an act of God. I suppose, in many ways, that's true. I was walking along the balanced tightrope until God showed up one day and pushed me off.

I have no idea how long things will last but I've made a vow that the revival inside me will never end. And, even if everybody else grows bored, I know I can always call on Ruby, Annie, Amanda and Kevin to come and join me in the secret place. In fact, the five of us will be hanging out at mine before the main meeting tonight. I'm still learning fearless love from Amanda's rat, cheesy jokes from Kevin, and childlike faith from Annie.

There are only a few weeks left until the summer holidays and, against all the odds, it looks as though Ruby and I are going to pass our course. Things have got much more interesting in this final term with a module entitled 'Wounded Animals.' We've healed seventeen rabbits so far. We're yet to raise the dead, although Belinda's drooping aloe vera plant has looked a lot perkier since we prayed for it.

We're still praying daily for Joey's mother. She's almost finished her cancer treatment and will soon find out whether or not it has been successful. It can be hard to believe God really wants everybody well when I see her at church looking so pale and weak and making slow instead of miraculous progress. But I've learnt I must take God at his word regardless of what I see otherwise everything gets rather *complicated*.

I would like to be able to say that all Jill's problems were fixed the moment she started following Jesus, but life doesn't always work like that. She is, however, happier than I have ever known her. She comes to church most Sundays and has joined a Life Group run by Sharon Sheppard. It's my private mission to set her up with Eddie's brother, Stevie, but Ruby keeps telling me not to interfere.

"That's not how Christians fight," she warned when I told her about my matchmaking plans. When I looked at her in confusion, she said pointedly, *"We pray."*

And so I am praying and trusting that God will set her up with somebody nice although, funnily enough, Jill no longer cries quite so much about being single.

Speaking of boys, I've noticed Ruby wanting to spend a lot of time with Mark recently. Of course, she would probably say the same about me and Joey. But she would be wrong. We're just friends. Although *'Livi Starling-Cashbottom: Revival Writer'* does have an interesting ring to it.

Even in the midst of an outpouring, things aren't always easy. Sometimes the devil tries to get me down by whispering things like, *'Don't you wish your mother was here to cheer you on?'* or, *'You do realise you're still so far from perfect, don't you?'*

To begin with, he would catch me off guard and I would waste a lot of time feeling miserable or even angry at God despite the wonderful things he was doing.

But, these days, I see the devil coming and, before he can get himself comfortable, I run at him and declare, "Devil, you've got nothing on me! It's true: I don't know why my mother had to die and God appears to be silent on the matter but I will trust him anyway because he is good. And it's true: I still make loads of mistakes and on my own I'd be a mess but I will keep flying anyway because the blood of Jesus is strong enough and I KNOW that he loves me."

The devil flees pretty swiftly after that.

There's so much that I don't know: whether I will ever have a one hundred percent success rate at healing, whether Ms Sorenson will remember me when she is old, whether any of my books will be bestsellers, and whether my mum is waiting for me in Heaven. But I do know one thing: I was made for love. There is no higher call than to love my Jesus. I am who God says I am and I want to be myself perfectly. Even more important than all the meetings and miracles is knowing that my name is written in Heaven.

Speaking of Heaven, I have been encountering a lot more of the 'more' that Sharon told me about. I am realising that just when I thought I had grasped how big God is, he is, in fact, even bigger still.

This very morning, I opened my eyes and found myself face to face with Jesus himself. He was just there, as real as my wardrobe— *more* real in fact— and all of eternity seemed to flow from his presence. My whole body felt as though it were in a state of trance and I would have wondered if I was still dreaming had I not been more aware of being awake than I had ever been in my life. It was like I had found myself existing for the very first moment. The veil that was torn over two thousand years ago was open before my eyes and all I needed to do was step in. Everything else faded away as I looked into his eyes of love. Nothing was between us. No distance. No sin. No separation. There were a million things I might have asked had I had any control over my senses but I was far too lost in awe.

It didn't matter anyway. His smile consumed me as he looked at me and said, *Everything will be alright.*

All my unanswered questions suddenly found their peace in him and it was in that moment that I realised I was genuinely grateful for the life that I've had, even the really sad bits that I wouldn't wish on anyone. I can be grateful because, although I cannot voice what they are, my spirit *knows* the plans that he has for me and I know that not a single drop of pain will be wasted.

The vision faded almost as quickly as it had begun but the last thing he said etched itself on my heart. I'm convinced that if it's true for me, then it's true for everyone:

I love you. I am coming soon.

~*~

Jesus is coming...
Get ready: E.T.A unknown

Dear Reader

Nobody knows the hour, but Jesus is coming back. Maybe it will be in your lifetime. Maybe you were born for such a time as this. Maybe every great adventure story is a mere whisper of The Greatest Story Ever Told: OURS.

Maybe the whole of Heaven is watching, waiting for the children of God to take their place, while angels are poised to write the tales of wonders yet untold— of countless broken wanderers found and healed and running home...

Maybe this will be the most glorious hour in human history.

All over the world, an End Time Army of unknown, unseen, hungry hearts is rising. These are the sold-out burning ones; living fearlessly, loving dangerously, face down in the secret place, choosing connection over correction, defined by Jesus instead of torn apart by division, daring to believe that God can use them to change the world.

It is time to take flight.

It only takes one person to start a fire.

And maybe, just maybe, God is waiting to be great through YOU.